© María C. Díaz

About the Author

ENRIQUE JOVEN holds a doctorate in physics. Since 1991, he has resided in Tenerife in the Canary Islands, where he works as a senior engineer at the Instituto de Astrofísica de Canarias. He writes regularly for various media outlets on subjects ranging from science and new technologies to the Internet. *The Book of God and Physics* has been translated into eight languages.

THE BOOK OF GOD AND PHYSICS

THE BOOK OF GOD AND PHYSICS

A NOVEL OF THE VOYNICH MYSTERY

Enrique Joven

TRANSLATED FROM THE SPANISH BY DOLORES M. KOCH

HARPER

NEW YORK · LONDON · TORONTO · SYDNEY

HARPER

Originally published in Spanish as *El castillo de las estrellas* by Roca Editorial de Libros, S.L., in Spain in 2007.

A hardcover edition of this book was published in 2009 by William Morrow, an imprint of HarperCollins Publishers.

FIRST HARPER paperback published 2010.

Designed by Richard Oriolo

Library of Congress Cataloging-in-Publication Data is available upon request.

ISBN 978-0-06-145687-9

10 11 12 13 14   OV/RRD   10 9 8 7 6 5 4 3 2 1

Anything that can be explored should certainly be interpreted.
—MAX PLANCK, GERMAN PHYSICIST (1858–1947)

INTRODUCTION

This novel is based on real people and events. Only the narrator of the story and his two friends are fictitious. I have respected to the maximum not only the history of the book, its avatars, its disappearance, and its later reappearance in the Jesuit libraries, but also the successive attempts at its translation. Gordon Rugg, for example, is quoted in the novel, from his article on the *Voynich Manuscript* in the distinguished *Scientific American*. I have also taken the liberty of "transtextualizing"—a recent term of reference—from Spaniard Francisco A. Violat, who, like the Englishman Rugg, believes the manuscript to be an elaborate hoax, and did indeed use a simple system of disks to generate, using triads, a series of fantastic words lacking any real meaning.

The *Voynich Manuscript* is an illustrated book that's about five hundred years old. It is unique in that it is written in a language that has never been identified or deciphered. One can only look at it as if it were an icon. Unlike other manuscripts, such as the much-quoted *Hypnerotomaquia Poliphili*—which inspired the recent and very successful novel *The Rule of Four*, by Ian Caldwell and Dustin Thomason—there is no known way to approach the *Voynich*. But the manuscript does exist. It is presently stored on a dusty shelf at the Beinecke Rare Book and Manuscript Library of Yale University, under the classification MS-408. One can peruse its images on the Internet and even buy a CD reproduction of its pages from the university. For those who prefer printed books, I recommend Gerry Kennedy and Rob Churchill's *The Voynich Manuscript: The Unsolved Riddle of an Extraordinary Book Which Has Defied Interpretation for Centuries* (2004), a paperback published by Orion.

Its existence really is no secret. But its meaning is. It was the most studied hieroglyph during the twentieth century and it continues to be so today.

Unfortunately, *Heavenly Intrigue* (2005), by the American author Joshua Gilder and his wife, Anne-Lee Gilder, is also real. Like the protagonist in this novel you are about to read, I myself used Amazon.com to obtain it and Google to learn a bit more about the authors' lives. The circumstances of Tycho Brahe's death comprise one of the strangest episodes in the history of astronomy, and his turbulent but fruitful relationship with Johannes Kepler is key to the development of modern scientific knowledge. Carl Sagan devoted a large portion of an episode in his memorable *Cosmos* documentary series to this singular intellectual alliance that produced, in a very short time, an authentic revolution in the understanding of the universe. The simultaneous existence of giants like Galileo, Johannes Kepler, and Tycho Brahe shaped a critical point not only in the history of astronomy but in the history of science itself.

As the author of this novel, I have tried to delve imaginatively into certain circumstances today, as disturbing as they are spurious, that attempt to undermine the credibility of science itself. The scientific community as a whole has been actively fighting this attack and its attempt to discredit and denigrate some of our most illustrious members, as in the case of Johannes Kepler. I have used real people and situations, as when the German professor Volker Bialas condemned this action at an astronomy conference in Austria. Bialas is perhaps the leading modern authority on Kepler, and he graciously provided me with a copy of his paper concerning the conspiratorial theory in the Gilders' book. I want to express my deep appreciation to him for this favor, and to Lotti Jochum, my colleague at the Canary Islands Institute of Astrophysics, who graciously translated the German text for me.

I also wish to express my profound gratitude to the staff of Roca Editorial, and in particular, to the director, Blanca Rosa Roca, for their confidence and assistance in the Spanish publication of this novel. I want to show my great appreciation, as well, to César Sanz, Ana Ruiz, and Antonio Cruz for their many valuable suggestions during the writing.

By coincidence, the *Voynich Manuscript* and Johannes Kepler crossed paths in the Bohemia of the early sixteenth century under Emperor Rudolf II. This coincidence has helped me to interweave a good many of the stories in this novel.

As far as I know, there were no connections developed between the two. But that is not to say they didn't exist.

LA LAGUNA, TENERIFE
OCTOBER 1, 2006

THE BOOK OF GOD AND PHYSICS

PROLOGUE

I became interested in the *Voynich Manuscript* shortly after being ordained as a Jesuit priest, more than two years ago. Poor Rafael, a fellow seminarian, was working on a biography of Father Petrus Beckx, one of our old fathers superior. Rafael is now a missionary in Southeast Asia. Not being very skilled in the use of the Internet, he asked me for some emergency instructions. I just told him how to use Google. To our surprise, in every single one of the initial results concerning Beckx, around five hundred, the *Voynich Manuscript* was mentioned.

Rafael continued with Beckx, but I was captivated by this other piece of nonsense, this manuscript. Since then I've belonged—along with another two hundred indefatigable researchers—to what is known as the Voynich List, a virtual meeting place where we share our meager findings and abundant theories. My real life is much more prosaic. I teach high school physics and math.

There are about 240 well-preserved and profusely illustrated pages in the handwritten parchment manuscript. The text could possibly be divided into sections; one of them seems to be about medicine, or at least medicinal plants; another about biology; a third about astronomy; and so on. It contains 170,000 characters separated into what appear to be words—around 35,000 in all. There are only 20 or 30 different characters. The structure of its language (we call it Voynichian) has no known historical antecedents and is totally cryptic. The traceable history of the book is of little help. On the contrary, it only adds to the legend. Its name comes from a Polish-American bookseller, Wilfred M. Voynich, who bought it in 1912. We Jesuits handed it to him. In order to cover expenses, the Jesuits were forced to sell some of their belongings at the beginning of the twentieth century (our situation certainly hasn't improved much). Father Beckx tried to pass off as his own a few of the items in his possession that belonged to the Jesuits, not out of self-ish malice but out of good common sense. In 1870 Rome was going through rough times, and King Victor Emmanuel's soldiers were about to confiscate our library. The pope dissolved the Jesuit order, and he had authorized Jesuit priests to keep only their personal belongings. Very little is known about the travails of the *Voynich Manuscript* before 1912.

Everything surrounding the *Manuscript* after 1912 is a mix of fancy and reality. Voynich was convinced that the author was Roger Bacon, and that he had encrypted it in the thirteenth century to protect his scientific discoveries. The bookseller energetically began to distribute photocopies of the work among scholars devoted to the famous Franciscan monk. No one was able to decipher it. But in 1919 a professor from the University of Pennsylvania, William Newbold, literally went nuts over the manuscript. He asserted that Bacon had discovered the microscope, and had made use of the telescope three centuries before Galileo.

He thought that the strange illustrations in the book were actually cells and galaxies. To demonstrate this, he explained that he had found a second text hidden in the first one, in a kind of shorthand, and, after six consecutive transcriptions of a code containing seventeen letters, he reached the conclusion that it was the anagram of a Latin text. This esoteric interpretation of the manuscript was considered valid until 1931, when another scholar, John Manly, discredited it, proving that Newbold's weird rigamarole was totally without merit. Voynich died that year and the book was inherited by his widow. This didn't dampen the efforts to decipher it. Things didn't get any better when a group of botanists analyzed the engravings and declared they represented plants on the new continent, America, which had been terra incognita. The challenge to decipher the puzzle reached the U.S. government, which after World War II gave the assignment to its best military cryptographers. William Friedman, who had cracked the coded messages of the Japanese Imperial Navy during the war, headed the commission. Using the first computers available, Friedman had deciphered other ancient texts, but about the *Voynich Manuscript* he could only say that it was written in a synthetic language that depended entirely on logic. More recent attempts are almost comical. In 1978 a man named John Stojko affirmed that the text was in ancient Ukrainian without vowels. In 1987 another scholar, Leo Levitov, declared it to be the work of the heretic Cathars, which was the panacea for mass-market paperbacks. Then came the Internet and the European Project for the Translation of the *Voynich Manuscript,* on which I am now working.

Voynich's widow kept the book in a locked security box until her death in 1961. It was sold to a New York antiquarian, H. P. Kraus, who bought it for $24,500 and offered it for sale at $160,000. Finally, tired of waiting for a buyer and fed up with the black legend surrounding it, he donated the manuscript to Yale, where it remains. The book became even more famous after its illustrations and legends appeared in an Indiana Jones movie as well as in the computer game Broken Sword, in which the manuscript is supposedly translated by a hacker who is then killed by the Knights Templar. The inventors of the game claimed that it included secret information about where to obtain geo-energy in various places on earth. That's all.

However, reality sometimes surpasses fiction.

I

On that particular Monday morning, everything seemed to be at a standstill. Perhaps the world had stopped, and if so, my trying to teach was totally useless. I had been standing by the board, chalk in hand, explaining the benefits of the law of gravity for more than half an hour, trying not to allow the ringing of a cell phone or the giggles caused by whispers that never reached my ears to distract me. I doubted very much whether Newton could have captured the minds of my fifteen-year-old students who, on Monday and at that early hour, were more likely to be interested in the progress of their love lives and the events of the weekend than in a physics class.

"To better understand this equation," I said, pointing to the very famous formula about the gravitational pull between two bodies being in direct proportion to their mass, and inversely proportional to the square of the distance between them, "perhaps it would be useful to review some history. Does anyone know something about Newton's life, besides his affection for apples?"

No hands went up. Perhaps if the question had concerned Keanu Reeves or Eminem, there would have been a forest of raised hands. But I wasn't disheartened. After all, who was Newton to them?

"Very possibly, Isaac Newton was the greatest thinker of all time," I said, answering my own question. "Things would be quite different today if

Newton had never existed. For instance, we wouldn't have satellites. And no cell phones would interrupt me while I'm teaching."

I searched the last row, from where the annoying sound was coming, and quickly saw a blushing female face. I didn't want to get involved in disciplinary issues, especially not when my talk was finally having an effect on my sleepy audience.

"But, Father, Newton didn't invent satellites."

"That's right," I answered, addressing the kid who spoke as he doodled distractedly on his notebook. "But I'd have a tough time putting one of them in orbit without an understanding of the law of gravity. And without satellites, there wouldn't be any digital television or global positioning, or a great deal of our communications," I said, almost too self-assured. "And not only that. Newton's laws explain the tides, the trajectory of projectiles, and, of course, the movement of the planets. All bodies in the universe exert the same kind of pull on one another. A couple of multiplications, a simple division, that's all you need."

I turned to the board, again pointing at the formula, and kept talking, deciding to change my focus from a mathematical to an anecdotal discourse, which usually worked much better with teenagers.

"In less than two years of studying on his own, Newton became the best mathematician in England. He was a solitary genius, cheerless and very forgetful. People said he often stayed sitting on his bed for hours, thinking, without being aware of whether it was time to get up or go to sleep. And that he poked his eye with a knitting needle to see what he could find there."

The kids laughed and began to mimic him with their pens, pretending to nail them into their eyebrows. In order to prevent any damage, I continued.

"Newton went into seclusion for two solid years so he could think. And this book was the result: it's known as the *Principia,* for short."

I had brought a modern edition of his masterpiece, *Philosophiae Naturalis Principia Mathematica,* published in English as *Principia: Mathematical Principles of Natural Philosophy,* to class. I held it up high for all to see and then put it on a girl's desk in the front row so that she could take a look at it and pass it along to the rest of the class.

"As soon as this book was published, Newton became famous. The scholars of his time realized immediately that it was something extremely special, the product of a rare intelligence. He was overwhelmed with honors for the rest of his life, becoming the first British scientist to be knighted. This book explains," I added, "the pull that sets the planets in motion, and also how they move, mathematically. Planets and satellites move in the same way. So if you want to know how our satellites orbit in space, you'll find the answer here."

The kids seemed doubtful. The book went around their desks almost without pause, some only trying to see how heavy it was, as if its credibility depended on its weight. Ironically, they were unaware that they themselves were subjecting the *Principia* to the laws of gravity.

"Newton did not make his discoveries from out of nowhere," I continued. "Other scientists before him provided the basis for his work. He himself admitted that if he could see farther than any man before him, it was because he stood on the shoulders of giants. He was referring to the four most important astronomers in history, whose lives had overlapped in the sixteenth and seventeenth centuries. I'm sure their names are familiar to many of you."

I paused.

"The Pole Nicolaus Copernicus was the first to assert that the Sun, and not the Earth, was the center of the universe."

Some students nodded, as if they had known this all along. I gave them the benefit of the doubt.

"The Dane Tycho Brahe spent forty years measuring the position of the planets with unprecedented accuracy."

Brahe produced a much less enthusiastic response among my students than Copernicus—which was not saying much.

"The Italian Galileo Galilei was the first one to make telescopes. And the German Johannes Kepler discovered that the planets don't move in circles around the Sun, but in ellipses."

"Father, was Kepler a murderer?"

The question startled me.

"Where did you get that from, Simon?"

"I read it yesterday in the newspaper," he answered offhandedly. The other students looked at him with disapproval. The bell rang, and they were running the risk of my launching into another explanation. Twenty-five cell phones were coming back to life.

"Don't believe everything you read in the papers," I said. "Now, all of you, out."

I picked up my *Principia* from where it had been left in the last row, chewing gum stuck on the cover.

Breaks, contrary to popular belief, weren't established so children could have a respite from teachers and classes, but most likely so that teachers could have a respite from students. I had a half hour free for a cup of coffee and for reading e-mail in my room. So I crossed the yard to our living quarters. The Jesuit building occupies four blocks in the center of the city. About half of this space is taken up by the school, almost a hundred years old now, with about eight hundred boys and girls. The school yard is in the middle, with its basketball courts and an open field for various sports. On one side there's a small building, about six years old, which serves as the gym. It rains often here, and politicians didn't like the idea of having kids deprived of sports, so they paid for it without protest. They had a totally different opinion about the science labs in the basement of the main building. No matter how hard we tried, we could never renovate them, and the kids had to work with test tubes and glass flasks that seemed to have come out of Dr. Jekyll's lab. We always met with the excuse of asking the appropriate funding organization, and we were sent to request support from independent groups instead. But since federal and local governments were controlled by the various political factions, they managed to pass the ball from one to another without ever giving us a penny. The third party involved was the city council, controlled by the power of the local contractors. Recently our administrator had received an unbelievable offer for us to sell and get out of there.

I got to the other end of the field without being hit by a ball. Minor success. I never know if they do it on purpose, but my good nature obliges me to think otherwise.

I said hello to Brother Matthew, the caretaker, who was on the phone arguing with the plumber—the eternal problem with the boiler. I got to the second floor fast, taking three steps at a time. On the way to my refuge, I stopped at the entertainment hall to pick up yesterday's paper. My room is somewhat bigger than the others because it's considered a communal space, with three networked computers wired to a broadband router. This is all we have, though it certainly isn't enough anymore. We just can't spend on infrastructure until we know for sure if we're going to move out, but the number of students who want to get online keeps growing every day. So I usually lock my door only during class time and at night. My personal cybercafé closes at eleven.

I turned on my computer as usual. The tower was always connected to the three computers in general use. I had several messages from the Voynich List waiting to be read—surely progress reports from my colleagues in the world outside. I would read them in the evening. There was an e-mail from Waldo, bypassing the filter. He often violated the List's protocol, using it to send personal messages. He lived in Mexico City, so our communications were in Spanish. To be honest, Waldo was often a little too much. Maybe it was because of loneliness, or because he had some unmentionable disease, but he always seemed to be glued to the screen. His contributions to the group were generally skimpy, misinformed, or naive. This one was no exception:

> Hector, I'm still reviewing old translations. I don't think they should have been rejected so lightly. "The Eye of God the Son strives through to the Great Void" could be a reference to the Star of Bethlehem. Tell me if I'm right, you who know so much astronomy. It could be a comet going through space. I didn't want to send it to the List before I checked with you. Waldo.

It didn't take me long to answer him. That phrase has been going around for more than twenty-five years, and the Stojko transcription was total nonsense.

> Waldo, forget that phrase, it's been discredited. It doesn't make any more sense than this other one: "The quick brown fox jumps over the lazy dog." Hector.

It would take Waldo a couple of weeks to discover, if he did at all, that the cryptic phrase I'd given him was just a test sentence for a standard QWERTY keyboard. In any case, he would forgive my joke.

I tumbled into bed and took a look at the newspaper. It wasn't until the last page, the one for odd news and gossip, that I found what I was looking for.

Kepler Under Suspicion

An investigation is under way to determine whether the astronomer killed his teacher in order to steal documents essential to his discoveries. According to the news agency report, the famous German astronomer and mathematician Johannes Kepler (1571–1630) is now in the ranks of the accused. A group of scientists from the Austrian town of Peuerbach will consider tomorrow whether the so-called father of modern astronomy was also a murderer. "The Poison of Publicity: Reaction to an American Thesis About a Kepler Murder Story" is the title of the special presentation by German professor Volker Bialas, who is to open the discussion. The Georg von Peuerbach Third International Symposium will be held in the above-mentioned town in the highlands of the Austrian Federation. The objective of the forum today and tomorrow, presenting distinguished scientists from several countries, is to discuss the successive stages in the development of the physical and mathematical models that finally provided the basis in the seventeenth century for Newton's work on the calculation and description of planetary movements around the Sun. The organizers titled the symposium "From Peuerbach to Newton. From Planetary Theories to Celestial Mechanics: Newton's Revolution." These researchers emphasize the importance of Kepler's work, among others, in this scientific development. But this time, besides the recognized contributions to human knowledge, the participants will study the possible accuracy of the theory presented by the American journalist Joshua Gilder, according to whom, Kepler murdered the Danish mathematician Tycho Brahe (1546–1601). Kepler met him in Prague, where Kepler had become a math professor after being banished from the city of Graz because he was Protestant. Brahe was the court mathematician to Emperor Rudolph II, and Kepler succeeded Brahe after becoming his favorite protégé and teaching assistant. This theory, which Gilder and his wife, Anne-Lee, proposed—and published in their book *Heavenly Intrigue*—is based on tests of Brahe's hair, seemingly proving that Kepler's teacher died of mercury poisoning. The American journalist concluded that the only likely murderer could be the German astronomer, motivated by his ambition to get Brahe's papers, which Kepler finally inherited and which now are considered essential to his discoveries. Moreover, Gilder found confirmation of his accusation in a letter Kepler addressed to a British scientist four years after Brahe's death, where he admitted indirectly to having stolen the Danish mathematician's intellectual property. Apparently, according to an ORF (Austrian public television) posting yesterday on its Web site, Kepler had taken advantage of the sorrow and ignorance of Brahe's heirs to make sure he got possession of his master's papers, though that did not prevent a legal dispute with them. The famous Kepler's laws, presented in 1609 (in his *Astronomia Nova*) and later in 1619 (*Harmonices Mundi*), made possible the understanding of how the planets move around the Sun, establishing models that are still valid today, an accomplishment that would have been impossible without Brahe's earlier findings. In his time, the Danish astronomer was one of the greatest scholars of celestial space, and for nearly forty years he recorded the first precise astronomical data in scientific history.

In all these months of research, I hadn't noticed a small, but important, detail, that two of the best mathematicians in history had worked under Rudolf II. But neither of them, as far as I knew, made any mention in his works, letters, or diaries of the strange manuscript. I looked at the clock and still had ten minutes before my next class. Since the scandal arose from a book written by an American journalist, it wouldn't be too difficult to find it on Amazon. Again I sat up in bed, facing my computer.

HEAVENLY INTRIGUE: JOHANNES KEPLER, TYCHO BRAHE, AND THE MURDER BEHIND ONE OF HISTORY'S GREATEST SCIENTIFIC DISCOVERIES, BY JOSHUA GILDER AND ANNE-LEE GILDER (2005).

I picked up the phone and dialed the administrator's extension. Fortunately Julian was right there.

"Julian, it's Hector. I need your permission to spend some money."

"How much?"

"Seventeen euros. No, wait. It's less. The price is in dollars."

"Come on, man, don't bother me with such trifles. I'm reviewing the construction company offer right now. There are so many zeroes that they roll across the table and fall off. You know the credit card number."

I filled out the form and selected the cheapest delivery. I continued reading the book summary, which essentially agreed with the newspaper review. Then I took a look at the readers' comments. One of them was quite eloquent.

Besides being an extraordinary book about the history of science, it tells about real-life murders. The authors open a window on a fascinating time, when astronomy, astrology, and even alchemy were all considered branches of the same science. The section devoted to alchemy is especially good, with an extensive investigation of mercury, which convinced the authors that it was the substance used to poison Tycho Brahe. The Gilders combine modern forensic techniques with a criminal analysis of the likely motives to show that Kepler—one of the most famous astronomers in history—is the more than probable murderer. [. . .] Brahe's obsession with perfection made him store away volume after volume of annotations. He was too busy looking at the stars to analyze his own data, and he needed an assistant like Kepler.

In contrast to Brahe's noble birth, Kepler had a difficult childhood. His father abandoned his family during trying times of continuous religious strife. His humble origins turned into an abnormal arrogance, and his extraordinary mathematical ability led him to come up with a new theory concerning the movement of the planets. The proof of his theory lay in the observations that Brahe had gathered over four decades, and obtaining them became an obsession that finally led him to murder. [. . .] I think the book deserves an episode of *CSI*. Many pieces of evidence easily lead you to agree with their conclusion. The authors don't assert they

can prove that Kepler poisoned Brahe, but everything points in
that direction. They have found many unpublished letters. If I were
on the jury, I would vote guilty.

This discussion perplexed me, a guilty verdict after a trial without proof. The story seemed more appropriate for the seventeenth century than for the twenty-first. Kepler's family had been persecuted in a similar manner when his mother was accused of being a witch by a neighbor, who alleged that she began to suffer terrible pains after the old woman had given her a wicked look. Kepler's mother came close to being burned at the stake. In any case, I would wait to read the book and judge for myself.

Now I had to go through my own martyrdom and lock myself in the classroom with the blessed children.

That evening I went back to the *Voynich Manuscript*. Messages from the List were accumulating every day, but each investigator followed a different direction. At least seven main lines of research were open, none advancing at a greater pace than the others. The oldest one established that the book simply used a ciphered alphabet. The letters had been replaced by symbols, and these had been scattered by various means of greater or lesser complexity. One need only to find the right algorithm to be able to reverse the process. This method was known before the earliest time the manuscript could possibly have been written, so this has always been considered a plausible hypothesis. The problem is that it's too simple, because today no cipher could withstand the speedy combinations and permutations of a powerful computer. Since the enigma hasn't been solved, the consensus is that the original system was terribly complex, introducing false spaces between words or eliminating the vowels. This is the preferred approach of the majority of researchers on the List.

Another small group of scholars believes that a second book is needed, or at least some kind of guide, in order to translate the text. The manuscript could be deciphered if an unknown second book containing codes could be found. But unless these codes had been hidden in the manuscript itself, translation would be impossible. Another approach has many advocates among newcomers. Though devised in 1499 by Johannes Trithemius, it is very often seen in computer-security manuals. Its technical name is steganography, and it means a message hidden in a sea of seemingly meaningless texts. This theory is very difficult to prove, or to refute, because the camouflage around secret messages could be as labyrinthine as you wanted to make it. For reasons that I can't explain, this is one of my favorite theories.

A large number of linguists—we really have them—favor another explanation. They flee, like scalded cats, from mathematical theories. Some believe that its words were written in an exotic language with an unknown alphabet probably originating in Asia. There are also partial translations, not making much sense, based on a variant of Manchurian Chinese because its short words follow patterns that change according to the tone of voice. The history of the manuscript could be a favorable factor if it could be proved that the book came from the Orient in one of Marco Polo's journeys or was brought by a missionary somewhat later—maybe a Jesuit—using the route first taken by Vasco da Gama in 1499. Although da Gama was associated with Jesuits, I don't favor this idea. Another group of linguists posits that it's a mixed polyglot language. It is here that the heretic Cathars enter the scene, because of the nature of the illustrations—all, according to these scholars, depicting religious rituals. Truly, this is the craziest of all the possibilities.

The most recent interpretation is the one offered by Friedman, the expert military cryptographer. He says the language, Voynichian, was devised following a certain logical pattern. The meanings of words could be deduced from the particular sequence of letters, and therefore, these new words would have enough prefixes and suffixes. This seems plausible, but the problem is that we don't know the meanings of these prefixes and suffixes, even though they could be rather clearly identified.

The last group is the skeptics. For them, the *Voynich Manuscript* is nothing but a ruse, a tremendous rigamarole without any meaning. A fraud created to ensnare Rudolf II, a naive and credulous king.

According to most reliable sources, Rudolf II (1552–1612) was the first owner of the *Voynich Manuscript*. He was king of Bohemia and Hungary, and emperor of what was then known as the Holy Roman Empire, rather an honorary title, since most cities and territories of the Roman Empire were even more autonomous than they are now. Rudolf was a nephew of King Philip II of Spain, the son of Philip's sister María and Maximilian of Austria. He spent his adolescence in the Spanish court, where he developed an interest in art, science, and mathematics, plus a dark and gloomy disposition that was to plague him all his life. Wanting to be away from the eternal disputes between Catholics and Protestants, and the threats from Turkey, he spent four years as a recluse in a castle in Vienna. Rudolf established his own court in the city of Prague, thus freeing himself from the oppression he had felt in Vienna. After his recovery from a particularly deep depression, he had built in his court an unusual museum that was visited by a few selected guests, but was never open to the public. Gallery after gallery exhibited thousands of paintings and sculptures, precious stones, coins, and all sorts of oddities, one of the most intriguing being a collection of pictures of dwarfs. It was also said that he had a regiment composed entirely of giants.

Between 1605 and 1606 he added two special rooms to his palace to hold his extensive library and his collection of clocks and scientific instruments. Along the passageways in this labyrinth of his dreams, a lucky visitor could see a multitude of exotic animals roaming free, or meet the most diverse personages. Rudolf collected all kinds of paintings, engravings, manuscripts, and books from his time, and he developed friendships not only with painters, philosophers, and mystics but also with scientists such as Tycho Brahe and Johannes Kepler, whose research expenses he gladly covered. The *Voynich Manuscript* first appeared in these magical surroundings.

An icon was blinking on the computer screen. A message was coming in, and I opened it to find out what the sender wanted to tell me.

Hi, Hector. I got new results with Joanna's program. See attachment. John C.

John Carpenter worked at Cambridge, a fact that gave his research an aura of prestige enjoyed by very few. His address never failed to impress: John M. Carpenter, PhD in Physics, Royal Greenwich Observatory, Cambridge, UK. John was thirty-four, like me, and judging by the photos on his Web site, we resembled each other. We had the same ungainly build and were blessed with incipient baldness. A couple of times each year, John visited Spain, or rather, the astrophysics laboratories in the Canary Islands. Thus, out of his extraordinary kindness, he would send messages in his no-frills Spanish.

The attachment he had sent this time was his transcription of two so-called astronomic folios of the *Voynich Manuscript*. We had been working on them for weeks, exchanging characters in every direction, trying to get some word in Latin, English, German, or Spanish that came close to what we supposed was known at that time. A star, a planet, a constellation, a zodiac sign, or the name of a month, anything we could use. We were applying an extended version of EVA (European Voynich Alphabet), a translation of the glyphs in the manuscript into Roman characters. The best-known version was created by Gabriel Landini and Rene Zenderbergen in 1990. The whole manuscript has already been converted this way, and it was easy to turn it into computer codes in order to study connections, coincidences, or simply statistics. EVA could be read more or less like this.

ꙮꙌ ꙗꙅꙁ ꙅꙅ ꙗꙅ ꙯ꙻꙶ꙰ꙁ ꙅꙅ ꙯ꙮꙩ ꙮꙅꙶꙭꙁ ꙮꙩ ꙙꙅꙶꙮ ꙰ꙅ꙯ꙶ꙰ꙅꙶꙁꙅ

This is the approximate form in which Cervantes would have written the beginning of *Don Quixote* in Voynichian. The reverse process, the one we were interested in, would allow us to write it this way.

> qotedy qoteedy qokedy ytedy okedor
> qosheol ochekdy qqochy okdy qotedy
> o keal qokalr shckhey qkolo dyqoche
> qoteeke ytedy okedor qoteedy qotedy

Spoken aloud, this sounds pretty silly.

2

week later we were enjoying a fun morning, or at least I was. It was a splendid day and I had just finished making a physics test for the kids. A sensation of sweet revenge for their many blunders in class sustained me. According to most of them, if we bored a hole through the Earth and dropped a stone into it, it would come out at full speed on the other side. I crossed the school yard at a good clip, thinking about this and shaking my head bemusedly while dodging the balls whizzing by. From out of nowhere, one dropped into my hands. Instinctively, I aimed for the nearest basket and made a shot. The ball traced a clean arc into the hoop, making a perfect parabola.

"Pure luck," someone said behind me. "I bet you can't do it again, Father."

One of my students passed the ball back to me. A few others smiled expectantly.

"All you need to do is apply the laws of physics," I said confidently.

And I threw the ball right back. Bull's-eye.

"Three more points for the priests' team," I said, raising as many fingers, like a referee.

I decided to challenge them on their own court.

"Well, for once I'll rely on Newton rather than on God. For every missed shot, I'll give all of you a point on Monday's test."

We agreed on ten shots from outside the three-point line. Word of the challenge spread like wildfire around the school yard, and soon I was surrounded by about fifty adolescents ready to enjoy booing me.

First shot. Basket.

Second shot. Basket.

Third shot. Circled the rim. Teetered. Basket.

The fourth and fifth shots touched the net on their way through the hoop. The booing had stopped; they would actually have to study for the test. So they began to be on my side as they realized that this ungainly priest knew his stuff.

Sixth shot. Rim again, various shouts, but finally the ball fell through the hoop. More applause than boos.

Needless to say, I won the bet. I had never played in the yard with the kids, so my victory changed their image of me as a stiff professor incapable of even glancing at anything but books and computers. I jogged toward our building.

Matthew was waiting for me at the door as if he were my trainer.

"What a ruckus you created, Hector."

I smiled and said nothing, just went up with great strides as usual. Matthew shouted after me, "There's a package in the mail for you. Here."

It was from Amazon. The book I'd been waiting for. I leafed through it while walking to my room.

The coffin was covered in black velvet with the family coat of arms in gold. The officials marched in front, carrying large heavy candles and holding up a beautifully adorned standard where his titles and honors had been written. Behind the coffin, his mount, followed by another horse in mourning, harnessed in black. Men followed, single file, carrying Tycho's armor and sword. Twelve noblemen carried the coffin. Behind them was his youngest son, accompanied by his Swedish uncle, Count Erik Brahe, and Baron Ernfried von Minckwicz. The funeral cortege continued with imperial chancellors, nobles, and barons, Tycho's aides and servants, his widow (leaning on two royal judges), and finally his three daughters, each one escorted by two noblemen. The

streets were so crowded that the cortege had to walk as if between
two walls, and the church was so filled with nobles and other
important figures that there was no empty space inside. When
the elegy ended, his helmet, armor, shield, and other combat gear,
indicative of his social position, were displayed in the crypt.

This was how Kepler described Tycho Brahe's funeral in Prague. In the
first pages of their book, the Gilders echoed this passage, often repeated
in Tycho Brahe's many biographies. He was, paradoxically, an important
historical figure in Denmark, where he died in exile and was buried. I continued checking the first pages of *Heavenly Intrigue* against a couple of
good books I had on the history of astronomy, and against a few others
I found in the old school library. At least for now, there was nothing to
scream about.

Tycho Brahe's death was very well documented in the bibliography. It's
unusual to see it recounted by his assistant, Johannes Kepler. The whole thing
started on October 13, 1601, only a few days after Kepler's crucial encounter
with Rudolf II, when the emperor contracted his services to carry out one of
the greatest scientific endeavors in history: the composition of certain tables
of astronomical events, to be named the *Rudolphine Tables* in his honor.
Tycho Brahe had probably accompanied a friend, Baron Minckwicz, to dine
at Peter Ursinus Rozmberk's palace. The protocol among nobles dictated
that no guest should get up from the dinner table before the host. This rule of
etiquette probably led Tycho to his deathbed. In his diaries, Kepler detailed
in full everything that occurred during those last fatal days.

Brahe remained seated, having to hold his urine much longer
than usual. Though he had drunk a lot, and felt the pressure in his
bladder, he was more concerned with proper good manners. When
he finally got home, he was unable to pee.

As a doctor, Tycho had some experience in such matters and tried several remedies, but to no avail. Brahe was in agony for five days and nights,
suffering intense pain and unable to sleep.

Finally he was able to urinate, but only a little and with tremendous pain. His bladder was still blocked. After insomnia came intestinal fevers and, gradually, delirium.

On October 24 his delirium ceased, and amid prayers, tears, and efforts by his family to console him, his energy failed, and he died peacefully.

Kepler continued his account, revealing intimate details that have become historical.

His celestial observations were interrupted, and his thirty-five years of work came to an abrupt end. During the last night of his delirium, just like a musician composing a song, Brahe repeated over and over: *"Non frustra vixisse vidcor"* (Don't let my life appear to have been lived in vain).

This prayer could be directed only to God, and to Kepler himself.

The Beinecke Rare Book and Manuscript Library of Yale University has what may be a truly valuable treasure in its MS 408. Not so much for what its pages might reveal—at first glance it's only a treatise on medicinal herbs—but for the fame accumulated over its five centuries of existence. I thought it was best to return directly to the source in order to see it with fresh eyes, and make strictly technical entries, free of commentary and subjective opinions. So for the umpteenth time I opened the Yale Web site.

MS 408. Encrypted manuscript. Central Europe (?) from the fifteenth or sixteenth century. Scientific or magical text in an unidentified language, apparently ciphered, perhaps based on Roman characters. Some scholars believe that the text was the work of Roger Bacon, since the illustrations seem to represent subjects of interest to him. [. . .] In parchment, 102 folios, with contemporary Arabic numbering—though not on every leaf. It includes five double folios, three triples, one quadruple, and one sextuple, folded to size 225 x160 mm, 240 pages in all. [. . .] Almost every page contains botanical and scientific drawings, many full-page, in ink and watercolor in various shades of green, brown, yellow, and red. With the apparent themes of the drawings as a base, the contents of the manuscript fall into six sections.

Part I: Botanical section, with 113 unidentified plant species, carefully depicting flowers, leaves, and root systems. Each drawing is accompanied by text; Part II: Astronomical or astrological section, with 25 astral diagrams in the form of circles, concentric or with radiating segments, some with the sun or the moon at the center. The segments are filled with stars and inscriptions, some with signs of the zodiac or naked females, some of them free-standing, others emerging from objects resembling cans or tubes; Part III: "Biological" section, with drawings of small-scale female nudes, most with bulging abdomens, immersed in or emerging from strange fluids or tubes and capsules. These drawings are the most enigmatic in the manuscript. It has been suggested that they symbolize the process of human reproduction or the process by which the soul becomes united with the body; Part IV: the "medallions" section, nine in all, very elaborate and filled with stars and cell-like shapes, with fibrous structures linking the circles. Some medallions with petal-like arrangements of rays filled with stars [. . .]; Part V: Pharmaceutical section, with about a hundred drawings of different species of herbs and medicinal plants, all with identifying inscriptions [. . .]; Part VI: Section of continuous text, with stars drawn on the inner margins. [. . .] Probably written in Central Europe, at the end of the fifteenth or during the sixteenth century. The origin and date of the manuscript are still being debated as vigorously as its puzzling drawings and undeciphered text. The identification of several of the plants as specimens from the New World brought to Europe by Christopher Columbus indicates that the manuscript could not have been written before 1493. This codex belonged to Emperor Rudolph II of Germany (Holy Roman Emperor, 1576–1612), who purchased it for 600 gold ducats, convinced that it was the work of Roger Bacon.

[. . .] Quite probably Emperor Rudolph acquired the manuscript from the English astrologer John Dee (1527–1608), who numbered each folio by hand on the upper right hand corner. It seems that Dee owned the manuscript along with other Roger Bacon works; it is believed that he lived in Prague from 1582 to 1586, a period in which he was in contact with Emperor Rudolph. In addition, Dee wrote that he received 630 ducats in October 1586, and his son Arthur noted that Dee, while in Bohemia, owned "a booke . . . containing nothing butt Hieroglyphicks [. . .] but I could not heare that hee could make it out." Emperor Rudolph probably gave the manuscript to Jacobus Horcicky de Tepenecz (who died in 1622). The inscription is still visible under ultraviolet light. In 1666 a man named Marcus Marci appears to have presented the book to Athanasius Kircher, a Jesuit priest (1601–1680). The book was acquired in 1912 by Wilfred M. Voynich from the Jesuit House at Frascati, near Rome. It was donated to this library in 1969 by H. P. Kraus, who had purchased it from the estate of Ethel Voynich, Wilfred's second wife.

This was practically all that was known objectively about the *Voynich Manuscript,* a cocktail of hieroglyphics, emperors, astrologers, and, to top it all, Jesuit priests. Enough to make anyone lose interest.

Early the next morning I had a message from Joanna waiting for me. It was short, very short:

Hector: Read *Scientific American*!

Joanna always writes from her small Swedish city whose name I can never remember. It was not really relevant, because, in our view, her world was reduced to a studio full of computers. That was the image we had of her, the only one we got through her webcam. She had the luxury of working at home for a computer company that paid well for her exceptional talent. As a defender of universal free software, she gave me constant problems because her programs were often incompatible with mine. John acted as intermediary, which allowed us to continue our joint research.

Scientific American was published in Spain as *Investigación y Ciencia*. Usually the English articles took a month or two to appear in Spanish. Our school subscribed to the original so that students who so wished—not many—could consult it in the library when it first came out. We also had a few computer magazines and these were the most popular.

I had nothing to lose by taking a look at the latest issue.

All of a sudden the power went out. I left my room in the dark and tried unsuccessfully to reactivate the circuit. Probably a fuse had burned out. Yet another reason to abandon our old house. Feeling my way, I entered Matthew's room and borrowed his ring of keys. Miraculously, the lights came back on at that moment. I decided then to take my morning constitutional, crossing the yard to the main building. It was still dark and chilly, mainly because there was no moon to reflect any sunlight. But the sky was beautifully clear and the stars stood out brilliantly against it. Under the bow of the always menacing warrior Orion, I opened the side door leading directly into the library. There was a magazine rack with the latest issues by the entrance. The September and October editions were already there, as if waiting for me. I found the article I wanted almost immediately in the September issue. Joanna's message had come to me quite late, but it saved me from having to do the research on the Internet.

"The Mystery of the *Voynich Manuscript*: A New Analysis of a Four-Century-Old Ciphered Document That Proposes It Is Only a Ruse," by Gordon Rugg.

It was six full pages long!

As I began reading, the lights went out again.

I heard running steps, a distant jump, and then a cry of pain accompanied by some epithets that, due to their scatological nature, probably didn't come from any regular occupant of the house. Somebody had probably been playing with the switches all along.

Surely one of the kids was the author of the prank, or maybe it was a ghost paid by the construction company to accelerate our decision. And it had cost him.

3

The biography of Danish astronomer Tycho Brahe was the least known of those that Newton considered giants. Perhaps this was because Tycho didn't make any concrete discovery as relevant as the sun-centered system of Copernicus, or the telescopic observations of Galileo, or the movements of the planets of Brahe's assistant, Kepler. Brahe's concept of the universe was erroneous, and the so-called Tychonic system was a pretty artificial combination of heliocentrism and geocentrism, the Sun and the Earth competing for control of the cosmos. History probably hasn't been fair to him. Even life itself, because many investigators have wondered what might have happened to astronomy had he lived even a few years longer. In ten years he would have shared the telescope with Galileo, and surely this would have changed his conception of the universe, perhaps even beyond Galileo's. His premature death was an irreparable loss for the scientific world. Though no longer a young man—in 1601 he was fifty-four, almost a senior citizen in the sixteenth century—he was still at the peak of his faculties.

As I read more and more of the Gilder book—which I interspersed with my own sources to avoid becoming too biased—I kept checking the details carefully, so as not to allow any mistakes whatsoever. One of their strongest arguments for attributing Tycho's murder to his apprentice, Kepler, was that the importance of Kepler's discoveries made it unlikely he would be the primary suspect for such a crime. Could a murder for the advancement of science be justified? This is the tricky question the authors pose throughout the pages of *Heavenly Intrigue,* leading the reader to conclude that in fact there was such a murder. Certainly a movie could be made of Tycho Brahe's fantastic life. He was born December 14, 1546, in Skane, to a noble family in *Hamlet*'s Denmark. One of the characters who inspired this masterpiece, Frederick Rosenkrantz, was a rather unfortunate cousin of Tycho's. (Rumor had it that Rosenkrantz was sent to fight the Turks in order to maintain his noble standing. He had impregnated a young lady. In the end, he died while attempting to intervene in a duel soon after receiving some economic help from his famous relative.) Today Tycho's hometown belongs to Sweden, but then, along with Norway, it was under the unstable Danish crown. Its rotten smell drove Tycho to exile and to seek the protection of Rudolf II, which was the fundamental event in this historical drama now raveling and unraveling in my notes.

It's not easy to classify Tycho Brahe. He is, no doubt, a prototypical Renaissance man. Considered a national hero by Danes, Swedes, Norwegians, and even Czechs, he cultivated the arts, letters, diplomacy, fencing, all kinds of luxuries, and above all, science. His poems are considered masterpieces of Scandinavian literature. His works in engineering, his instruments, and his inventions could well compete with Leonardo's. His disfigured face is proof of his devotion to the sword, the result of a youthful duel. Chronicles of his time say that Tycho tried to settle, by swordplay, his supremacy in mathematics over another Danish nobleman from the city of Wittenberg, a student like himself. His rival surely lost the passion for numbers over time. This didn't happen to Brahe. Quite the contrary. He did, however, lose his nose in one slash, and it nearly cost him his life. Infections were very difficult to cure back then. Tycho survived, but he had to wear a prosthesis on his face for the rest of his life. He made several himself, and would normally wear a light one, made of copper. On important occasions he wore an expensive one made from an alloy of gold and silver that closely resembled his skin color. Unfortunately, plastic surgery didn't exist yet.

Tycho Brahe's birth occasioned a series of peculiar events. His mother, Beate Bille, wife of a Danish gentleman, Otto Brahe, gave birth to twins. Tycho didn't know about his twin until many years later. His brother was stillborn. According to a prior family agreement, one of the boys was to be adopted by Otto's brother—Jorgen Brahe, who was childless—and would be educated among nobles so that he could inherit his uncle's wealth and bountiful estate. Fate caused a rift in the powerful Brahe family. At only two years of age, Tycho was kidnapped and taken to live with his uncle's family, who raised him as a son.

Paradoxically, this had some benefits. His aunt and adoptive mother, Inger Oxe, belonged to a cultured family. There was a sharp contrast in their way of thinking from Otto's, whose vision of life for the boy didn't go beyond a military education and a career of service to the king. Thus young Tycho was given an academic foundation that he wouldn't have had living at home with his contentious brothers. Tycho soon excelled as a student and, by the time he was sixteen, was capable of discussing any scientific matter with the top academic authorities. He probably entered the University of Copenhagen in 1559, when he was twelve. Such precocity was not so rare then. Life was different, and so was life expectancy. Lutheran university education went beyond the classic instruction in Latin, Greek, Hebrew, logic, rhetoric, and dialectics. The influence exerted by Philipp Melanchthon, friend and follower of Martin Luther, was evident. Understanding biblical texts demanded a knowledge of literature and history, while the ancient and the sacred made the knowledge of geometry and arithmetic indispensable. These disciplines inevitably led to astronomy, the science considered closest to the heavens. Astronomy established the ecclesiastical calendar and was the practical basis for astrology. Melanchthon, like many other thinkers of his time, saw no distinction between the two; he believed that man's fate was intimately connected to the stars and planets. So Tycho Brahe soon began to practice astrology. Kepler did as well, a bit more wholeheartedly, and to a lesser extent so did Galileo. The Pole Nicolaus Copernicus was the only one of the greats who never wrote a horoscope.

Though both Kepler and Tycho believed that planets exerted an influence, they didn't accept predestination. Man's will, if strong enough, could conquer the dictum of the stars. They both gained fame and fortune with their predictions, which were largely based on logic and what is known today as psychology. They weren't fools and didn't wish to disappoint their kings and protectors, whose only interest in astronomy was astrology. Once, when Tycho was accosted by a nobleman who had received radically different readings from two different astrologers, the Danish sage simply explained it away by saying that the astrologers probably hadn't used the same ephemeral charts. He evidently knew the differences between the so-called Alphonsine and Prutenic tables. The first were published in Toledo in 1252, elaborated by fifty Arab and Jewish astronomers under the patronage of Alfonso X (the Wise), king of Castile. They followed Ptolemy's classic model with the Earth as the center of the universe. The other tables were based on the Copernican model, and owed their name to the king of Prussia, to whom they had been dedicated. Neither of these models satisfied Tycho, so he created his own. He began by measuring anew the positions of the stars and planets. He was only sixteen.

Sixteen is the average age of my students, and barely half a dozen of them have been able to pass the physics test. Nonetheless, correcting the tests brought quite an unexpected joy for me: one of them was simply perfect. I couldn't find a single error in any of the concepts or development of the formulas, not to mention his good penmanship. Of course, the author just happened to be the kid who asked the impertinent questions, the one who read the newspaper. Naturally curious, he was as extremely irritating as he was intelligent. I decided to talk to him after class. I had no intention of embarrassing him in front of the other kids, most quite proud of their ignorance and lack of concern about their future or about life.

I was heading to class when Dean Damian met me in the tutoring room.

"Hector, do you have any idea who did it?"

"Who did what?"

"You haven't been in the yard?"

"Not yet. I was on my way."

We went out together. A huge graffiti covered the side wall. I was shocked.

"It appeared this morning. I imagine some mischievous kids did it last night. I'm going to put an end to this once and for all."

Damian wasn't kidding. This sort of thing was happening more and more frequently, and meetings with parents were dishearteningly ineffectual. Their kids were angels, and in their eyes we were devils incarnate. They lectured us on how to be more flexible, how to motivate the students. They gave ridiculous excuses for tardiness and absences. The parents were actually accomplices to their kids' misbehavior.

But this was different.

I couldn't open my mouth. Or close it, for that matter. I was flummoxed.

"It's just covered with scribbles!" Damian shouted, raising his arms to the heavens.

The whole wall was certainly covered with large characters written in Voynichian.

I told Damian about the blackouts last night and the sounds of running and jumping. I copied the characters into my notebook, but I didn't tell Damian what the graffiti was. I needed to find a sensible explanation.

I canceled my first class. Meanwhile, the kids were locked in the study hall. You could see the mixture of satisfaction and fear of punishment for their anonymous mischief.

I compared the characters with EVA. Some were not perfect, but the transcription was clear.

ACHILLES' RAGE WILL FALL UPON YOU

And unfortunately, so was its meaning. Someone was threatening me; I had no idea why. It could very well be one of the kids. I didn't think they were particularly skilled in classical Greek texts, but a movie about Troy was very popular, and it was possible they knew that Hector, the Trojan hero, died at the hand of Achilles, the Greek hero.

But this didn't really seem to fit. I don't believe in punishment, and a failing grade was of no concern to them, so why would they hate me? Besides, if anyone were capable of using the Voynichian alphabet in such a way, he would be a straight-A student. I tried to come up with a list of possible enemies. It didn't take long.

I've got no enemies. What was going on?

* * *

That afternoon I locked myself in my room. I knew something that the others didn't. The problem was, I didn't know enough. It was simply a graffiti-covered wall at a school. Did I need to worry about it? After all, students threatened their teachers every day, most without any real intent. But in this case, the students were surely not to blame. They weren't capable of something so subtle and complex. Ignorance and innocence usually travel together.

Since I'd become a priest, my contacts with the outside world had greatly diminished. My new family was within the seminary and monastery walls, in parishes and religious retreats. My real family led a quiet life, away from the city, devoted to the peaceful work of orchards and warm chats with neighbors. Every afternoon at this time, my father would play dominoes in the casino, and my mother would be watching television with my aunts, perhaps planning an exciting shopping trip to the capital. Life there was simple.

More than once I had requested being sent away for missionary work. The answer was always the same: everything in its proper time. Teaching provided practically the only income for the Jesuits. Donations were becoming scarce and grants from a non-Catholic government depended too much on political fluctuations. Without money there were no missionaries, so someone had to mind the store and the rear guard. But I'm not complaining. Here I have enough free time for my devotions and my passions. I don't think I could live far from books and mathematics for any length of time.

Comforted by these thoughts, I managed to convince myself that it was a practical joke; that someone had copied the characters from some folio perhaps forgotten in the printer, so I decided to continue with my usual work. Egged on by Joanna, we had changed the direction of our theories, which had proved to be useless, blind efforts. We were attempting a free dive into the turbulent waters of cryptography. John was enthused by the possibility of finding something relevant in that senseless sea of text, and even more so if the discovery related to ancient astronomy. The old way of making substitutions in classic cryptography seemed obsolete. Algorithms had become so complex that even programming them was difficult. It didn't seem logical for someone in the fifteenth century to be capable of reproducing those intricate tabulations from memory without making mistakes. One of the most disturbing characteristics of the *Voynich Manuscript* is its perfection. Impossible as it may seem, the book has no corrections, no crossed-out words. Its author was able to encode more than two hundred pages by hand without making a single mistake. It seems impossible.

The idea that one or more messages could be hidden under a pile of garbage was more logical. It was easy to write something that made no sense: you couldn't make a mistake. We could teach a monkey to type, and although there's a very faint possibility that it could become a novel, it's much more likely that the result would be total nonsense. The problem of defining the garbage in the *Voynich Manuscript* is that it seems to depend on chance, but in fact does not. That monkey knew what he was doing.

I was looking at the article by Gordon Rugg, PhD, in *Scientific American*. According to him, the author or authors of the manuscript had used a sixteenth-century method to generate nonsense. Following this method, Rugg and his assistants managed to produce pages of text resembling those in the book, something to keep in mind. But we had produced almost identical results and, on certain pages, exact copies of the originals. The only problem was that our own model for codifying the gibberish would not reproduce the whole text. And that small irreproducible part was driving us crazy. Something was not gibberish. A needle in a haystack, a diamond in the rough.

Joanna was excited that part of the British psychologist's arguments coincided with ours. Rugg had already published them in a prestigious magazine, so we wouldn't be the first. The Voynich List was filling with messages from skeptical collaborators. Some proposed abandoning the whole thing. Others urged us to finish what we had started, supporting Rugg's ideas for developing a powerful, divisible code. This code would be distributed on the Internet in the same way as genetic sequences or the famous project known as SETI (Search for Extraterrestrial Intelligence). The manuscript's recent popularity would make it easy to gather hundreds of volunteers to execute the new algorithms in their spare moments. In a few months, the proponents claimed, everything would be finished. Then we would have an exact copy of the *Voynich Manuscript,* but no translation.

Neither Joanna nor John, nor even I, wanted to entertain this prospect. Perhaps because we knew more than other people, perhaps because our own model was better than Rugg's. It was simpler and had produced better results. Above all, because we couldn't abandon the idea that the *Voynich Manuscript* was more than just gibberish devised to deceive a foolish king. The publication of Rugg's model had revealed some of our tricks, but everything was not lost. On the contrary, the fact that he independently developed a similar theory of the gibberish text served only to reinforce our thesis. From another angle, now there were more of us thinking the same way. Or almost.

Again I thought of the monkey. It was clear that no matter how many potassium-rich bananas he ate, he could never produce the degree of regularity found in the pages of the manuscript. He couldn't, for instance, write two or more times, consecutively, any of the most frequent words. Rugg agreed: How could he write "*qokedy qokedy dal qokedy qokedy*"? Not in a million years, not even if he had all the available keyboards, could the monkey reproduce my favorite typing exercise, "*The quick brown fox jumps over the lazy dog.*" Such consistency couldn't be found in any known language. Not by chance, not even by sheer will. Besides word repetition in the Voynichian phrases, there were surprisingly regular patterns in the words themselves. Some syllables appeared only at the beginning of words, some at the end and also at the beginning, but never in the middle. And so on for a multitude of combinations.

Tired of trying different schemes, I went to bed. "Early to bed and early to rise." God must disapprove of his priests staying up late playing with hieroglyphics.

4

S imon, will you please stay for a moment?"
     I hadn't yet given him the test results. We'd lost a whole day
     with the matter of the graffiti scandal, and were already much too far
behind schedule. Besides, Christmas vacation was upon us, which meant leisure for them and retreat for me. In both cases, physics would be sidelined.

The kids, with the usual uproar, went out to the yard.

"I want to talk to you about your exam."

"Is it that bad?" Simon asked, surprised. He was pretty self-confident, and the possibility of failure would totally upset him.

"Quite the contrary," I answered.

"Honestly, I didn't copy."

Of course he didn't. From whom?

"No, I already know that. It's perfect, you got an A," I said with a smile.

"Thanks," he mumbled.

"I just wanted you to know. It's the first time in two years that I've given an A."

Simon kept staring at the floor as if he were guilty of something. Then he glanced up and made a strange request.

"Father, give me a B."

"What?" I couldn't believe my ears.

"Give me a B, or better still, a C. Nerds don't cut it," he added.

"Okay, I'll give you a C plus, but only for the sake of appearances. For the final mark, I'll average it as an A. No problem," I promised him.

"Great, thanks." He sighed, relieved. "By the way, do you know any more about the murderer?"

"Who? Kepler?"

"Yes, I've been researching this on the Internet. My father helps me, and we've found some interesting things."

"Really?"

The kid kept surprising me.

"I'll tell you another time, if you want. Now I've got to take a leak."

He hurried off. If there's anything more humiliating for a kid than getting an A, it's wetting his pants. Etiquette hasn't changed much since Tycho's times.

Simon was American. His father worked at the U.S. consulate and his mother was a Spaniard who always came to the parent-teacher meetings alone. I had never met the elder Simon, and I hadn't pressed. I imagine he probably had an aversion to Spanish priests as teachers. Evidently his wife was the one in charge of their children's education.

That same afternoon after lunch, I began taking notes on Kepler. Not so much on his universal discoveries but about his life. He was born December 27, 1571, at exactly 2:30 in the morning in his grandfather's home in Weil der Stadt, a small city near Stuttgart. The great influence of astrology in those times made the precise recording of these details very important. Kepler himself, years later, concocted his own horoscope.

The same month that Kepler was born, Tycho Brahe turned twenty-five. With a generation separating them, their relationship years later was one of master and apprentice, a kind of paternal-filial love-hate. It was never the camaraderie of peers. In addition to the age gap, there was an even greater social difference. Tycho belonged to a powerfully influential Danish family, and he could afford the luxury of replacing his lost nose with a costly gold prosthesis. Kepler belonged to a noble but impoverished German family. His grandfather, Sebald, head of the clan, still had the family home and some prestige, but little money. His father, Henry, was, in Kepler's words, stupid, perverted, quarrelsome, and rude. According to his diaries, Kepler saw his mother, Katharina, in a much better light. He had saved her from being burned at the stake as a witch.

In the spring of 1575, Katharina left Johannes and his kid brother with some relatives and went in search of her husband who, after beating her severely, had abandoned the home to follow his fortune as a mercenary. Johannes contracted smallpox, which was often a death sentence back then. Though he survived, his health was much impaired, especially his eyesight. No one would have placed any bets on this cross-eyed kid becoming one of the most important astronomers in history.

Kepler's hometown, Weil der Stadt, was an autonomous imperial city of the Holy Roman Empire, which in fact was neither holy nor Roman despite its pompous name. It was also an exaggeration to say that Rudolf II ruled over the group of duchies, free cities, bishoprics, and other territories that later became modern Germany, Austria, and Czechoslovakia, as well as parts of what are now Poland, France, and Holland. With the old Spanish empire sinking everywhere, Europe was an intricate maze of religions and wars, ecclesiastical and political interests.

As a free city, Weil der Stadt enjoyed tax privileges and commercial treaties. It was also a Catholic city, loyal to the Hapsburgs. But all the area around it, including nearby Leonberg, where Kepler grew up, belonged to the belligerent Protestant duchy of Würtemberg. So Kepler was always caught between two fires. In 1555, only sixteen years before Kepler's birth, the Treaty of Augsburg was signed, solving the religious problem in a Solomonic way: "*Cuius regio, eius religio.*" This meant that the governor of a territory would choose its religion. The Keplers were devout Lutherans, and being the first Protestant family in an officially Catholic city wasn't always easy. In fact, not at all, particularly when the Counter-Reformation became more virulent. Ah, the Jesuits!

The history of the *Voynich Manuscript* meets that of the Jesuits. Somehow we were everywhere. Perhaps this desire to be everywhere explains our eagerness to take the teachings of Jesus to the four corners of the world.

In modern times the *Manuscript* appeared at the end of 1912, when Voynich found it in the House of the Society of Jesus in Mondragone, near Rome. A Jesuit priest, Athanasius Kircher (1601–1680), had left it there two hundred and fifty years before. Kircher received it from Marcus Marci, not really an ordained Jesuit, but a physician and professor at the University of Prague. In 1638 Marci traveled to Rome and met the noted scholar Kircher. They maintained a close friendship for twenty-five years, keeping up a copious correspondence. The last letter that Marci sent to Kircher would accompany the *Manuscript* on its journey. Both are now at Yale.

Though Kircher was German, he lived most of his life in Rome. Perhaps inspired by Kepler's curiosity, or Tycho's—or even Rudolf II's—he was interested in practically everything under the sun. And beyond. After eight years as the math teacher at the Collegio Romano, he managed to devote himself wholly to science. He was visited by dozens of scientists, clergymen, and members of royal families, from all over Europe, and received countless books, artifacts, natural curiosities, and mechanical inventions from them. Emperor Rudolf II had a famous, albeit lost, museum in Prague that came to life again in Rome through this Jesuit scholar. Even without dwarfs or giants, the Kircherianum, or Museum of the Collegio Romano, became a tourist attraction in the seventeenth century.

Nevertheless, neither Rudolf II in Prague nor Athanasius Kircher in Rome ever mentioned among his possessions what later became known as the *Voynich Manuscript*. The Kircherianum opened to the public in 1651, and the book didn't get to Rome until 1666, fifteen years later. When Kircher died in 1680, his successors at this museum created detailed catalogs of its contents. But the book never appeared among them.

Then the problems started. In 1773 the Society of Jesus was dissolved and its possessions confiscated. Thousands of books owned by the Jesuit order were dispersed, mainly thanks to the librarian at the Collegio Romano, a man named Lazzari who championed Cardinal Zelada, one of the primary instigators of the anti-Jesuit movement. Zelada took a large quantity of books and manuscripts to Toledo. However, Father Pignatelli saved the archives of the Society of Jesus during the Napoleonic invasion. With the end of Napoleon in 1814, the Jesuit order was reestablished, and most of its possessions restored in 1824, including the museums, libraries, and even the Vatican Astronomical Observatory. The manuscript is believed to have stayed in Rome, though nothing is known about its whereabouts during those times.

It had taken me a few sleepless nights to summarize the vicissitudes of my Jesuit predecessors for the members of the Voynich List. The order isn't secretive at all, and it's not difficult to consult our archives—they're even accessible on the Internet. Neither power nor greed has motivated us; we have nothing to hide. Otherwise, I wouldn't be here. If any Jesuit wouldn't answer my questions, I would leave. Our history has no romantic mysteries about the Illuminati or the Rosicrucians.

There are many interesting connections and relationships in Jesuit history. For instance, it's said that as a young man, Ignatius Loyola, founder of the order, had accompanied the royal treasurer of the king of Castile on a trip to Tordesillas, where Loyola met Queen Juana of Castile, later known as Juana la Loca (the Mad One). She was the great-grandmother of Rudolf II, the central figure in the history of the manuscript and the protector of Kepler and Tycho. Perhaps it was from her that Rudolf inherited his tendency to depression, eccentricity, and madness. All of these came to him, it must be said, from an unfortunate combination of family bloodlines.

The story of the Society of Jesus cannot be told without at least knowing a little more about its origins. Those were not easy times for Rome, particularly with the schism caused by Martin Luther. After Pope Leo X excommunicated him and encouraged the son of Juana of Castile, Charles V (who by then was Holy Roman emperor, king of Spain and Naples, Hapsburg lord of the Low Countries, and also a devout Catholic), to go against Luther and his followers, to capture and execute them as heretics. Emperor Charles V accepted but, aware of the risks and of the large number of converts in Germany, demanded in return that the pope help him conquer the French possessions in Italy. He succeeded in battle until the inconvenient and unexpected death of Pope Leo X, whose successor, the fainthearted Clement VII, sided with the French. This infuriated Charles. If the pope had wanted to punish the Lutherans, now the Lutherans would punish the pope. The troops of Charles's brother, Ferdinand of Austria, mostly comprised of cruel and bloody mercenaries like Kepler's father, entered Rome, first under the Duke of Bourbon, who died in the siege, and then under Juan de Urbina.

The repression was horrible. Everyone in their path was tortured, robbed, and killed. It was even worse for the priests; they were ripped open and their guts scattered in the streets. The Lutherans were possessed by a hellish hatred. They invaded hospitals and threw the sick into the Tiber. They forced Catholics to celebrate heretical masses, and killed those who refused to give Communion to donkeys. Sacred relics were desecrated, and thus Saint John's head was used as a football. Men were hanged by their genitals, and women, particularly nuns, were raped. Rome, the eternal city, no longer seemed eternal. With most of its inhabitants dead or dying, its stores closed, and the streets overflowing with cadavers, its glory seemed gone forever. These horrors lasted until 1534, when Pope Clement VII succumbed to fevers. Little by little, the city recovered, and the new pontiff, Paul III, obtained funds for artisans to reconstruct castles and palaces. Michelangelo painted *The Last Judgment* in the Sistine Chapel. Ten years after the tragedy, Rome was visited by Emperor Charles V, the man who from the shadows had engineered the sack of Rome.

A Rome that wanted to heal its wounds received Charles V with full honors. Pope Paul III had recovered the air of the Renaissance, and Rome was reborn. In 1540 Paul III approved the founding of the Society of Jesus, whose members promised a devoted allegiance to the Holy Father. He convoked the Council of Trent, setting the reluctant Church on the road to the Counter-Reformation. He ended the demonic sale of indulgences and spiritual privileges. Luther's reasons for rebellion were finally accepted, but only in order to combat him. Attention turned again to the Gospels, to religious writings by the founders of the Church. Luther got what he wanted, but it was too late.

When Pope Paul III died in 1550, he was succeeded by Julius III and then by Paul IV, who was a strong supporter of the Inquisition. He hated nakedness, burned homosexuals at the stake, and nearly ordered Michelangelo's frescoes erased. Later Pius V, another Dominican like Paul IV, continued his harsh, austere policies. He banished prostitutes from the city and Jews from papal territories, and ordered the creation of a list of forbidden books. Kepler was born under his successor, Gregory XIII (1572–1585). Tycho began his observations, and Rudolf II became Holy Roman Emperor. Pope Gregory reformed the Church and the calendar—the Gregorian calendar, inspired mainly by Copernicus—and founded the Collegio Romano, a great Jesuit school that would impart knowledge as far as China and Japan, and which in time became the Gregorian University. Galileo occasionally visited the Collegio Romano, where he made many friends as well as enemies. The giants on whose shoulders Newton stood years later were all together there, in that space and time.

5

ector, there's someone asking for you at the office."

It was barely dawn when Matthew woke me. After working pretty late, I'd expected to sleep in since I had no classes before noon. I splashed my face with excruciatingly cold water –the old boiler was on the blink again—and quickly put on a clean shirt, combed my hair, and started downstairs. I had no idea who it could be. Maybe a mother headed for her usual grocery shopping, to let me know her child was laid up in bed with a cold, had a broken collarbone from a bicycle accident, or was hung over after a night out drinking. A quick peek through the glass door confirmed my suspicions. A tall, dark woman, about thirty-five, with a huge black suitcase—incredibly heavy I found out later—was waiting for me. Quite beautiful, I had to admit.

"Good morning, ma'am. You're the mother of . . . ?"

Just as I was reaching out to shake her hand, it hit me that nobody takes a suitcase to the supermarket. At that moment there was a loud clap of thunder.

"That's quite a storm coming!" I said. "Come on in so we can keep dry."

She still hadn't spoken. She seemed shy, or maybe frightened. Perhaps she'd just left her husband and was stopping by the school to pick up her son and take him with her. In my sleepy state I imagined all kinds of scenarios.

"Hi, Hector. I'm Waldo," she said with a sweet-sounding Mexican accent.

A second, even more deafening, thunderbolt brought me back to reality. It was an impressive storm.

"Waldo? From Mexico, from the Voynich List?"

"Yes," she said, answering all three questions in a word. "I'm really Juana Pizarro. Waldo's my computer; my father named it after himself. He's also Waldo."

I couldn't believe it. That idiot guy was actually this idiot girl. And here she was, from out of the blue. I tried to cover my confusion.

"How good of you to come!" I exclaimed with my best fake smile.

"You also knew me as Joanna, in Sweden, on the Voynich List."

Third lightning bolt. They seemed perfectly timed. Who knows, maybe this apparition from the great beyond was summoning them at will. I rubbed my eyes, silenced my internal dialogue, and ushered her in.

"Come on in, Juana," I said, taking her arm. "We'll have some coffee in the visitors' room. And you'll be able to tell me everything calmly."

Matthew had turned on a couple of electric heaters very early, so the gigantic room where the chairs and tables, like the building itself, were nearly a hundred years old was warm and cozy. I tried to find a steady chair for Joanna, or Juana, among the relics.

"You must be wondering what I'm doing here."

I nodded as I prepared the coffee. For a couple of minutes, the percolator was the only sound. We were alone in the room, the kids were in class, and Matthew's transistor radio needed batteries, thank God. My own were beginning to feel recharged as we started talking and sipping our coffee.

Two and a half cups later she was well into her story. Juana was using two, three, and even four different identities on the Voynich List. From what she told me, that was often the case with the others. She obviously thought it was naive of me to have just one. She said using multiple personalities was a simple means of supporting or discrediting others, or even ourselves, as John did. Apparently our British friend had a second, parallel theory concerning the *Voynich,* so far-fetched that he didn't want to acknowledge it as his own, but so provocative he didn't want to let it go. That was one of Juana's reasons for coming to see me. The other one struck me, along with—or rather *as*—a new thunderbolt.

"I've received threats. Death threats."

She didn't know why, had no idea, but she was really frightened. She wanted to warn John and me personally and, at the same time, find a safe place until the storm subsided.

"Both literally and figuratively," she laughed, pointing at the window.

Obviously she didn't live in Sweden or work for a multinational company, or have any children. Her webcam was a fake, but she did speak perfect English after spending years studying at an American university. Her family had plenty of money and therefore she didn't need to work at all. She had devoted the past three years almost exclusively to attempting to decipher the *Manuscript*.

"So when those e-mails also started coming to my personal e-mail address, which I give only to my closest friends, I got really scared. Maybe it's just a joke, but whoever it is knows a lot of stuff about me. Much more than you could possibly imagine."

Then she smiled. "Of course you had a secret too. Don't you have to wear a habit?"

"People say clothes make the man. But they don't make the monk." I smiled back.

"I like you in person, Hector. You aren't what I'd pictured."

"Well, you certainly aren't what I'd imagined."

"Do you think I'm being hysterical?"

I walked over to the window and motioned for her to come and look. It had stopped raining. I pointed to the graffiti on the wall of the school yard.

"Read it."

She focused on it and started mumbling the translation. She was much more fluent than I in Voynichian.

"'The rage of Achi—'"

"'The rage of Achilles will fall upon you,'" I finished for her. "I had no idea what it meant until you came."

A new explosion sounded just then, and looking at me, Juana turned pale. Then she exclaimed, "But the storm's already gone by!"

"That's only the kids," I explained. "It's break time, and they're all going outside now."

We were safely above them.

* * *

Juana was staying at a very luxurious hotel nearby. She was en route to the Canary Islands, where she planned to meet John, or rather seek shelter with him. So she was really going to devote herself to the stars. I was getting the sensation of being a silent statue in this story, with FOOL stamped on my forehead. Evidently there was more than friendship between Juana and John. Of course this was none of my business, but I was a bit bothered that they'd kept this a secret for so long. John had gone to Mexico last summer, and then she'd gone to London. At least I had the whole story now, or I hoped I did.

She tried to convince me to accompany her to Tenerife and meet John too. He was doing some astronomical observations there at the end of the month, and had decided to arrive earlier in order to have more time with Juana. They thought of me, she said, before selecting the place. My country helped them decide on which island, and they took care of the rest, including the rent for the luxury villa—paid for by Waldo, the real Waldo; her father was covering all the expenses. Once again I felt like a complete idiot. I made up a dozen reasonable excuses (though the main one, my academic obligation to my students, was sufficient) and politely refused. I was almost ready to abandon the situation, even the *Voynich*, except the discoveries they hinted at had piqued my curiosity. Anyway, I didn't want to be the third wheel on their tryst.

We could continue e-mailing and even phoning to discuss questions strictly related to the research. If the time came, I could even perform their wedding ceremony. As for the recent threats, we wondered whether it was advisable to notify the police. Judging by the spectacular arrests of Internet pedophiles, terrorists, and con artists, we decided it might be better to leave them in the dark. Finally, there was nothing more than a scrubbed wall that Matthew, of course, had whitewashed that afternoon. With the evidence erased, our worries vanished too. And everything returned to normal.

"Look, Father. We downloaded this from the Internet."

Simon hung back while his classmates jostled and shoved each other out of the room. Simon brought me a printout of a recent article in a Danish scientific review. The authors, with truly Nordic names like Jacobsen and Petersen, headed a natural science museum and a planetarium, respectively. An impressive body of historical research backed up their findings. The title was self-explanatory: "How Tycho Brahe Really Died." Simon couldn't wait for me to read it, and started giving me his thorough recap.

"It seems that even if somebody has a tremendous need to pee, his bladder never bursts."

As he continued, I remembered that the first balls were actually animal bladders inflated with air.

"So Tycho must have died from some other cause," Simon went on. "Since his symptoms were like those from poisoning, people started to be suspicious."

The factual details of Tycho Brahe's agony had been well described by the aforementioned Kepler, as well as by his doctor, Johann Jessenius: extreme pain and urinary disorders from uremia, together with insomnia, fevers, and delirium. Those are the same symptoms produced by heavy metal poisoning, or by certain plants. According to the authors, the motive might have been either political or religious, since neither the Catholic Council nor the nobility felt comfortable with the great influence this Danish astronomer had gained over the weak Catholic emperor Rudolf II.

"There was an autopsy performed in 1991," Simon said. "They found a metal nose but no bladder stones."

Simon wasn't aware of Tycho's youthful incident with the sword and he was very excited when I told him about it. He didn't expect to find D'Artagnan among the best scientists in history. This first medical investigation that Simon was describing was done with the remains of Tycho Brahe's beard. It seems that Tycho's tomb in Prague was opened in 1901, in commemoration of the third centennial of his death. The authorities attempted to restore the sepulcher and make sure that the astronomer's corpse was still in place, amid rumors that it had been exhumed in 1620 when the Catholics took Bohemia. Fortunately, the remains were still there, along with those of a woman, probably his wife, Kristine, who survived him by some years. Then they took out a few fragments of his shroud and of his beard, the same ones that ninety years later were given to the Danish government by the Czech National Museum. When these samples arrived in Copenhagen, they were immediately taken to the Institute of Forensic Medicine of the state university in an attempt to shed light on the old rumors concerning the possible assassination of the Danish national hero. Using an absorption spectrometer, they measured the concentrations of arsenic, lead, and mercury.

"And they found lots of lead, as if he'd been shot—but not enough for bullets," the boy joked.

The analysis of the beard hairs revealed an abnormally high lead content, in the range of being a possible cause of death. This theory had been rejected because human remains of that period often had a high lead content. It was commonly found in kitchen utensils, pipes, and also as an ingredient to sweeten wine. In addition, the material in his coffin contained lead, possibly contaminating his beard posthumously.

"And there was no significant amount of arsenic, the classic poison," he added.

"Then came mercury, isn't that right, Sherlock?"

"Elementary, Father Watson," Simon joked. "The symptoms agree exactly with mercury poisoning. And it also seems that this Tycho guy, besides being an astronomer, was an alchemist."

Tycho had actually studied practically every branch of human knowledge; he was familiar with alchemy and medicine. Following Paracelsus, an unconventional doctor of the sixteenth century, Tycho concocted his own remedies, many of which he prescribed for Rudolf II himself, attempting to ease his mood crises and bouts of depression. Mercury was a very common ingredient in those days, and it must have been abundant in his laboratories. It's possible that the prolonged ingestion of mercury-based medicines may have been responsible for the high concentration of this metal found in the forensic analysis. Could this have killed Tycho? Simon continued.

"Since they didn't know if mercury definitely caused his death, they took some additional samples of Tycho's beard. This time they took hairs with the roots intact, which made it possible to check, based on beard growth, how long before death he had ingested the poison. They used a device at the Swedish University of Lund to test it in 1996.

"I read that it involved a modern analytical approach based on the PIXE, particle-induced X-ray emission, technique. The conclusions were definitive. The day before he died, Tycho Brahe had ingested a large quantity of mercury, which caused his death. The reason? Today we'd probably call it self-medication."

"And what part does Kepler play in all this?" I asked.

"He was around," Simon answered. "In all the movies there's got to be a bad guy, and crime never pays. At least in American movies."

After math class but before dinner, I went to say good-bye to Juana. When I arrived, she was already at the door of the hotel with her suitcase at her side, waiting for the taxi to take her to the station. She would spend the night in Madrid and fly to the Canary Islands early the next morning. John would be there waiting anxiously for her. His charter, on a direct flight from London, had arrived in Tenerife this morning.

"Forgive me for getting here so late. I was delayed talking to some parents—" I said, trying to apologize and noticing that she kept nervously checking her watch.

"I've nothing to forgive you for," she cut in. "On the contrary, I'm really indebted to you. After all, I'm the one who showed up unannounced and full of secrets."

She smiled and made a face, as if to show sorrow and beg forgiveness. Her cab had just turned the corner, heading toward us. She kept talking.

"Hector, you don't know how much I've enjoyed finally getting to meet you. You're so kind and smart—very smart. I'm sure you understand me."

She handed me a manila envelope and kissed me on both cheeks. I blushed a little.

"I'm sorry I can't stay longer. We've hardly had any time to talk about the *Voynich*. Are you sure you can't come to Tenerife for the weekend and meet John? There are some very inexpensive charter flights."

"I'm sure," I answered. "I've got a ton of work with the students, and we're up to our ears in meetings. We have to decide about moving the school, and a million things more. I really can't. Maybe some other time."

Juana had already climbed into the cab, and the driver was struggling with her unwieldy suitcase. This accidental battle gave us a few more seconds.

"Well, then, write every day. And think about what I've given you."

"I'll do it, don't worry. Give John my best."

"*Ciao.* And take care."

"You'd better get going. Good-bye."

The taxi pulled out. I stayed there a few moments, watching the car disappear. Then I looked at the envelope. It was sealed and nothing was written on the outside. I tore it open as I started walking back to the school. Inside was a CD and another envelope, also sealed, together with notes giving instructions on what to do with both items. Juana had been in town for barely a day and a half. The weather was calm after the storm, and we'd spent the afternoon going around the city. A touristy visit to the old churches, the cathedral, the history center, and the Roman ruins. During our walk we scarcely mentioned the threats, and she monopolized the conversation, telling me about her years as a student in the United States and, of course, how much she loved John.

We joked around over dinner in a Mexican restaurant. That was about all. We hadn't mentioned the threats or even the *Voynich* except in passing. I supposed that all this top-secret information she had alluded to would be on that CD and in that envelope.

She was a very intriguing woman.

6

The dining room was in an uproar. The only moment of silence was during grace, before we ate.

"So they're going to kick us out, Julian? Have they gone nuts?"

"That's how it seems, Matthew," he answered. "With the law on their side, they can do it. The judge and his minions are the ones who decide what's a fair price for the property. We've got to leave anyway, like it or not," he added.

"What about the real estate offers?" I asked, astonished.

"They withdrew them after they found out that the city council was going to evict us for what it's calling 'works of social concern.' I'm afraid I smell a rat."

"More likely a rat's nest," Matthew shot back. "Or else vultures. They're all in cahoots, we've got to do something; I've called the lawyer. He'll be here this afternoon. But it's not looking good."

"Then how much do you think we could get?" Carmelo, the prior, spoke. The rest of us were eagerly awaiting the administrator's opinion.

"With luck, a quarter of the offer we had," Julian answered quietly. "Less than half of what it's really worth. And this supposing that the notice I got this morning from the city council goes into effect on the terms it recommends."

"Will that be enough for a new school?" Dean Damian wanted to know.

"Barely. Perhaps for the land and construction, but not enough for the furnishings. Later we'll need a mortgage. And we'll have to look into grants and seek credit anyway."

"And how much will we have left?" Matthew still wanted to know.

"To send to the missions?" Julian answered with a question. "Nothing, for at least three or four years. Assuming we can maintain the same number of students, of course."

All our faces reflected helplessness. Carmelo intervened once more, trying to rally the troops. "Let's wait till we see what the lawyer says. We can still pull some strings."

I had no idea what our prior could be referring to. Perhaps to some well-connected old friends. Carmelo had spent almost twenty years heading our Jesuit community, and in all that time he'd met a lot of people and many owed him favors. He was a good man who never said no to anybody asking for help.

"Hector, will you stay at the chapel after the prayer? I need to talk to you. Unless you've got a class, of course," he asked me.

"No problem, Carmelo. This afternoon I've got only one support group, and that's at six. I'm all yours till then."

The prior came to meet me at four. He brought some old papers in one hand and a flashlight in the other.

"Hold this."

I took the flashlight while he pulled a bunch of rusty keys out of his cassock. Then he turned to the altar and gently moved a part of the baroque altarpiece aside. There was a door that looked like it might lead to a storage area or perhaps a small, old dressing room where the first Jesuit priests had kept their vestments. Though that door was familiar to all of us, we took for granted that it was permanently shut.

Carmelo opened it with one of the keys. Then he asked for the flashlight, turned it on, and went into the darkness. I followed him.

"What you see here, or rather what you can imagine, is an old passageway that pre-dates the construction of the school," he explained. "Hector, watch your step on the stairs just ahead."

I looked at the floor and the walls. It was very humid.

We went down about sixty feet. Puzzled, I didn't say a word during our descent, trying to digest the fact that this catacomb had always been right under my feet. And in the middle of the city.

"End of the path," Carmelo said when he reached a broad landing. "Or at least as far as I've dared to explore. Beyond this are tunnels with sewage and rats the size of dogs. That's about where the modern sewer joins the old one."

He pointed to an area where large, hewn stones supported a vault that looked very old, really ancient.

"Aren't those the Roman sewers?" I asked.

"Right, Hector. The old Jesuit monastery had an underground labyrinth. Not that this could be Rome, but there's a resemblance. Those were tough times."

"Surely. And I suppose the city council doesn't have any idea this exists."

"No clue. A single phone call to the people at National Heritage would be sufficient to halt any construction, whether ours or the council's. The school was actually built with considerable secrecy. I've brought you something concerning this."

He handed me the papers he was carrying. I could hardly read anything in the scant light.

"It's a series of notes by the prior then, together with some letters. His complete diary is in the archives. You'll figure out why I brought you here."

"I'm trying to guess. I suppose I'm a notorious detective."

"Sort of." The prior laughed. "I want you to study it all and see what we can do. Whether it's really a good idea to reveal these old ruins."

I kept thinking. Buying our property would be bad business, either for the city council or the real estate firm, if the ministry was finally going to intervene. We really had to fine-tune our strategy.

"Let's go back. I'm feeling the dampness," Carmelo complained. "Hector, all that you've seen and heard here is like a secret of the confessional of course." He smiled.

I smiled back understandingly, and we started the narrow ascent in silence.

* * *

There were three piles of papers on my desk. For the first time in months, I completely shut down my computer. To my left, the mystery of John, Juana, and Joanna—*los Juanes*, as I called them; to my right, the ancient history of the monastery. And in the middle, graffiti included, a few of my latest translations of Voynichian texts. I also had the printouts Simon had brought me, which I'd only just started to read. There was nothing I could postpone for long. I would take it all calmly, with a cup of coffee. It was Friday night and we priests didn't usually go out drinking. It was enough of a novelty for me to have been out last night with that beautiful yet disturbing Mexican woman. Now I was back in my room, alone with several unsolved puzzles awaiting me. And the whole night ahead.

Suppose that I opened a box with a gigantic jigsaw puzzle. One practical approach would be to separate the pieces by color. Here the sky blues, there the tree greens, over there the people pieces. There are only four corners, and also just a few edged pieces. But nothing prevents us from being guided by shapes or by simple intuition. Some pieces have a bit of sea and a bit of sky. They aren't easy to classify but, paradoxically, it's no problem if they fit incidentally. Normally several of them form a line, or several lines, that usually converge. With this analogy we could say that instead of trying to solve shape problems individually, first we have to look for the connections among the pieces.

I was a Jesuit priest and the *Voynich Manuscript* had once belonged to the Jesuits.

I belonged to the Jesuit order and so did the monastery where I lived. And there were hidden secrets. But no syllogism resulted from these and the preceding items, because the *Voynich* had never been hidden within these walls. I studied astronomy and taught physics and math at a provincial school. Kepler and Tycho Brahe were real astronomers and mathematicians. I was trying to unravel an old mystery from Tycho and Kepler's times. And this book might have actually passed through their hands. Conclusion: I was a fool if I thought myself capable of deciphering something that those two giants couldn't manage to crack. This was an impossible proposition.

But I couldn't stop thinking about the puzzle. Did the alleged poisoning of Tycho Brahe have anything to do with all of this? That was implausible. It seemed clear that he had unintentionally taken his own life. Or not? Why the insistence by the authors of *Heavenly Intrigue* on demonstrating the opposite four centuries later? And why was there a similar effort to get rid of the *Voynich* issue once and for all? Many questions without an answer. I didn't like these last pieces. We were being threatened. By whom? Why and what for? It was a line I didn't want to cross. Then I'd go back to Tycho's death.

What did I know about alchemy and medicine at the end of the sixteenth century? My idea of alchemy, of the search for the philosopher's stone—for an unknown substance capable of converting any metal to gold—wasn't much better than Harry Potter's. For Tycho Brahe and many others, this search was a waste of time. Just as he approached astronomical ephemera, Tycho chose to investigate the practical applications of alchemy himself rather than chase fairy tales. Many other alchemists of his time did the same; they concluded that it was simply chemistry applied to medicine in order to cure diseases. In this regard, Tycho, like the rest of the "physicists," was a follower of Philippus Aureolus Theophrastus Bombast von Hohenheim. A figure known today simply as Paracelsus.

Paracelsus attempted to end fourteen centuries of Galenic medicine. Galen's medicine—like the ancient astronomy that Tycho was equally set against—was based on Aristotelian concepts. Sickness came from an imbalance among the four humors, or essential body fluids: blood, yellow bile, black bile, and phlegm. The humors produced vapors and were responsible for a person's physical and mental characteristics. Blood basically had a positive aspect. It pertained to a friendly, even temperament. Yellow bile related to ill humor, anger, and violence. Black bile was associated with melancholy and laziness. And phlegm with serenity. We still use the term *phlegmatic* to describe a person who has this tendency. The four humors, in turn, had to do with the four basic qualities of matter: cold, hot, dry, and wet. So curing disease was based on the regulation of the humors through the application of the required quality. Thus the doctor decided whether it was necessary to bleed, purge, prescribe diuretics, heat, chill, or apply salves.

Seeking equilibrium was the most common means of fighting the worst malady of the epoch: the plague. Right after the discovery of America, a new illness, syphilis, proved equally devastating. Paracelsus declared that new illnesses required new cures, and his theories began to attract followers. He proposed that the human body was itself a reduced model of the cosmos, a microcosm. And for that reason, the same notion of balance applied equally to big and small things. Thus, there were seven planets in the heavens because there were seven metals on Earth, and there were seven principal components of the human body; so it followed that their nature and behavior had to be similar. What applied to the chemistry of metals applied also to the organs of the body. And what one could observe in the sky could equally influence one's health. Because the Sun and the Moon were considered planets (wandering bodies), this singular correspondence remained unquestioned through the late eighteenth century, until William Herschel located Uranus in 1781.

Naturally, the Sun was associated with gold and the heart. All was very evident. The Moon was connected with silver and, perhaps for its grayish color, perhaps for its emotional component, with the brain. Back then the heart, rather than the brain, was considered the fundamental part of an individual. Transplants were of course unknown, but Tycho's doctor, Johann Jessenius, was the first surgeon to conduct a public autopsy—in Prague in 1600, a year before the death of his friend.

Jupiter had associations with tin and blood, although in classical mythology Mars was associated with blood, war, and death. In alchemic medicine, Mars was connected with iron and the gallbladder. Venus related to copper and the kidneys. Saturn, to lead and the spleen. And finally, Mercury—the mythical messenger of the gods—with, of course, mercury. In the human body it was related to the lungs.

Today we don't see many advantages in the newer alchemic medicine over Galen's classical model. By then it was already known that many of the metals, such as lead, antimony, and mercury, could be poisonous at a certain dosage. Tycho, as a follower of Paracelsus, made sure that only the pure essence of metals was extracted in his ovens and stored in glass flasks. The difference between the medicine and the poison depended on the purity of the mixture and the amount administered. A very fine line.

The line between life and death.

7

I hadn't slept much, but this morning was actually sunny and its warmth revitalized me. I wanted to devote the weekend to exploring the subterranean labyrinths. I supposed that the prior wouldn't have any major objection. I would also review the bundle of old papers in the archive. I decided to have a look at Juana's envelope before I went down to breakfast.

The instructions were simple.

> Insert the CD and follow the steps. If you're unable to get to the
> end, only as a last resort open the small envelope.

Okay. I didn't understand why all the mystery, but it amused me. I inserted the disc in the computer drive. It contained one file. A very eloquent HECTOR.EXE. The computer hummed as the disc spun. The monitor blinked and went dark. Then a message appeared on the screen.

> Hi, Hector. We have to make sure it's you who's reading this disc. We'll give
> you access to the subsequent screens by means of simple codes. Click Enter.

I did. A mathematical puzzle appeared. I had five minutes to solve it in order to get the code for the next screen.

You're in a group of one thousand people who are going to be executed by the following method. You will be lined up in a row, and the executioner will blow off the head of every other prisoner, starting with the first one, and so on. The survivors will stand in line again in the same order, and the executioner will repeat his actions again and again until there's only one left. Which position in the row will you select?

I didn't much feel like thinking. Number 501?

There was a sound like a cannon shot.

I quickly lowered the speaker volume. A new message appeared on the screen.

Incorrect response. You have a second chance, but now only one minute to solve it. You cannot turn off the computer. If you do so, or if the time runs out, the CD will self-destruct. Be thankful that we won't do the same with your hard drive. Because we could.

Wham. Not even enough time for coffee. This was no pair of turtle-doves—they were a couple of sadists. I'd picked a stupid answer. Since 501 is an odd number, I would be executed in the first round. I started thinking, desperately searching at full speed for a pencil among the hundreds of papers on my desk. Without intending to, I wound up with a single heap. Thinking out loud, I started scribbling on a blank sheet of paper.

Before the execution starts, we're 1,000, after the first round, 500. Then 250, 125, 62, 31, 15, 7, 3, and finally, just me. There are nine rounds of shooting in all and I always had to place myself in an even position. If we were divided by two each time, that would mean, in order to survive, that I had to multiply my position by two, and do this nine times ($2 \times 2 \times 2 \times 2 \times 2 \times 2 \times 2 \times 2 \times 2$), or 2 raised to the 9th power, which is 512.

I still had fifteen seconds. I double-checked the answer by repeating my reasoning in reverse.

If I'm in the correct spot, my position before the first shot will be 512. Then after the first round I'll be 256. Then 128, 64, 32, 16, 8, 4, 2, and finally, I'll be in the first position. I would survive. Voilà!

I inserted "512."

Bravo, Hector. Do you want to go on, or should we have some coffee?

They knew me too well. As I shut down the computer and finally went downstairs to the kitchen, I wondered if I really knew them. I was going to need at least two cups of coffee. What had I gotten myself into?

I came across the prior in the kitchen. He looked glum, and as if he'd hardly slept last night.

"Good morning, Hector."

"Good morning, Carmelo," I said. "I was wondering if you could leave me the key to the chapel door. I'd like to check things out down there."

He looked at me somewhat despondently.

"Yes, of course," he answered, handing me the keys. "Take it out, it's the smallest one. This is probably pointless."

"Why do you say that?" I asked, struggling with the unwieldy bunch of keys.

"We had a long meeting yesterday with the lawyer, well into the night."

"And?"

"The city council's project involves the construction of a gigantic underground parking lot. Over five hundred spaces."

That didn't clarify much for me. If they were planning a deep excavation, they most certainly would have to expose the Roman ruins. That would bring the project to an immediate halt, causing a fiasco for the developers, along with the promoters of the risky venture.

"I still don't understand," I insisted.

"There are too many interests involved. Foreign capital. On top of the parking lot, they're planning a large shopping center. If anything halfway suspicious comes up, they'll cover it with cement. As much as is needed, well seasoned with money."

"But not everything can be bought," I protested. "Some archeological ruins that come to light can't be allowed to go unnoticed by the press or by the universities, not even by the government."

"And who's going to let the cat out of the bag? Us?"

"Why not?"

"There's one overwhelming reason the lawyer gave me yesterday. If we try to oppose the expropriation, they'll remove our license as an educational institution."

"Can they do that after a hundred years?"

"Possibly not, but it makes no difference. They can get to whoever decides this in Madrid. In fact, it looks like they've already been there because the threat is firm. Nobody knows how much money the enterprise is prepared to spend, but they're clearly able to move mountains. They've even threatened our lawyer. Anonymously, of course."

My astonishment must have struck Carmelo. Threats were becoming the order of the day.

"Yep, that's how it is, Hector," he continued. "Yesterday he said he'd no longer be working for us. He has a family and plenty of less problematic clients. There aren't many other ways out. You must be wondering if we can get to Madrid in time and reveal what's hidden below us." He pointed at the floor. "They could just as easily accuse us of hiding our archeological patrimony. The lawyer doesn't know this, but I'm filling you in. Acting in bad faith also gets punished, even more severely. So we're really forced to head for the hills with whatever they give us, and start all over again."

"I'll keep the key anyway," I said cautiously.

"Do whatever you like. At least take some pictures of the hole before the cement mixers bury it for good."

"I can always post them on the Internet," I joked, trying to make light of a very serious issue. But the prior didn't crack a smile. He spoke again.

"There's a deadline. We have until the end of the term in June, a little over six months. No extensions."

"Where will we hold the September exams? In the city council main hall?" I protested. "We don't even have time to secure architects."

"They already have the solution for that. They'll lend us classrooms in an abandoned public high school through the next term. And they'll be charging us rent, of course." He stopped. "I'm giving it up for now."

He stood up. I couldn't see clearly, but it seemed to me he had wiped his eyes with his hand. He left without another word.

Our library holds some twenty thousand volumes. Neither our collection nor our space is very large. We jokingly call the visitors' room a "space solution," but it is important to a city as poor as ours. The eviction is shameful for my entire community. The local savings bank, supposedly in a disinterested role, would take charge of all the holdings, transferring them to a building more in keeping with our circumstances. The books would remain on deposit, we would find anything else unacceptable, and they would preserve the library's name, not out of respect for the donors, but as a precaution to let the small number of visitors and associates continue to read their favorite books. Needless to say that the savings bank doesn't try to spread culture for the love of art. Rather, it is counting among its future plans a few wonderful deductions for expenses in the euphemistic category of cultural promotion. In view of this, not a week goes by without a visit from a mellifluous-voiced representative of this entity, insisting on our need to update and modernize our installations.

The library, like much of the school, is in very bad shape. In the past few years we've used it as a junk room. A rotten table and an ink-stained desk were inevitably transferred to the reading room, where they were used to replace less-abused pieces of furniture that were then taken out for use in other parts of the school. It had become nearly impossible to sit anywhere without ending up on the floor, surrounded by sawdust, or tearing one's pants on a treacherous nail. Our assets were rarely replenished, partly because we had no money and partly because there was less and less interest in maintaining this small repository of knowledge. Mea culpa. I myself had advised against investing in its upkeep on numerous occasions, always opting to spend our scarce resources on computers. Through the Internet we could access any source of knowledge in the world. That's what I always said. But anyone can make a mistake. That very afternoon I learned that the Internet wasn't always the best solution.

The library was deserted. Despite its being open to the general public, and at the token price of an associate membership card—free to students and alumni—nobody had come that Saturday to consult anything. The occasional visitors tended to show up on Sunday mornings, and the principal attraction was our collection of old comic books, the whim of a group of Jesuits who started the compilation in the postwar period and continued it for the next thirty years. Sadly, one has to admit that today these constitute the most valuable and sought-after treasure in our collection, and we have no shortage of offers to purchase them. Besides the worn-out old comic books, there're a considerable number of old books for teaching. Early in its existence, the school provided textbooks to students who were unable to buy them. Then we got them back, all full of notes and doodles, poems and obscenities. Now they've accumulated by the dozens on the top shelves.

Also found on the upper shelves are the reference books, classical literature, philosophy, and natural sciences. As a complement to the last group— and reminiscent of a time before television and the Internet—about twenty dried, stuffed animals adorn the shelves. There are crows, owls, doves, a couple of cats, a fox, and even an eagle. Last year a shelf fell due to its combined weight and deterioration—we donated another curiosity that had been with us for decades to the university: the jars containing tapeworms, scorpions, mollusks, spiders, and all types of invertebrates preserved in formaldehyde, most of them brought from exotic places by the missionary brothers. That day several of the specimens spilled onto the floor and seemingly came to life—especially an extremely rare green octopus that nobody dared touch, except Matthew, armed with a mop. It was quite spectacular.

I went down to the basement, where the documents of the Jesuit order and of the house are stored in the archive. The room was locked (Carmelo had just given me the key) and couldn't be opened by anyone outside the order except by special permission. The only express prohibitions are against making photocopies of the documents and removing them from the building. Since the photocopier was ruined (it had unfortunately stood beneath the shelf that collapsed, and didn't survive the impact of the mineral collection that went through it like a meteorite shower), that's no longer an option. Whatever our destination, the archive will be separated and go with us. It isn't going to end up parceled out to us, subject to bank payments and the like.

The papers I was seeking were connected with Anselmo Hidalgo, prior of the community from 1915 until he died of pneumonia in 1922. The shelves held boxes and portfolios, an orderly accumulation of old documents, files, letters, and diaries of successive members of the Society of Jesus who had lived in, or at least passed through, the house, from the founding of the monastery in 1751 until now. The only original buildings remaining, just barely, are the church and its annexed chapel. Their artistic value protects them from the wrecking ball. That's no problem for the city council, since they are located at one end of the building and won't be too much of a nuisance. The house, as such, was built a hundred years later, and the construction of the school, which occupies the largest portion of the land, started early in the twentieth century. The house is on the verge of collapse, and the school has fallen into disrepair. It was Father Hidalgo who undertook the ambitious school project, ordering the destruction of much of the ancient structures—stables, a small inn for travelers, and the vegetable garden that helped sustain the community. He was an enterprising man who counted on the unconditional support and approval of his superiors.

The school quickly gained fame in the neighboring provinces, and the students' residence hall was always full, except during the Civil War, when all the installations were closed. Today there's neither a residence hall nor any boarders, since times have changed, but in essence the school retains the same spirit and the same pedagogical principles that it had when it opened in 1916.

The box labeled P. ANSELMO HIDALGO, JESUIT PRIOR 1915–1922 was quite voluminous. At first glance it contained at least four volumes that seemed to be diaries, a huge roll of plans (possibly for the construction of the many buildings that he oversaw, and obviously the school itself), and a bundle of letters tied with a red ribbon and sealed with wax. It seemed that nobody had reviewed this correspondence for at least eighty years. I unrolled the bundle of blueprints. Quite a few of them matched the floor plans of the school, and others, those of the house and the church. Still others showed older, long-gone buildings. One smaller, even more ancient master plan included a series of underground paths. Surely they had something to do with the labyrinth that Carmelo had shown me. It was a good starting point, and I wouldn't have to go back and grope blindly through those narrow, gloomy passageways. The last person to examine those papers was probably the archivist priest. The position of archivist and of librarian had disappeared, like so many other things, over the years. And now I took care of most of those responsibilities. The cybernaut priest with the cybercafé in his cell.

Clearly an archivist was still needed. One portfolio in Father Hidalgo's materials was completely out of place. It was very old, possibly the oldest in the archive. On its spine was the inscription P. LAZZARI, 1770. The name was familiar; Lazzari had actually been the librarian of the Collegio Romano during the first suppression of the Society of Jesus. Three years before Pope Clement XIV declared the order "extinct in perpetuity," it seemed that this Roman priest had been here, actually in this monastery. Fortunately for us, the extinction was not at all perpetual. Part of the archive had arrived in Toledo by the hand of Cardinal Zelada; another part had been saved by Giuseppe Pignatelli; and of a third part, the one that must have included the reference to the *Voynich Manuscript,* nothing was known.

I blew the years of dust off its cover and untied its strings. Inside were a Bible and two classical books, *The Confessions of Saint Augustine* and a small volume of writings by Thomas Aquinas. Personal items, of no interest. Lazzari may have attended some religious meeting in those days, perhaps a retreat or, say, a strategy meeting in less-turbulent Castile. No wonder those were very complicated times for the society. Only three years earlier, in 1767, the Jesuits had been ousted from the New World by King Charles III, and the already mentioned papal dissolution came only three years later. There was little I could use here, but no matter how superficial the connection, the idea that someone related to the *Voynich* was once in my own monastery made me smile.

It was dim and shadowy in the basement, and there was so much dirt, I decided to take Father Hidalgo's box with me so that I could examine its contents in detail. Strictly speaking, the house and the library are two separate buildings (the library, as stated, was built inside the school), so I was violating one of the principal guidelines of the archives. However, since I was the person deciding on their use with the total confidence of the prior, I didn't think twice about it. That was a big mistake. Things are always safer under lock and key. I left the heavy box in the only uncluttered corner of my room and went to wash up. I had gotten really filthy rummaging through those years of accumulated dirt and dust. When I came out, the towel still in my hands, the box and all its contents had disappeared. I couldn't believe it; it had vanished in less than five minutes. Possibly the running water masked the sounds of footsteps or any other noise made by the thief. My door, as always, was open. I didn't see anybody when I stuck my head out, and when I checked with the other priests, none of them had seen strangers wandering around the long hallways of the old house.

* * *

Carmelo's lack of surprise when he learned what had happened certainly surprised me. I expected some kind of reprimand for my imprudent action, but he barely managed a few words, as trite as they were brief.

"It couldn't be helped."

"But aren't we going to call the police? It's still a robbery," I protested.

"Maybe a petty theft. Papers that were old a century ago."

I kept insisting, hoping to remind him of the conversation we'd had barely the day before.

"What about our strategy?"

"I already told you it wouldn't make any difference. Let it be, Hector."

I must have looked about to cry, because he put his hand on my shoulder to console me. *He* was consoling *me*.

"Don't torture yourself. Come with me and we'll say a rosary together in the chapel."

I reluctantly obeyed, not understanding this sudden indifference after he had so recently insisted on searching for new arguments to avoid our exile. The boxer seemed to want to throw in the towel. Or to limit himself to praying, so as not to be slapped around anymore.

Even so, the news of the theft greatly affected the rest of the community. Above all, because the box contained the first master plans for the school and possibly deeds, notarized documents, engineering reports, appraisals, and all sorts of commercial papers. They all assumed—especially the always belligerent Matthew, and Julian, our administrator—that the robbery had been sponsored by the city council or by the construction company itself, whose financial backing was still a mystery to everyone. That was another mystery; we didn't really know who exactly wanted us out of the school. The community also immediately associated the incident with the graffiti, since I had reported somebody snooping around the library that night. On the surface, it all seemed to be an attempt to not only steal our official deed but also to discredit us.

Not long ago somebody had reported in the moronic local newspaper, which was, of course sponsored behind the scenes by the savings bank, that the Biology Department of the university had found, among the specimens donated by the Society of Jesus School several months ago, a human fetus! (Actually it was the fetus of a calf, but that story didn't serve their purposes.) Needless to say, the same paper had echoed the story about Kepler's alleged murder of Tycho Brahe. And this bothered me because none of the pieces of this puzzle fit together.

The blue sky pieces always look alike.

Putting them together could take me forty years, almost as many as Tycho had spent observing the sky. Pieces that Kepler had later arranged to function as perfectly as an old-style watch mechanism.

I was in a foul mood when I headed back to my room. This time I shut the door, though now I had little to safeguard. I turned on all the computers and went online. John's and Joanna's programs (maybe I should get used to calling her Juana once and for all), and my own, were running again. I had no clear idea of what I was doing because not even the codes were activated. For days I hadn't looked at any algorithms or familiar patterns from the pages of the *Voynich Manuscript,* and I also didn't know whether *los Juanes* themselves were following that line of investigation or, as the pretty Mexican had insinuated, something totally different. I wasn't in the mood to solve any more puzzles in order to figure it out. Not for the time being anyway.

Thinking about this, I started to laugh. Just a little at first. Then a roaring, silly, falling-down kind of laughing fit. And I couldn't stop. Because I'd been threatened. Because they'd come into my cubbyhole and robbed me from right under my nose. Because, after so many years, the prior was seized by a strange apathy and now seemed indifferent to what might happen to us. Because I couldn't get Juana out of my mind, with her long black hair falling over her eyes. And because I was sitting here, like an idiot, in front of the computer while my entire world was undergoing a seismic shift. What did God want? To test me again? Choosing to enter the society at an earlier pivotal, uncertain stage of my youth had been a considerable test. Did I really have the calling to be a priest? Hadn't I exceeded the limits of common sense with my ecological and radical libertarian impulses, with my obsession to save the world and love the dispossessed, to become a champion of social justice? And now, even so, I was shut up in this ridiculous room. How do I go out into the world? How do I stay here? God wouldn't just give me the answers. If He did, none of the science we know today would have made sense.

It's one thing to have faith and quite another to confuse faith with reason. Newton, Brahe, Galileo, Copernicus, Kepler. All of them had faith. In God and in their work. None of them died in vain. At that thought I stopped laughing and rubbed my face. I'd found some relief. The answer to the last question—the most important one—was blinking on the computer screen now, winking at me. I could go out into the world through the Internet. Everything was there except for a few dust-covered pieces of parchment that were undoubtedly in the desk of a city councilman. It wasn't all that important. Not enough to make me give up. I wouldn't have another crisis of faith now. If Jesus had once spent his days amid cooking pots, surely now He could be among computers. To start with, who were those journalists, and why were they so determined to ruin the reputation of Johannes Kepler, the most extraordinary mathematician of the early seventeenth century? I still hadn't given much thought to this. Not exactly a minor question.

So I opened the largest encyclopedia in the world, where we all have an entry, no matter how little we have done. Sometimes being born is enough for us to be mentioned. Whether in a telephone book, the yearbook of your nursery school, an online article, a message sent to a forum on Turkish cuisine, or an explanation of how to brown French toast without burning it. Everything is there, and you only have to know how to look for it.

GOOGLE: GILDER AND *HEAVENLY INTRIGUE*

Nothing overly surprising. On the contrary, only 10,400 mentions. This number may seem large, but it was strangely small for a supposedly prestigious journalist and a presumed best-seller. I checked a few links. The majority were reviews from publishers and online bookstores, so they didn't add anything new to my search. Another group of links took me to a press release (in several languages), the same one I had seen in the local rag. It was from an international press service, so it appeared in newspapers around the globe. But this didn't add anything new to the story either. Some panel made comments on the book, generally no more substantial than the ones I'd read on the Amazon Web site. There didn't seem to be much else. Gilder and his wife, who was of German descent, wrote the book together. Their biography was very brief. Barely three lines on the dust jacket, the same ones that were repeated word for word everywhere else. However, those three lines were a world in themselves. *Joshua Gilder has been a magazine editor and a speechwriter for the White House, and has occupied high-level positions in the State Department.*

The third line made reference to his only novel, *Ghost Image,* which had gone practically unnoticed. Oh, well. With the exception of the pseudoscientific essay *Heavenly Intrigue,* he was clearly not the named author. It appears that he had been what we'd normally call a ghostwriter or the "as told to," or even a speechwriter responsible for writing the requisite statement to be read prior to any unnecessary military invasion. A character entirely in the shadows. If that was the case, perhaps 10,400 mentions were too many for national security.

8

I had planned to save Sunday for my subterranean exploration. I intended to examine the labyrinth after the noon Mass, when everybody else had left the church, but I decided to postpone the excursion. Without Prior Anselmo Hidalgo's old floor plans, the task seemed more complicated. I didn't even know what to look for. It would just be a blind search, and maybe it was better to at least have a starting point. Perhaps I could find a clue in the few papers that had escaped the thief. I could study those later and instead spend the day on any of my other unfinished projects.

I decided to play a bit more with *los Juanes* since there was still an hour before our meal.

Back in my room, I inserted the CD and repeated the same operations. For some reason the program hadn't saved my place in the game (which seemed to me an unpardonable mistake for such consummate experts in the technology), but I finally got to the proper screen.

Bravo, Hector. Do you want to go on, or should we have some coffee?

Of course I already had a cup, so I pressed ENTER.

We carefully reviewed the theories of Gordon Rugg. They're quite a lot like ours, and this is something we've already noted by e-mail. Rugg suggests that the *Voynich Manuscript* is a deliberate ruse. We'll discuss who the author of this deception *could be* on the following screens, provided, of course, that you solve the puzzles. We already know that the characters used in the manuscript are ordered in too sophisticated a manner to be a mere assemblage of random words.

I had no doubt of this. We spent months combining syllables, prefixes, and suffixes. All kinds of variations and permutations. I went on to the next screen.

Some patterns in the Voynichian words can be reproduced. The three of us have managed it without too much effort. But not all of them. Gordon Rugg put himself inside the skin of the possible bamboozler and posed the following questions: What methods are available to generate a language that seems real? What technology, if we can call it that, was used in the sixteenth century?

"Punch cards?" I joked to myself, having seen them used a long time ago when I was a kid.

The deceiver must have used some method other than statistical randomness. Moreover, in that century little was known of statistics. Perhaps a rudimentary apparatus capable of generating varied patterns—many and different—but which would finally end up repeating themselves. Are you aware of anything like this in the sixteenth century?

I truly wasn't. I could of course make a search. And surely Rugg himself would have talked about it in his *Scientific American* article that I hadn't had time yet to review in depth. But I supposed they were going to tell me. I was right, though it still wasn't going to be easy.

We need to put you through another test, Hector. We're sure you understand.

I was afraid of this. It wouldn't be any help for me to curse their parents, his and hers. Families that the Church would be uniting in a short time, given their current relationship.

A new puzzle appeared. It was more difficult than the first one, because now I had only ten minutes to solve it. At this point, I couldn't turn back. I had no choice but to go on or lose everything.

At the end of a crushing battle, the soldiers regrouped. They were sad, because a large number of them had been mutilated.

We're going on with the stylish sadism, I noticed.

70 percent of them had, at least, lost an eye. And 75 percent had lost at least one ear. A full 80 percent of this army had, at a minimum, lost an arm. And 85 percent of the soldiers had lost one leg. The general wants to know how many of his men, at a minimum, had lost one eye, one ear, one arm, and one leg. So he can order medals to honor these men as the very bravest.

I knew the puzzle. I'd read it as a boy, in a book by Lewis Carroll. *Los Juanes* had embellished it a bit.

I glanced in vain at my shelves because the book was still at my parents' house. I had to think. The solution was based on group theory. As before, I thought out loud.

"In the worst of cases, which would be that the same unfortunate 70 percent of the soldiers who had lost an eye had also lost an ear, an arm, and a leg, we would have to decorate exactly 70 percent of the soldiers. But this is the maximum number, and the general is stingy and wants the minimum."

I was doing well on time. I reviewed my thinking.

"Now let's think in reverse. Exactly 30 percent didn't lose an eye, so if 25 percent also didn't lose an ear, this means that 55 percent, as a maximum, didn't lose both an eye and an ear. With the same reasoning, 20 percent more still have both arms, which makes 75 percent. And 15 percent more have their legs. In all, a maximum of 90 percent of the soldiers haven't lost everything at once. Thus, a minimum of 10 percent had the worst wounds and would receive an honorable discharge—and a medal."

I wrote "10" as my answer.

You're brilliant, Hector. In only seven minutes. Do you want to go on, or should we have some coffee?

Before the coffee, I needed to eat something. So I left the computer on and went down to the dining room—smiling from ear to ear, as if I'd just won a championship with flying colors, defeating a formidable opponent.

For our Sunday repast, we usually take our time. On the Lord's day there's always better meat or a better stew. In addition, there's excellent wine and a scrumptious dessert prepared by the Carmelite nuns, whom we take special care of since they're all past sixty now. For a long time they've depended on their luck and pastry-making talents, which are unsurpassed. We delight in their excellent cream roll with truffles followed by an espresso and a liqueur. We're no hermits to be depriving ourselves of small pleasures. Conversation is one of these. And the subject at that Sunday gathering was the usual.

"No, Damian. We can't take on that expense. We'll have to accept."

The administrator was as inflexible as the Department of Finance.

"We can't put the kids in those barracks. The council condemned the building a year ago, by order of the Department of Sanitation. And it's a dangerous neighborhood," the dean of the school insisted. The city council proposal was almost an insult.

"The only profitable businesses there are bars. We'll lose the kids. As if they weren't rebellious enough," Damian declared.

"On the surface it seems like they're doing us a favor. Or hasn't that son of a gun told you yet that we priests also have to take care of alcoholics and prostitutes?"

"C'mon, Matthew. Don't talk like that," the prior cautioned. "Besides, social work is as much a part of our job with the marginalized population as with the kids at school. At bottom, the city council does have a point."

"That's hogwash," Matthew insisted, getting angrier by the second. "The politicians and councilmen love spending money on trips and stipends and garbage. Have you been to the Municipal Museum of Modern Art yet? It's beyond shameful—those four scraps of iron and some haystacks stuck to the wall. For half of what that cost, we could have a new school. And to top it off, they bring their mistresses to Mass."

"Enough already, Matthew, let it go."

Obviously, Carmelo didn't want to keep arguing, since local politics was a scandal in many places, unmentionable in some, and just tolerated in others.

"And if I catch whoever wrote that we Jesuits are putting fetuses into jars, I'll throw him in the river," Matthew threatened, pounding the wooden table with his empty cup.

He smiled bitterly as we all got up from dinner.

Back in my room, I continued my investigation of Gilder. There were a number of Web sites for me to check, and perhaps some links to scientists or historians who had tried to rebut the libel. The press notice cited a small conference in Austria, and a paper read there by a German biographer and expert on Kepler's work, Volker Bialas. Judging by its title—"The Poison of Publicity: Response to an American Crime-Story Theory About Kepler"—this was presumably unfavorable to the Americans' thesis. As much as I searched, I couldn't find the text on the Internet. Then I wrote to John, asking him to try to locate it for me. This was a small conference of astronomy scholars. Surely he could easily find a transcript of the talk. So I left Bialas for the moment and returned to the Gilders and their careers.

I soon found the short autobiography that Joshua Gilder had used to promote his first novel. Politically correct in every sense. He was born in Washington, D.C., in 1954, the son of a military psychoanalyst. The portion about his childhood captured quite cinematically his great struggle to conquer dyslexia and become a successful writer. Quite an achievement, really. Despite his great problems with spelling and learning to write words correctly—Gilder said he once had a 30 percent error rate—the contents of his first articles pleased the magazine editors of such publications as *The New Leader*.[1] Gilder later worked as an associate editor at *Saturday Review*, which went bankrupt in 1982. Through a friend, he met Peter Robinson, the person in charge of writing speeches for George H. Bush, who was then vice president of the United States. Robinson had to draft between seven and ten speeches a week

---

1. The American preoccupation with spelling isn't well understood by Spanish speakers, whose language has a close match between its written and spoken sounds—unlike English, as demonstrated by the famous anecdote of a vice president not recognizing the correct plural form of potato. I also recall an episode of The Simpsons involving a "spelling bee," and the national spelling bees evidently have a broad following, something unthinkable in Europe, or at least in Spain. (Author's Note)

for him, and he took Gilder on as an assistant to share the load. Robinson was soon promoted, becoming President Ronald Reagan's ghostwriter, and Gilder followed in his footsteps a year later. He wrote the actor's speeches for the next four years. He recalled jokingly that one of his (and his boss's) most famous lines—"Go ahead. Make my day!"—was taken from Clint Eastwood's *Dirty Harry*. Ronald Reagan used the line during a dispute with Congress over taxes. Other than this brief story, there aren't many references to what Gilder wrote, illuminated, or inspired. He did mention, very proudly, a speech at the 1988 Moscow summit, in which, very shortly before the collapse of the old Soviet Union—and via Ronald Reagan—he urged the Russians to better themselves. After that year, he was named assistant secretary of state for human rights. Following several death threats that he believed were from the Bulgarian KGB, he resigned and entered the private sector, opening a consulting firm. His wife, Anne-Lee, was a television reporter for a German network.

Joshua Gilder had produced only a single work of fiction. His other entry into the literary world, *Heavenly Intrigue,* was published by Doubleday in the fall of 2003. And this is the house that gave us *The Da Vinci Code,* no less. With these connections, the American reviews of the Gilders' book can only be described as cloying, not to say openly biased. Here are a few, caught on the fly, among many circulating on the Internet.

> "*Heavenly Intrigue* is a delight, a fascinating read . . . a murder investigated four centuries later. Entertaining and informative."
> —*WASHINGTON POST BOOKWORLD*

> "The Gilders have written a brilliant, original, historical work, which ought to convince its readers that one of the greatest scientists in history committed cold-blooded murder."
> —*NATIONAL REVIEW*

> "Kepler had the motive, the means, and the opportunity to do away with his mentor, from whose observations he derived the laws of planetary motion. The authors make a historical restoration of a fascinating time."
> —*KIRKUS REVIEWS*

What about the astronomers? What did they have to say about this?

It took me almost an hour to locate a documentary review of the book. This was in the *Journal for the History of Astronomy,* the most serious scientific publication concerning early astronomy. In volume 35, the February 2004 issue, Marcelo Gleiser writes as follows.

> There are many ways of telling a story, especially when its characters are dead and can't return from the great beyond to defend themselves or accuse others. The Gilders assert that Tycho ingested a lethal dose of mercury thirteen hours before his death, and that the poison was coldly administered by a calculating, half-crazed Kepler, determined to obtain Tycho's observations by any means. There are three aspects to the authors' argument: the large dose of mercury; the fact that this substance was administered to Tycho with murderous intent; and, finally the explicit accusation of Kepler. The first point is credible, the second doubtful, and the third simply ridiculous.

Gleiser, naturally, doesn't receive any echoes in the press, and his article was probably read by only a few curious persons such as myself. He proceeds to crush the journalists' arguments one by one. He accepts poisoning as the ultimate cause of Tycho Brahe's death, something the Swedish investigators had already proved through the forensic analysis of remnants of the Dane's beard, agreeing word for word with the facts that nosy Simon had supplied me with several days back. Gleiser then analyzes the Gilders' next arguments with erudite rigor.

> Was Tycho murdered? The authors of the book go all out, page after page, praising Brahe, an honest, friendly, magnanimous man, incapable of harming anybody, including himself. Kepler, on the other hand, is described as mentally ill, a frustrated, neurotic, and egotistical man, capable of going to any length in order to prove his geometric ideal of the cosmic order. Nevertheless, among science historians there is absolute evidence that Tycho wasn't exactly generous, but instead rather aggressive and ill-tempered,

pretentious, and even tyrannical with his apprentices. And that Kepler was a complex, emotional, and very religious person. There is nothing in his writing that gives one the impression that he was capable of murder. While we agreed that Kepler coveted Tycho's observations, we don't see the evidence that he was homicidal.

Marcelo Gleiser ends his review on familiar ground concerning Tycho Brahe, whose biography has been carefully reconstructed during the past four centuries, helped by the fact that the Dane and his followers recorded absolutely everything. It isn't unwarranted to say that Tycho is possibly the first great experimental scientist. Gleiser speculates—in a manner equal or superior to the Gilders', and in much less space—about Tycho's possible suicide or his, more than likely, accidental death. I decided to continue pursuing all of this in greater depth. I turned off my computer for the night and prepared my math class for the next day.

I was getting back to my routine.

9

Or maybe I wasn't.

Simon had worked through the whole weekend. Class had barely ended, his classmates stampeding out with the usual frenetic, polyphonic background music, when he came to my desk.

"Father, I've got an odd story to tell you, though maybe you won't care for it."

"Why won't I like it?"

"Because it's a love story."

"Did you finally meet a girl?" I kidded. He was trying to make fun of me.

"I'll never meet a girl now. I got hooked on the computer because of you."

"Then I'm sorry. Maybe I'm leading you down the wrong path, and we should've gone out for a few beers and hooked up with some babes. I'm not that old."

"I know. The news got around about your fancy dinner at La Tasca Mariachi. In good company, so I hear." He laughed.

I felt myself turning red. "She was only a friend. Go on, tell me."

"It's about Tycho Brahe."

I was already interested. This wasn't going to be as I'd thought—an actual love story about Tycho, who was always faithful to his wife, Kristine, the daughter of a humble Protestant minister. It also didn't have any direct connection with his death, or his final slow agony, as suggested by the historian and astronomer Marcelo Gleiser.

"Tycho had a sister who was an alchemist. She fell in love with another alchemist, but he was a real good-for-nothing. A scumbag who would do almost anything for money."

Simon was referring to the strange story of Sophie Brahe.

Sophie had the honor of being considered in many books on the history of science as the first woman devoted to studying astronomy. In those days, when gender equality wasn't even a concept, Sophie Brahe was an exceptional woman. Chronicles of the times describe her as the most cultivated woman of her day. She was an expert at gardening, horticulture, art, astrology (though she couldn't be defined strictly as a fortune-teller), alchemic remedies based on Paracelsus's ideas, literature, and especially genealogy. She was Tycho's kid sister, twelve years younger, and his favorite. Even at fourteen she helped her brother with his observations of a lunar eclipse, and starting then, she shared his passion for the stars. Sophie played an unusual role in her brother's life. Given that Tycho's wife was a plebeian, she couldn't sit beside her husband at official gatherings that he attended as a nobleman, nor could she receive kings and princes at his observatory on Hven Island. Thus, Sophie was called upon to take on this diplomatic role, while her sister-in-law sadly had to take a backseat.

"Sophie Brahe's whole life was like a poem," Simon went on. "Maybe that's why some of Tycho's most beautiful verses are dedicated to her. They're still preserved in Danish literature."

All of this reflected very well on my student, and his knowledge of science and literature combined with a quick wit. He continued.

"Following the customs of the time, Sophie's marriage was arranged while she was still almost a child, to a very old, very rich nobleman. When Sophie was widowed, not yet thirty, and with a baby, she became emotionally dependent on her dear brother Tycho. This continued until Erik Lange came on the scene. It seems the two of them had met on the island of Hven, which King Frederick the Second of Denmark had given Tycho to establish an astronomical observatory. Tycho governed the island and everything on it, teaching his apprentices to use the instruments and apply his techniques of observing stars and planets."

"Yes, I know very well the history of Uraniborg, the fantastic observatory you're talking about," I interrupted. "One of the most brilliant episodes in the history of astronomy. There's probably never been any place like it. I promise to tell you all about Uraniborg sometime, but now go on with your story—your classmates are so eager to learn math they might come back early from break," I said sarcastically.

"Tycho and Erik Lange were friends—they shared their experience and knowledge of alchemy—and Uraniborg had a laboratory for this research. Lange, a nobleman like Tycho, was convinced it was possible to convert any metal into gold. During one of their encounters, Sophie came in, and Cupid's arrow struck its mark. But almost as fast, their relationship soured. In those days there were a lot of con men taking money from kings and nobles, pretending to look for the philosopher's stone."

This made me think of the *Voynich Manuscript*. I'd read somewhere that the most likely explanation for how Rudolf acquired it was that a couple of swindlers, who claimed to be capable of turning lead into gold, had sold it to him for six hundred ducats. A connecting point I had overlooked. Finally there was a first puzzle piece that connected the sky to the sea. Meanwhile, Simon kept talking, faster and faster.

"What happened was that Lange went broke and had to run all over Europe avoiding his creditors. He even ruined his family, all his friends, and was on the verge of doing this to his loving fiancée. If he didn't succeed, it was only because her properties belonged to her son. Sophie and Lange didn't get married until 1602, a year after Tycho died. During that time Lange's finances miraculously improved, but he didn't give up his obsession. Again he started traveling and went broke, leaving Sophie all alone. Like Tycho, Erik Lange also died in Prague. In 1613."

Simon was checking his notes. By then he'd almost finished.

"Sophie Brahe lived a lot longer. She died at eighty-four, extremely rich. Not because Lange finally found the philosopher's stone, but from her son's and her first husband's income."

"And what conclusions can you draw from all this you've told me?" I asked.

"Well, that Tycho was rich and Lange was broke. Tycho's sons were considered illegitimate by the nobility, because his wife was a commoner. So Tycho Brahe could have trusted his sister and his future brother-in-law to manage his estate in case of his death, as it happened."

"That's pretty far-fetched, Simon."

"So are the Gilders' proofs," he protested. "All the way to the stubble of his beard. Besides," he added, "Kepler didn't have any knowledge of alchemy or of medicine, or of mercury, except that it is the name of the first planet from the Sun."

"Right. Lange wasn't lacking a motive or the means. But it's rather anti-climactic, let alone unprofitable for Doubleday."

"For who?"

"Nothing, forget about it. I'm just thinking out loud."

I had Monday afternoon off and spent a couple of hours taking care of chores in town. Extremely mundane tasks, such as going to the doctor with Matthew—his ulcer was acting up again—and stopping by the attorney's office to pick up some forms that Julian needed to fill out. I also took the opportunity to buy some new shirts, and a sweater that was on sale. I'd felt extremely awkward when Juana took me by the arm while we were walking and I pulled away from her. She probably thought it was because I'm a priest, but in fact I was ashamed, afraid that she'd stick her hand through one of the many holes in my old sweater. I spent so much time in the company of teenagers and other priests that I hadn't kept up my wardrobe. Coming out of the main shopping center, I found myself in the middle of an impressive traffic jam. Luckily, being on foot, I could move along much faster than any of the trapped vehicles. But the conversation I overheard left me feeling depressed and alienated.

"Ma'am, move out now."

"I can't, Officer. I'm waiting for my son—he's coming from his English class. At five o'clock on the dot."

"But can't you see the traffic jam? Can't you see the cars piling up? Move on. Forget about the kid. He'll manage."

"I've got the right to stop here for a minute. If you don't want me to, let the city council put up the parking garage they keep promising," the woman replied angrily.

"But what if the priests don't want to sell? You know how they are. They gamble like the next guy, and then claim they're broke."

"Well, throw 'em out then," the woman at the wheel fired back. "Besides, think of all the scandal they're causing. Imagine what the parents thought when they saw that picture in the papers of that creature preserved in a jar. Some of my friends plan to take their kids out of there. They don't want their own children to be a party to anything like that."

"They're really not that bad. I studied with the Jesuits," he said, sounding less annoyed as the traffic finally started to move, "and I've got no complaints."

"Well, see how you've turned out. Intolerant and dictatorial. Don't worry, I'm leaving," the woman kept shouting, getting even more upset. "Here he comes. Now I've got to rush him to his religion class so I don't miss my yoga session. Today I've got a lot of negative energy, it must be below zero. Fuck the hotels, fuck the restaurants—we can't even find a place for the boy's First Communion. I've had it up to here with priests!"

"So, move on, ma'am. Next time I'll fine you," the officer said, and walked off, shaking his fist at another car that had just run a red light.

The woman waited for her boy to open his afternoon snack before she started the engine. After threatening to smack him if he tossed the sticky wrapper inside the car (it was left behind on the sidewalk), she finally put her foot on the gas and pulled out. As cheesy television hosts say, that afternoon I'd taken the pulse of the man on the street. At least our ex-student had no complaints, though the woman at the wheel had too many.

I returned to the challenging CD.

Again I had to answer a familiar question and sip cold coffee before moving on to future revelations.

You're brilliant, Hector. In only seven minutes. Do you want to go on, or should we have some coffee?

I went on.

The Manuscript was written between 1470 and 1608. In this period we covered the earliest archeological dating as well as the hypotheses about the depictions of certain plants from the recently discovered America. In addition we came to the first solid references to the possession of the manuscript by Rudolf II. If we give more weight to its possible authorship by John Dee or Edward Kelley . . .

There they were—the possible deceivers. Ambitious alchemists like Tycho Brahe's brother-in-law, Erik Lange.

. . . we then come to the Italian cryptographer Girolamo Cardano. In 1550 Cardano describes a system for codifying messages, known as "Cardano's grid." This grid is merely a piece of paper or board with slot-shaped perforations, so that an entire text can be covered up, except for the letters visible through the slots. You write a key sentence, word by word, in the spaces revealed by the slots. Later the rest is filled in with nonsense text. The only possible means to discover the original message is to have the paper to block out the superfluous letters and show only the key sentences.

This was quite simple, and the diagram made it easier to understand. My joke about using punch cards was right, the first computing systems in the sixteenth century.

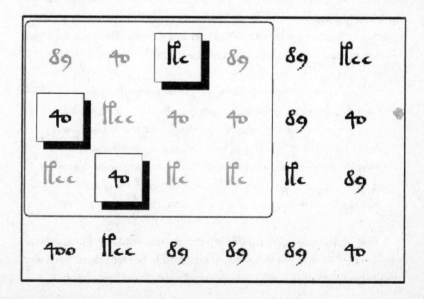

This method can also be reversed. Suppose we construct a three-column table, filling each column with prefixes, intermediate syllables, and suffixes— all meaningless. And we even leave some of the table spaces blank. We can then generate words in an almost random fashion, moving a Cardano-type grid with three slots—one for each column—over the table. Because of the blank spaces, not all the words would have three syllables. If we move the grid in different directions, rotating it, flipping it, or moving it in any way we can think of, the patterns change in a nearly unrepeatable manner, almost at random. According to Gordon Rugg, the swindlers would have done something like this, very carefully copying each word generated by this method. One after the other.

Los Juanes went on to explain in detail the findings of the English research psychologist. In scarcely three months, two people could have generated the whole manuscript, adding roughly executed but fantastic drawings. Then they insisted on binomial distributions, repetition of patterns, various statistical concepts, and all manner of modern reasoning to assure that, in fact, the proposed explanation published in the respected American journal contained a credible semblance of truth. There was one problem. Yes, this method could reproduce something like the *Voynich Manuscript,* but by accepting this we denied the possibility of finding any hidden meaning. This method implied acceptance of the deceit. And it wasn't 100 percent accurate. There was a margin of error, and that encouraged us to continue following our own direction.

We've worked for a time on our own triadic pattern, the one that you suggested, influenced by Friedman's findings in the 1950s. Our computer gives us results far superior to his, and far closer to the original than Gordon Rugg could obtain in years of using grids. But let's be realistic, Hector. There were no computers in the sixteenth century; the most we could hope to obtain from creating millions of combinations would be a copy of the Manuscript. The message, if it exists, would remain forever hidden.

They made sense. We'd already reproduced, word for word, several pages of the *Voynich.* But there was no relationship between them. Each was the product of hundreds of hours of computation. Sheer brute force.

> We had to start thinking in another way. Finally, we believe we've got
> something promising. To participate, you need to show us you're truly capable
> of thinking outside the box.

Those shits! Hadn't we spent more than a year working together? Where was this sudden distrust coming from? I was tempted to turn off my computer, destroy the CD, and erase it from my mind. But my curiosity overcame my irritation. So I clicked to continue. The new puzzle was, of course, more complex than the others. The time allotted for solving it, twenty minutes, was more than generous.

> A bear leaves his cave. First he walks six miles to the south. Then he turns
> and covers an equal distance to the east. Finally, he travels another six to the
> north. When he gets tired and decides to end his walk, he discovers that he
> has returned to his cave. What color is the bear? Insert code and press Enter.

At first this seemed like a senseless puzzle. But then I realized it was pretty easy.

If the bear's cave is exactly at the North Pole, initially it can only walk southward along a meridian. Then, moving east or west, it would actually be crossing meridians. Since all the meridians converge at the Pole, it can only walk home again. In less than two minutes I knew it had to be a polar bear, which is what color? White, of course.

I inserted "white" in the answer box and pressed the key.

The loudspeakers roared. A terrifying sound.

> Incorrect response, Hector.

The program allowed only me one minute for another attempt. Otherwise, it warned me of the fatal unraveling. What remained on the disc would be erased.

I was frozen, exactly as if I were at the North Pole and that huge bear were breathing down my neck. My answer had to be correct. Was the program out of whack? Not likely, knowing the authors as I did. What other colors fit bears? Not too many. There are gray bears and brown ones. Also black, I think. And pandas, but their color combination doesn't seem real. Thoughts were racing through my mind. I had to decide on an answer. Fifteen seconds. Ten. Five. I keyed in the first thing that came to me.

> Congratulations, Hector. Do you want to go on, or should we have some coffee?

Whew!

I'd actually followed their advice, reasoning in the most direct manner without using any arithmetical operations or geographical knowledge. The answer was there. The oldest trick in the world. The most obvious solution.

Not for nothing was John a fan of Tolkien and *The Lord of the Rings*.[2]

Logically, what I'd inserted in extremis was "code."

---

2. In *The Lord of the Rings*, when the heroes stand facing the stone doors of the mines of Moria, they find them shut. Above them one can read the sentence "Say Friend, and enter." The password is obviously "friend." (Author's Note)

10

T he trigonometry you see on the board is nothing new. It's about two thousand three hundred years old."

That didn't impress them much. I persisted, directing my attack at their self-esteem.

"Kids in Greece in the year three hundred B.C. were already studying Euclid. They had to sit on stone benches until they solved the triangle problems," I threatened. "Business in those times depended on navigation. There were no GPS satellites to tell people where to go. And no Americans to invent them. America didn't even exist. In fact, Columbus discovered the New World because he made a big mistake in his calculations. Geometry wasn't his forte."

"What was his mistake?" one of the girls in the front row asked.

"He miscalculated the circumference of the Earth," I answered. "By this time, scholars at the University of Salamanca already knew the accurate measurements made by the Greeks, approximately twenty-five thousand miles. Columbus thought there were only about twenty thousand, and therefore, sailing from Spain to Asia, east to west, was a shorter distance. Halfway there, he found an unknown continent."

"But didn't people then think that the Earth was flat?" Simon broke in.

So I had to explain. "No, not at all. In ancient times it was already known that the Earth is a sphere. It wasn't necessary to go out into space and take photos in order to prove it. Something as simple as seeing ships disappear on the horizon showed the curvature of the Earth. The masts were the last to disappear from view." I returned to my main theme.

"Trigonometry means, quite simply, the measurement of triangles. Using Euclid's formulas one could perfectly measure distances or heights. Maps could be drawn with these formulas, and one could calculate the position of heavenly bodies, that is, the stars and planets."

I decided to drive the point home.

"All the diagrams and drawings made by Copernicus, Tycho, Galileo, and Kepler were based on Euclid's theories. In fact, geometry remained unchanged until a couple of centuries ago. That's why it's still being taught in schools, because it enables us to make most of the calculations we need for daily life."

It was no use. My students could not care less about the benefits of mathematics. So I pointed again to the board, full of every sort of triangle, and ended the class with the usual instructions.

"For tomorrow I want you to do the problems at the end of the lesson, numbers ten through fifteen. And no excuses."

"But the Champions are playing this afternoon!" a straggler protested.

"Well, that sounds like an excuse, so you'll be first at the board. Tough luck. Now, everybody out."

The bell rang. I was erasing the board when I heard Simon's voice behind me.

"Father, tell me more about ancient astronomy. I don't understand why Kepler would want to kill Tycho. Was there maybe a hidden love triangle?" he joked.

"It's pretty simple. Until the sixteenth century, astronomers used Aristotle's model of the heavens. The Earth was at the center of the universe, and everything else revolved around it. It was a simple concept and it worked pretty well. In fact, they were able to use the stars as navigation guides without getting lost."

Simon's face told the story. He didn't quite get it.

"If we look at the night sky," I continued, "we notice first that the stars move from east to west, but we get the impression that we're standing still. The Sun is one more star. After sunrise its light keeps us from seeing the rest.

At sunset, night falls and we can see that this stellar movement continues. It doesn't matter much whether we think the Earth or the Sun is at the center of everything."

"I see," Simon said, still not convinced.

"But some stars didn't follow suit," I added. "They showed some erratic behavior, so the Greeks called them planets. The word *planet* meant precisely that: 'wandering body.'"

"Did they disappear?"

"No. But their displacement wasn't the same as that of other stars. Sometimes their trajectory reversed itself. Especially playful, if you'll pardon the expression, was the planet Mars."

The kid was listening attentively.

"Mars was the main topic of discussion between Tycho and Kepler. Tycho had been tracking the position of this planet in regard to the fixed stars for more than thirty years, but no matter how he tried, he couldn't fit its trajectory into any known curvature. He asked Kepler to work for him on this and other tasks. It goes without saying that once Kepler had this data, he realized that Mars moved along an ellipse, with the Sun as one of its focal points."

"It seems simple," Simon commented.

"It wasn't at all. I'm skipping a lot of details. When ancient astronomers discovered the planets and saw that they moved differently from stars, they decided to associate them with different spheres. The sky was no longer a single vault with the fixed stars moving in unison and revolving around the Earth. The firmament was composed of a series of concentric, crystalline spheres set inside each other and moving harmoniously. Like the Sun and the Moon, each planet had its own sphere. The Earth remained motionless, at the center of everything. The fixed stars occupied the last sphere."

"If each planet revolved according to its own sphere, their strange movements were justified," the kid intelligently concluded.

"Yes and no. Theoretically, the model worked. But it didn't work geometrically. There was no way of finding the exact movement of the spheres that were inside other spheres. There was no way to predict with certainty where and when the planets would move. The model grew more and more complex. From the eight initial spheres, it went to more than fifty. Some depended on others in a very sophisticated way. Finally, in the second century, Ptolemy of Alexandria developed a series of tables and calculations that helped predict the precise orbits of the planets. He created a beautiful geometric model full of curves and elements with suggestive names such as epicycles, equants, and deferents. Geometry had triumphed. This model was used for fourteen centuries and no one doubted Aristotle's cosmological view of the Earth as the center of the universe."

"It seems too long," Simon said skeptically.

"Not that long if we take the times into account. The Church wasn't always as open and marvelous as you know it to be now," I joked, pointing at myself. "The Aristotelian model established the Earth as the center of divine creation, and man within it. Christian philosophers and theologians, like Thomas Aquinas, adapted Aristotelian ideas to Christendom, and faith replaced science. It was one of the biggest mistakes in the history of the Church."

"Galileo was almost burned at the stake, wasn't he?"

"Galileo was, in fact, accused by the Inquisition and forced to renounce Copernican theories. A few years earlier another contemporary of Tycho and Kepler, Giordano Bruno, was indeed burned at the stake. The first modern astronomers were more guarded," I went on. "The clearest example is Copernicus. When he published his new model of the cosmos, with the Sun at the center of the universe rather than the Earth, he was very prudent. So much so that he dedicated his book to the Pope, just in case. Copernicus died in 1543, only a month after he saw his theories published in *The Revolutions of the Heavenly Spheres*. They had taken him twenty-five years. Even now we usually call any great change a revolution or a Copernican movement, no matter what it's about. Astronomy is that important."

"And when did Tycho and Kepler enter the scene?"

"Only a few years later. The Copernican model had no success at all when it came out, though now it might seem like an extraordinarily brilliant intuition. Copernicus first considered the orbits of the planets to be perfect circles, and therefore his calculations were inaccurate. When he realized this and tried to adjust his experimental data, he again had to make use of epicycles and deferents. Like Ptolemy. But his tables of astronomical events, based on his model, were no better than the existing ones. So navigators and scholars continued to believe in the geocentric model, which also happened to agree with the religious ideas of the times and didn't contradict the great Aristotle. In fact, Tycho never adopted the Copernican model. He began from scratch, jotting down the positions of stars and planets with incredible precision. But he went only halfway."

"What do you mean?"

"That he wasn't able to adjust geometry to reality. He didn't have time. Tycho had his own vision of the universe, with the Earth in the center and the Moon and the Sun revolving around it. But the rest of the planets were then considered to revolve around the Sun, not the Earth. He had made the right observations, but his model wasn't right. By that time Johannes Kepler had become a brilliant mathematician, though he was burdened by the problems of his strict Lutheranism. You know most of the rest."

"Was Kepler a follower of Copernicus?" Simon interrupted impatiently.

"Yes. And this was a main point of contention with his teacher. Tycho wanted Kepler to adapt his careful measurements to his own model. Kepler was reticent and only pretended to agree with the work he was doing. That was why Tycho passed on his data to him so slowly."

"I see. Interesting, very interesting."

"Yes, it is. Astronomy changed the way we look at the heavens. And when astronomy changed, science itself changed, and society with it. In time, faith and reason became opposites. Nobody doubts that things would be very different today had it not been for the work of these giants."

Simon was satisfied at last. We had been talking for more than half an hour, and other students were at the door waiting to get back into the classroom. Perhaps one or two of them had been listening.

"Father, would you let me look through your telescope?" the inquisitive girl from the first row asked me from out of the blue as she reached her seat.

"Of course." I had no objection.

Right away, a chorus of teenagers demanded, "Can I look too? Pl-e-e-e-a-se!"

John Dee's name can be found everywhere in connection with the *Voynich Manuscript*. Tycho Brahe's several biographies mention him, and that was even more meaningful for me. Dee shared some lines with Tycho because, besides the famous Dane, he was one of the astronomers who reported on the appearance of the supernova of 1572.

Before getting into the search for data on this great alchemist's life, I wanted to know more about the famous stellar explosion, better known today as Tycho's supernova, and justifiably so. On the evening of November 11, 1572, while Tycho was coming home from his alchemy lab for dinner, he looked at the sky. He probably always looked at it, being so tenacious. But this time Tycho saw a new star—he knew the position of the visible stars very well, about four thousand of them, more or less, visible to the naked eye at that latitude. And he was astonished. There was a star where before there was nothing. It was much brighter than any of the others, much brighter than Sirius or Vega, even outshining the most brilliant planet, Venus.

Tycho did the prudent thing. He called his servants, apprentices, farmers, and anybody else he could find—remember that Tycho was the lord and master of the island. They all looked at the sky where Tycho was pointing, and they all confirmed his discovery. Tycho observed his star very carefully during the following nights. Surprisingly, contrary to his initial expectations, the star didn't move, didn't develop a brilliant halo, didn't have a tail, and didn't become blurred. It definitely wasn't a comet.

The discovery of this *nova* star, as he called it, was a historical event. It wasn't simply that there was one more star. Since ancient times no new stars had appeared. (This wasn't exactly so, because in 1054 another supernova had arrived in the sky, what we know today as the remnants of the Crab Nebula. It had been seen—or at least reported—only by Asian astronomers in China and Japan, so Tycho was unaware of its existence.) In Aristotelian cosmology, the skies beyond the Moon were immutable, and in fact comets were considered atmospheric phenomena occurring within the sphere of the Earth. Tycho already had doubts about the infallibility of the Aristotelian hypothesis, and this event strengthened those doubts. They were confirmed some years later when he measured a comet's parallax and correctly placed it well beyond the Moon's orbit.

I suddenly remembered another of the most surprising coincidences in the history of astronomy. The advent of supernovas is a very rare phenomenon in our Milky Way galaxy. They're produced when a star of great magnitude, larger than the Sun, grows old and begins fusing the chemical elements in its nucleus to get the necessary energy to stay alive. This goes from hydrogen to helium to carbon, and then to heavier elements like iron. The iron particles can't fuse, so the energy is used up and the star collapses very quickly upon itself due to the tremendous gravitational force. This creates a colossal explosion. Though the Milky Way contains a hundred million stars, this phenomenon occurs only an average of three times in a thousand years. In the last millennium, only some Asian astronomers were able to see the first supernova. Tycho Brahe witnessed the second, and only a few years later, in 1604, the third was seen by none other than Johannes Kepler. No stars have collapsed in our galaxy since then.

I was reviewing Tycho Brahe's most extensive biography, Victor E. Thoren's *The Lord of Uraniborg,* when I noticed a curious detail. The author describes the Danish astronomer's many travels all over Europe before he built Uraniborg, the first astronomical observatory in the world. In these trips Tycho made friends and shared his uncertainties with a good many contemporary scholars. In the autumn of 1577, Tycho decided to stay longer in Regensburg, in northern Germany. He wanted to attend the coronation of Rudolf II as head of the Holy Roman Empire, the same man who years later during Brahe's exile would become his mentor and friend. But at this time Tycho Brahe was simply a distinguished young nobleman, conducting some diplomatic missions for his beloved Frederick, king of Denmark, while at the same time broadening his own scientific knowledge.

It was then that he met Thadeus Hayek, a physicist from Bohemia. This would have had no importance except for the fact that Hayek was a known follower of Paracelsus. He was also a famous alchemist, just the sort of person Tycho sought out. A few years later, according to Tycho Brahe's biography, Hayek wrote that he had witnessed John Dee, and a mysterious accomplice, convert mercury into gold, probably in 1584. And it was precisely between 1584 and 1585 that John Dee and Edward Kelley spent some time in the court of Rudolf II in Prague.

It seemed these stories were bent on converging.

It was time to delve into the lives of these two sinister characters. I closed Thoren's book, and again logged on to the Internet. The strange lives of both Dee and Kelley, their connections with the occult, esoterica, unexplained events, and all kinds of fantasies took me through an endless trail of nonsense. It wasn't going to be easy to separate fact from fiction in the lives of these men who said they could speak with the angels in the language of Adam and Eve. I made myself some coffee and began taking notes.

It was very late, but my curiosity exceeded my need for sleep. John Dee, at least, was well known enough not to take me very long. Or so I thought. Dee, or according to his formal title, Dr. John Dee, was born on July 13, 1527, in one of the watchtowers of London, though we don't know why his mother was there. His father was a textile merchant, a gentleman, and tailor to Henry VIII, so that could be a connection. His forebears were from Wales, where the word *dee* meant "black"—which may have been significant for someone many times accused of practicing black magic. As a child in Essex and a youth in Cambridge, he was a brilliant student. Dee excelled in Latin, Greek, arithmetic, geometry, philosophy, and, of course, astronomy. Like Tycho and Kepler, he was particularly fascinated by astrology. Dee believed that the planets exerted their force over other bodies, especially over humans, a shadow of what later became known as the force of gravity, first postulated mathematically by his countryman Isaac Newton a century later.

John Dee traveled on a quest for knowledge, just as Tycho did. For years he worked with Gerard Mercator, the famous mathematician, geographer, and mapmaker, and some time later he took Mercator's mapmaking techniques to England. Mercator is considered to be the first to apply Euclidean geometry to navigation, drawing on his maps the farthest navigational straits, both in the northwest and in the northeast. Dee later translated Euclid's magnum opus, titled *Elements,* into English.

The coincidence made me think. The same day that I had chosen to teach my students Euclidean geometry, I came across one of its main champions in Europe. Up to that point, John Dee's record as a scientist was spotless. The bad part would come later.

Dee returned to England. The king, Edward VI, then a nine-year-old child, died at fifteen in 1553. John Dee was serving under the Duke of Northumberland, who had commissioned a horoscope for the child-king from an Italian physicist, Girolamo Cardano. It was rumored that Cardano thought about it for a long time, and even then hesitated, fearing the repercussions, and finally decided to keep silent. Other sources said that the Italian mathematician was mistaken concerning the young king's cruel destiny. Possibly he didn't want to take any risks; he could be accused of being a spy.

This was certainly an obscure episode. There were endless English intrigues during the sixteenth century. For me, the most interesting piece of information was, as Gordon Rugg supposed, that John Dee and Girolamo Cardano had worked together. The theory of codifying the *Voynich Manuscript* using the Italian's method was gaining momentum.

Upon the death of Edward VI, things got complicated for Dr. Dee. King Edward was succeeded by his half sister Mary Tudor, who restored Catholicism and devoted all her energy to destroying the Protestants, which, back then, amounted to burning them at the stake. John Dee was arrested, his books and belongings confiscated, and his house sealed. It was 1555, and his crime was his astronomical calculations. Everything that had to do with numbers was related to the kabbalah, numerology, and other magic and heretical arts. He was also accused of belonging to a secret Protestant sect, of casting horoscopes for the queen and her consort, and even of sorcery against her.

Dee was judged and condemned to death, but mysteriously set free some brief time later. He was absolutely ruined.

Somehow he kept the queen's favor. The following year he proposed to her the project of constructing the biggest library in England, a grandiose royal library. He was rejected, naturally. Despite this, John Dee collected volume after volume on his own and managed to amass around four thousand books. In the context of that era and keeping in mind, for instance, that the University of Cambridge had only a few hundred books, his collection was enormous. It covered philosophy, alchemy, astrology, and astronomy—then indistinguishable from each other—not only medicine and theology. If the *Voynich Manuscript* was included, that remains a mystery. In 1558 Queen Mary died and was succeeded by Elizabeth I. England's course changed again.

Elizabeth was Protestant, and England followed. John Dee was called upon to determine a favorable day for the coronation of the new queen. He chose January 15, 1559, and judging by history, he chose well. Elizabeth was queen for a long time and she was good for England. This helped Dee's position in the court. He became the official astrologer, benefiting from the fact that every European monarch had an astrologer and alchemist, and took the matter of finding the philosopher's stone very seriously. It seemed that, in addition to this task, Queen Elizabeth asked Dee to take on some less magical, more prosaic assignments. The most interesting one was acting as a double agent during the war between England and Spain. And his secret identity was none other than 007, very cabalistic *and* cinematic. It's been rumored that this anecdote inspired Ian Fleming to give this identity to his famous character James Bond.

There was another clue linking John Dee to Tycho, and then to Girolamo Cardano. It had to do with the appearance of the supernova. Dee's work explains his trigonometric method to measure stellar distances—known as parallax—which Tycho considered admirable. But Cardano, the third astronomer, disagreed. He rejected the idea that the supernova was a new star. He believed it was the same star that guided the Magi to Bethlehem and had remained hidden since the birth of Christ, due strictly to its divine nature. Nevertheless, John Dee was basically a Copernican astronomer, and his writings on the science of the stars are closer to Tycho's than to Cardano's. Dee's contribution was the observation that the supernova was slowly growing more distant from the Earth.

After this, Dee underwent a complete change. He began talking to the angels and doing a lot of silly things concerning religion. It seemed so even to a man of the cloth like me. So I decided to go to sleep and leave my research on Dr. John Dee's magic life, and that of his even more incredible associate, Edward Kelley, for another day.

II

I had not heard from John and Juana since I said good-bye to her at her hotel. No e-mails, no postcards from the Tenerife beaches or Pico de Teyde. Nor had John acknowledged my asking for Professor Volker Bialas's paper on the Gilders' book. Following a paternal impulse, I tried the cell number our charming Mexican friend had given me, but it was disconnected or out of range. This was the first time in a year that I had completely lost contact with them, just when we had begun to know each other. They hadn't given me the address of a rented villa or of any hotel where they would be. After all, I had refused to accompany them, so why would I need it?

I didn't know whether I should worry. It was understandable if they wanted to be alone for a few days, away from the rest of the world. They had the right to a private rendezvous. But so much mystery seemed odd. My only contact with them was through the ciphered CD that I hadn't finished solving. The last screen had almost defeated me. Even though I was enjoying their game, I almost didn't want to go on with it now. Failing would mean finally losing communication. I'd keep trying with the phone and e-mail. Maybe they didn't have Internet access. Hard to imagine.

I had other urgent business to attend to, my community's future. That night we received another graffito, this time on the other side of the wall, the street side, to make sure people would see it. And this one in perfectly legible Roman characters.

SPECULATORS MURDERERS

Naturally this caused panic. It's hard to understand how the inability to find a parking space in the center of town could make some people call us murderers. And we had been educating their children, and maybe themselves as well, for almost a hundred years. Plus a few more years comforting their souls in the old church.

The old parish church. My exploration of the underground passages was still pending.

Though the box with the documents and the old prior's floor plans hadn't been found, I still kept a few papers that Carmelo had given me the day of my first trip there. The mess on my desk, particularly these last days, was such that these papers were now buried somewhere under all the others. After recovering them, I lay down on my bed and looked them over.

A few pages were only Anselmo Hidalgo's account of his daily activities, pretty mundane. A simple but detailed *ora et labora* from those days. Masses, classes, the usual visits to the sick and the faithful, and a few to politicians, master masons, or officials from various departments, plus a painstaking record, in red and blue, of expenses and income. There was a page with an attempt at a poem. The old prior's poem seemed like a poor imitation of Saint John of the Cross. And there were drawings. Many, and badly done, like doodles. They didn't seem to mean anything. A horse, a dog, a man smoking a pipe. Some fat naked women inside barrels or cans.

Fat naked women inside cans?

I jumped out of bed. It didn't make much sense for a Jesuit prior to be drawing naked women, particularly when he was far from being an adolescent. The drawings were familiar, very familiar.

When I compared Anselmo Hidalgo's doodles with the drawings in the *Voynich*, the resemblance to some of the figures was astonishing. They were not exactly alike, but there was enough similarity for me to be sure that he wasn't a deviant. It was evident that this old Jesuit, a former prior of the monastery where I now lived, had also been captivated by the *Voynich Manuscript*. And the most intriguing part, that he probably saw it with his own eyes.

I checked the images carefully against my printouts of the original. The women Hidalgo had drawn were similar to those in one of the "astronomical" pages of the *Voynich Manuscript*. They were not exact, but they followed the same norms of beauty, such as they were. Unlike the book, there were no Voynichian characters, only the women. That was another difference to keep in mind. There were a lot of fat or pregnant women, about whom the *Voynich* scholars had made numerous hypotheses. Another heavily decorated illustration presented the same group of women bathing or submerged in various fluids in communicating vessels. The most interesting theory suggested an allegory about the union of body and soul. Perhaps at the moment of birth. Or about their separation at the moment of death.

It was time for a new exploratory trip.

I got the key to the passages and a flashlight with new batteries, and went directly to the chapel.

It was deserted at this time of night. A few friars, not yet retired for the night, would be in the television room. Or perhaps around a table in the kitchen, relentlessly discussing how to face the difficult situation before us.

There was a preliminary agreement with the city council. We had finally consented to leave quietly. But the two parties still differed greatly on the

compensation for the forced expropriation. We also hadn't agreed to resume instruction in the decrepit old institute while the new school was being built. Damian, Carmelo, and Julian held endless meetings with the legal representatives of the councilors involved. Many ended disastrously.

It wasn't easy to open the door. No doubt, Carmelo knew better than I the tricks to working the lock. I left a piece of cardboard as a door stopper. I didn't trust the rusty old lock mechanism. I felt my pants pocket. My cell phone was there, though it might be out of range a few steps down. And I had no bread crumbs to leave behind. Nor any rope to guide me through the labyrinth.

Theoretically, there was nothing to fear.

I retraced Carmelo's route of a few days ago. There was no choice. The steps led in only one direction, always down, naturally. The path didn't branch out. So I went on until I reached the ample landing where we had ended our first exploration. The sound of running water could be heard. There were also sounds of little feet. I shouldn't have shone my flashlight on them. A rat dashed madly between my legs and I yelped with revulsion. I tried to kick it, but needless to say, I didn't even graze it. I'm only good at basketball.

Then I looked at my cell phone screen. Of course there was no signal. That scared me, which made me feel a bit silly. I just had to turn around and climb back, no big deal. Then I tried to make a mental map of the location and figure out exactly what was above me. I couldn't. I had turned several times going down, and the straight stretches were of different lengths. I decided to bring a GPS receiver next time. Lack of technology wouldn't stop me. Then I realized the foolishness of my thinking. If the cell phone was of no use, the GPS would be totally worthless at this depth. How idiotic of me.

I stepped off the main path, giving myself fifteen minutes to get back to the same point. I would always turn right—whenever possible, of course. I would turn left only when I couldn't turn right. And I then would reverse this, only turning left on the way back. I didn't consider myself a bad explorer, I had a pretty good sense of direction, but I missed not having the North Star overhead.

That first incursion didn't produce any interesting results. More rats, a nauseating stench, and little else. The Roman section was almost intact, but it was only a series of connected blind wells, and the trickle of water running through the ducts was just filtration from the recent excavations a few yards above. I was surprised that the municipal architects hadn't discovered the Roman sewer system in various places.

Well, maybe they had, who knows? I wished I knew which building was really above me. I first suspected it was the modern art museum, built a couple of years ago on a piece of land formerly owned by the mayor's family.

The next day my classes seemed to drag on interminably. The theory of the inclined plane wouldn't penetrate their heads, and the square roots were becoming round in mine. I decided to cut the afternoon session short with the excuse that I didn't feel well. My head really was pounding.

I lay down for a while before going to dinner. I wasn't sleepy, but exchanging the inclined plane for a horizontal position was a relief. The aspirins worked. The throbbing in my temples stopped and I could think clearly again. Should I go back to the CD? I was worried about my friends. I decided to go ahead and open the envelope that had come with the disc. I had locked it in the drawer of my night table right after Father Hidalgo's belongings disappeared. But come to think of it, if the thief managed to take that big box, carrying off the whole piece of furniture would have been even easier for him. Fortunately, it was still there. The thief probably decided that he would find only a Bible, a curious custom in American hotels. Juana's envelope was separating the Old from the New Testament in the beautiful Bible my mother had given me the day I was ordained. Like before and after Jesus came into this world, they would be my own before and after.

Then I recalled another detail. Reviewing the archives of librarian Lazzari's belongings, which he left in our community house in 1770, I had found only a Bible and a few classic books. Had I bothered to leaf through these books? Of course not. I was too interested in Father Hidalgo's floor plans to think of that. Now I had the chance to know whether Hidalgo himself had seen the *Voynich Manuscript*. Could there be anything in Lazzari's belongings?

The idea was so simple it almost scared me. When the Jesuits fled, in the desperate effort to keep their enormous collections of books and documents, the main librarian decided to hide them in various places. Some ended up in Toledo, Spain; others were hidden in Rome; some in France. Why couldn't Lazzari have also thought of our humble and almost unknown monastery? The Society of Jesus had just settled here, the building was new, the town was small, and there were a minimum number of visitors. It seemed as if it could have been a very safe place.

I set aside Juana's envelope, got out of bed, and went back down to the archives. My headache was totally gone.

The folder with P. LAZZARI, 1770 was right where I'd left it. I untied the ribbons holding the cardboard covers and, perhaps for the second time in a hundred years, these old volumes would see the light of day.

I leafed quickly through the pages of Saint Augustine and Thomas Aquinas. There was only dust. Not even an annotation. They were cheap editions with nothing significant in them.

Then I opened the Bible.

Who said the Holy Spirit is a fable?

Right between the Old and the New Testament, I found a sealed envelope.

I dropped it into my pocket, locked the archive, turned off all the lights, and dashed back to my room.

This time I made sure the door was well closed before examining the contents of that mysterious second envelope.

There was a folded paper with a sentence written on it.

In Latin, for added torture. And not even in very academic Latin; there clearly were some missing letters: "Haec immature a me jam frustra leguntur oy."

At first glance, the meaning of these words could be something like this: "I tried to read this in vain, too soon."

This meant nothing to me. Except that in fact he had tried to read something and failed. And perhaps too soon. If it weren't written with a goose feather pen on eighteenth-century paper, and hidden within the walls of my monastery for nearly two and a half centuries, I'd have thought that the Machiavellian *Juanes* were behind all of this.

It made sense if applied to the *Manuscript*. A lot of sense.

After all, nobody had managed to decipher the *Voynich*. Not even the many Jesuits who had temporarily possessed it. Perhaps the most intriguing part of the message was "too soon." Too soon for what? And why? Was it necessary to wait for something or someone?

I put aside these ancient ponderings and prepared myself to face more modern ones. The CD was scrolling again on my computer screen, spewing the familiar panels at great speed—it was good to know the old solutions to the first riddles beforehand, and to anticipate the new explanations provided by *los Juanes*, soon to be parading across my monitor.

Congratulations, Hector. Do you want to go on or should we have some coffee?

Since I already had my coffee, I pressed the key to continue.

We usually don't see the obvious. What part of the Voynich *Manuscript* would be the easiest to decipher?

We had asked ourselves that question many times. For John and me, the astronomical diagrams were naturally the simplest. The names of the main constellations, the signs of the zodiac, the months of the year, and the many stars were old enough to be included in the *Manuscript*. I guess that if we were botanists we'd think likewise about the plants. The problem for them was that the botanical figures had no labels, and that was why we had an advantage.

I suppose you chose the astronomical diagrams, as usual.

Smart guy. And smart girl, because the disc had been made by both. The perfect Spanish in which it was written was surely Juana's contribution.

That is where we looked again. But in a different way.

Which way? Looking at the characters as reflected in a mirror? Reading them from right to left, like Arabic? Deleting the vowels, like Hebrew? All of these had been tried, time and again.

Maybe the most famous diagram in the *Voynich Manuscript* is on page 67. One can distinguish twelve divisions. Apparently they refer to the twelve months of the year, or to the twelve signs of the zodiac. The central figure seems to be the Moon. The three of us have reviewed this page over and over.

True. And each of the twelve divisions seems to have two parts. One part has words (perhaps the names), and the other, some stars, though badly drawn. This page is so famous that it even appeared on the cover of what is known as "The Astronomy Picture of the Day" on the Internet. A group of astronomers chooses an outstanding picture of the skies or of space, either because of its beauty or its mystery. Out of simple curiosity, I searched for the reproduction. In fact, on August 26, 2002, that drawing was the leitmotiv of the well-known Web site.

That is where we looked again. But in a different way.

These guys repeated themselves too much, but I looked at it again. Nothing new under the sun. Or around the moon.

Think of the polar bear, Hector. Do the stars keep you from seeing the sky?

Was there something else besides stars in the drawing?
Yes, there was.
Three concentric circles around a star, and many words. And the circles, just like Aristotle's spheres or Copernicus's planets, could revolve around the central star. The solution was so obvious I was astonished that nobody—except John, of course—had noticed it. This astronomical engraving in the *Voynich* was just an artistic representation of what could be the combination lock on an old safe. By moving the circles in a particular way so that the mechanism engaged, one could open the door and get at the hidden treasure. The problem was, we didn't know the combination.

Frankly, Hector, as you probably have guessed, it's all a combination of three elements. Except that this time we are a bit closer. There are fewer syllables that we need to combine.

This was an optimistic way of looking at it. The number of possibilities was still astronomical, pardon the pun. Anyway, I was fascinated by their discovery, simply brilliant.

And now, open the envelope. But before that, destroy the CD. Adiós, Hector.

I obeyed. Took out the disc and broke it. To make sure it was completely destroyed, I put some alcohol in an ashtray with the disc pieces and set them on fire. After a while, the only thing left was a stinking mound of plastic.

Then I went to the night-table drawer and took Juana's envelope from inside my Bible. It was the second secret envelope I would open that day. But this time I had some idea of what it contained.

I opened it carefully, knowing that if I tore the tickets, Iberia would not refund them. For days I suspected that the envelope contained a plane ticket to the Canary Islands.

That night I slept like a log. At least a few of the issues on my mind during the past days had been resolved. The CD was gone.

12

Los Juanes had found out when school vacations began and booked my flight exactly for that day. Presumably they would be at the Tenerife airport to pick me up. I imagine they assumed I'd be able to solve every riddle on the disc, or that my ego would force me to take the plane in order to find the final solution. My shrewd friends knew that all of this intrigue would get me totally hooked on the *Voynich Manuscript*. My prior didn't object at all to having me start my Christmas vacation a few days early. "You've earned this," he said. And he added that a change of air and getting away from books for a while would be good for me. If the students needed a break, the long-suffering teachers were twice as deserving.

Since I still had a week before leaving to see John and Juana, I could use that time to rotate—never a better word—the circles in the diagram of the stars. It didn't seem very easy. The words around the moon spokes didn't look to fit anything in astronomy or in astrology. At first glance, they were only random characters in Voynichian.

They did follow the regular pattern of prefix-syllable-suffix, but without repetitions. That would have made it easier to decipher. In any Romance or Germanic language, some months of the year have the same ending. But not in Voynichian; it was more complex.

Actually I didn't know what I was trying to accomplish by rotating the discs. I only knew that there were three and that most words in Voynichian were triads. This diagram could be the key to deciphering the rest of the book. Or not. It could also be the only key in the manuscript, with the rest just unintelligible text to derail an impatient translator. It could have a thousand meanings, or none at all. There was nothing to celebrate. Besides, it might be impossible even to identify the twelve months, or the twelve constellations, or—to be completely ridiculous—the twelve apostles. There was no clue as to which direction the disks rotated. Start from sunrise? Or from sunset? Must the diagram be interpreted on a particular day, like a solstice, for example? On an equinox? Was it too early or too late?

I'd leave these questions for another time. Now I was thinking about something much easier and more fun.

Who was Edward Kelley?

I began searching on the Internet. Soon I'd found the biography of a character straight out of a novel, an authentic rascal from the Middle Ages.

Edward Talbot was born in 1555, more or less, in Worcester, England. As a child he was an apprentice to an apothecary, and maybe that was where his interest in herbs and alchemy originated. Then he became an amanuensis, and later a notary in Lancaster. That's where his deceptions started. He was caught falsifying documents and was arrested and banished. In addition, as a gruesome reward, he received two ears, like a matador. Unfortunately they were his own. It seemed that the traditional punishment for this kind of offense was the public amputation of the earlobes. He was always depicted in engravings and drawings with long hair, a beard, and wearing a big hat. Pure vanity, I thought.

Talbot hid in Wales, and changed his name to Kelley. He began talking about a manuscript he had—the *Voynich*?—that nobody could read. Except him, of course. The book explained how to find the philosopher's stone. Kelley also said he had been guided by a spiritual creature—an angel, no less—to a place called Northwick Hill. There, in the ruins of an old abbey, and in a bishop's tomb, he had found the book and a strange red tincture that served as a base for converting metals into gold.

Because this singular story was so incredible, many people believed it. It was widely thought that the Catholics had hidden in the tombs of priests and bishops a good many treasures to keep them out of the Protestants' hands. The belief in the existence of angels was so widespread that cherubim and seraphim, plus other angelic fauna—God forgive my looseness of speech— were thought to be the real movers of the celestial spheres. Even John Dee, a competent mathematician and scientist, really believed in them.

Dee and Kelley met in 1581 or 1582. Dee was already trying to talk with angels, to no avail, and Kelley was famous for doing it easily. Dee didn't have much money—Queen Elizabeth was not very generous—but he had valuable contacts in the court, which made him a desirable target. Kelley took advantage of this and visited Dee with a crystal ball.[3] Edward Kelley claimed he could communicate with the spirits through this magic mirror. So, for a while, Dee believed him and recorded everything Kelley told him he heard from the great beyond. Dee also thought that only the good angels could be summoned, and that through them he would acquire knowledge and security. He used Kelley as a medium. Kelley would talk to them in the language of angels, the so-called language of Enoch.

Enochian was obviously an invented language, but it had its own alphabet and is fully documented on the Internet by a sizable group of nincompoops. Its structure, as could well be imagined, is very similar to English, into which it can be translated practically word for word without difficulty. Enochian characters could also be easily replaced by Roman characters. It had its own peculiarities, like having words without vowels or without consonants. In this sense it shared some characteristics with the kabbalah. It had less than a thousand known words, in nineteen symbolic poems. Unfortunately, any resemblance between Enochian and Voynichian would be a pure coincidence. Enochian is completely legible, Voynichian, well, let's not talk about it. For a time it was thought that the *Voynich Manuscript* was written in this new, invented language, surely by the Dee/Kelley duo. Sadly, it was later proved that this speculation had no merit.

Again fleeing from justice, Edward Kelley convinced John Dee to leave England. They began a long journey, first through Germany and then Poland, invited by a mysterious prince—or count, it's not clear—named Laski. The alchemist prince suggested that they join the strange court of Emperor

3. This magic ball later belonged to John Dee and is in the British Museum in London. (Author's Note)

Rudolf II in Bohemia. He was a gullible, depressed king who spent exorbi-
tant sums attempting to become rich through experiments with the—by then
already stale—philosopher's stone, as well as trying to improve his personal
condition. He felt besieged by misfortune. And so to Prague they went. Not
only these two rascals, but also various oddballs who had joined them along
the way, like Catholic renegade Pucci, who regarded Dee as a prophet.

John Dee and Edward Kelley must have arrived in Bohemia's capital in
1585. Dr. Dee told Emperor Rudolf that in his conversations with the angels,
specifically with Uriel the archangel, on September 21 and 22, 1584—one
had to be precise in heavenly matters—he had been informed of the stone's
secret. Thanks to the manuscript (the *Voynich*?), the red tincture, and divine
intervention, they could obtain gold. More or less. During the time Dee and
Kelley stayed in Prague, a series of vague, fantastic events resulted in very
different outcomes for each of them. While Kelley became the emperor's favorite, John Dee found only bad luck. A year later, in 1586, Pope Sixtus V
banished him along with some of his followers, like Pucci. They were accused of practicing black magic.

I found all of this quite amusing.

I still hadn't come anywhere close to finishing this research. I decided
to dig deeper into the religious aspect. According to a Middle Ages school
of thought, God himself had given alchemy to Adam, through an angel, of
course—in this case, the Angel of Mystery, also known as Raziel. Adam
surely passed this bit of knowledge on to Enoch. Then, from Enoch to Abra-
ham, to Moses, and then to Job, who after much suffering owned the philosopher's stone and received a sevenfold increase—the magic number—of his
initial riches. The character of Enoch is confusing because he appears twice
in Genesis, the first time as Cain's son. His relationship to Adam makes sense
because he would be Adam's grandson. But the second mention has more to
do with alchemy. According to this, Enoch was Jared's son, Methuselah's
father, Lamec's grandfather, and Noah's great-grandfather. Going back to
Genesis, it says that he was an honest man who "walked with God," lived
for 365 years, and then disappeared, "because God took him away so he
wouldn't have to die." That's all.

When I was a child, these Bible stories fascinated me. That was Holy
Scripture. Today, *Wikipedia* tells us more about this famous Enoch.

Enoch was the first to invent books and various forms of writing. The ancient Greeks believed that Enoch was the equivalent of Hermes Trimegistus, and that he taught the children of men the art of building cities while proclaiming some admirable laws. . . . He discovered knowledge of the zodiac, and of the planets' trajectories; he taught the children of men that they should adore God, that they should fast, pray, give alms, make votive offerings and tithe. He deemed some foods abominable, as well as liquor in excess, and he established festivals for each sign of the zodiac to offer sacrifices to the sun.

Enoch also appears as a prophet in the Koran under the name of Idris, and according to the Book of Enoch, the apocryphal Hebrew text, God had taken Enoch and converted him into the angel Metatron, a colleague of Uriel and a favorite of John Dee and Edward Kelley. Enoch's importance for alchemists was his supposed invention of an entire alphabet and a complete set of symbols. And that all of these, properly combined, could convert metals, and even transform human beings, angels, and spirits.

I think that neither Tycho nor Kepler would have accepted what *Wikipedia* says—a quote attributed to Bar-Hebraeus, a Syrian theologian of the third century—concerning Enoch's discovery of the trajectory of the planets, as well as his studies of the zodiac. Though they both probably knew about this. For two astronomers like them, any matter relating to the heavens had to have a sounder basis.

I explained everything about Enoch to Simon, without mentioning, of course, the *Voynich Manuscript*. This was an additional lecture about the forgotten Holy Scriptures, that now, for better or for worse, are no longer studied. I imagined he would be thrilled to know more about the origins of alchemy.

"Were you taught that Adam and Eve are our first ancestors?" he asked.

We had grown friendlier. I told him that for the rest of the semester he could stop calling me Father. All that formality made me feel old and creaky.

"To be honest, in my time I felt a bit schizophrenic. Just imagine," I continued, "that you're in a natural science class. And that your professor, a young priest like me, talks about Darwin's theory of evolution, and says that we originated with apes. Then, in the next class, an old priest says quite the contrary, that God created Adam and Eve."

"That's how it's taught in the United States."

Simon had read the local rag.

"I told you not to believe all that the newspapers say. It's not really like that."

"What is Intelligent Design?"

"Exactly the opposite of what it seems," I said. "It's a messed-up version of the theory of evolution, much closer to the creationist view. It talks about man first appearing on Earth by the will of God, and not as the random result of natural selection. But Darwin demonstrated that the evolution of species was a natural phenomenon, not directed by a supernatural power, and that its results depended on circumstance and chance."

"Then why is it called Intelligent Design?"

Simon was again firing questions.

"Because its followers think that life is too complex to be a product of chance, so they assume that a superior intelligence must have guided evolution. Obviously, God. It's a kind of Christian fundamentalism," I added. "They don't do us a favor, really. Everything is simpler when religion and science are kept separate.

"Look at the disaster the obscurantism of the Middle Ages brought to the Church. The blame for Galileo's trial still follows us, so many centuries later."

"What are American fundamentalists looking for?"

"In the first place, it's a small portion of the population," I pointed out, "though quite influential. In some states, like Kansas for instance, this belief is taught as an alternative to Darwin's theory. They are convinced that evolution doesn't really mean progress. They don't agree that there is no specific goal to attain, or that there was no prior design. They reject the idea that everything could change according to chance and circumstance. Intelligent Design is an outrageous silliness that their scientists and universities don't even want to talk about. But the most recent American presidents, except

Clinton, a Democrat, have been very receptive to the demands of the various powerful evangelical groups."

"I don't understand how they can convince so many followers. Americans were the only ones to reach the moon. And they're so creative, they invent almost everything," Simon said skeptically. "If anyone knows about science, it's the Americans. I'm half American myself."

That was true. I remembered that his father worked at the U.S. consulate.

"Ask your father then. They've got money and influence. They've got lawyers and politicians. And television networks with skilled ministers who impress the less educated. They don't just rely on the Bible, some groups have their own bizarre mythology."

"For example?"

"For example, let's go back to Enoch. For the Mormons, who are just a small sector of the creationists, Enoch founded the pure city of Zion in the middle of a sinful world. He and all the inhabitants of that city were taken by God, vanishing from the face of the Earth before the Flood. They left behind Methuselah and his family, including Noah, so that God-fearing people could continue to populate the earth."

"Taken where?"

"To a happy Arcadia, I suppose."

"And what is Arcadia?"

"Oh, Simon, you're driving me crazy." I was frustrated. "Don't you understand what I'm saying?"

"No."

"Well, I'm going to play basketball for a while. And you should do the same."

For the rest of the day, I continued with the known history of the avatars of the *Voynich Manuscript*. From the court of Rudolf II to Marcus Marci, and then to the scholar Athanasius Kircher, and by then it was already in the hands of the Jesuits again. But after Kircher died in 1680, and until 1773 when our society was dissolved the first time and all of our archives were moved, we don't know anything. The *Manuscript* doesn't appear in the catalogs, museums, or libraries of the Jesuits. Was it hidden, or the object of a pact of silence because of its content? Perhaps. Of course, many of its illustrations, especially those of the nude pregnant women, as well as the map of the heavens, could be seen as relating to the devil. Any of these could make the manuscript seem like a witches' treatise, with its drawings of strange plants, unknown constellations, and of course its strange, cryptic characters. The type of book that's usually forbidden to the unprepared reader. Someone had to have decided to hide this unintelligible manuscript rather than destroy it. Perhaps it contained something of value, and eventually the right person, armed with the required knowledge, could decipher its mysteries.

It didn't have to be me, naturally. Though the idea was enticing.

The book had not been in the hands of the Jesuits for long. In 1853, following the death of Father Roothan, general director in the years after the first restoration, Petrus Beckx was named to succeed him. That Beckx had the book at some point is well documented. When Wilfred Voynich bought it in 1912, it still had a label on the cover that read FROM THE PRIVATE LIBRARY OF P. BECKX. In 1870 Victor Emmanuel's troops entered Rome and captured all our belongings, except personal effects. Perhaps they were afraid of the large contingents of Catholics who were Roman citizens and who had befriended the Jesuits. So the soldiers must have looked the other way. Despite this, the new government took over about seventy libraries holding more than four hundred thousand books. These went to the national library. Among these volumes was the correspondence between Marci and Kircher, as well as Kircher's belongings, formerly in his own museum. There was nearly total plunder. Later, during the second restoration of the society, our possessions were only partially reordered and classified.

Villa Mondragone (Dragon Mountain) was built in 1577 outside Rome, by Cardinal Altemps. It was sold in 1613 to Cardinal Scipione Borghese, later to become Pope Paul V. Then, in 1865, the villa was given to the Jesuits, and that's where our general director took refuge during the difficult years of the second dissolution. And his books went with him. In 1896, with the Jesuit order restored thanks to the generosity of Pope Pius X, the villa was finally purchased to stay in Jesuit hands forever.

There was only one problem. The building was falling apart and it would be expensive to restore. Something had to be sold, which was a dangerous decision because the Jesuits have always been criticized for being too money oriented. Our libraries had more than a thousand volumes and the sale of some of them would be kept secret. Only two antiquarians and Pope Pius X himself could bid for them. Pius X pulled rank and bought about three hundred books for the Vatican libraries. This was in 1912. That same year, an unknown American book collector of Lithuanian origin, Wilfred Voynich, secretly obtained another thirty volumes. He never revealed where he got the *Manuscript;* that was the agreement. Only when Voynich died would his widow discover the provenance of the book in his will. Voynich thought he had bought a very old manuscript, a fantastic, ciphered book probably containing the first scientific discoveries of the British Franciscan monk Roger Bacon.

Not much more is known about the travails of the manuscript through Jesuit monasteries and libraries. It all began when the book got to Rome with a letter from Marcus Marci. Probably this happened in 1666. From that time until Voynich got it out of Villa Mondragone, also in Rome, there was a period of 246 years. Almost two and a half centuries, during which time the mysterious volume could have gone from hand to hand in a useless attempt to decipher its secret, or it could have remained on an obscure shelf somewhere, gathering dust.

I kept wondering why librarian Lazzari had come to our brand-new location. Did the envelope inside his Bible have any meaning related to the *Voynich Manuscript*? And why early in the twentieth century did another Jesuit, Anselmo Hidalgo, copy drawings from the *Voynich*? Too many unanswered questions. And on top of it all, someone had stolen the box with Prior Hidalgo's belongings.

Right out from under my nose.

13

Almost everybody had come.

There were hors d'oeuvres, refreshments, a thermos with hot coffee (my personal suggestion), gloves, hats, scarves, and such.

The winter sky was spectacular. And the proceedings promised fulfillment for those courageous souls keeping their eyes peeled. The "performers" never failed to show up, and the weather helped, fortunately. It was naturally cold in Castile, Spain, past the middle of December. But the night was clear and the stars were shining bright.

The bus driver took the whole trip slowly. We weren't going far, barely thirty miles from the city, just enough to leave its annoying lights behind. The idea was to go up the hill to the ancient castle and set the telescope next to its old walls. The road was duly paved, so it was easy. The only trouble was that I had to carry the telescope. The tripod wasn't light at all.

The bus left us right there.

"This all right, Father?" the driver asked.

"Yes. But please try to park the bus so the wall can be a windbreak to protect us from the breeze."

He skillfully maneuvered the bus, edging its back next to the stone wall, and turned off the motor.

"It's going to take a while," I warned him. "If you want to leave, I can always reach you on your cell, and then you can pick us up."

"And miss this celestial event?" He laughed. "No. If you don't mind, I'll stay. I want to see this too."

"No problem. Surely the kids will give you something to eat. They brought lots of food and drinks."

I began setting up.

It was early, around seven thirty, but the sun had set a while ago. I had brought a few sky charts to distribute among the kids. And I'd brought my laptop too, so I could easily predict when a particular star would appear in the sky. I was playing to advantage, but wasn't trying to repeat the feats of Tycho, Kepler, or Galileo. Just trying to be practical. Any teacher's dream is to see one of his students become an important man of science. I was no exception.

"Okay," I shouted to the kids. "While I mount this, you find the cardinal points. Then look west and tell me what you see."

This caused a great commotion among the two dozen kids who had come with me, trying to find the cardinal points. Finally Miguel, the extremely nice driver, was the one to answer this question. It so happened that to the north was the Northern Turnpike, and he knew the roads well. In the meantime, I struggled with my Celestron telescope.

It took me about fifteen minutes to aim it properly. Once I found the North Star, it was easy to adjust the inclination to the latitude, and to set the axes of rotation and elevation. Using this as a reference, the equatorial mounting of the device did the rest. I connected it to a port in my laptop and keyed in three equidistant stars as guides for the calibration. The software controlling the telescope created its own sky map. I had to try twice because, not surprisingly, I had initially used the wrong time.

Then I set the telescope to point toward Venus. To everybody's fascination, the motors for raising and lowering the lens began working at full speed.

"This looks like a gimmick."

"It's technology. Or did you expect us to solve triangles in this cold?" I joked.

Then I began teaching.

"Okay. Here's the first stop on our trip through the solar system. The most brilliant point you can now see, to the west, is Venus. It will soon set and disappear. It's the evening star."

Nearly all pointed their fingers toward the most brilliant body in the sky after the Sun and the Moon. Though it wasn't especially luminous that evening.

"Venus follows the Sun and it will soon disappear on the horizon. So take a look, one at a time. Anyone who moves the tripod will get a ten-point penalty on the next test," I warned them.

One by one they looked, with almost religious respect. The first ones didn't say anything. And then it was Simon's turn.

"Why do we see so little of Venus? It's only a crescent."

"Because Venus, like the Moon, has phases. Galileo discovered them, and it has been fully proved that the Sun, and not the Earth, is at the center of the planets."

After a while I aimed it toward the east. Mars was beginning to show. So the girls and boys again lined up to look through the telescope. Most of their comments had to do with the redness and size of Mars, no bigger than a lentil. Simon shrugged after taking a look, and offered his opinion.

"I don't think I'd kill for this, to be honest."

"Neither would I," I replied. "And there weren't any telescopes then. There was only patience."

Infinite patience. The night was just beginning and many of the kids were already getting restless. While they were eating, I encouraged them to just look at the sky with the naked eye.

"Over there, very close to Mars, you'll see a group of stars. How many?"

Someone said four. Others, five. And the girl with the light blue eyes— I've no idea whether eye color has anything to do with perception—said seven.

"They're the Pleiades. According to Greek mythology, they were the seven daughters of Atlas, changed into doves by Zeus so they could fly to heaven and escape from Orion."

"Escape?" asked the girl with catlike vision.

"Well . . . yes," I said, hesitating. "Orion wasn't exactly good company. He was an arrogant bully."

So I told them the story of Orion, the bravest warrior. His constellation could already be seen from the east. They all agreed they could see his belt and his bow, and its most brilliant stars: blue Rigel and Betelgeuse, the giant red one that sits on his shoulder.

"To me it looks like a coffeepot," Miguel joked.

"True. Today it would be called the Coffeepot Constellation, but they were more poetic then. Now look at the Moon, it's already coming up; see the small bright point that comes first? The one that doesn't twinkle? A reward goes to anyone who guesses what it is, using the chart of the heavens."

I sat on a rock with a thermos of hot coffee, mesmerized by the sky. Miguel joined me.

"It ain't easy to handle so many kids."

"Easy it's not. But sometimes it's worth the effort."

"I believe you," Miguel agreed. "I've got a kid about the same age who must be out drinking himself silly. I can't control him at all."

"It's a bad age, they are easily led astray," I kidded, "by any idiot like me."

Miguel laughed and gazed again at the sky.

"Look, Father, I'm not really a believer. But there must be something. Someone had to put all those stars out there."

Then it was my turn to laugh. I remembered saying the same thing to my father the first time he showed me the stars. I was ten and didn't want to do my First Communion. Later I changed my mind, of course.

"Hector, could you point the telescope at the Moon?"

The kids were demanding my attention again.

I got up to fix the computer and aim the telescope. The Moon was in its first quarter, bright but almost ready to disappear. Before allowing them to look, I added a filter to reduce the amount of light reaching the eyepiece. I didn't want anybody to be blinded. They thought I was exaggerating.

"Damn, what a rock!"

Of course he got a rap on the head. But he just laughed. The kids who followed toned down their expressions of awe.

"It floats!"

"Can you see the American flag?"

"It's full of pimples, like you."

"What a trick."

"Let me look again, asshole. It's my turn."

And so on, while Miguel and I kept discussing matters human and divine, and ate some of the snacks and sodas. When they got tired of looking at the moon—actually they never got tired of it, but other performers were already onstage—I shifted the focus of my Celestron.

"Well, has anyone guessed yet what doesn't twinkle next to the moon?"

Not a peep.

"Okay, I tricked you. The planets don't show on the cardboard planispheres. Let's start the next round. Girls first."

"Shit! It's Saturn!"

The foulmouthed girl didn't get a rap on the head but a yank on her ponytail that moved her away from the telescope. She thought it was funny.

"Oh, Hector, don't be such a meanie," she squealed, turning eagerly to look again.

Maybe I could turn one of them into an astronomer, but as an educator I was a total failure. Was I allowing them to be too disrespectful? I shook my head and went back for another cup of hot coffee. Before returning to my rock, I put in a stronger lens so they could enjoy the other *Lord of the Rings*.

Time was flying. My watch read two in the morning and the planets were following the usual path. Mars was already setting in the west, and Saturn was passing overhead.

"Aren't you cold?"

"No!"

They were unanimous, so I didn't insist. I returned to chat with Miguel, who'd just taken his turn observing Saturn.

"It's incredible. I can't imagine how we could send that thingamajig so far."

"Well, we did. And even farther," I added. Then I looked at my watch again and mentioned how late it was. We were supposed to be back at the school by three.

"I'm not in a hurry. I don't have to return the bus until eight in the morning. When is Jupiter supposed to appear?"

I asked the computer. It wouldn't be visible until five.

"Fine with me. I'm having a terrific time, and we've got more than enough ammunition," he said, referring to the goodies.

I gathered the herd and told them Jupiter was worthwhile. And if they wanted to finish up, Mercury would appear at seven, right before sunrise. We could leave after daylight. They didn't take out their cell phones and send text messages to their parents. Not even one refused to spend the night there without sleeping.

"Let's have another soda and another snack, Miguel. We still have ham—Ibérico, no less."

"These kids are very pampered. In my time, there was sausage, that's all."

14

There they were. Smiling and holding hands. I also smiled at them through the glass. My suitcase was taking a long time to come out.

The trip had gone smoothly. I'd arrived with plenty of time before my flight from Barajas International Airport. So I took some time to wander around its grandiose installations. Of course stopping and wandering are mutually exclusive, but this kind of reasoning was beside the point for me now. The prospect of a few days' vacation free of kids and parents excited me. For a week I'd be myself again, like before. The indefatigable world traveler who deliberately took the less traveled routes to witness extreme poverty in many countries. The planes were filled with tourists. Lonely men in search of cheap, quick sex, nothing more. Shopping tourists. Tourists in search of wild, unspoiled nature to tame with their sophisticated hiking equipment. Insatiable tourists ready to devour ruins—architectural or human, it made no difference. A countless number of tourists from many different countries with one thing in common: the chasm between the rich and the poor.

This trip was different, however. It was true that after I became a priest, because of the seminary and my university studies, there weren't many opportunities for travel. At least, not as often as before. That was the reason I purposely chose the best missionary order. I was lucky enough to meet admirable people in remote places in Africa, Southeast Asia, and Latin America, always ready to sacrifice themselves for others. Being so often in these countries, I also contracted the high fever and insomnia that were the main symptoms of their disease. Doctors call it malaria. We preferred to characterize it as solidarity.

The flight lasted less than two hours. The tailwind pushed the Airbus so hard that we arrived in Tenerife twenty minutes ahead of schedule. The time saved was completely used up waiting in the baggage claim. Following Murphy's Law nearly to the letter, my suitcase took the longest to come out. When it finally appeared, I was already afraid of the worst. It brought me more joy than if it had been the first one out.

With the same smile on my face, I hugged both *Juanes*. First, Juana, even more stunning than the first time, tanned from days at the beach. And then John, taller than I'd imagined from his photos. And he spoke Spanish much better than he wrote it. I supposed Juana had something to do with that.

"How wonderful that you finally made it, Hector," Juana said, smiling, bringing back memories of our earlier meeting and kissing me on both cheeks. They were burning. I couldn't help blushing from embracing her again. John looked like a lobster, red all over, like an authentic British *guiri* in the Canary Islands. So my color wasn't too noticeable.

"Hi, Juana. Hi, John. Together at last."

"Yes. Like three Mouseketeers," John said, beaming.

Juana and I laughed hysterically at that, until the poor guy grimaced and we finally controlled ourselves. John seemed to be easygoing, a truly sensible and peaceful man.

After a few hurried words, the usual small talk among people who don't know each other well, we left the arrivals terminal. Juana took the lead.

"Come, Hector. Our car's parked right here."

Juana was driving. John didn't dare. First, because of the roads, which were hellish, like going around traffic circles, and especially for those like him, used to driving on the left side. And second, because Tenerife traffic is extremely chaotic in its mix of tourists in rental cars, who obviously don't know the roads, and locals, who drive so slow that they annoy the impatient Spaniards.

I knew Tenerife only a little. I'd been there as a child with my parents. The Teide, an imposing volcano in the center of the island, was still there. The rest of the island was all built up. Rows of houses, hotels, and apartments had robbed nature in more ways that one could imagine.

We took the North Road. After crossing Puerto de la Cruz, we climbed a few miles toward the Orotava Valley. In the middle of a spectacular land-scape was the plush neighborhood in which Waldo, Juana's father—"Papá," she said—had rented an impressive chalet, or bungalow, as she called it.

"This is it."

The air was clean and fresh, but the temperature was not at all like that of the city I'd come from. I glanced up and looked for a while at the snowy peak of the volcano, over twelve thousand feet high. To its left, resembling small mushrooms, one could see the towers and cupolas of the observatory.

"When do you have to go up to work?" I asked John, pointing at the white peaks above us.

"Oh, in a few days. But not here," he answered.

John explained that the British telescopes were on the neighboring island of La Palma, in the observatory called Roque de los Muchachos. The one in Tenerife was devoted to the study of the sun. I didn't know that. John was a cosmologist and worked nights.

"I would very much like to see it, really."

It sounded like a plea. Certainly I had no intention of returning without a few photos from the giant telescopes on La Palma. My students would never forgive me.

"Well, if that's what Hector wants, so be it."

Juana kept on directing our plans. John thought it was wonderful to go to the other island a few days ahead of schedule, and besides, he knew a lot of the astronomers there, which would save us the annoying visitors' permits. Surprisingly, Juana wasn't interested.

"To be honest, it's all the same to me. I'd just as soon stay on the beach while you two look at the sky."

We didn't pay much attention to that. It was John's work and my hobby. Although she was totally devoted to her Englishman, Juana wasn't at all involved in the world of astronomy. While in college in the States, she'd studied law and English philology. When she got bored with this, she switched to computer science. She didn't need to work for a living. Judging by the comforts of her chalet, her family must have their economic needs well covered.

* * *

We spent the first two days as tourists. Beach and mountain, because Tenerife has both. We went shopping and to restaurants, of which there are plenty. In this way we forgot about the *Manuscript*, the threats, the routine, and any other problems. We didn't turn the computer on at all. They held hands all the time, except briefly during meals. There was no other way for them. They even fed each other. It was a little too much for me. So, after two days of playing the "invisible man," I decided I'd seen enough landscapes and more than enough cuddling, and that it was time to go back to work.

"What else do you have?"

They both gave me a completely blank stare.

"What else have you found out?" I insisted.

They shook their heads.

"Very little," Juana said, while John rose to get his laptop. "I suppose you guessed the meaning of the concentric circles," she said, wanting to know.

"Well, it's a good idea," I answered. "It could give us the key to deciphering the whole book. Or maybe not."

John logged on. In no time the words, in Voynichian, on the three circles around the big central body and its apparent constellations, appeared on the screen.

"Look, Hector. We've recorded some statistics."

He opened a page of calculations. Juana put on her small eyeglasses, which detracted greatly from the charm of her marvelous dark eyes. For a while I was silent, thinking.

"Hector"—John's voice brought me back to reality—"look at this. On the outside ring there are about a hundred twenty syllables, mostly grouped in triads. About a hundred on the middle ring, and about eighty on the inner one."

I did a quick calculation in my head.

"That would make . . . almost a million possibilities."

"Nine hundred seventy thousand, to be exact," Juana pointed out, quite transformed. Now she looked like a strict math teacher.

"That's not too much for a computer. What's the problem?" I asked.

"The problem is that we don't know what to look for. We can put together a million triads, but how do we know which ones have any practical value?"

Juana completed her beloved John's reasoning. "We'd need to check them one by one. Computers don't think, they don't perceive relationships."

"They've got no senses or feelings," I added.

"So, what do you suggest?"

John looked at me intently, as if I'd brought the answer with me to Tenerife. I had only figured out what they already knew. I thought out loud.

"This time we won't need to use force. Safes aren't opened with explosives. The money would be burned."

"Nice metaphor," Juana said, removing her eyeglasses, which were now holding her hair like a crown, restoring her devastating beauty. I tried not to let her distract me. I thought I was immune to such things; I was a priest, for God's sake.

"I suggest we go back to the historical clues. Most people on the List seem to go for the idea that it was a fraud perpetrated by John Dee and Edward Kelley. Perhaps with the support of Cardano's theories."

"If it's a fraud, there's no message," John objected.

"Well, then, let's suppose that they ciphered it to hide something. Let's be positive. Let's begin with the central body. What is it?"

"Everybody seems to agree it's the Moon," Juana replied.

"Not me. The Moon isn't at the center of anything."

"And the Sun?" the young woman asked.

"No, we can't have stars and the Sun at the same time," I observed.

"A planet? A special star?" John suggested.

Of course. That was it.

A thought suddenly struck me. I jumped off the sofa and landed a resounding slap on John's red back. He didn't object, despite his sunburn, he just wanted to hear my epiphany. I was so pleased with my discovery that I teased them.

"Okay. I'll tell you if you can keep from kissing each other for ten minutes."

They looked at each other as if they were actually weighing the decision.

"All right," Juana conceded, speaking for both of them. "Come out with it, you confounded priest."

"Tycho's supernova."

Juana looked at me blankly; she knew very little about astronomy. But John was intrigued. He continued my line of thinking, using the same clues that I had found in the past couple of weeks.

"It was in 1572. It appeared as the most brilliant star in the sky. Tycho saw it, John Dee saw it, and they compared their parallax results. Cardano too."

"Yes," I agreed. "Cardano didn't want to accept it as a new star and thought it was the legendary star of Bethlehem. It's possible that the date of the supernova's appearance coincided with the development of the *Manuscript*."

"I suppose the positions of the stars are measured in degrees," Juana suddenly piped up. "So that could be the key to turning the disks. You know, twenty to the right, five to the left, and there's our treasure."

We were truly working as a team. John quickly gave a brief summary of stellar cartography to his girlfriend.

"Yes, Juana. We need two angles to know the exact position of a star in the sky."

"Then we have one circle more than we need, darling," she countered.

Another acute observation.

"Have you noticed this?"

They looked carefully at what I was showing them.

On the top part of the diagram, there was something strange. The words

didn't close the circles; there was a gap between them. And in the middle circle there were four marks. I asked John for a compass.

"I'm sure there's one in the kitchen," Juana kidded.

To her surprise, John took out a compass from his backpack. I gave her a teasing look.

"Your man is almost perfect. A gem!"

I measured carefully, moving the compass over the diagram. The gap, as John called it, was about five degrees, more or less. It was as if an angel were whispering the solutions to an endless hieroglyphic in my ear.

"If you maintain your abstinence for another ten minutes, I'll tell you what I think it is."

"I don't know whether I can," Juana protested. "How can you priests do it for your whole lives?"

I ignored her last question and explained my theory. "A circle has three hundred and sixty degrees. If we stretch this a little bit, three hundred and sixty-five."

"Then the two unmarked circles would be incomplete, right?" John inferred.

"That's why they cover only three hundred and sixty degrees and we can safely assume that they correspond to the two angular coordinates of the star."

"And the other circle would refer to something that had three hundred and sixty-five parts," Juana said, completing the thought, and, with her glasses back on, looking like a professor.

"Bull's-eye," I exulted.

John jumped up.

"The two coordinates and the date. And that's it, right, Hector?"

It wasn't difficult to find these details on the Internet. The date was very well known: November 11, 1572. Therefore, the inner circle had to be revolved 316 notches—one per day until the eleventh day of the eleventh month—out of the possible 365. But in which direction? We quickly came to an agreement. Time moves clockwise. We'd revolve the disks in that direction.

The supernova coordinates presented a small problem. Since it was a star that had barely existed, for just a few months, it couldn't be found in the classical record. We knew it had exploded very close to the constellation of Cassiopeia, but that reading didn't work at all. Finally we found the pertinent data. Recently the remains of the supernova had been photographed from a space satellite, capturing its remaining X-rays. The coordinates accompanied the NASA photo.

Right ascension: 00h 25m 17s
Declination: 64° 8' 37"

These were obviously equatorial coordinates.

"We'll have to put ourselves in the year sixteen hundred. And not only know what coordinates were used then, but also correct them if needed," John suggested.

"Yes," I agreed. "The precession may have changed the declination about two degrees. It's not much, but it could correspond to a position ahead or farther back on the wheels."

"What the heck are you talking about?"

Juana looked annoyed. They say that ignorance is bliss, but not in her case. Since John was completely engrossed in looking for equations, I explained.

"The absolute equatorial coordinates were devised to avoid the problems presented by local coordinates, which change with the time of year. These coordinates refer to the celestial equator. The declination is the measurement along the arc of the body's hour cycle between the celestial equator and the body of the star. It's measured from zero to ninety degrees starting at the equator, positive in the Northern Hemisphere, negative in the Southern. And the right ascension is the arc measured from the Aries Point to the meridian where the star is. It can vary from zero to twenty-four hours."

Juana knew her math, so she was able to follow.

"What is the Aries Point?"

"It's the intersection of the celestial equator and the ecliptic, or point in the sky where the Sun appears at the spring equinox, on March twenty-first. It's also known as the vernal equinox. For astronomers, it's like point zero," I noted.

"You got it," John proclaimed. "The vernal point is of course point zero for Tycho Brahe, and supposedly also for his contemporaries. At least it appears to be so according their astronomical tables of 1598."

"And what coordinates do you think he used?' I asked, a bit worried.

"Hmmm ... as I feared. Ecliptical," he continued, addressing Juana. "This refers to the ecliptic, the plane in which the sun and the planets move. This is more practical for planetary astronomy, what existed then. We now have to convert all the data about declination and right ascension into celestial longitude and latitude, the ecliptical coordinates. Longitude also started at the vernal equinox, or Aries Point, and that makes things easier. It goes from zero to three hundred and sixty degrees, so that is clearly how one of the disks should be turned."

"And the celestial latitude?" she asked.

"That would be between zero and ninety in our hemisphere. Well," John offered, "does anyone want to solve a trigonometry problem, or should I find a program to do it?"

"We're in a hurry," I urged.

John clicked the numbers on his laptop.

"Voilà! Done! Write this down. Correcting it for the period, the latitude is about thirty-seven degrees. And the longitude, almost fifty-four."

Juana wrote the numbers on a piece of paper and continued.

"In brief, we have to rotate one disk thirty-seven positions. Presumably the smallest number, but we don't know in which direction. On the middle circle, three hundred and sixteen positions clockwise, and on the outer one, fifty-four. In the same positive direction."

' "The combination 37-316-54 sounds as if we were experts in the kabbalah," I said, laughing. "John, do you have a pair of scissors and some paper so we could draw these characters and then turn them?"

"That won't be necessary. It's already been done," Juana remarked. "Believe it or not, we have made time to work with the *Manuscript* these past days."

They showed me the fruits of their labor. There were three cardboard disks the size of 45s. On the edges they had carefully copied all three hundred words in the original diagram. Except for the ones they had broken into syllables and rotated in order to make them legible horizontally. It was very simple to form words that way. John rotated the device and posed a question.

"Roulette, anyone?"

Juana volunteered, cautiously.

On the first attempt, she got about a hundred new words. We separated them one by one, and in blocks. They made as much sense as the rest of the *Manuscript*.

None. We decided to try again. We rotated the first disk the other way. Then we reversed longitude and latitude. Then we tried reading the new words inside out, and not only backward.

After two hours of this, we decided it was necessary to go out for a few beers and sit on a terrace by the sea. It wasn't bad.

If we had plenty of anything, it was patience.

"So you think the *Voynich* could have been in your own Jesuit monastery for some time?"

"No. That would be too much of a coincidence," I told John. "I'm sure Father Lazzari spent a few days there, but I don't know why. Possibly he was inspecting the new location for the society. I also learned that our old prior, the one who built our present school at the beginning of the twentieth century, got to see the book. But he could just as well have seen it in Rome."

I also told them about the theft of the diaries and documents that had once belonged to Anselmo Hidalgo. They were astonished, and right away associated this incident with the threats. Out of loyalty, I avoided mentioning the discovery of the subterranean tunnels.

"All of us at the monastery think that this happened because of the real estate problem. The box was full of architectural plans for the buildings being constructed on the land, and for the present school. Who other than the new construction company, the newspapers, or the city council would want those? I don't see any connection with the *Voynich*."

"But you received some threats, like Juana, didn't you?"

"I didn't get e-mails or phone calls, only that mysterious graffiti covering the whole wall and written in Voynichian."

"And that's not enough?" our Mexican friend said. "I'm afraid to go back home and have the phone ring again. I've changed my cell phone number three times already."

"You can stay with me as long as you want, as you know. My flat in Cambridge isn't great, but the city's small and cozy. And it's very close to London, which I know you love."

"Thanks, darling, but I have to go back to my dad. You saw him. He's old, and he misses me a lot."

I was beginning to feel uncomfortable. Now they were hugging each other and kissing affectionately, as if I weren't there. So I decided to let them be alone. I paid the bill and got up from the table, leaving them there. Besides, I felt like going for a walk on the beach, alone. I wanted to think. The night was beautiful, inviting some of us to meditate, and some others, fatefully, to expressions of love.

I came back an hour later, licking an ice-cream cone. It felt pretty decadent to be having ice cream in the middle of December. At the monastery, the heating systems would be going full blast by now. And here I was in the Canary Islands. I had taken a good walk alone on the beach, enjoying the sea, the breeze, and the landscape, and then returned, going across town. Everywhere, there were lots of people of all kinds, mostly tourists on vacation, having fun. Like myself. When I got back to the table, John and Juana had left. I put two and two together, and delayed my arrival at the villa for another hour to give them time alone. I finally got tired of walking and eating ice cream and returned to the villa, making plenty of noise to warn the lovebirds.

"Don't make such a racket," John said as he opened the door. "Stop being a typical Spaniard."

I thought that "typical Spaniard" sounded funny.

John was working with the diagrams again, alone in the living room. And he went back to his computer immediately after he let me in.

"Where's Juana?"

"Up in her room. She has a headache. So do I," he added somberly.

It was evident that they'd had a spat. Probably their first.

I found an old newspaper on a shelf and pretended to be completely engrossed in it. After thirty minutes of silence, John burst out, "I don't understand it."

"You'll figure it out," I answered cautiously.

"No. I don't think so. I've never seen her like this."

I took a breath and played confessor. "You had an argument?"

"Yes. Maybe you could understand her, being a pastor."

"Well, perhaps if I were a pastor, I could help," I joked. John didn't get it right away.

"Oh, I see now." He smiled. "Pastor or priest, what difference does it make?"

I tried to explain that it wasn't exactly the same. In English-speaking countries, a pastor is more akin to a preacher, and this is more common in Protestant churches. In Catholic countries, we are less inclined to preach, though quite capable of long sermons when the occasion presents itself. We prefer the word *priest*.

"What is she upset about?" I asked him.

"She thought I was making fun of her. She really let me have it and stormed upstairs."

"So tonight I won't have to force you two to focus on the task at hand," I joked again, trying to lighten the mood. But John still wanted to discuss their fight.

"I didn't know she was so religious. I'd have been more careful."

"Hey, I'm the religious one. But rushing things isn't good, no matter what."

Again I was mistaken. John wasn't referring to sex at all. Oddly, priests think of this first when couples have problems. Maybe because we can't give much advice in that department.

"Don't be an idiot, Hector. It isn't that."

"Oh."

"Juana has some strange ideas. Old-fashioned, maybe, I can't tell."

"Just try to explain them."

"She began to sound like Waldo. You remember him?"

"Yes. Her alter ego on the List."

"Yes, the one who wrote only silly things."

So it wasn't only me who'd noticed this. Waldo was peculiar. He was especially obsessed with the magical origin of the *Voynich Manuscript*. He loved to think about angels and the divine origin of the book. All its symbology had some relationship with the Bible for him, well, for her—with ancient sacred texts not yet translated, and with Enoch and the fantastic stories of John Dee and Edward Kelley.

"We were talking about the possible connection between the key to the puzzle and the star of Bethlehem. Cardano supposed that the supernova could have been that star."

"It's not such a bad idea to try December twenty-four instead of November eleven," I said. "Just in case."

"We did just that. As you can imagine, we still didn't find anything. So as a joke, I also suggested we try the date of the Annunciation. When the archangel Gabriel appeared to Mary."

"I can't see any connection with the diagram. And I don't get the joke either. And least of all, her reason for getting mad," I added.

"Well, that's not exactly what I said. I expressed some doubt about Mary's virginity," he admitted.

"You're the idiot, John."

He deserved this. I thought the man had more common sense.

"Forgive me, Hector. I didn't mean to offend anyone. Not you or her. Let me go on."

"Go on. But if you continue like this, I'm going to storm upstairs too," I threatened. "There are two types of nonbelievers: the atheists and the morons. I thought you were in the first group, and I'd very much regret having to include you in the second."

"Call me an idiot, if you want, but please listen to me. When I said it, she slapped me across the face. Hard. And then she got really worked up. She said I was a stupid scientist, that I had no values, that I didn't believe in anything. That I'd be better off reading the Bible. That I surely did come from a monkey."

"She might have a point there. You acted like a gorilla."

"Then she ran off crying and locked herself in her room," he went on. "She's still there. I tried to apologize, but she wouldn't open the door. She says she won't let me touch her ever again."

I didn't know what to say to comfort him. He really did love her. A pious exit, maybe, because we priests are well trained for that.

"Leave her alone for tonight. Tomorrow I'll talk to her. And if you manage to solve the *Voynich* in the meantime," I added, "she'll forget all about it. You've got to atone for your sins, my dear old Brit." And I went to bed.

The next morning, breakfast was like a funeral.

"Hector, please tell that Englishman to pass the marmalade. He doesn't speak a Christian language," Juana said sarcastically.

John not only passed me the marmalade, but also the butter and the chocolate buns he'd bought especially for her. Juana wouldn't even look at him.

"Your marmalade, Your Majesty," I said, offering her the whole tray, and the brightest smile I could manage under the circumstances. But she didn't smile back. Quite the opposite.

"That idiot doesn't understand anything. I said marmalade. *Just marmalade.*"

I put the tray down. I tried to change the subject but only made it worse.

"So tomorrow we'll be going to La Palma?"

"Not me."

Juana's answer was definite. John resigned himself.

"Of course, Hector. I promised to show you the observatory. We'll go together."

And they didn't speak to each other for the rest of the day.

15

It was a four-engine prop plane, making hourly round trips between the islands of Tenerife and La Palma. Its cabin barely seated thirty people, and the flight took a scant thirty minutes. Just enough time to eat the complimentary chocolate bar. We bought same-day tickets at the terminal. John hadn't lost hope that Juana could get over their tiff and make up with him before going back home. Less than fifteen minutes before boarding time, John's cell phone rang, and our plans changed.

"Hey—a message—I was just about to turn it off."

He stared angrily at the Nokia screen.

"What's going on?"

"Juana's at the other airport, south of the island."

"Has she changed her mind? Did she make a mistake?"

"No, nothing like that. She sent me her itinerary: TFS-MAD-MEX. Not even a good-bye," he said, sighing. Pretending to be calm, he took a deep breath and suggested we change our return tickets.

"Let's go to the counter, Hector, and see what we can do."

Such a rushed trip made no sense now.

We settled our new itinerary on the go. John would stay at the observatory lodge (he had brought his suitcase) for his scheduled two weeks' work. With no chance of a reconciliation, it was pointless for him to go and come back the next day. He offered me an entire night in the observatory, a privilege usually denied to visitors.

"Don't worry, you can easily pretend to be on a research fellowship." He laughed. "Of course you'll also have no chance to sleep if you're flying back early in the morning."

I didn't mind. On the contrary, I almost relished the opportunity. I was used to staying up all night. And the flight to Tenerife linked with my return flight to Madrid. I looked forward to getting back to Spain and spending the Christmas holiday with my family.

John's cell phone beeped again.

"What now? Has she changed her mind?"

"No." He smiled. "Just sending kisses. To you, of course," he added ironically.

After several fruitless attempts to contact her, he finally gave up and turned off his phone. We climbed into the small plane, and took off into a blanket of clouds. Rising above them, the snowcapped volcano was a spectacular landscape.

No less spectacular were the vistas of the island of La Palma. Known by its inhabitants as la Isla Bonita (the pretty island), like the one in Madonna's song, it consists of a volcanic formation around a giant crater called the Caldera de Taburiente. From the air, one has the impression that a supernatural being dug a colossal spoon into its core and scooped out a large portion of the island. Near the observatory, at the highest point on the crater rim, the strange basalt formations, called *roques,* have an almost human quality, which explains the observatory's name, Roque de los Muchachos. Marco told us about this and many other things during our ascent. He drove skillfully on the nerve-racking highway that took us from sea level to the scientific installations at 7,200 feet. Marco Giuliani, an Italian, and an astrophysicist like John, had an assigned time to use one of the telescopes at the observatory.

By the time we arrived, I was having trouble keeping my chocolate bar down. We said good-bye to Marco until dinnertime (which had zero appeal for me at that moment), and using the inner road that linked the various buildings, we continued on foot. The altitude made this more difficult than I expected. It took me a while to adjust, and at first I could speak only between gasps.

"It's strange"—I puffed—"that from the start . . . astronomical observatories were built on islands."

"Not so strange, it's really logical and practical," John said. "The two best places in the world for observing the heavens are volcanic islands with high peaks and clear skies. Hawaii in the Pacific Ocean and the Canaries in the Atlantic. Look over there"—he pointed, changing the subject. "That huge beehive of mirrors, nearly fifty feet in diameter, is used to capture Cherenkov radiation."

I'd never heard of that, and I was thinking of something else.

"Did you know that Tycho Brahe had an island all to himself?" I asked.

"Oh yes. The isle of Hven in the Baltic Sea," he answered. "Between the main Danish island of Zeland and the Scandinavian peninsula. No more than a few square miles. The young king of Denmark threw him out of there, and later demolished the observatory to build a cozy love nest for his mistress. A good thing Tycho didn't live to see it," he added.

He didn't seem very interested in the Danish astronomer, since he went right back to his comments about Cherenkov radiation.

"Last year we nearly had a disaster with that contraption when the motors controlling the mounting's movement went haywire and left the entire mirror pointing a fifty-foot lens directly at the Sun. It burned all the shrubs nearby."

There really was a sizable patch of scorched ground. But I kept thinking about the connections between insularity and astronomy. I suppose isolation is a good way to get work done.

John took me to his assigned workplace. It was in the building of the William Herschel telescope, named in honor of the famous British discoverer of Uranus, of the Sun's place in our galaxy, and many other things. He was also the first man to design really large telescopes. John told me this as we walked in. The wooden door to the building with the giant Herschel spherical cupola was, oddly, almost identical to that of a church, and I mentioned it to him.

"Don't be surprised, Padre. It's not for nothing that telescopes are called temples of the sky."

Going into the Herschel telescope actually felt like entering a cathedral. Something intangible enveloped me, elevating me, bringing me to a higher plane, closer to the divine. This really was a cathedral, an imposing monument of glass and steel devoted exclusively to contemplating the heavens. I was mesmerized by the towering vault, and its supports for the nearly perfect mirror, greater than 130 feet in diameter.

"Wait till you see it move tonight. It's like a ponderous clock."

"Of course I'll wait," was all I could say, amazed.

The dining room of the residence was a Tower of Babel. It was filled with the sounds of conversations in German, Italian, and even a sprinkling of Spanish. Marco joined us there, as well as a couple of Spanish engineers working on the immense Canarias telescope.

"Hi, John. Back again?" one of them asked. He was a slim, bearded fellow with dark circles under his eyes from staying awake studying the stars for days.

"Hi, Enrique. Yes," John answered, "tomorrow I'm starting my two weeks of observations. I'm still working on my gravitational lenses. I'd like you to meet Hector," he added.

John introduced me to the two engineers, and we cordially shook hands. They had been struggling for several days with one of the Osiris detectors that was acting up. Osiris, the god of the dead, was the strange name given to a complex instrument on the Canary Island telescope. I sat silently through the meal, paying close attention to everything, fascinated by the astronomers' singular world. My only contribution was an offer to get coffee for everyone.

"No way," Marco fired back. "That machine's a piece of shit. Let's all go up to Galileo and have a real cappuccino."

We climbed into Marco's car and rode to the very top of the observatory site. The Nazionale Galileo telescope, the jewel of Italian astronomy, is there. It's in an odd-shaped building, like a granary, and not at all like the other white-dome telescopes. However, it's a technological marvel, shaped in a wind tunnel to obtain the greatest possible service from its mirrors and instruments.

Our host took us to a small enclosure apparently used as a meeting room, with a table in the center. The walls, crowded with posters from various astrophysics conferences, also had magnificent framed photos of nebulae and galaxies captured by the Galileo itself, and a small tribute to the famous Venetian astronomer. An inscription told all about his life.

Then, with my steaming cup of coffee in hand, I felt a stunning déjà vu.

"*Haec immature a me jam frustra leguntur oy.*"

This was included in the inscription.

At that moment I lost my sense of time and place, as if in a dream. John's voice pulled me back.

"*Cynthiae figures aemulatur mater,*" he added.

"What's going on? Are we electing a pope here?" Marco joked, overhearing our Latin. "Would anyone like more coffee?"

"Not yet," I said, coming out of my trance.

"*Cynthiae figures aemulatur mater amorum*. That's how I think it is in the original, but don't quote me," John said, completing the sentence.

"The mother of love imitates the shapes of the Moon?" I tried to translate.

"More or less. That's what Galileo wrote when he discovered the phases of Venus. It has rising and waning crescents, like the Moon."

"What are you talking about?" Marco interrupted, intrigued.

John gave him the relevant background.

"Apparently Galileo liked to wrap his discoveries in an aura of mystery. It's not known whether he did this out of fear of his enemies, or simply because he liked to play with language. The fact is, upon finding the strange shape of Venus, that's how he described it, with the sentence in the inscription."

"Which is an approximate anagram of the actual sentence," I noted.

"According to legend. A simple dance of letters," John remarked. "The emperor's mathematician couldn't correctly solve the puzzle. And Galileo didn't want to reveal the true meaning except to the emperor himself, who had to plead for the answer in order to relieve his mathematician's concern."

"And who was that mathematician?" I asked, already knowing the answer.

"Kepler, of course. Mister Nobody." John smiled.

* * *

A night of on-site observations in a large telescope can be very tedious and disappointing for an amateur astronomer. Especially if the objective that night is for the instruments to collect spectroscopic data, a frequent occurrence.

There's not much to see in these techniques, at least for us novices. But for astrophysicists, this data is exciting. Maybe it's here that one finds the dividing line separating astrophysics from astronomy, as happened many years back, when Kepler, Tycho, and Galileo began drawing the line to separate astronomy from astrology. Nowadays, scientific instruments that scrutinize the heavens devote most of their time to obtaining "spectra," separating the light received according to its energy source, thus gaining varied information as to the chemical components of a star, or the speed at which a galaxy is receding from our own.

"So that's it? Is that all?" I impatiently asked John after seeing a series of quite fuzzy parallel lines displayed on the instrument monitor. We'd been waiting more than a half hour for the detectors' reading.

"Doesn't seem like much to you?" He snorted. "It's spectacular."

John tried to explain to me, with faint success, the relationship between these lines and the slippage toward red of his galaxies, which he already considered as his own. After all, there are stars and galaxies for all who seek them.

"Man of little faith." He laughed.

He opened several files of images he had stored in the hard drive. The photos had been taken six months ago by an infrared camera located on the Herschel telescope. Compared to the bunch of lines now coming on the screen every thirty minutes, these were much more interesting.

"These are galaxies," he said, pointing at some blotches in the center. "And these too. But much more distant."

Using a pencil, John indicated some arcs of light surrounding the central group of objects. The light coming from the more distant objects had changed its trajectory, curving and producing this singular effect.

"The closest galaxies warp space," John explained, getting more and more excited. "Light from the distant galaxies penetrates that warped space, curving through it, and finally reaching our mirror."

"I remember hearing something about this," I answered, recalling one of the most startling statements of modern physics: "Light has no mass, but it has weight."

My viewing that night palpably proved to me that Newton's gravitational theory had been corrected and completed. For this, more than two centuries had to go by, and the world needed to give birth to an intelligence nearly commensurate with the English genius. That of Albert Einstein. No longer did bodies simply attract one another with a force directly proportional to their masses. Now, by the effect of its mass, a body warped its surrounding space. Other entities (even those lacking any mass, like light) would inevitably have to move through that invisible, elastic tapestry. And not necessarily in a straight line.

John and I discussed this while waiting for the next reading from the detectors. He gave me a curious riddle to illustrate the difference between Newton's and Einstein's concepts of gravity.

"Suppose that the Sun suddenly disappeared. What would happen to the Earth?" he asked.

"I suppose it would say good-bye and head for outer space, no longer subject to the big star's attraction."

"Yes, but at the same time?"

I kept thinking.

If the Sun disappeared for a moment, its force on the Earth would vanish with it. Newton would have said so. The Earth would begin its interstellar journey at that moment. Obviously the correct answer was the opposite.

"With the Sun's disappearance, the shape of space would change," John said, answering his own question. "But this disturbance wouldn't reach the Earth immediately. In the same way that the waves in the ocean take a certain amount of time to reach the shore—"

"I guess we have a limit on that velocity," I interrupted. "Some eight minutes?"

"About."

"But since that's the same time it takes the Sun's light to reach the Earth, we'd also take eight minutes to notice the Sun's disappearance."

"You're getting there." He smiled encouragingly.

"So, in practical terms, we'd leave our orbit just as we last saw the Sun's light."

"Exactly, Hector. We'll end up solving the *Voynich* together, you'll see."

* * *

The night was dragging. The instrument had to repeat the same measurements over and over, making checks, corrections, and calibrations. The telescope moved in silence, always pointing with prodigious precision to the same spot in the sky, moving with it. But this was, as John had explained that morning, only the simpler part of its clockwork mechanisms. In addition, its mirrors and sensors adjusted and moved to compensate for gusts of wind, variations in atmospheric pressure, and their own weight. There were monitors and gauges all around, recording these fluctuations. Nothing very alarming in John's judgment. Then our conversation turned to the *Manuscript* for a while.

"I'm intrigued," he said, "by your finding Galileo's remark in Lazzari's Bible."

"When I saw it again in the inscription this afternoon, it totally stumped me. I had no idea of its origin. I thought it was a clue concerning the *Voynich*."

"If you translate it literally, it could also mean"—John smiled before he repeated—"'I tried to read this in vain, too soon.'"

"But that's the translation of the undeciphered anagram. A ruse to throw the Italian Inquisitors off track."

"Then what sense does it make for it to be written in a Spanish Jesuit monastery and left in a sealed envelope tucked into a Bible in 1770?"

"No idea," I simply said.

"Was that librarian an astronomy buff?" John wondered.

"I don't know," I admitted. "Not necessarily."

"Unless he had a motive for developing that interest. Like wanting to decipher one of his most treasured books."

"It could be," I conceded. "I can even think of another explanation, if that's what you're thinking."

"What?"

"Kepler."

"Kepler?" he asked, puzzled.

"Yes. I keep thinking that it seems incredible for the imperial mathematician to Rudolf the Second not to ever mention the existence of the *Manu-*

script in his writings. Especially considering the fortune it cost the emperor. If I spent that much on a ciphered manuscript," I suggested, "wouldn't I want to crack the code by every available means? And wouldn't I ask my best mathematicians?"

"Tycho and Kepler."

"Exactly. Lazzari would have tried to leave a clue for whoever might open the envelope. Written under the same circumstances as Galileo's. Persecution from Rome."

"And using the same remark, but with an additional meaning. His reference to a book. Our book," John threw in, following his habit of taking possession of things, be they volumes or galaxies.

"Galileo had no connection with the *Voynich*. But Kepler possibly did. The famous Latin quote surely links them," I continued, eagerly speculating.

"Ergo, we've got to investigate Kepler a bit further," John concluded.

A new spectrum appeared on the screen, the last one for the night. The support technician came into the control room and told us he was about to move the cupola. It was dawn already. John shut down the program that was moving the instrument. Then, working together, they adjusted the position of the telescope, leaving it pointed at the zenith. That finished the night's work.

We went outside. It was cold as hell. We got in the car and the technician drove slowly to the residence. There was still time for a last cup of coffee, at a table with a mix of the people who hadn't yet gone to bed and those just up. It was easy for me to get a ride in the small caravan of astronomers and maintenance people at the observatory. They were changing shifts and going back to town. I'd be let off where I could take a cab to the small airport on the outskirts. I hugged John good-bye.

"Write to me, old Brit. You know I open my mail five times a day."

"I'll do it, Padre. And don't forget to pray for me. I'll accept any kind of penance for my sins." He smiled a bit sadly.

We had no news from Juana, who by this time must have been crossing the Atlantic toward Mexico.

16

Why haven't you put up the crèche?"

The little girl shrugged her shoulders.

Her twin brother was more forthcoming.

"Mom punished us."

"I'll talk to her. Meanwhile, go and look through your toys for things we could use."

It was Christmas Eve. It was snowing in town, and it all looked like a winter wonderland. People bustling in and out shopping for dinner, buying last-minute presents, and sending greetings. My father still hadn't come home. His card game was taking longer than usual.

He thus managed to avoid bothering people in the overcrowded house. My mother worked incessantly in the kitchen, and my sister was helping her with the dinner preparations. My brother-in-law, like my father, had prudently distanced himself from the culinary frenzy, and was comfortably watching television in the living room.

"Sister," I said, walking into the kitchen, "how come my niece and nephew don't have a crèche? Did you forget what we're celebrating today?"

I pulled her braid, and of course she got mad. But she didn't insult me the way my students did. And not in front of my mother.

"Still like cats and dogs," she joked. "Come on, Hector, get out of here. And put up a crèche for the kids. So you can stop annoying us."

"I punished them because they were fighting. They don't let up for a second," my sister explained.

"Like the two of you when you were their age," our mother put in. "I can't see why it surprises you."

"Come on, Uncle. Help us. Don't be like an old guy," the young boy said.

"What did you find?" I asked them.

Alicia was carrying a bunch of things in her small arms. We agreed that the best possibility for the Virgin would be Barbie in a wedding dress. Her brother, Daniel, insisted that one of his G.I. Joe figures had to be Joseph. Then they started fighting, and my sister seized the opportunity to throw it in my face.

"See? And on top of that, you laugh at their shenanigans."

I finally got them to make peace. At last the little boy, gritting his teeth, accepted a Jedi friar, cowl and all, for the role of Joseph. The laser sword would serve as his cane. The G.I. Joes were included too; we put them crouched amid the piles of sawdust representing the desert dunes. Armed to the teeth.

"Like that," I said. "Just like the real twenty-first-century Palestine."

My mother came out of the kitchen with the salad bowl right as my father walked into the house. They both started laughing at the peculiar montage.

"Your son's just as revolutionary as when he left," Father said.

"Let him be," Mom answered, planting a big, happy kiss on his cheek. "Because today we're all together. Hector," she went on, "I've told our parish priest you'll be celebrating midnight Mass with him. So don't get any stains on your jacket."

Nothing seemed to have changed much at home.

"What about the star?"

Little Alicia had noticed something was missing from the crèche.

"We don't have one," I answered. "We'll have to make it. Bring me some scissors, glue, and silver paper. And a compass," I suggested, smiling to myself.

* * *

Making the star of Bethlehem entertained us for a good while. The famous star that's been bothering astronomers for centuries, and even now remains unexplained.

Perhaps it was a comet, a meteorite, or maybe even a supernova. No astronomical event coincides with the birthday of Jesus of Nazareth. The most plausible analysis came precisely from Johannes Kepler. Matthew's Gospel—written about seventy to eighty years after Christ's birth—says "the star served as a guide to the Magi and remained stationary above the baby's birthplace." Kepler, a man of faith but also a scientist, supposed that Matthew had adorned the event with some astronomical phenomenon. Kepler himself had observed a supernova in 1604 that formed a triple conjunction with Jupiter and Saturn, the apparent coming together of three heavenly bodies. So he went back in time and looked for the conjunction of these planets closest to the year zero. The result was 7 B.C. The historical clues approximately agree with this date. Luke says that "then a decree of Emperor Augustus ordered a complete census." The decree was issued in 8 B.C., and was the reason for Joseph and Mary's journey. The death report of Herod III, the Great—ruler at the time of Christ's birth—said that this occurred shortly after a lunar eclipse in 4 B.C., according to Jewish historian Flavius Josephus. This and other records confirm the historical hypothesis. The result, paradoxically, is that Jesus Christ's birth occurred—at a minimum—five years prior to his celebrated birth date.

The calendars, in addition, have changed greatly in an attempt to fit things together. The Julian calendar, the one used throughout the Middle Ages, was replaced by the Gregorian calendar in order to match astronomical time. In Catholic areas, among them Spain, France, and of course Rome, the reform was imposed in 1582. In Protestant ones, it was adopted only in 1700, and in England one had to wait until 1752 for the official acceptance of the Gregorian calendar.

This led me to think about the *Voynich*.

The supernova of Tycho, Dee, and Cardano appeared in 1572, only ten years before the introduction of the new calendar in Rome. Was there a possible error in the dates? Was it really November 11, 1572?

I pondered all of this while I was drawing the star. To the astonishment of my niece and nephew, the compass perfectly divided the circle into six equal parts, and as the points were joined, the Star of David appeared, the Jewish star with six points, formed by two intersecting triangles. It was the amazing result of mathematical exactitude—numbers and geometry. John Dee was a consummate geometrician. If he had to draw a star and assign its date, he needed to be precise. The Gregorian reform had been established in 1582 by Pope Gregory XIII after many years of study. Its purpose was to make congruent the Julian year, the one already used in the Roman period—since 45 B.C., to be precise—and the so-called tropical year. This is the astronomical year, since it measures the elapsed time between two successive passages of the Sun through the Aries Point. And it lasts 365 days, 6 hours, 9 minutes, and 10 seconds. The Julian year had an error rate in relation to the astronomical year of 3 days every 400 years. It wasn't a lot, but by the time of Gregory XIII (also of John Dee, Tycho Brahe, and Johannes Kepler), the error already amounted to about 10 days. Little by little, the religious calendar was getting more out of phase with the astronomical one, and that was a problem. So the reform consisted, in the first place, of erasing those 10 days in one blow. Thus, in Catholic countries in 1582, October 4 was followed by October 15. History reports that Saint Teresa died that night, October 4, and wasn't buried until October 15. The next day.

After returning from Mass, I stayed alone in the living room for a while, working online with my laptop. Everyone else had gone to bed. I discovered something truly interesting. John Dee, during his time as adviser to Queen Elizabeth, had tried to have England change its calendar to the one adopted by Catholic countries, thus following the astronomical criterion. This was also, according to his calculations, more precise. The queen, influenced by the archbishop of Canterbury, adamantly opposed this. They believed that it would mean bringing England back into Catholicism. So, for another 170 years, the British persisted in their error.

Could the authors have represented a real astronomical date in the diagram in the manuscript, and not one that was out of synch with the Sun's position? In their shoes, it made sense to think so. The eleventh day of November would thus be changed to the twenty-first. I didn't have the disks prepared by *los Juanes* handy, so I decided to make an assignment for my little niece and nephew the next day. The poster paper and scissors, and especially the compass, had fascinated them. Now they would have a project for Christmas Day.

The following night I began testing my theory. I now had some disks nearly identical to those made by *los Juanes;* well, actually with quite a few surplus glue drippings, from the little ones' kinetic enthusiasm. But the result was the same. To represent Voynichian, I used the original characters, and not the substitute alphabet known as EVA, though that is more useful for constructing program algorithms. I thought that it could compromise an experiment as simple as the one I was preparing. The characters in the *Voynich* are quite clear. Many resemble Roman letters, such as o or α. Others are like numbers: 9, 8, or 2. At one point it was thought that the numbers mixed with letters could be related to possible alchemical formulas or astrological dates. Then it was found that their frequency was similar to that of letters, and they were seen simply as characters. The ones actually resembling numbers were attributed to the draftsperson's random chance. There are other unfamiliar signs, such as a kind of double letter: ᴨᴨ; a question mark ?; or even something similar to Greek letters: nu, iota, rho, and others used in mathematical formulas. They don't have any apparent significance. Keeping in mind their frequency of use in the manuscript, a Roman letter was assigned to each. To the symbol c, the letter "e" was assigned, for being the most used. To the symbol o, the letter "o," to 2 the letter "s," and so on until the alphabet was complete. The Voynichian characters are apparently grouped into syllables, and these into words, much more easily distinguishable.

On the island of Tenerife we used this combination:

37-316-54

If my new theory was correct, one had to add ten extra steps to the middle circle:

37-326-54

Once the three wheels were turned to the corresponding positions, I took paper and pencil and began the slow transcription of characters. The majority of the words formed with the three syllables drawn on the wheels lacked any sense. But there were twelve of them—exactly coinciding with the twelve points of the star in the astronomical diagram—that presented a common pattern upon being reordered. I located similar. syllables at the beginning as prefixes, and did the same with the suffixes at the end. The unknown syllables were left in the middle.

t ⎯va⎯r ivs	o⎯ kj ⎯ver
t t ⎯kj ⎯ver	d⎯va⎯r ivs
s⎯va⎯r ivs	y⎯ kj ⎯ver
t s⎯ kj ⎯ver	x⎯va⎯r ivs
v ⎯va⎯r ivs	vt ⎯va⎯r ivs
q⎯va⎯r ivs	vt t ⎯va⎯r ivs

Breaking the translation down to EVA, the majority of the words made sense. Not only did the most frequent characters almost coincide with the Roman ones, but the numbers also served as numbers.

¶⎯ₐₐ⎯Ɽₙ2	«t—va—rivs»	January
2⎯ₐₐ⎯Ɽₙ2	«2—va—rivs»	February
x⎯ₐₐ⎯Ɽₙ2	«x—va—rivs»	March
4⎯ₐₐ⎯Ɽₙ2	«4—va—rivs»	April
^⎯ₐₐ⎯Ɽₙ2	«v—va—rivs»	May
¶¶⎯ₐₐ⎯Ɽₙ2	«vt—va—rivs»	June
¶¶¶⎯ₐₐ⎯Ɽₙ2	«vtt—va—rivs»	July
8⎯ₐₐ⎯Ɽₙ2	«8—va—rivs»	August
9⎯ l¦s⎯ₐₑ2	«9—kj—ver»	September
o⎯ l¦s⎯ₐₑ2	«0—kj—ver»	October
¶¶¶⎯ l¦s⎯ₐₑ2	«tt—kj—ver»	November
¶2⎯ l¦s⎯ₐₑ2	«t2—kj—ver»	December

Of the twelve words, eight had the ending "ius" with some variations, which was quite simple to translate: *Ianuarius, Februarius, Martius, Aprilis,*

Maius, Iunius, Julius, Augustus. Most of the others ended in "ver." Thus they corresponded to the remaining four months: *September, October, Novembris, December*. The numbers were also related and permitted a certain order.

I needed to get in touch with John and Juana as soon as possible. Finally we had something that made sense in that tremendous hodgepodge of scribbles. Some texts in the *Voynich Manuscript* were not pure inventions. At least one of the illustrations with words had a logical structure. It remained to be seen whether other diagrams in the book were created in this manner as well. And, above all, the fundamental question remained to be answered. Because we all know the months of the year. Even children.

What exactly were we looking for?

Juana limited her answer to a concise "*Felicidades*" (Congratulations), and saying she wanted to compare the translations I'd made to the symbols. She added jokingly that in case I was mistaken, her congratulations could serve just as well as a late Christmas greeting. John, however, was euphoric in his answer to my letter detailing the findings. "You made my day!" he told me. It had snowed at the observatory and he lost two nights without being able to open the cupola of the telescope or connect his instruments. In addition, he was spending the holiday far from his parents, who lived in London, and above—or beneath—it all, he hadn't heard from his beloved Juana, who still refused to take his calls.

Anyway, at least John had truly expressed his joy.

His comment brought back the time I'd read Gilder's remark to him, or rather, that of the Reagan/Gilder duo. Maybe the Reagan/Gilder/Eastwood trio. And this quote perhaps accounted for a strange dream I had that night. In the dream, Johannes Kepler drew a huge Magnum revolver from his holster and pointed it at Tycho Brahe, who, taken aback, could only unsheathe a small sword. The first bullet took his nose away. After killing Tycho, in my dream Kepler went through all the boxes in the famous Dane's room until he found a cardboard portfolio with a label on top that read: I TRIED TO READ THIS IN VAIN, TOO SOON. Inside was the *Voynich Manuscript*. Kepler smiled at the sight and took it with him.

* * *

My niece and nephew woke me up.

"Let's go, Uncle. Mom said you're taking us to the movies today."

I looked at my watch. "At ten o'clock in the morning?"

They innocently shrugged their shoulders and insisted, "Come on, get dressed. You promised."

I didn't recall any promise, but the young ones did deserve a movie treat. It was the last day of my brief Christmas vacation before returning to the monastery and school. Our whole community had agreed to a New Year's reunion, and to reaching a final decision regarding our forced move.

"Which theater do you want to go to? Have you already picked the movie?"

My two silly questions made it perfectly clear how little I had gotten around. The town council provided a single gathering place, crowded with folding chairs for neighborhood meetings and, occasionally, for a community-theater production, political rally, or movie, as in this case. The two small cinemas I'd known years ago were closed, like so many other things in this steeply declining area, where even the high school could barely keep enough students to escape closing. It also depended on kids from the surrounding, sometimes even smaller, towns and the children of immigrants, the only hope for revitalizing the countryside and the scant commerce and industry remaining in the region.

"Yes, they want to see a documentary. There's an excellent Turkish film about Kurdistan in theater fifteen," my sister joked, pouring my coffee. "The original, with subtitles—the way they like it."

"*Star Wars*," little Daniel answered in perfect English, oblivious to his mother's remarks.

"They're still showing it? Is that how far behind this town is? Can't you elect a new mayor?" I laughed.

"*The Revenge of the Sith*," the boy said immediately. "It's the end of the trilogy."

"That one I haven't seen," I admitted. "What time does it start?"

"Eleven on the dot. So hurry up to get good seats. And don't buy them candy, or they won't have any appetite later."

"Morning movie?" I protested.

"Yes, for this weekend. In the afternoon it's rented for the evangelical baptism."

"Do I have to take them to that too?" I thought my sister was still teasing me.

But she wasn't joking.

"Don't you know how the town's changing, son?" my mother interrupted, having just come into the kitchen with the kids' coats and mufflers in hand. "They've even got a preacher."

"Did Porretas retire?" I retorted, laughing, still not believing this conversation. Porretas, an old man who took care of his neighbors' small amount of livestock, had earned his nickname naturally from his eccentric behavior. He would smoke a strange mixture of plants personally gathered on the hillside and then sunbathe completely nude in the meadow. This didn't bother the sheep—or us kids either.

"The town's growing some with Latin American immigrants. They're good people, very hardworking. Mostly from Honduras, Colombia, Bolivia, and Ecuador."

"That isn't bad," I said.

"They're taking our business away from us," my sister complained. "While you Jesuits are going to Latin America, they're coming here. And they care less and less about Catholic priests. You're a bunch of slowpokes."

"Well, I'll take the kids to the movies," I said, cutting short the exchange. "When are we eating?"

"When you come back, dear," my mother answered, giving me a kiss.

I liked being king of the roost again for a few days.

The popcorn was great (naturally I disregarded my sister's advice), and the movie very entertaining. Few laws of physics escaped its vengeance, but the kids didn't care. They saw the speed of light as something quite ordinary. For them, one need only run up and find the right black hole. Asteroids seemed to have the Earth's gravity, except they were hollow and less than a thousand feet in diameter. Stellar battles were authentic pandemonium in Dolby Surround Sound. With space being a vacuum, it was puzzling how they got sound waves to move out there, maybe through wormholes, membrane fluctuations, or negative energies. "Energies even less than zero," I said to myself sarcastically. But it made no difference because imagination broke all barriers and the kids finished the movie clapping like crazy for that display of fantasy and special effects.

A really strange thing happened when the film ended. A well-dressed young man, in suit and tie, came out of the front row and spoke to the children. An unmistakable name card on his coat identified him.

"Who is he?" I asked Daniel, to make sure.

"The religious history teacher."

"What does he want?"

"To collect our drawings for the contest," little Alicia said, pulling a folded paper out of her coat pocket.

"What is *this*?" I asked, pointing to the contents of the paper.

"Noah's ark," she answered proudly. "I put in all the animals I know."

"But aren't there any dinosaurs?" I asked gently but with a touch of mischief.

She paused to think for a moment, and then answered. "I forgot them. Can you help me, Uncle?" she asked, handing me a pencil.

"Of course."

And to her brother's delight and my own, I drew a huge *Tyrannosaurus rex* in the middle of the boat.

17

Before the age of forty, Tycho Brahe was already known and respected among all the sages of Europe. And by 1589, his fame was at its peak. That year Johannes Kepler, at sixteen, was about to enter the University of Tübingen. He was the opposite of the rich aristocrat Tycho.

Kepler brought only a few books with him, and no money. He realized very soon that theology and mathematics, obviously including astronomy, went together in his search for truth. In Tübingen he became a follower of Michael Mästlin, an astronomer who had gained the respect of the notable Tycho, then considered the leading authority on the subject. Although the official teachings in the field were still based on the ancient Ptolemaic model, Mästlin was among the few who believed in the new Copernican system, in which the Earth itself revolved, as it still does, around the Sun. Kepler quickly adopted the idea. In his mystical thinking, it made sense that the Sun, the most brilliant star, source of light and life, should symbolize the Creator, center of everything. A universe created by God couldn't be anything but perfect. His search for harmony was to become a lifelong obsession.

Kepler graduated in 1591, hoping to have been destined by his tutors to propagate Lutheran doctrine. But despite his Christian devotion, his defense of Copernican movement raised doubts among his religious superiors. These were times of division, strict dogma, and ceaseless controversy. He was regarded as having Calvinist tendencies, which cast doubt on his suitability for the pulpit. Years later he would also be accused of developing friendships with Catholics, especially among Jesuit scientists—here we are again—and for that reason he never gained the complete confidence of Lutheran reformists. Against his wishes, and frustrating his religious vocation, Kepler was sent as a mathematics teacher to a small high school in Graz, Austria. That was a radical change for him. So drastic, according to his biographers, that even the calendar there was different. Tübingen followed the Julian calendar, but east of the Bavarian border, the Gregorian calendar was used. Moreover, the journey took ten more days than expected.

Fine, this fits in with what's already known, I thought.

The school where Kepler taught was built in 1574 in response to a Catholic school founded a year earlier, by Jesuits, of course. Again Kepler was caught between two fires. The seeming harmony between the two congregations in Graz was only superficial and would end in time. Meanwhile, the young Protestant developed parallel pursuits to his teaching, especially astrology. Kepler famously defined astrology as "the madcap kid sister of astronomy." Later he would write: "If astrologers sometimes hit the mark, it is purely by chance." Nevertheless, like Tycho, Kepler believed there were tenuous connections between the stars and people. As the official mathematician of the region, he was in charge of writing the required predictions on the calendars of those years. For 1595, Kepler announced a very cold winter, an uprising in the countryside, and a Southern attack by the Turks. This all proved to be correct, making him very popular. These weren't very risky statements. Kepler—and Tycho even more so—kept strict records of all the meteorological changes. And in rural areas, as well as among the Turks, there was continuous turmoil.

That year Kepler made an exceptional (though strangely erroneous) discovery that would greatly affect his life. He was studying the conjunctions of Jupiter and Saturn, that is, the point at which Jupiter would overtake Saturn in the zodiac. These were the most distant, and thus the slowest, planets known in those days. Every twenty years, Jupiter, moving slightly faster, passes Saturn. Kepler drew the successive known conjunctions of his time and saw that these formed triangles, which moved, rotating around a central point. This same drawing can be produced with a looped string stretched tight between equidistant nails inside a circle, if we keep the end of one triangle as the beginning of the next. The result of all this was a second circle inside the triangles. Kepler was impressed by this, and it raised many questions for him. Why a circle? Why are there only six planets, no more and no less? Why do they move at a certain rate? Why do they move at a speed that changes in a consistent pattern? Two thousand years after Aristotle, Kepler believed he was seeing the order of the universe before his eyes, the perfection of God in the harmony of the cosmos in that diagram. Nothing random or senseless could exist in the sky. Having discovered the relation between the orbits of Jupiter and Saturn—the triangle, geometry's primary figure—he tried a similar system with the remaining planets. He attempted to find a square between Mars and Jupiter, a pentagon between Earth and Mars, a hexagon between Earth and Venus, and so on.

Kepler was a lover of geometry, and a formidable mathematician.

But the basic planar shapes didn't really match planetary orbits. Then, using polyhedrons, he experimented with volumes. Only five of these could be fitted within a sphere: tetrahedron, cube, octahedron, dodecahedron, and icosahedron. For Kepler, the Earth's orbit was the universal standard. Around it he drew a dodecahedron. The sphere that would contain it would be the orbit of Mars, in turn circumscribed by a tetrahedron. It was the same with Jupiter and the cube, whose outer sphere would represent Saturn's orbit. He reasoned that the same would apply to the inner planets, Venus and Mercury. Everything had its own order. Five perfect solids, and the sphere for the six planets. The distances separating them were thus prefigured. He only needed to match experimental observations with the theory, and the grandeur of the divine design would be confirmed.

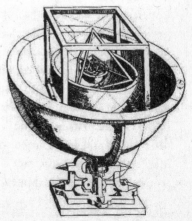

By far the best celestial observations on Earth were Tycho's. Kepler wrote to his admired teacher, Michael Mästlin, who responded enthusiastically, encouraging him to publish his discovery. This could enable Tycho to study Kepler's work. Kepler's theories were published in 1597, in a book as small as its Latin title was grand: *Introduction to the Cosmologi-*

cal Tests, Containing the Cosmological Mystery of the Marvelous Proportion of the Celestial Spheres, and of the Truth and Particular Causes of the Number, Size, and Periodic Movements of the Heavens. The work is better known under the shortened title *Mysterium Cosmographicum.* Kepler hastened to send copies of his *Mysterium* to other astronomers of his time. Galileo was teaching then at the University of Padua but wasn't yet well known. The invention of the telescope was just a few years away. Though Kepler didn't send him his book, his essay did reach the Italian's hands. Galileo then wrote for the first time to Kepler, telling him in a letter filled with praise that he was already an adherent of the Copernican model, but still hesitated to admit this publicly, in fear of reprisals and jeers from his colleagues. Kepler replied, encouraging him in this, and asked him for an objective critique of his *Mysterium.* Galileo didn't answer. Thirteen years elapsed before the brief correspondence of the two giants resumed.

And what about Tycho? In an obscure episode in the history of astronomy, Tycho Brahe suffered the plagiarizing of his own planetary model. Ursus, another astronomer of the time, published the Tychonic model as his own invention. (Ursus was to precede Tycho as imperial mathematician in the court of Rudolf II, a post that Ursus, Tycho, and Kepler held consecutively.) Kepler sent his book to Ursus and was unwittingly entangled in a controversy that nearly dashed his hopes. Tycho hadn't yet met young Kepler, and thought of him as the upstart friend of his enemy Ursus. Fortunately, the *Mysterium* reached Tycho through Michael Mästlin. In this way, Kepler gained the great Danish teacher's respect, the only opinion that really mattered to him. Despite the unpleasant mix-up, Tycho showed interest in Kepler's theories, but politely rejected the polyhedral model contained in the *Mysterium* for its failure to match his experimental data (which was strictly correct). However, he praised Kepler's ingenuity, encouraging him to use his mathematical abilities to adjust his observations to his own Tychonic model. Soon afterward, they began working together. These were the most interesting facts I found among the three greats. An endless chain of misunderstandings and delays mixed with a pinch of pride and self-involvement. Maybe e-mail would have made all of this easier.

Meanwhile, I had a new message.

From Juana.

Hi, Hector,

Your explanation of the *Voynich* astronomical disks is truly impressive. I've precisely followed your solution, step by step, with the same results. There's no doubt you're on the right path.

But I'd be lying to you if I didn't admit I'm discouraged.

It's not so much about the *Manuscript* but, as you must suspect, about John. So I think it's best at this point for me to bow out of our shared project. I don't want to suffer, much less cause others to suffer.

I really thought he was different. Noble, intelligent, and kind. And handsome, of course. A real English gentleman. I was wrong. He's as idiotic and foolish as the guys I met at the university. There's a lot he doesn't know about me. Had he known me better, maybe he wouldn't have spoken to me as he did. But maybe he simply wouldn't have bothered to say anything to me at all.

Hector, can I make a confession?

I'm assuming you've said yes.

I suppose you both must think I'm nothing but a spoiled little rich girl whose father, maybe because of guilt feelings over her mother's death, always catered to her every whim. When I finished high school, I went to college in the United States. I needed an excuse to get away from home. For over a year I went to party after party, getting drunk and hopping from one man's bed to the next without ever stopping to think about what I was doing. I started taking drugs and had the money to buy whatever I liked. I became a walking pharmacy, and would invite anybody around to join me.

One night I had a breakdown. I hardly remember anything about it before waking up in a hospital bed. The doctors said that some backpackers had rescued me, lying naked and unconscious next to a highway. Later I learned from the police investigation that some other young men from the university had left me there, thinking I had died. Too much sex, alcohol, and drugs for them to risk taking me to a doctor. Eventually I went into rehab. My father sent me to the best clinic in Texas, which he paid for entirely. That's where my life started to change and make sense. I came to know the Gospels there, to become one with my faith in Christ, and learned to live following the Bible.

You understand all of this, being a believer. You've totally devoted your life to your faith. But John can't and would never be able to. I'm exasperated by his cold rationalism, and just can't accept his disdain.

Anyway, I went back to the University of Texas, quit law, and got really involved in computer science. You think of them as organizational tools, and I think that best defines what I'm trying to explain to you. My life gained order among the machines. At our study center we tried to fill the gap between the worrisome questions we all have and the profound answers given in the Gospels. The Bible was inspired by the Holy Spirit, is the infallible word of God. Jesus is God, the Living Word, made flesh by His miraculous conception and birth. He lived His life without sin but atoned for all of ours and died on the cross. I can't be with someone who mocks the one who brought me back to life. To real life.

I hope that, if John asks you, you'll know what to say to him. You have the same beliefs as mine.

Somehow I'll manage to forget him, though I'll pray for him every day.

Now you understand why it's best for everybody if I step out of the research on the *Voynich*. I don't want to make it harder; it's tough enough by itself.

Be sure to tell me when it's all worked out. I'll celebrate the day.

Lots of kisses, and take care,

Juana

"Hector, come down when you're finished. Most of us are in the chapel."

Matthew had come up to let me know. Being so wrapped up in reading Juana's letter, I'd completely lost track of time. My return to the community after Christmas was filled with uncertainty. The prior had decided to meet in the chapel instead of the usual hall. Thus, no coffee.

Carmelo began with an Our Father, followed by a brief prayer invoking the intercession of the Holy Spirit to guide our decisions. This was neither a council nor a conclave; the future of twenty persons and the education of several hundred children all hung in the balance.

"Brothers, you already know why we're gathered here. There's no better place," Carmelo said after finishing his prayers. We nodded in silence. He took a breath and continued speaking, with noticeable effort. The prior was visibly affected. It wasn't a good sign.

"Many of you have spent these few days off with your families, celebrating our Lord's birth in the company of parents and siblings. Some of us for whom God provides our society as sole family, have remained here. These haven't been easy days."

Most of us thought Carmelo was referring to his own existence. His very elderly mother had passed away a year ago. He only had some distant cousins left. We were everything for him. Even so, this wasn't his main cause of distress.

"Two days ago we received a new judicial order, pressing us to vacate our house."

A lot of us were unaware of this extreme measure. I looked at Dean Damian, who seemed just as bewildered as I was. Almost in unison we asked the prior for more information on this. Julian spoke on his behalf, having been forced to return to the monastery earlier than expected, given the gravity of the predicament.

"That's how it is, exactly as Carmelo says."

His voice sounded funereal. The administrator took up explaining the details, to relieve the prior's discomfort.

"The city council has acted in bad faith. It hasn't respected the mandatory periods for the notifications of expropriation. There's been no attempt to mediate between the parties. In fact," he concluded, "it has maneuvered behind our backs."

"If it's as you say," Damian spoke up, "we need only to give notice of appeal in order to halt the expropriation."

"The appeal was filed and rejected on technicalities," Julian again informed us. "Besides, we're now without legal representation. I've had to petition our house in Madrid to provide us with legal support."

Then it was my turn.

"Where are the pressures coming from?"

"If we knew that, we'd know where we stand," Julian said. "In the past week, the local paper has devoted three editorials exclusively to us. 'Phoenician ecclesiastics' was their kindest label for us. The real estate developer has started signing up workers for the project. More than a thousand people are on a select list, waiting for employment that has been assured them. From simple carpenters to administrative and security personnel. In a few cases, there are signed labor contracts, and salaries advanced."

"What about the politicians?"

"All the doors are closed," Julian responded with even more devastating news. "And not only of buildings. Whoever isn't on a skiing vacation is with his secretary at a party meeting. Nobody knows or wants to know. Meanwhile, time keeps pressing in on us."

"What's our option now?"

"Nothing," a very pessimistic Carmelo answered me. "Only prayer."

"Apart from that?"

My question must have struck the prior badly, judging by his disapproving look. Everybody waited in silence, expecting a public rebuke. This, however, didn't happen. After several seconds of silence, the administrator again took the floor.

"In fact, the buildings forming the Jesuit complex, except the school, must be vacated before the first of March. The school, obviously, will remain open until June thirtieth for everyone involved in teaching. 'The modification of the development plan approved by the Corporation, making legitimate use of the emergency procedure'"—Julian was now reading from the official paper—"'anticipates the cession of the lands, with exception made of the Church of Santa Marta and its annex'—this chapel, where we are now—'to the successful developer, chosen by the opening of competitive, sealed bids, which shall be witnessed before a notary on December thirtieth of the current year.'" He finished reading and said, "That is, the day after tomorrow." Then he added, showing both sides of the paper, "No getting around it."

"So the day after tomorrow we'll know who's behind this," I pointed out.

"Don't you believe it," Julian said. "It's a dummy corporation. I wasn't able to find out who they actually are. Everyone says it's foreign capital, but nobody knows for sure."

The prior took the floor for the last time.

"Julian is negotiating accommodations for us in the Carmelites' old convent. It's a gigantic building and, though it's dilapidated, we'll make some investment in its renovation. When we move from there to the new school, God willing, the twenty-odd rooms we're to occupy will be sufficiently decent for us to convert them into a modest inn and somewhat relieve the sisters' financial burden. They've eagerly accepted our proposal. And now," he ended, "let's get back to work."

"At least over there we'll have some pastries to go with our coffee," I said to myself, getting up from the uncomfortable wooden bench. Then I glanced at the side door and again felt compelled to go there. I decided to return the next day with some good boots, refreshed and in a better mood.

18

I didn't want to reenter the chapel's underground without first checking to see if I could find some kind of map to help me. I returned to the archives and went through the few remaining papers, both old Prior Hidalgo's and those of Father Lazzari, the mysterious visitor. I leafed through his old Bible, where I'd found Galileo's puzzling quote that led me to Kepler and, perhaps, to the *Voynich*. There weren't any more papers or annotations. Nothing even underlined.

So it seemed at first glance.

I was right that Lazzari hadn't written anything in that book. But maybe he hadn't because it simply wasn't his. That old Bible had a different name on its first page: Giambattista Riccioli. And a date: 1666.

This was strange. That was the year the *Voynich* was sent to Rome, where it landed in the hands of Athanasius Kircher, before it vanished for nearly 250 years. I couldn't see why Lazzari would have brought an old Bible, which didn't even belong to him, to Spain. It was our archivist who stored it among his possessions. Books are often left behind on night tables.

Or they could instead be left there deliberately.

Especially in the case of Bibles and the Gospels.

Giovanni Battista Riccioli wasn't unknown to me. And I supposed, not to John either. The Englishman was right when he implied the Jesuits' connection to astronomy. Riccioli was considered the author of the most important scientific work written by a Jesuit in the seventeenth century: the *Almagestum Novum,* published in 1651. The first *Almagesto,* its precursor, had been an Arabian compilation of the observations of Ptolemy, the father of ancient astronomy and of the geocentric system. In this revised work, Riccioli undertook to recover and reconstruct the old theories and adjust them to the new discoveries resulting from the invention of the telescope. Though he rejected the Copernican system (these were the hard times of the Inquisition and the trial of Galileo), he wasn't an absolutist. It's thought that deep down he favored the heliocentric doctrine. So he compromised, teaching both systems at the University of Bologna, the oldest in Europe. Emphasizing, out of obligatory piety, that the system used by Copernicus and Kepler could only be considered a hypothesis from research that ran contrary to Church orthodoxy. He's most remembered for his detailed maps of the lunar surface, carried out with Francesco Maria Grimaldi, another Jesuit, and also for his support and mentoring of a third great Italian astronomer of the seventeenth century: Giovanni Cassini. The names of Riccioli and Cassini are intimately linked with the development of astronomy.

To speak of Cassini is also to speak of Christiaan Huygens. They were the first astronomers to study Saturn with a telescope, a few years after Galileo thought he saw some strange forms at its sides, like earlobes, that he mistook for two satellites. Huygens clearly distinguished the rings and discovered its largest satellite, Titan. Cassini observed the central system of rings, which now bear his name, and found four additional satellites: Iapetus, Rhea, Tethys, and Dione. The Cassini-Huygens mission to Saturn, with its Huygens probe, parachuted to Titan's surface, jointly honors these scientists.

Cassini was a devout man who came very close to becoming a Jesuit. He studied in Genoa at one of our schools, from 1638 to 1642. From there he attended the prestigious University of Bologna. At twenty-five he was already teaching astronomy. For his precocity and brilliance, he could be compared, so the history books say, only to Tycho Brahe. Like him, Cassini observed a comet—in 1652—and, like the Dane, confirmed that it was much more distant than the Moon. A new contradiction—this time in Catholic territory—of the Aristotelian doctrine of the immutability of the celestial orb that was still prevalent in his time. Cassini gained in his era the recognition denied Galileo, and only because of Galileo's towering stature has Cassini's been partially overshadowed. He adjusted the new Gregorian calendar, measuring the tropical year with total precision. He accomplished this thanks to a heliometer that he installed in the Basilica of San Petronio, in Bologna. He also calculated the tilt of the terrestrial axis, approaching perfection, within less than 0.005 degrees.

In addition, he proved something else. He demonstrated the validity of Kepler's second law, which states that the closer celestial bodies are to the sun, the faster they move, and the farther away, the more slowly they travel. Decades later, Newton was to add a physical explanation of this phenomenon in his famous *Principia*.

Once more I met with old friends.

Again Kepler. Cassini and Kepler. Jesuits and Kepler.

The *Voynich Manuscript* had to appear somewhere.

Just like my first exploration, I used a piece of cardboard to keep the door from locking behind me, and made sure it was tightly wedged in. This late after supper, nobody would come to the chapel. The first stretch was already familiar. Long flights of stairs to the ample landing where the branching began. On the previous trip, I had decided to always veer right, only going left when I couldn't avoid it, and then to reverse the process on the way back. This time I turned left as I went on.

For the first ten minutes, nothing caught my attention. More blind wells, old underground channels, and rats all around. I allowed myself another ten minutes of exploration. Some segments were already familiar. Maybe the paths were interwoven. Sometimes, at first without noticing it, I was retracing stretches covered on my prior visit. Anyway, since my maneuvers were almost always the opposite of those taken before, my path didn't repeat for more than a few yards overall.

Until I heard distinct footsteps. I stopped.

"Carmelo?"

Who else could be down here?

"Carmelo, is that you?" I asked again, more forcefully.

I kept listening, but nobody answered. The steps grew faster, soon turning into running. I ran toward them, following the sound and abandoning the Boy Scout motto that I'd adhered to so scrupulously till then. To my surprise, I was soon back at the main landing. Clearly, I'd been traveling in circles, like a fool. I wanted to kick myself for not bringing a compass. I could still hear the fugitive, whoever it was, running up the steps at a fast clip.

I did the same.

Then I got a hard bump, literally, as I collided with the door. I couldn't help but howl. Whoever it was certainly wasn't coming back to let me out. The key turned, but the door wouldn't open, and I realized that this person had bolted it from the other side. Meanwhile, my community was fast asleep in bed. I checked my watch. The earliest-rising brothers would come to pray in the chapel around seven in the morning. I had a few hours to kill before anyone would hear my shouts. Armed with a good supply of batteries and ample curiosity, I decided to go back down.

Again on the main landing, at the start of the forking paths, I sat on the ground, took out pencil and paper, and made a rough drawing from memory of the known passageways, left and right. I got up and, following my scrawled layout, took what I thought was the most direct route to the main section of the Roman sewer. Except for a couple of minor errors that I corrected on the map as I went, there was no problem. At this new broad space, I again sat down. This time on a huge ashlar now dislodged from its original support in one of the vaults but, amazingly, still standing. I turned off my flashlight, to save the batteries, and thought, in the dark, about where to go next. One option was to abandon the known path and follow the trench that held a trickle of the foul seepage from the newer channels above. I intended to focus on completing the map and abandon combing the passages. I was almost finished when I came upon some writing.

ALTISSIMUM PLANETAM TERGEMINUM OBSERVAVI

It was carefully engraved on the wall in large letters. I copied it. The literal translation was simple: "I saw the highest planet with . . . three shapes"? Figuring out what it meant was another story.

What did it mean? And who had written it?

I retraced my steps to the main space, sat down, turned off the flashlight, and tried to relax for a while. I still had two hours before anybody would open the door.

"What were you doing in there?"

"It's a long story, Matthew," I answered the early-rising friar. I should have figured that, as the one in charge of our house provisions, he'd be the first one up. "The important thing is, you've gotten me out of a jam," I said between gasps, having shouted myself hoarse through the door.

"Hector, you're not the one I'm most concerned about now," he said. "I guess you probably haven't heard what happened while you were in there."

"What happened?" I asked, curious.

"Carmelo collapsed shortly after supper. We were having coffee in the living room and he just passed out."

"Oh my God," was all I could stammer.

Matthew gave me the details. At midnight, our prior was hospitalized, in critical condition. The latest news on his condition (two priests were standing by all night at the medical center) wasn't at all encouraging. This greatly upset me. Not only because of the deep friendship that bonded me with my prior, but also because he clearly couldn't have been the one who locked me in the basement that night. I cursed my mistrust, feeling dirty inside and out. Without another word I went to my room to shower, drank my coffee standing up, and left for the hospital with other brothers.

When we arrived, Carmelo had just passed away.

The next several days were tough for all of us. First we were engaged in a bitter dispute with the local authorities over having Carmelo buried in our chapel. They cited sanitation laws. Underlying this was the shadow of the expropriation itself. We renounced our ecclesiastical privileges and accepted a compromise permitting the cremation of the old prior's remains. Then we placed the urn containing his ashes in the chapel itself, in a small niche where Carmelo had prayed so many times, and where just as often he had reflected on the best possible outcome for our tiny community. We needed to elect a new prior. For the mandatory selection of a father superior, we proceeded to a secret ballot to determine Carmelo's replacement. The place chosen for this was, again, our old chapel. Julian, our administrator—and the man most trusted by the deceased—was elected on the first ballot. The designee humbly accepted his new responsibility, and immediately got to work on the matters still causing us countless headaches. Matters that had certainly undermined our former prior's frail health, thus contributing to his demise.

The day after his election, Julian summoned me to accompany him to Carmelo's room. He opened the door with the master key, and we went in silently, as if afraid to disturb the memories of our dear, deceased brother.

"Hector," he told me, "since you're the one in charge of the archives, according to custom you'll need to collect his belongings, sort, and catalog them. Then you must put them with those of the other Jesuits, in order that future generations will be able to study his life and work. Which was significant," he concluded.

I nodded, briefly surveying the overburdened shelves. Carmelo had accumulated a considerable book collection. On his desk were various notebooks filled with commentaries, along with his prolific diary. All handwritten. He never wanted to own a typewriter, let alone a computer. An abundance of work lay ahead of me.

Then I saw it. There it was, exactly as I had taken it from the archives. The box containing Anselmo Hidalgo's floor plans and files.

I said nothing, closing the door behind me.

19

ector, someone's asking for you at the office."

Hearing Matthew on the phone, I immediately thought of Juana. Another surprise visit? News concerning the *Voynich*? A change of attitude about John? On my way down the stairs, two at a time, I raced through these and other questions.

I was nearly right.

I can't say I felt cheated when I got to the door.

"John!" I shouted, hugging him. "I thought you were back home."

"Hi, Hector," he greeted me, smiling. "No, I've still got two days left. It was impossible for me to finish my observation period on La Palma. Everything was covered with snow. I'd never seen weather like that at the peak. It's already here too." He laughed.

It had, in fact, started snowing hard. If Juana seemed to bring rain, then John certainly brought snow.

"I changed my flights so that I'll leave for London the day after tomorrow from Madrid. And what better way for me to spend this time than getting to see you on your own turf. I'm welcome, right?" he asked with some hesitation.

"Of course, old boy," I answered. "No need for a hotel—we've got plenty of rooms in the house. Actually, too many," I said, recalling our prior's recent death. "Besides, this way you can help me with the latest *Voynich* clues, including the old Jesuits' cat's cradles."

"That's great, Hector. I'm still amazed that you found the twelve months in that astronomical diagram. As far as I know, it's the first bit of sense that's ever been found in the manuscript."

"Thanks, John. But, for now, it doesn't lead us to anything new. Finally we'll have time to talk about everything. Come with me. I'll find you a room, and then a cup of coffee."

"Whatever you say, Padre," he said, smiling.

Julian had no objection to our putting John up. He even encouraged him to stay longer, for the chance to practice his English. We gave him a room with a bath in the renovated, such as it was, section of the building, and made the introductions to members of our community, crossing paths in the hallways or going by their rooms. We also filled him in on our former prior's death and our ousting by the city council. John was aware of the exile from earlier conversations, but knew nothing of the death. He expressed his most sincere condolences to Julian, hoping his presence there wouldn't disturb our mourning. For those two days he fit right in.

That afternoon we went for a walk in town, essentially retracing the same touristy route I had taken weeks before with his beloved Juana. It wasn't long before he asked about her.

"C'mon, you must have heard something," he probed when we stopped at a café, weary of going through old churches and ruins.

"Only a few lines," I said, evading his question with a measure of mercy. There was no point in revealing her confession at this moment.

"What does she say about me?" He wasn't giving up easily.

"Nothing," I lied. "She only talks about the cryptographic discovery of the names of the months written inside the astronomical diagram. She's keeping at it, and promised to tell me whatever she finds."

Not a word of this was true, but I decided it was best for now. Not only had Juana explicitly declared that she wouldn't get back together with John, but she had also—as if it were all of a piece—decided not to continue working on the *Voynich*. She had trusted me to explain things to John when the time was right. I didn't want to detract from John's renewed enthusiasm for the investigations.

He finally seemed to accept what I said, and was soon immersed in the Jesuit intrigue that was, or seemed to be, connected with the famous book. In addition, now relieved of my promise of secrecy to Carmelo, I told him about the ancient ruins beneath the monastery.

"What about the stolen box you mentioned?" he asked.

"You'll hardly believe it, but I found it in the prior's room. Don't ask me why or how it got there," I said. "Carmelo was actually the one who urged me to go through those papers, and then he kept me from seeing them. I've no idea why he did this."

"Can I take a look with you?" he asked.

"Of course. You'll be a big help. Four eyes see better than two, and it's all a jumble of old papers that need a careful review."

After supper we went down to the archives.

Burned as I was by my first blunder there, I had returned Anselmo Hidalgo's documents to their original place to avoid more problems. Whoever wanted to enter the archives, even the new prior, now had to ask me. It was safe there.

We turned on the lights and locked the door. The old wooden box made a dry thud as I set it on the floor, raising a dusty cloud that filled the room for a few seconds, making me sneeze.

"Bless you!" John shouted, laughing.

"Thanks," I responded automatically. "Look, these are the floor plans."

I unrolled the old papers. The first one to catch our attention was the layout of the underground passages. It wasn't a very detailed drawing. Its anonymous author had barely bothered to use a ruler. Even the relative distances didn't seem very exact. I pulled out my own drawing of the labyrinth and we compared the two for a while.

"I wasn't too far off," I said finally. "Looks like I only missed a few of the side forks and a couple of rooms at the edges. I was afraid to go that far."

"What's this cross?" John pointed to the place on my map where I saw the inscription in Latin. The old drawing had nothing marked there, so I explained.

"'*Altissimum planetam tergeminum observavi.*' It's inscribed on a wall there, and I jotted it down. I suppose it was a Roman inscription related to some deity. Maybe Jupiter, the chief of the Roman gods."

John stared at me, surprised. He smirked and then knocked on my head. "Hey, anybody home?" he shouted in my ear.

I turned around. "Have you gone nuts, John?"

"Don't you get it?"

I didn't. It didn't suggest anything special to me. "I saw the highest planet with three shapes?" The largest planet, or Jupiter. That's what I thought.

"It's another of Galileo's famous quotes, my friend. Another of those riddles about his discoveries with the first telescope. So it's not about Romans or anybody else."

"Which is the highest planet?" I asked.

"In those times, the most distant. Saturn, of course," he answered. "When Galileo says three shapes, he's referring to the planet itself and its two satellites he thought he saw through his instrument. Later, with better means, Christian Huygens distinguished the now-familiar system of rings. They weren't satellites or lobes on the planet's sides, but the famous rings."

"Yes, I knew about this," I noted. "The first comment, the one I found in Lazzari's Bible, seemed to be leading us to Kepler. What about the second one? Very possibly by the same Jesuit librarian," I suggested.

"Let's keep looking," John said, momentarily putting aside the Saturn question. "This is clearly part of a church."

He had uncoiled a second floor plan, much larger and more detailed than the first.

It represented the ground floor of a basilica, which obviously wasn't our small Church of Santa Marta.

"'Floor plan of the Basilica of San Petronio in Bologna,'" he read. "The date is 1655. And it's signed by '*dottor Giovanni Cassini genovese.*'"

"That's it!" I exclaimed. "It makes perfect sense."

John waited for my explanation.

"Cassini and Riccioli. It's clear as day," I said, raising my voice and getting up from my cramped position on the floor.

"Riccioli the astronomer? The one with the first maps of the Moon?"

"The same. He was a Jesuit and one of the greatest scientists of the time. Cassini worked under his sponsorship in Bologna. And for an unknown reason, through Lazzari, his Bible ended up inside these walls."

"That could also explain the pending Saturn question. The Cassini mission brought us all the way here," John joked playfully. "This old librarian's clues don't seem so complicated," he added, alluding to Lazzari. "I suppose, at the bottom of it all, he was trying to lead somebody to the *Voynich*."

"Could be. It's thought that during that period the manuscript was hidden in Jesuits' hands. Lazzari could have thought it might never come to light again, and he intended to leave clues as to its existence. Except," I admitted, "it's not mentioned as such anywhere."

"What about this line, and these numbers and points?" Again John was pointing at the floor plan of the Bologna basilica.

"The superfamous meridian line. We'll have to search the Internet for something about it, John. Let's go upstairs."

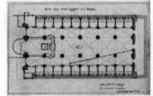

The first surprise, a happy one, led us to confirm, even without any explicit mention of it, that the *Voynich Manuscript* was clearly related to our latest discoveries. The book disappeared after its transfer from the hands of Marcus Marci to those of Athanasius Kircher, surely in 1666. It's likely that this Jesuit scholar attempted to decipher it. He had already made similar successful attempts, interpreting some Egyptian hieroglyphics. He made sense of those found only the year before, in 1665, on the recently unearthed Minerva obelisk, which the famous Bernini later mounted on the back of his sculpture of a small elephant in Rome.

Kircher was a learned man of his time who attempted to embrace all areas of knowledge. He studied and wrote on subjects as varied as music, optics, hydraulics, magnetism, and philology. One of his principal efforts was an attempt to create a unified geography of the planet, in the same way that he fought successfully a few years earlier, at least in the Catholic orbit, for the unification of the Gregorian calendar. His ambitious mapmaking endeavor (called *Consilium Geographicum*) had a reason for being, since Jesuits already were all over the world, from the Americas and Africa to China and Japan.

His work dealt not only with knowing where to go, but also with being aware of one's position at all times. It was quite difficult to find a specific geographic location. Kircher attempted to identify the longitudinal and latitudinal coordinates of all the Jesuit missions and schools. For this he drew on the scientific knowledge of the priests, surely the best of their time, who had taken up the mission of collecting the pertinent measurements for Kircher to interpret and compile. His mail during those decades was copious. It's believed that he maintained routine correspondence with nearly eight hundred persons, an almost incredible number even now with the Internet. In Rome alone, there are still more than two thousand of these letters in existence. In reference to his vast project, the latitude calculation was quite simple, requiring only the measurement of the elevation of the Sun at midday or of Polaris, the North Star, at night. But the difficulty of calculating longitude at sea seemed insurmountable.

Kircher trained his correspondents in the measurement of the so-called magnetic declination, but the results weren't as good as he had hoped. The failure of this geographic project, which was finally dissolved, was one of the reasons for his encounter with the—also Jesuit—astronomer Giovanni Riccioli, the other great scientific authority in the Catholic pantheon of those years.

"It's really strange," John said as we read the screens the computer kept popping up. "But what do we know about the plan of the basilica?" he asked.

" 'The construction of the Basilica of San Petronio began in 1390 and was completed in 1659, though its main facade was never finished,' " I began reading. " 'Its original design is by Antonio di Vincenzo, and its style is late Italian Gothic. It owes its name to the patron of the city of Bologna. It was the place selected for many historical occasions, the most important of which was perhaps the coronation in 1530 of Charles the Fifth as head of the Holy Roman Empire. San Petronio was also the church of the University of Bologna, the oldest in Europe and, by extension, in the world. The Dominican Ignazio Danti was there in 1575, serving then as Cosimo the First de Medici's cosmographer. Danti taught mathematics and astronomy, and formed part of the committee of experts who prepared the new calendar.' No wonder, since Pope Gregory XIII himself was born in Bologna."

"We know this calendar entered the Catholic world in 1582," John said, reiterating the too-familiar point for us. We continued skipping from screen to screen.

" 'The study of the Sun's movement throughout the year and the precise dates of solstices and equinoxes were essential to determining the tropical year. Danti had already designed an instrument in the Basilica of

Santa Maria Novella in Florence: a meridian. A blaze of light'—the image of the Sun—'was projected on the floor of a large church when the solar rays penetrated the interior through a small orifice fashioned in the roof, which permitted a much more precise definition of the distinct positions and variations in the movement of the Sun's path than the methods known till then. The most common of these was the gnomon, or pointer, for projecting the Sun's shadow on a sundial—'"

"The meridian is based on the principles of the camera obscura—" John again interrupted.

"Don't tell me." I cut him short. "Kepler."

"For a change." My friend laughed. "'Though it really isn't known who discovered this effect, the basis of photography. Often its invention is attributed to Leonardo, who—like Dürer—used it as an aid for his drawings. The hole in the wall projected an inverted image of the object being copied. But it's Kepler who first explained how this worked, around 1604. Or a bit later.'" He frowned. "This page must be in error. Kepler was the one who explained the physics of Galileo's telescope, in his treatise on optics."

"Maybe," I said, "but our friend always seems to show up as an ingredient in the sauce."

"'In the Bologna basilica, Danti reproduced the instrument he had built earlier in Florence,'" John continued reading. "'Years later, those responsible for San Petronio—the Jesuit scholar Riccioli being the most prominent— commissioned the brilliant young astronomer Giovanni Cassini to construct an improved, more precise meridian.'"

"Which is the one that appears drawn on the original floor plan and also on a ton of Internet pages. It's still there, in Bologna," I remarked. "The heliometer or meridian of San Petronio."

"What is its floor plan doing in this box?"

"I suppose it got here through Lazzari, who apparently loved to mess around with Riccioli's papers," I joked, remembering the librarian's Bible.

"But these are the papers of another Jesuit closer to us—Hidalgo himself," the Brit reminded me.

"Right. In this holy house papers move around, appearing and disappearing as if by magic," I went on, a bit confused after so many stories. "So what?"

"Isn't he the same friar who made drawings from the *Voynich*?"

"So what?" I repeated.

"Well, maybe all of this is somehow connected," John answered. "Let me see them," he asked.

I showed John the rough sketches of naked women copied a century ago, God knows how and where, by Anselmo Hidalgo. After closely examining them, he made an offhand comment.

"There's got to be something else down there."

John's request to return to the underground passages presented a serious problem. Supposedly only the deceased Carmelo had known of their existence. It was true that Matthew had gotten me out of there the last time. To explain, I'd told him that the door in the chapel was only the entrance to an old dressing room where albs and chasubles were kept. He didn't ask any more, and I didn't think he had any further interest in it. As a result, I should be the only one who knew about the labyrinth. Should I inform the new prior of its existence?

For reasons I couldn't explain, I decided not to.

I would keep this to myself, violating a fundamental norm of the society.

And that forced us to act secretly.

We chose the following night, New Year's Eve.

Nobody asked us why we were staying up so late. A couple of hours after midnight, earlier than expected, everybody in the house had gone to bed. We geared up with the usual flashlights and extra batteries, and I also took a hammer and a large screwdriver. I couldn't be sure that the ghost from last time wouldn't come back to repeat his antics. I put a compass, the maps (both Hidalgo's and my own), a small notebook to jot down whatever might appear, and some chocolate bars in my small backpack. John happily ate his as we were leaving, not at all worried about possibly being locked in. It seems that the English are addicted to Mars bars.

We carefully wedged the door. And we got to the main landing, where the path branched off, with no major difficulties. All of it impressed John, especially the remains of the ancient Roman sewer.

"Everything's in order up to here," I said, looking at my map. "Now we can choose our path."

"To the left, of course," John kidded, starting on his way without pausing to wait for me.

We inspected the passages for about a half hour. Everything matched the maps. I took John up to the Galileo quote carved on the wall, but this was the only thing of interest that we saw. Then I suggested we explore the more remote areas where I hadn't ventured, but which appeared on Hidalgo's sketch. John agreed. We supposed that after a couple more turns to the right, we'd reach an expanse with a fork in the path. Taking the left branch we'd be able to return without retracing our steps, since it connected to another passage parallel to the one we had covered. The opposite fork wasn't on the map; the drawing ended there. Rather, the paper ended. We noticed it had been torn.

"It doesn't matter. Let's go and see," John said assuredly.

We went and found nothing. A big wall over fifteen feet high, clearly built much later than the passages, blocked our path. John felt it with his hands before he spoke.

"We can't go on. Nobody can get past this. Hector, don't bother taking out the hammer."

Then he added:

"We're up against something like a Planck wall."

20

John left for London the next day. Before he did, we chatted for a few hours. He talked about Juana and how he missed her, as well the diagrams and how much he always enjoyed visiting Spain. He promised that, as soon as he got to Cambridge, he would look for the proceedings of that conference in Austria that discredited Kepler, especially after we agreed on Kepler's fundamental place in the history of the *Voynich Manuscript*. And of course we spoke about the wall.

Planck's wall, that is.

John explained the cosmological significance of that wall.

"The world probably began in a state of extremely high density, pressure, and temperature. So intense that a new theory was required to explain it. Not only should this include quantum mechanics, but it must also be consistent with the force of gravity in order to be understandable. These initial instants are known as the Planck era, a period of time that starts with the first tiniest fraction of a second in the life of the universe. A decimal point and forty-three zeros followed finally by a 1. Unfortunately, nobody had been able to develop such a theory. Therefore, the known laws of physics were incomplete since they failed to explain that moment.

"Today we have a lot to do, still lacking the proper tools. Traditional physics proposed a universe that, at least in theory, could be known and predicted in full detail. We could assume that with Newton's and Maxwell's laws, knowing the initial state of all bodies as precisely as possible would be all that was needed in order to be able to tell their position at any given moment. However, this determinist vision of the cosmos, quite attractive philosophically for unbelieving scientists, was torn to shreds with Planck's, Schrödinger's, and Pauli's quantum physics, which doesn't allow us to know the present and future position of a single electron around an atomic nucleus, but only the possibility of its being here or there. How, then, to answer questions about the creation of the universe, and where it's headed?

"The greatest problem facing physics today is that the laws of the macrocosm and those of the microcosm are different. Since gravity explains how stars, stellar masses, and groups of galaxies form, it would therefore also be useful to know about the future of this vast expanse of heavenly space. But when you rewind the film of the universe, and everything that exists in it gets so compressed that the operative laws become those of the microcosm, quantum mechanics falls short. The first photogram that modern physics is capable of producing by means of equations resides in this tiniest fraction of a second. And there is the wall. We came in after the movie had already started."

That wall fascinated John, a barrier that prevented us from seeing beyond it, and from knowing the instant of the birth of the cosmos. The exact moment of the great explosion. We also spoke about the Jesuits, of course, since the Jesuits educated the one who became first a priest, and later the father of the theory of the primeval atom, the Belgian Georges Lemaître. This theory, as we know it today, was scornfully renamed the very famous, or notorious, Big Bang by the British astronomer Fred Hoyle. The English and Catholic priests were always at odds with one another. John and I laughed together, and said good-bye with a big hug that broke this strange tradition.

I decided to devote the rest of the day to my old prior. At some point I had to begin putting his papers in order, and to see to my obligations to the community. So I decided to go to his old room, using the master key to open the door, and closing it behind me. I drew back the curtains, and sunlight came in through the window, flooding everything in the room with light so I could begin my work.

* * *

First I classified the books. Many were familiar. Some about theology, philosophy, pedagogy, and ethics had identical copies in our library. An interesting series of volumes on the history of the Society of Jesus caught my attention. There also were a few novels. Carmelo found solace reading Agatha Christie. I made a pile to take downstairs.

Once I finished with the books on the shelves, I sat at his desk. A detailed diary and a ledger were still open. I set them aside to take to Julian. I was also taking him a portfolio with documents relating to our house, like receipts, checkbooks, letters from the city council, and such, the usual for someone in charge of a community like ours. I carefully separated everything related to administrative chores—papers to be checked by the new prior—from anything merely personal, which I would have to read and archive. Or, in case I judged a document to be totally irrelevant, destroy. Among the personal documents that Carmelo had kept was an old diary, surely from his days as a novice. Quite tenderly, he told the story of his parents, modest Castilian farmers raising a few pigs, and of how he began to feel his calling, entered the seminary, and was finally ordained as a priest. He told about a brief mission in Asia, an unwelcome sickness, and his coming to this house. As he went on, his entries grew farther apart, until the diary was interrupted in 1973. I suppose his increasing responsibilities prevented him from continuing this task. What a pity.

In a couple of hours, I was able to put his desk in order. But when I got up, thinking my job was done, I had to sit down again.

I had forgotten about the drawers.

The first was locked. And the second.

It made no sense to waste time looking for the small keys. The old friar probably kept them in his pocket. And his clothes had been taken away by the nuns. At this point, those keys might be jingling in some poor man's pocket.

I tried to jimmy the lock. The lock on the first drawer broke off and popped out, attached to a chunk of wood. If Mathew couldn't repair it somehow, this piece of furniture would be totally ruined for future service. All part of the archival work, of course.

I dumped the contents of the first drawer on top of the desk.

There was an envelope with old photos, possibly of his closest relatives, all of them gone. A watch. A leather wallet with a couple of bills. A pack of eucalyptus cough drops.

Altogether, it didn't amount to much. Once the first drawer was out, I could get to the second without needing to force the lock. Reaching down and groping, I felt the bottom. There was only a folder. I took it out carefully, and the moment I read the title on the cover, in Carmelo's handwriting, my hands started to tremble.

"VOYNICH"

It got worse when I opened it, because it was totally empty.

The next morning I got up dizzy and confused. I'd barely slept three hours. Finding that folder, even though it was empty, left no doubts about the relation of the *Manuscript* to the monastery where I lived. I had already believed that Anselmo Hidalgo, the old prior, had seen it, but I didn't know where. Now I also knew that during my years in the house, Carmelo had some knowledge of the book as well. There were still a few mysteries. The first, of course, had to do with the contents of the folder. Had they been stolen? And in that case, perhaps on the same night Carmelo died? By the same person who locked me up in the labyrinth? I couldn't let go of the idea that maybe Carmelo himself had hidden those documents for some reason. That would explain his nervousness during his last days.

Another item that didn't quite fit into the whole scheme was my own role in it. To my knowledge, nobody in the house was aware of my interest in the *Voynich*. It was a mathematical exercise in which I indulged in my free time. Since none of the other priests was much involved in ciphering techniques, or even knowledgeable about computers, which they used only out of necessity, it wouldn't have made any sense to speak about it. Especially not now.

Our library had to be open to the public that day.

I wasn't expecting any visitors, but I had to follow the schedule. To my surprise, Simon was waiting outside the door.

"Hi, Hector. Happy New Year," he said, greeting me with a smile.

"Same to you, kiddo. What brings you here?"

Simon was dying to tell me all about the results of his latest research. He had continued on his own, reading everything he found on the Internet about alchemy and Enoch, which was quite a lot.

"You were right, Hector. For many believers, Enoch is one of the fathers of alchemy, which he learned from the angels."

"That is more than even a priest can accept." I laughed.

"Okay. But some sites also say that Enoch is the father of writing. And they all talk about that guy you mentioned, John Dee."

I remembered telling Simon about Dee and Kelley—the supposed authors of the *Voynich*—and their relationship with Enoch and his conversations with angels. There was certainly nothing innocent in this. I didn't remember telling him anything about the *Manuscript* itself, so I was careful on that point.

"And this English wizard wrote in his diary that the Enochian alphabet was conveyed to him through his medium, Edward Kelley." The kid went on, so impassioned that he was almost incoherent. "This happened in 1582. Later, living in Bohemia, they contributed to a book in that language. And that happened"—he checked his notes—"in 1585."

"What book?" I asked innocently.

"It was called *Voarchadumia*. And its main writer was"—Simon was again trying my patience, leafing through page after page of his scribbled notes—"Johannes Augustinus Pantheus. Another priest."

I sighed in relief. It wasn't the *Voynich*. So I let Simon blabber on to his heart's content. He'd made some interesting discoveries, but they were so muddleheaded they could be called alchemic.

"In the Middle Ages, the study of alchemy was on two levels, the *espagiria* and the *archemy*," he said with difficulty. "Archemy is the same as *voarchardumia*, and that's the part that teaches how to transform one metal into another. Espagiria is the part that teaches how to classify bodies and identify their properties, by natural or violent means. Its objective is changing and purifying bodies. Basically, medicaments."

"Interesting," I said, truly amazed.

"So Paracelsus was a pioneer in all of this. The first alchemists had only the transformation of metals in mind, but later they tackled many other matters. In their pride, they believed they could be like God and create all sorts of animated beings. They took very seriously the legend of Albertus Magnus, who built a kind of wooden automaton that came to life by means of a strange spell. Paracelsus went beyond this and claimed to be able to create a real being, which he named *homunculus*. In his treatise *De natura rerum,* he explained that by putting together various amounts of animal humors and body fluids, under the favorable influence of the planets and with just a little heat, the mixture would gradually take human form. The small creature would start to move and talk, and thus the homunculus came to be. In his writings Paracelsus explained in all seriousness the services this creature could do for us, and how to feed it.

"Sounds like a story by Lovecraft," I remarked.

"Love who?" Simon asked, confused.

"An early twentieth-century writer known for his sinister stories about unpleasant extraterrestrial beings," I explained. "I'll lend you one of his books."

"I'm sure I'd like it." He smiled. "Thanks. Do you want me to finish telling you about my research? I only have two pages left," he claimed.

"Of course, go on."

"All the alchemists recognized the influence of the planets on metals. Paracelsus went further. According to him, each metal came into being thanks to the planet that represented it, and since each of the six planets was related to two signs of the zodiac, the metals also received certain properties. Thus the Moon, silver, owed its hardness and its pleasant sound to Aries, ruled by Mars, and Pisces. And to Venus with Gemini and Libra, its malleability and resistance to form alloys. And finally Saturn, with Scorpio and Capricorn, got its density and homogeneous body. And so on, more or less, with the rest of the metals." Simon cut short his explanation.

I was already aware of all this, but I let Simon finish his lecture. He really worked hard during the Christmas break.

"We also owe to Paracelsus the introduction of the powers of the kabbalah into alchemy. The kabbalah breaks words down into the numeric value of their letters, and from there, according to special rules, we have the various possible interpretations. I'm sure you knew this."

That was true. I nodded in agreement.

"After Paracelsus only two writers continued working with the alchemic kabbalah. Pantheus, who is the Venetian priest I mentioned earlier, and later John Dee. Dee tried to create his own kabbalah with the help of alchemic symbols. And that's all," he finished.

"Did he succeed?" I asked him.

"I'm not too sure about it. Some say all of this appears in the treatise *Monada Hierogliphica*. Others insist that it's in the already mentioned *Voarchadumia,* from which Dee copied and improved findings from Pantheus and others. He later hid his discoveries in a very famous book that has gone around for centuries without ever being deciphered. Maybe it doesn't even exist. They call it the *Voynich Manuscript*."

I looked at him for a while, considering. Then I admitted, "Yes, it does exist."

That afternoon I tried to make some sense of Simon's notes, comparing them to my own. As a reward for his efforts, the following day I invited him to have a soda with me outside school. We both still had a week left of the holiday vacation, and it wasn't any good for either of us to be shut in all day in front of the computer. According to his findings, there was a book—the so-called *Voarchadumia*—in which we could find Enochian described by Pantheus, and later by Dee. Enochian characters were related to the kabbalah and deciphering them didn't pose major problems. Enochian was an invented language, perfectly translatable, which Dee and his crony Kelley used to dupe Rudolf II, trying to make him believe they possessed the secret of the philosopher's stone. Their first book would deal with archemy, the part of alchemy that attempts to turn lead into gold.

And then the *Voynich* appeared. It was unintelligible, not in Enochian, but possibly written by John Dee himself—or by Dee together with Kelley. Then the purpose of the *Voynich* would have been, as Gordon Rugg and other scholars suggested, to continue their deception of Rudolf II, or to hide some kind of alchemic knowledge concerning Paracelsus and his medicinal concoctions. After all, the drawings of plants, naked women, fluids, stars, and planets seemed to point in that direction. This second book would be related to the other branch of alchemy, the espagiria. This led directly to

Tycho Brahe, a great admirer of Paracelsus's medicaments. And Tycho went to Bohemia shortly after the English tricksters.

What about the astronomical circles?

Until then, they were the only key uncovered in the whole manuscript. A pretty obscure key, but it surely connected John Dee to Tycho Brahe. The only known relationship between them was perhaps some correspondence about their observations of the famous supernova. Dee may have reflected it in the *Voynich*, but for what purpose? On my desk were the three disks of heavy paper that I'd made with the help of my niece and nephew. I rotated them again into their correct position. What else did this puzzle hide? The syllables that precisely corresponded to the twelve months of the year made no sense outside that diagram. With various programs and algorithms, John had covered two dozen more pages, exchanging the newly found prefixes and suffixes, but that didn't help at all. Up to now, the only explanation was that the manuscript didn't entirely consist of useless scrawls, paradoxical as this might sound. There seemed to be an implicit message that said, "Keep on looking."

There were many more papers on my desk, more pieces of that puzzle that seemed to grow day by day. I thought about the most probable hypotheses. There was an undeniable fact to begin with, the presence of Lazzari, the general librarian of the Jesuits in Spain. First in Toledo, then shortly before the suppression of the society in my own house in 1770—according to the archive—supposedly to protect the most valuable volumes in the Jesuits' vast collection. It seems pretty sure that the *Voynich Manuscript* was among them. First because it disappeared in the hands of a Jesuit, Athanasius Kircher. And second, because it reappeared, almost 250 years later, in one of our communities, Villa Mondragone, near Rome.

Meanwhile, the manuscript could have been passed from hand to hand, but was always in our possession. Intelligently, Lazzari had made use of Galileo's ingenuity to leave two clues concerning this book. The first one, the quote in the envelope in Riccioli's Bible: "I tried to read this in vain, too soon." This was Kepler's translation of the anagram in Latin that referred to the phases of Venus that Galileo had hidden from profane eyes. A double meaning, perfectly understandable by someone like Lazzari, relating directly to Kepler and to the manuscript. The second phrase, also an anagram by Galileo, was in the underground labyrinths below me, and it was about Saturn. From Saturn to Cassini there was only one missing link, and that had clearly come up in the old papers of the house that included the floor plan for the Basilica of San Petronio in Bologna. But why these two quotes? Why two different clues?

I made some coffee. I always think more clearly with a cup of coffee in my hand, pacing slowly in my room.

In order to take one more look at the pages of the *Manuscript,* I went to my computer. A hundred and two folios, adorned with writings and drawings on both sides. I checked the pagination. There are 5 double folios, 3 triple, 1 quadruple, and 1 sextuple. Supposing the initial pagination was consecutive, it doesn't come out right. There are 28 folios missing, or 56 pages. I checked the entries of some scholars on the Voynich List. In fact, they supposed that the book consisted of at least 234 pages, or of 252 at the most. Considering that there might be some multiple folios, the number of pages could reach up to 310. That simply meant that the *Voynich,* as it exists today in the Beinecke Rare Book and Manuscript Library of Yale University, is incomplete.

But where is the rest?

The very question was thrilling. Many on the Voynich List have suspected that the key pages for deciphering the manuscript were torn out. In this way, only by joining the two parts would the translation be possible. We had been able to unlock one diagram, but maybe it wasn't the only one. Or it could be, perhaps, that the part to be deciphered wasn't there. Someone—or several people—could have deliberately removed the pages. But this implied that when it occurred, the meaning of the *Voynich* had *already* been deciphered.

Again I paced the floor, with another cup of coffee.

Had anybody else reached the same conclusion?

Was this person looking for the missing part of the *Voynich*?

Did any such person—or persons—know that the whole book, or parts of it, could have been hidden for some time in my own monastery?

If so, many of the strange things happening around our house suddenly acquired a new meaning. A chill ran down my spine as I started to write John a long e-mail.

21

The next morning I already had John's answer. That English guy didn't sleep much either.

Hi, Hector,

Very, very interesting!

Always a bull's-eye, you devilish priest! There must be a second part of the *Voynich* somewhere, though not necessarily in your monastery. It would be too much of a coincidence to be able to solve the *Manuscript* without leaving home. That certainly would make me suspect you had some pact with the Evil One! I tend to think—actually, I'm almost sure—that the missing pages could still be hidden in Italy. What else did we find from Lazzari? Cassini's floor plan in the Basilica of San Petronio in Bologna? What does that show us? The meridian. And what does a meridian show us?

See you soon,

John C.

I never understood John's habit of leaving me with a puzzle to solve. At least this time he didn't send a codified CD for me to crack.

Holding a very hot cup of coffee, I looked out the window. Everything was absolutely quiet outside. I still had a week without kids, screams, and basketballs hitting me from out of the blue. My community was in a tense calm, waiting for what would happen after Christmas vacation. The councilmen and their powerful friends must have gone skiing. They had no need to rush. But they couldn't afford to slip.

A meridian is a line that connects the centers of the roughly circular images that the Sun projects on the floor of a church when its rays come in through a small opening in the ceiling. This always happens when that celestial body reaches its peak, that is, at noon. A simple way to set the clock, and that was how the sixteenth- and seventeenth-century faithful knew—having no watches—the time for religious services. This was the "civic" application of the invention, though it really was more religious, and of course, astronomical. So the answer to John's question about the meridian was obviously a date. The Sun follows the meridian as days go by, and along the same line, the seasons, the solstices and equinoxes, besides other things like the months of the year and even the zodiac.

Another date? Or the same date?

I decided to answer John's e-mail.

Hi, John,

Okay, the answer is a date.

Now, pray tell, what date?

Hector

My British friend probably wasn't far from his computer, since he took less than ten minutes to answer.

Hi, Hector,

Naturally, the same one we found in the *Manuscript*.

John C.

John was already connected to IM. We had the same idea, so we started to chat online.

"Hi, John."

"Hi, Hector."

"Why the same date?"

"Because it's the most logical."

"Why?"

"Look, Hector, if you deliberately break a book apart, taking out the code page with keys to the text to be transcribed, wouldn't you keep the same code as a clue to guide others to that text?"

"Sure. Except John Dee didn't live in Cassini's time, but a hundred years before."

"Right. But Dee wasn't the one who hid the book, it was Lazzari. We can assume that the Jesuit priest already knew the meaning of the diagram. If not, tell me why he would want to break the book apart."

"Right, I agree. Let's suppose it's the same date. That gives us a point in a straight line. Then what?"

"I haven't the slightest. So I already booked flights. We'll have to see it in person."

"You did what?"

"Your flight leaves Madrid for Rome tomorrow at four in the afternoon. I'll get there directly from London at five. There are several afternoon trains to Bologna."

"Thanks for checking with me."

"You're welcome. I'm sending you an adjunct with the electronic reservation."

"I see I can't say no."

"No, you can't. Oh, and another thing. Please tell Juana."

"What?"

"Write to her. Maybe she'll listen to you. She won't answer me."

"I'll try, old chap. Over and out."

I sighed with relief. John's idea was simply brilliant. The idea of the meridian, of course. The second, about Juana, made no sense. Our Mexican friend wanted nothing to do with him. But still, I decided to try. Before getting up from my desk, I sent her a short e-mail saying that John and I were going to meet again in Rome, and that we had new clues about the *Voynich Manuscript*. No other details, no mention of Lazzari, Bologna, or Cassini and his meridian.

Why bother if she wasn't going to come?

* * *

"Then, are you going to Rome to see the pope?"

It was the perfect excuse, both for Simon and for my community. A few extra vacation days, well spent, before coming back to the same routine with the kids. Besides, I had never been in Italy.

"Well, that's what I intend to do. Tomorrow I'll leave for Rome with some friends, but I'll be back in time for classes."

Simon looked at me in amazement, sipping a soda through a straw. And need I say it? I had ordered a cup of coffee, or rather, a cappuccino. It sounded more appropriately religious, and I needed to get into the mood.

"How did Tycho Brahe make it to Prague?" he blurted out. "He died there. Or he was killed, it's not clear. So you still have a lot to tell me."

"Well, as they say, it's a long story," I told him. "If you like, we'll begin at the beginning. That'll probably be best."

"Okay with me."

"Trying to tell all of Tycho's life briefly is pretty difficult," I began. "After he finished his university studies and traveled extensively all over Europe, Tycho wanted to establish himself in Basel. Then King Frederick the Second of Denmark, well aware of Tycho's fame and talent, called him to his court—"

"It sure sounds like a fairy tale," the kid interrupted me, laughing.

"Don't interrupt, and order another Coke. You're making me nervous slurping on those ice cubes." It was distracting. "King Frederick appealed to Tycho's national sentiments, to the Brahe family ties with the Danish crown, to his own friendship, and above all, to a financial offer that was obviously astronomical in order to make Tycho stay in his homeland to do his research. In total, the offer included several feudal estates in Scania and Norway, a couple of castles, more than fifty farms, several small towns, and an annual cash income that would increase with time, besides—and this is the best known—the whole island of Hven. It wasn't very big, hardly three miles long and two miles wide, but Tycho would be its lord and master. He could put its inhabitants to work on his own project, building the incredible laboratory-palace of Uraniborg."

"Does it still exist or is it a myth?"

"One could think it was a fantasy, because this one-of-a-kind castle has completely disappeared. Even its famous instruments, some of them really large, have been lost. To locate its remains, the land had to be excavated a century later, and even then, only part of its foundation was found. The laboratory was totally ransacked and destroyed by the Hven citizens, just after Tycho was forced to leave. They ended up hating him. It's also rumored that for a time the isle served as a love nest for young King Christian, the main instigator of the astronomer's fall from grace. King Christian used to join his lover there. But many engravings of the time represent Uraniborg, and there are chronicles and stories galore, and of course dozens of diaries with observations and experiments in almost any field of knowledge, not only astronomy. Naturally alchemy was also included. You yourself found very specific details about his sister Sophie and his brother-in-law Erik Lange, a sponger. Uraniborg did look like a fairy tale. Tycho planned and designed everything to the last detail. Sumptuously and with elegance, without worrying about costs.

"The most important European nobility of the time visited Uraniborg, and of course, anyone who had something to teach or to learn. Uraniborg was the first scientific laboratory established in Europe. Tycho was a real Renaissance man. Even today, those who like to put a price on things believe that no government, now or ever, has given a single scientist more in research grants. About one percent of all the Danish wealth at the time, which included the whole Scandinavian peninsula, not only Denmark but also Norway and Sweden, went to Tycho. Not even the American Apollo Project to take man to the Moon received such a percentage of a country's income."

"You're exaggerating," Simon managed to say.

"Maybe, but it's all part of Tycho Brahe's legend."

"Why that name, Uraniborg?" he asked.

"Because Urania is the muse of astronomy," I replied. "He also built Stjerneborg, or Castle of the Stars, when he thought his palace wasn't large enough for him. The construction of Uraniborg began in 1576, and it was the center of world astronomy until 1597, when Tycho Brahe went into exile. After more than twenty years of astronomical observations."

"Why did he have to go into exile?" Simon again wanted to know.

"When King Frederick the Second died, he was succeeded by his son, Christian the Fourth, who was young and impressionable. Tycho and his family held an important position in the court, and that created a lot of enemies for them. The famous quote from *Hamlet* could well apply here. 'Something is rotten in the state of Denmark.' It fits perfectly."

"Did he throw Tycho off the island?"

"He made Tycho's life impossible. He stopped paying him, confiscated part of his lands, humiliated his family. The citizens of Hven didn't help much either, because they saw Tycho Brahe as a tyrant who forced them to work without pay. Then Tycho collected as many instruments as he could, and together with his family and those faithful to him, began his sad peregrinations over northern Europe. Tycho had friends and tremendous fame, so he soon found refuge, and in the best place possible: the court of Rudolf the Second, king of Bohemia. It was then 1599, and Rudolf was still lucid, passionate about science, literature, and art. He named Tycho imperial mathematician. He assigned him a pension, which Tycho rarely received on time, and a castle very close to the Prague court where he could have his new observatory, Benátky."

"And what about Kepler?"

"That's when Kepler came on the scene. Tycho began working at Benátky with a dozen helpers, and resumed his astronomical observations around June 1600. But he needed a good mathematician. Looking at Johannes Kepler's published book on perfect solids and the planets, Tycho saw him as young and knowledgeable, the perfect candidate. Besides, Kepler's economic and family situation was almost desperate, so he quickly accepted the Dane's offer. Or perhaps it was Kepler who asked Tycho for a job. There's a strange group of letters between them on this, full of misunderstandings. And pride, lots of pride."

I paused to finish my second cup of coffee, which was already cold.

"You know the rest of the story. They worked together for a year, until Tycho's strange death. During that period the famous Dane assigned Kepler the job of determining the orbit of Mars. To that end, Tycho shared almost three decades of his amazingly precise observations with Kepler. Kepler thought he could solve the problem in a week, but it took him more than eight years."

I put my cup on the table. Simon seemed satisfied with my explanations and the two sodas.

"Well, unless you have more questions, I'll pay so we can leave," I quickly suggested. "I have to pack for tomorrow."

"Thanks for the sodas and inviting me, Hector," Simon said, getting up. "I promise I'll find out some more before you come back."

"I hope so," I said, smiling and holding his arm. "Wait. Don't forget the book I brought you."

Simon read its title. "*Tales of the Cthulhu Myths,* by H. P. Lovecraft."

"You'll like it."

"Sounds good," he said.

"So, how long will you be in Italy?"

"Four—five days, max. You've met John, quite generous but impulsive."

Julian wasn't interrogating me, strictly speaking, but I sensed that my sudden trip was making him uncomfortable. Even so, he had no objections. It wouldn't interfere with my classes.

"Yes, of course. A charming person, and very intelligent. Have fun in Rome, and be sure to visit the Vatican museums, the Forum, the Colosseum, the Pantheon, and so many other places. I was there many years ago, and every corner of that city fascinated me. If you like, I can make a few phone calls and find you lodging," he offered. "The society has plenty of houses in Italy. And oh," he reminded me, "the Holy Father holds audience on Wednesdays. Don't forget."

"No, but thanks, Julian. John already made all the reservations. We also want to take advantage of this to make a meteoric trip to another city. There's no Italian city without a duomo, and practically no duomo without a meridian."

I wasn't really sure if Julian understood that I wanted to visit churches not only for religious purposes but simply for fun. I didn't even know whether the prior was familiar enough with astronomy to know about meridians. But he did.

"In fact, you could find one in Santa Maria degli Angeli, in Rome. And speaking of duomos, I remember visiting the meridian in the Milan duomo, and the one in Florence, in the fabulous cathedral with the Brunelleschi cupola. There is another in Palermo too, but Sicily would be too far for you. If you want to see an authentic meridian, you'll have to go to Bologna. A famous astronomer built it, as you must know."

He hesitated, trying to remember the name. I had to help him.

"Cassini."

"That's right. Giovanni Cassini. One of our protégés."

"We're planning to go to San Petronio, of course."

"Those instruments, and the building of them, reached their peak in the seventeenth century," he went on, and I was pleasantly surprised by Julian's extensive, detailed knowledge. "The exact date to celebrate Easter had to be determined. Even here, in our small Church of Santa Marta, the idea was to have a meridian, but its final dimensions made it impossible."

"Really! I had no idea," I exclaimed, totally amazed.

"Yes. If you go deep into the archives, you'll find papers with the sketch. It couldn't be done. When the church and the old monastery were built, high-ranking officers in the society were our guests. At first they wanted to build a large church on this land, and give the house a great library. But because of the persecution we were suffering, the money evaporated right before the first suppression of the society. Or at least it was hidden until the situation improved. By then, it was already too late, and the Jesuits had decided to turn strongly to missionary activities. They postponed the construction for a more propitious occasion, which never materialized. That's why the Church of Santa Marta didn't amount to much. And we don't really have a library, except the small place that you take care of. Carmelo could have told you many stories about this."

He sighed, showing a deep grief that seemed sincere. I was reminded of the only revelation the former prior made to me, a few days before he died: the existence of the underground labyrinths. Did Julian know about them?

I didn't dare ask.

It was still more prudent, I thought, not to reveal their existence to anybody, not even him. I was aware of violating a fundamental norm of living in the Jesuit community, but at that moment I didn't feel safe about anything or anybody.

"Take a lot of pictures in Italy, Hector. We'll enjoy seeing them, especially me."

"Of course I will."

Then I recalled another piece of advice Carmelo had given me, the need to photograph the labyrinth before it was condemned for good. Strangely, I hadn't taken the camera with me on any of my previous expeditions. Maybe I could find time for a last visit before leaving for Rome.

I planned to spend only about thirty or forty minutes underground. I had many things to do, papers to put in order, errands to run. John's invitation—or rather, his command—had really caught me by surprise. I had scheduled my time almost to the minute. As a result, I had only a couple of hours left for sleep, so I decided to skip that, and instead take a nap on the train to Madrid. Knowing the usual chaos at Barajas International Airport, I much preferred to be early than to risk missing my plane to Rome.

Well after midnight, I went down to the chapel. I took the usual backpack with the map, some hand tools, a flashlight with extra batteries, a couple of chocolate bars, and—this time of course—my digital camera. Perhaps taking food on a thirty-minute exploration was a bit much, but I had become increasingly cautious, to the point of being obsessive.

No one was in the chapel. Not a soul.

Except maybe Carmelo's.

I glanced sadly at the niche where his remains lay. Involuntarily, I commended my soul to the old prior as if he were a saint. And I began the descent from the same place where, just weeks before, he had been my guide.

Everything went smoothly. First I took a shot of each landing, and then of the branching out of the corridors. The flash briefly lit each spot. In the Roman section I took pictures more carefully. I also photographed the engraved Galileo quote, which was almost certainly made by the former Jesuit librarian Lazzari. The last step of my exploration was to reach the Planck wall. I had labeled it under that name on my map, in honor of John's comment when we got to it.

I took pictures until the batteries told me to stop.

Then I retraced the same steps coming in. Everything was left as it was, and I went back to my room to pack.

Dear Juana,

Go with them.

There is nothing wrong with this. As long as you are firm and serene.

Even though you and I know that John isn't the man you deserve, the man with whom you could finally form a truly Christian family. He is just an atheist who makes a living with grants from his country. A country that, in its imperial way of thinking, believes it can give birth to another Newton, or another Maxwell, by feeding this kind of parasite. Hundreds of them are draining the British public funds daily, sinking their fellow countrymen into what we could call, without fear of being mistaken, scientific misery. Victims of Eurosclerosis. The subsidies given to scientists pervert the desire to work, undermine the patriarchal family, and erode religious fervor, which are the three sources of prosperity. Hector, the Spanish priest, in contrast, seems like a man in the full sense of the word, though he might be too influenced by his religious fervor.

Our interest in finding and deciphering the *Manuscript* is still intact. We still need you as much as you need us. First we helped you, and now you're more than returning the favor. You can't know how grateful we are. You've done a wonderful job on the Voynich List and mustn't stop now. At least not for sentimental reasons.

So it's necessary for you to continue your sacrifices, which are at once a means of personal retribution and, at the same time, a way to get closer to the Creator.

My secretary will take care of your trip to Europe. I gave her very specific instructions that she will e-mail to you. We'll be with you at all times, though we don't think you'll be at any risk.

Be discreet. Just act normally, like a woman, and they won't suspect anything. Control your impulses. You know what you've already suffered. Take the Gospels with you and reread them whenever you're in doubt or your spirit falters.

You know where and how we can meet again.

Please let us know immediately of anything new, any clue or any new findings.

He is always with you.

We're praying for you.

A brotherly hug,

Thomas

22

John was waiting for me in a self-service coffee shop at Fiumicino Airport in Rome. My flight was a bit late, but his had arrived exactly on time. We hugged and ordered espressos.

"Together again, like lovers," I joked.

"No way, lad," John replied, still smiling.

"Well, what are our plans?" I asked him while reactivating my cell phone after the flight. On the train to Madrid, I had kept it on roaming, just in case there was any unexpected news from our house.

"We can go directly to Bologna this evening," he said. "There's a Eurostar at nine. We can also stay in Rome and go see something in the morning. Or, if you like, there's a third possibility, a stop in Florence. It's halfway, and it also has a meridian."

My cell phone alerted me to an incoming message. I stared at the screen, mesmerized. John noticed but went on with the usual jokes between people getting reacquainted.

"Your girlfriend?"

"More likely, yours," I said, to his surprise. "She'll be here from Miami at eleven tonight. She wants us to wait for her."

Of course we did. John was euphoric. And he became more and more nervous after several espressos. He didn't want to switch to decaffeinated, like me, as I hoped to get some sleep that night. I supposed he wasn't planning to. We took advantage of the wait to make reservations online for a good hotel on Via Principe Amadeo, very close to Termini Station and the Church of Santa Maria Maggiore. Three separate rooms, just in case.

Juana's imminent arrival totally unsettled us. It was useless to try to make our itinerary without her. John had practically forgotten our initial reason for meeting in Rome. His only concern at the moment was to make up with the beautiful Mexican. And I was sincerely hoping for that too. More than anything, to regain some order on this strange vacation, and resume our investigations of the *Voynich Manuscript* with a sensible plan.

At eleven thirty Juana appeared at the gate. She seemed to me taller and more slender. She had a new haircut—very short, like a boy's—and she barely smiled. Her clothes were much more sober than before, a long skirt and a large sweater under an ample coat, almost too big for her. In other words, she looked quite different from the young woman in a tiny bathing suit on the Canary Islands beaches.

Her greeting was laconic.

"Hi, Hector," she said, first greeting and kissing me on both cheeks. "Thanks for waiting for me."

As if John didn't exist. Finally she turned to him.

"Hi, John."

He tried to embrace her, but she quickly stepped back, snubbing him.

"Don't even think about it. We broke up for good," she added, pushing him away. "I'm only here to help solve the mystery of the *Manuscript*. I like to finish what I start."

John seemed to accept this, but he looked at me, seeking help. I shrugged, and changed the subject.

"We're staying in Rome tonight," I told her. "We made reservations at the Universo."

"How fitting for astronomers," she said, and laughed for the first time.

"Purely by chance," I said. "Come on, let's find the taxi area before it gets too late."

On the way I told Juana some of our conclusions. Part of the Jesuit story that I'd discovered in the past few days, mentioning the underground labyrinths, without much detail, and something about Cassini's life.

"We intend to visit Bologna," John said, breaking his silence.

Juana didn't even look at him. Things weren't beginning well for them. So she asked me directly.

"Why Bologna?"

"We want to see if we can find something in the San Petronio meridian. It appears in the old documents from my monastery. And it was built by Cassini with the help of Riccioli, a Jesuit scientist who knew Kircher."

"Who surely possessed the *Manuscript*," she quickly pointed out.

"Yes. Everybody on the List seems to agree on that."

"It's not a bad plan. Though a bit vague," she said to me.

"There's more, Juana. But all in due time." We were already at the hotel, and I thought it wasn't right to talk about this in front of other people. It wasn't that I didn't trust the taxi driver. Quite honestly, Juana's presence intimidated me. She seemed like a completely different person. At the hotel café we had some sandwiches, and then went up to our separate rooms. We agreed to meet early in the morning for breakfast and to see the city.

As I expected, John hadn't slept a wink. There were large, telltale dark circles under his eyes.

"What do you think?" he asked me before Juana joined us for breakfast.

"Think about what?" I answered as I buttered my bread, not wanting to get in the middle.

"You know what. She has changed, hasn't she?"

"She's annoyed, still very annoyed," I told him. "I suppose she'll get over it somewhat, or it'll spoil my trip."

At that moment Juana appeared in the restaurant. Things weren't much better than the night before. She too looked poorly rested, more than the usual jet lag. With those two souls in purgatory, I was preparing for one of the most exciting moments a Catholic priest can experience: seeing the Holy Father in person, the Vicar of Christ on Earth. It didn't matter if it was from afar, in the rain, in windy or cold weather. In Rome at the beginning of the year, the weather was not exactly splendid.

However, despite everything, the morning turned out to be unforgettable for me. I tried to disengage from them as much as possible, in order to enjoy my first hours in Italy. They kept silent as I walked ahead of them, sometimes crossing the street in search of a better angle for a photo. There was so much to see! From Santa Maria Maggiore we took Via Cavour to the Forum, with the grandiose Colosseum on our left. Then we took Vittorio Emanuele to the Tiber River. Of course we crossed the Sant' Angelo Bridge, which leads to the famous castle where Emperor Hadrian is buried. And following Via della Conciliazione, we faced Vatican City. When we got to Saint Peter's beautiful ellipse, the piazza was crowded with a mix of the faithful, onlookers, and tourists. We were a bit like them. I was the faithful one, Juana the onlooker, and John obviously looked like a real tourist.

I proposed we each take an hour on our own, and agree to meet in a downtown restaurant for lunch. They didn't object. We could do whatever we wished until then.

I merged with the crowd.

There was something marvelous in that place.

We all prayed together. The young were singing—and I with them—while the pope led the prayer, and time seemed to stand still. Nobody wanted to leave. Not even after the pope said farewell and blessed the whole gathering.

I felt totally refreshed by the time I approached our meeting place. But the clock said I was an hour late, so I would surely be the last one to join the group. During my delay, they had probably exchanged some unpleasantries.

To my surprise, John and Juana were engaged in a lively conversation and drinking martinis.

Things seemed to have improved.

Or maybe not.

"Tell me why."

John hesitated.

"Not without Hector—look."

"Hello, young couple," I said euphorically, and perhaps a little too condescendingly, as if I were the pope. It was an egregious error.

"We're not a couple, Hector. Not anymore," Juana said bitterly. "How was it for you?"

"Unforgettable," I said. "What did you do?"

"I tried to visit the Vatican museums, but no luck," John lamented. "They're not open when the pope is granting a public audience."

"We'll see the Sistine Chapel another time," I tried to console him.

"Maybe we'll have time after we return from Bologna. When are we leaving?"

"When you guys tell me why we have to go there," Juana interrupted, growing more aggressive. John looked at me in amazement, not knowing what to say and obviously asking for help. It seemed clear to me that before I'd joined them, Juana had purposely become more accommodating in order to drag some information out of the naive Brit. But apparently John had withstood her attacks. Though everything seemed to indicate that he was about to fall apart.

So I took the lead.

"You don't have to come," I said.

Juana didn't expect such a curt answer.

"I didn't mean I don't want to go. Quite the opposite." She attempted to soften her position. "But I would like to know what we're going to look for there. If I don't, I won't be good for much."

"The idea of writing to you was John's, not mine," I insisted. "And the idea of the trip also. If you want to help," I concluded, "go back to being the way you were."

John was flabbergasted and looked at me, wondering how far I intended to go. His eyes were begging me not to press Juana any further. Then she answered me.

"I haven't changed, you have. When you decide to let me in on what you know, please call. I'll be at the hotel."

She picked up her handbag and her coat, paid for the martinis, and left without another word.

We ate very little; neither of us was hungry. Feeling tired, we hardly talked. I silently regretted my attitude with Juana, but John didn't complain. On the contrary, it was he who tried to lighten the situation and made a proposal for the afternoon.

"Come on, Hector. Finish your coffee, and let's visit the Basilica of Saint Mary of the Angels. Later we'll see what to do about Juana."

Neither of us had ever seen a meridian except in books. We'd better be well prepared for Bologna. And the Basilica of Santa Maria degli Angeli dei Martiri was fortunately very close to our hotel, right across from the train station.

It was built on part of the Diocletian thermal baths, the Caldarium. And it was designed by none other than Michelangelo during the last months of his life.

"Look, there's the meridian."

It was really there. A straight bronze line inlaid in the marble floor, more than 120 feet long. The signs on the wall explained that the meridian was designed and built by Francesco Bianchini in 1702, following the one created years before by Cassini in Bologna.

"I say, it's marvelous!" John exclaimed, immediately starting to walk on it, one foot behind the other, like a child. "It's too bad it's not noon now," he said.

"True. But we could come back tomorrow. It's so close."

It was Juana.

She was behind us, as if spying. When she saw my surprised, almost angry expression, she responded logically.

"I wanted to pray and the hotel concierge told me this was the nearest church."

I gave her a skeptical look. If she wanted to pray, why hadn't she done it a few hours ago in the Vatican with the pope himself? But she kept up the pretense.

"I also searched the Internet. I knew that one of the most famous meridians is here. Our meeting is just a coincidence," she added with a conspiratorial wink that disarmed me.

"Okay, Juana," I said. "We'll talk more later."

We all had dinner at a nice pizzeria in the Piazza della Repubblica. I started my explanation there.

"The meridians were first built in order to determine the exact date to celebrate Easter, the Resurrection of the Son of God. According to the Council of Nicea, that day must coincide with the first Sunday after the first full moon after the spring equinox."

"Then they're a very exact calendar," Juana said to confirm.

"Absolutely, the most precise in their time. The straight line marks the trajectory of the Sun exactly at noon during the whole year. Or if the meridian isn't long enough, only part of the year. For example, in Florence," I went on, "the opening in the impressive Brunelleschi dome is so high that sunlight filters inside the cathedral for only a few weeks around the summer solstice. But the projection of the solar disk, on the other hand, is magnificent."

"And what about the *Voynich*?"

"We have some leads," I replied.

"To what?" she insisted more anxiously.

I looked at John. He put his fork on his plate, wiped off the tomato sauce with his napkin, and began talking. Very slowly and deliberately.

"We suspect there are two books. Or perhaps that the book was divided into two parts by Lazzari, the Jesuit librarian who hid the manuscript."

This didn't really surprise Juana, but she wanted to know the whole story.

"The key to the astronomical disk could lead to something hidden in the unknown part of the manuscript," John went on. "My idea is that, in addition, Lazzari used the same date and the same key in order to hide it."

"Do you mean that on November eleven, the Sun will give us a clue on the floor of the Basilica of San Petronio in Bologna?"

Juana reached this conclusion very fast. She was smart.

"The eleventh, or maybe the twenty-first. Who knows? Perhaps it's only a false lead," she added.

Her face lit up. Finally our friend was smiling openly.

"Let's go to Bologna then. Tomorrow."

> Dear Thomas,
> Everything's going fine. Tomorrow we leave for Bologna. They discovered a connection between the Jesuits who had the *Voynich* and one of the buildings of the Society of Jesus there.
> I stand firm. With the help of the Lord, who has come to our aid so often. I just finished reading about the final deliberations of the Kansas State Council on Education. A first victory, of many more to come.
> Many kisses,
> Juana

"What are you doing here?"

Juana was in the lobby, sitting at one of the hotel's two courtesy computers with access to the Internet. The clock, in the shape of a sun, showed a half hour past midnight.

"The same thing you are, I guess. Catching up on e-mail." And she attempted a smile.

"Yes," I admitted. "I have a kid at the school doing historical research. He's so enthusiastic, it's great."

She looked at me quizzically.

"Tell me more,"

"It's a very interesting and exciting thing. It's not directly connected to the *Voynich,* but could very well end up being related," I explained, noticing that Yahoo had no new e-mails for me.

"I won't be able to sleep tonight till you give me the details." Juana smiled at me. In a few hours her attitude had totally changed.

"A book on Kepler's life was published a few months ago. Ordinarily this wouldn't be news, since there are many very good biographies of the German scientist."

"Aha!" she said, pulling her chair closer to mine. This unsettled me a bit. Along with her sense of humor, she also seemed to have recovered her former beauty.

"But in this case the authors presented something new. They asserted that Kepler was a murderer. That he killed Tycho Brahe."

Juana looked shocked.

"Wow!" she burst out. "As far as I knew, Kepler never got along well with his master, but to say that he murdered him seems like too much."

"I think so, and so does almost everybody in Internet forums and universities. The authors' conclusions," I continued, "are based on the forensic analysis showing that Tycho died of mercury poisoning."

"Is this true?"

"It seems so on the surface. The Danish scientists certified this when they analyzed the astronomer's remains—after his tomb was opened—in preparation for the quadricentennial of his death. But they also admitted that mercury was a common medication in his time. And Tycho Brahe was an expert in its healing powers. He was a follower of Paracelsus and of his so-called alchemic medicine."

"Then, what really happened?" Juana prodded. Her dark eyes were brighter than ever. At least that I'd ever noticed.

"Probably he poisoned himself," I stammered. Then I managed to recover my natural tone of voice to finish the story. "He suffered from a urinary infection after a banquet in which he wasn't able to leave the table to go to the bathroom. Maybe pain and desperation made him increase his own recommended dosage."

"I see. But why do you say that this could have any relation to the *Voynich Manuscript*?" she insisted.

"Simply because as imperial mathematicians, both Tycho and Kepler belonged to the court of Rudolf the Second, one of the few known owners of the *Manuscript*. Besides, Kepler comes up again in one lead we're following now. It's known, for example"—as I went on I couldn't shake the feeling that perhaps I shouldn't divulge everything—"that Kepler had good friends among the Jesuit scientists of his time—"

"I remember someone from the Voynich List mentioning this," she interrupted.

"It was me." I laughed. "With another name, of course."

"You too?" Now she laughed. "You claimed you didn't do such things."

"Why shouldn't I be like you? Bad habits are acquired quickly," I said with a wink.

"You shouldn't do that," she protested, her lips still smiling.

"What? Write under a pseudonym?"

"No, wink at me. It's not proper for you in your position."

I blushed, turning back to face the computer screen so she wouldn't see my face. Juana pretended not to notice.

"Hector, I'm leaving for now. I'm sorry." She laughed again and stood up. "By any chance, did you bring that book with you? As you can see, it's not easy for me to get to sleep, and even less with this horrendous jet lag."

"Yes, I did, along with a bunch of papers. I'll bring it down for you tomorrow at breakfast."

"Thanks. Then I'll see you at nine in the hotel restaurant."

"Good night, Juana. Sleep well."

The next morning Juana and John came down for breakfast before me. They weren't able to sleep either. Neither together nor separately. But their attitudes seemed to have improved overnight. I greeted them cheerfully, and on my way to the buffet table, I left the book next to Juana.

"Thanks, Hector," she said, starting to read the title on the cover out loud. "*'Heavenly Intrigue: Johannes Kepler, Tycho Brahe, and the Murder Behind One of History's Greatest Scientific Discoveries,* by Joshua Gilder and Anne-Lee Gilder.'"

John joined the conversation, glancing at the book.

"This must be the volume you were telling me about, right? I also brought you a copy of the Austrian symposium paper you wanted."

I gave him a WHAT-WERE-YOU-THINKING look, and John understood.

"Forgive me," he apologized. "You know, I've got a lot on my mind these days."

After cramming my plate with toast, butter, marmalade, and a hard-boiled egg, I returned to the table. Juana was still looking at the book jacket, a puzzled expression on her face.

"Anything wrong?" I asked.

"No, nothing," she finally said. "This couple seems somehow familiar."

I didn't make much of this and changed the subject.

"What's our schedule?" I asked.

"First, the postponed visit to the meridian at Saint Mary of the Angels. We have to be there exactly at noon," John said.

"And then we'll go to Bologna," Juana added. "I saw the train schedule. We have easy connections, but the trip will take us a little over three hours. Provided we skip the visit to Florence."

She was obviously sorry about that.

"Maybe on our way back to Rome. First things first." I tried to sound convincing.

That's how it was. We had scarcely three days to do a million things. And we didn't even know what lay ahead for us.

23

The Eurostar took us straight to Bologna, the old university capital. To get there, we crossed central Italy, with a few minutes' train stop in Florence. From the window we could see perfectly the three big buildings at the core of one of the most famous artistic centers in the world: the cathedral itself or Duomo, the Baptistry, and the Campanile. Before leaving Rome, just across the street from Termini Station, we had witnessed the miraculous daily spectacle of the sunlight landing on the meridian at Santa Maria degli Angeli. Exactly at noon, the image of the King of the Skies was projected onto the marble floor of the nave, right in the center of the chromium-plated band that marked its trajectory. We couldn't keep from applauding, which must have seemed rather odd to the faithful attending religious services.

At dusk we reached Bologna.

We walked out of the station dragging our luggage. The hotel we had chosen was only a few blocks away on Via dell'Indipendenza, a major historic avenue. Bologna, all brick buildings and porticoed streets, welcomes the traveler. Medieval palaces surround its two main squares, the Piazza Maggiore and the Piazza di Nettune, surrounded in turn by the two most important churches, San Domenico's and San Petronio's.

That evening we dined in a trattoria on Via dell' Indipendenza. There, while enjoying delicious Italian cuisine and an exquisite wine, we planned our activities for the next day. Obviously we included a close inspection of the famous basilica where Cassini built his meridian.

"What does the book say?" I asked John, who was immersed in reading the art guide we bought at a huge bookstore next to the ancient university.

"Many things. That the Basilica of San Petronio owes its name to the patron of the city, a bishop from the fifth century. That it's one of the largest medieval brick buildings in Italy, begun in 1390 but never finished," John said, handing me the book.

I started reading out loud. "'At first the church was intended to be bigger than Saint Peter's Basilica in Rome, but it had to be reduced drastically when church authorities decided to shift their financial resources to the nearby Archiginnasio. This kind of thing—this one in particular—is rumored to have moved Martin Luther to confront the Catholic powers. From the sixteenth to the nineteenth century, the university was located there, in the Archiginnasio, and then San Petronio became its church. The interior of the basilica is in Italian Gothic style, with twenty-two chapels on both sides of the immense central nave. The pillars that support the vault, and that separate the different chapels, seem to have been built with the singular meridian in mind, measuring over two hundred and twenty feet, the longest in the world.'"

"That number must mean something," Juana observed.

"Of course it does," I replied. "Cassini studied the path of the sunbeams in relation to the church walls very carefully. Finally he decided to place a small hole, less than an inch in diameter, on the ceiling of the fourth chapel on the left side, as can be seen in the illustration."

That illustration in the book was identical—or at least very similar—to the one we found in my monastery. The floor plan of the basilica as Cassini had drawn it.

"And?" Juana begged me to continue.

"He placed a small hole at the height of a thousand feet, according to what it says here. Or a little over twenty-seven meters."

"That's wrong," John protested, knowing something about inches and feet, yards and meters.

"He used the French metric system of his time. I'm sorry, John," I said with a smile, and went on. "'At ground level, as Cassini had predicted, the length of the meridian represented one six hundred thousandth of the Earth's circumference That is exactly 66.7 meters. That is the reason for its size,'" I finished reading.

"I really want to see it," Juana announced, "but I'm exhausted. What if we leave now, go to sleep, and get up really early tomorrow?"

We agreed that was the best choice, so we paid the bill and went back to our hotel.

At nine in the morning we were already on the steps to the Basilica of San Petronio. The facade, left unfinished, gave a poor impression of the building. An uninformed tourist could very well overlook it. Behind us was the Fontana di Nettune, with its impressive bronze statue of the God of the Seas by Giambologna.

"Did you bring your camera?" Juana asked me nervously.

Both John and I had ours. And all sorts of notes about Cassini's calculations.

We went in silently. The church was dark and only a murmur of prayers could be heard coming from one of the back chapels with scarcely a dozen people attending Mass. John pointed at the ceiling. High above and framed in gold, imitating a resplendent Sun, was the "eye" that gave life to the meridian.

It didn't seem like much.

The straight line began right below the small opening.

Like the one in Rome, the meridian consisted of a metal strip, bronze inlaid in the marble slabs. Alongside, another series of slabs crossed the strip at right angles. They seemed to indicate distinct places on which at noon the Sun's rays would be reflected according to the various signs of the zodiac. The meridian marvelously bypassed the pillars of the enormous nave, giving the impression that the basilica was built especially to accommodate the meridian, and not the other way around. None of the pillars had to be moved.

The line of the meridian miraculously joined north and south.

Waiting until noon, we explored the rest of the church. Nothing stood out especially. There was a towering belfry, an exquisite choir in the Chapel of the Holy Sacrament, and little else. We noticed that most of the walls were not covered with the usual frescoes, but were painted in light colors, pinks and whites, as if to improve the scant light. Perfect for astronomy, but a little too dreary for religious services. When the time was near, we sat on a wooden bench next to the meridian to be able to see the movement of the incoming Sun's rays.

The image wasn't circular. It was winter, the beginning of January, and it had the clear shape of an ellipse, with its main axis along the meridian. The degree of deformation of the solar circle changes drastically as the months go by, since the Sun's height changes. This happens in the same way that the shadows of trees and buildings become elongated with the approach of darkness. When the Sun occupies its highest point in the sky at the summer solstice—Saint John's Day in June—its image is practically circular. The opposite happens at the winter solstice in December, when the elongation of the image is greatest.

"Have you noticed?" John asked, pointing at the floor of the basilica.

"Noticed what?" I asked back. I didn't understand the Brit sometimes.

"The floor pattern. Hexagons. Like a great beehive."

"So?"

"Nothing in particular. It just caught my attention. Like the great modern telescopes, made up of hexagonal mirrors. It seems like a premonition."

"Right," I agreed. "This place seems to be especially blessed for astronomy."

"Can you be quiet?"

Juana was mesmerized by the movement of the sunbeams on the marble. At exactly twelve fifteen, the ellipse of light was cut into two identical halves by the meridian line. That was the expected time, taking into account the fifteen-minute difference from Bologna to the meridian of reference. Then the sunbeams slowly drifted away.

"Fine," I said, breaking the silence. "Have we learned anything new?"

I stared at John, and so did Juana. After all, he had been the one with the idea, the initiator of our trip. We were now in Bologna and had seen Cassini's meridian.

John finally spoke.

"We need to explore the whole line."

"It's over two hundred feet long," I protested.

"Well, only the segment that corresponds to the period from the eleventh to the twenty-first of November. That's not too much," he said.

"Maybe we need to be here on those days," Juana interrupted. And then added, "Maybe the solar image would clarify something."

I thought about it. John shook his head. He seemed sure.

"No. There are no possible shadows, only a luminous disk. Besides, that would be almost a year from now," he added.

Then, staring at the meridian and going back to his initial idea, he had a question.

"Where on the meridian line would the eleventh of November fall?"

"According to the classic division, in Scorpio. This sign covers until the twenty-third, so both dates fall on the same section of the line," I noted.

The three of us went to the section of the meridian line marked with the sign of Scorpio. There was nothing different there. Nothing at all.

In the afternoon we argued over whether it was better to go back and spend the couple of days we had left in Florence. John didn't want to give his opinion. He felt frustrated, and somehow guilty for having brought us all the way here. Besides, Juana hadn't shown the slightest interest in him whatsoever, even though she had grown more cordial and friendly with both of us, especially me. She was the one who suggested we stay in Bologna one more day. I accepted, and John had to resign himself.

That night the two of us again met alone in the hotel lobby, in almost the same circumstances as two nights before in Rome.

"Hi, Hector." She smiled at me. "Here I am, finishing an e-mail."

"Are you missing anybody in particular?" I ventured clumsily, thinking that perhaps it hadn't been too hard for her to get John out of her life. She got the point and smiled again at me.

"No, there's nobody else," she told me. "What I wrote to you is true. I'm not going back to John," she repeated, the smile on her lips changing to a serious, annoyed pout.

"What a shame. You looked so happy together—"

"Don't bother. It's really over," she interrupted, while at the same time clicking the mouse to send her message. "We can be friends. Even solve the *Voynich* together, if we make the effort. That's why I'm here. Nothing else."

"Well, as you say. I won't insist. I've no right to."

"Thanks," she said.

"And related to this," I asked her, "have you become evangelical? You weren't interested in seeing the pope in Rome," I pointed out. "We've never seriously discussed religion, you and I."

"I'm Christian, like you," she replied. "Though I don't believe in the pope anymore, as you saw. No, I'm not Catholic. I've delved deeply into the Bible from the beginning, trying to recover my faith."

I looked at her in disbelief. She realized it.

"Good friends in Mexico and in the United States helped me through my crisis. And my father too," she added. "I owe them a lot. I think I already explained that to you in my e-mail."

That was true. I didn't want to continue questioning her about her beliefs, which, after all, were not so different from mine. I changed the subject, going to what had brought us to Bologna.

"There's something that escapes us in this meridian. That's what I feel," I said.

"I agree. That's why I didn't want to leave. It's a pity John gave up so quickly. He wasn't like that before," she added.

But she was wrong, because John suddenly appeared on the stairs, not even aware he was in his pajamas. He was that excited.

"It's that fucking Kepler!"

"Hey, watch it," Juana and I both said at the same time, annoyed by John's improper language. "Let's keep our civility," I said curtly.

"Kepler," John repeated. "The key is in Kepler."

"Definitely. There are lots of clues related to Kepler," I admitted. "But not in the meridian."

"Oh, yes, in the meridian too," he insisted, smiling.

"One of the most important results Cassini gained from that meridian line was the confirmation of Kepler's second law. The one that says that an orbiting planet covers equal distances in space in equal amounts of time," I reminded John, but he shook his head.

"No, that isn't it. Remember what you told me about Lazzari?"

"What was it?" I stammered.

"That he possibly knew the meaning of the book before he separated it into two parts. And that a clue in one part could lead us to the hiding place of the second."

"That's what *you* said," I emphasized. "And that was our reason for coming here."

"It doesn't matter who said it," John argued, clearly upset. "The fact is that Lazzari knew that the astronomical diagram was Tycho's supernova. A bit later John Dee drew it, making the date of its appearance in the sky the key we're looking for. Or maybe one of the keys."

"I'm getting lost here," Juana pleaded. John turned to her.

"Kepler had friends among the Jesuits and perhaps he had something to do with solving the problem, if they had a solution," he said, "and Lazzari could have used that same key to camouflage the second part of the manuscript. A very clear clue."

"Crystal clear," I joked. "I'm still not sure where you're headed, old chap."

"What do Tycho and Kepler have in common?" he asked.

"A thousand things!" I shouted, losing my patience. "Practically everything. They worked together, remember?"

"There could even be something else," Juana chimed in, surely referring to the book I had lent her. She was smiling, but I'm not sure whether it was because of my irritation or John's arrogance.

"How many supernovas have appeared in our galaxy in the last thousand years?"

"Not many, as you know," I answered, more in control now. "Not counting the one in China, only two. Tycho's and—"

"Kepler's, you idiot!" John said, insulting me affectionately.

I didn't know what to say. Put this way, it seemed very simple.

Kepler had really seen with his own eyes the explosion of a second supernova in 1604, only three years after Tycho's death. This is a rare case in the history of astronomy, that two of the greatest scientists—master and apprentice, no less—had each witnessed such a wondrous event. This second supernova is the one known today as Kepler's supernova, obviously. It's the latest supernova to explode in the Milky Way, and can still be seen through X-ray and infrared telescopes.

Knowing what we needed to do the next day, we went to our separate rooms for the night. But none of us, no matter how hard we tried, could sleep a wink.

"Uh-huh," John said. "Let's look for the section that corresponds to the ninth of October."

The ninth of October, 1604, was the date Kepler's supernova appeared in the sky. We'd gotten up very early that morning to be able to have a whole day for our investigations. We had to wait for the basilica to open for the eight o'clock Mass.

"Libra, next to Scorpio," Juana observed as she rushed to the zone marked with this sign of the zodiac. We followed her, constantly looking at the floor.

But there was nothing special there either.

The day before, there were scarcely a dozen people attending Mass, but now, so early in the morning, there were only three besides the priest. So we were two equal groups. The priest came to us, asking if we needed any help. In a mix of Italian and Spanish, I explained to him that I was also a priest, actually a Jesuit, besides being an astronomer, fascinated by Cassini's meridian. My Italian counterpart smiled, and as I thanked him, he invited me to join him in the celebration of Mass. Since the investigation didn't promise any revelations that morning, I accepted and abandoned my traveling companions for a while. Giovanni—that happened to be the name of the good priest—handed me the proper vestments and invited me up to the altar with him.

Looking at the whole nave of the basilica gave me a totally different perspective. I could see clearly the ten enormous pillars supporting the vault, five on each side. To my right, the meridian line passed closely by two of them. My friends were crouching next to the first pillar, the closest one to the main entrance. Then I smiled and looked up.

And I thanked the Holy Spirit.

After the Eucharist I rejoined my friends.

"What? Anything new?" I asked in a mocking tone.

"No," they answered, unaware of my derisive tone. "There's nothing here either," John answered, even more depressed.

"This Brit isn't a very good astronomer," I said, watching Juana, who gave me a puzzled look. "Because astronomers always look up, never down," I added, raising John's chin and forcing him to take his eyes off the floor.

The answer wasn't on the floor. We had to look at the pillar.

Because right next to the sign of Libra, the straight line of the meridian coincided with the first of the enormous pillars. This one had a base about six feet high and twelve in diameter, rising about fifty feet to a classic Corinthian-style capital. And before it joined the support lines of the arches, there was a prominent ledge.

"Could something be there?" Juana wondered, reading my thoughts.

"I've no idea. But I hope no one has cleaned that area for a long time. About three centuries or so," I remarked.

"Last year."

It was Giovanni's voice, behind me.

We all looked helpless. But the Italian priest kept smiling.

"The light color of the walls had darkened a long time ago," he explained. "And the temple was even more somber than it is now. With a little help from the diocese, we contracted a cleaning company. The workers had a simple, compressed-air device to blow off all the accumulated dirt on the capitals from two hundred and fifty years. Then we repainted a little, as much as the budget allowed," he explained.

"I suppose nothing unusual happened," I suggested very cautiously.

"No," he said. "Some things fell down, like old pigeons' nests and nails. They also found a plumb weight on top of one of the pillars, surely left there since Cassini's time, I suppose. It's the only thing I didn't throw away. Perhaps it was on this pillar, I don't know."

That wasn't much, a forgotten plumb weight, probably one of many that they used to level that enormous basilica and later to build the perfect astronomical instrument. Still clinging to some hope, I asked him to show it to me. He had no objection.

We sat in silence, waiting for the priest. Juana seemed aloof, absent, perhaps exhausted after so much traveling and so little sleep. John looked at her, totally lost, not knowing what to say. I was about to propose a tour of the beautiful city of Florence for our last day, when Giovanni finally appeared with the requested object.

"Here it is. I kept it wrapped in this old newspaper."

I handled it with care. It was a rusty iron cylinder, about six inches long, and pretty heavy.

"Let me see," John said, holding out his hand.

John didn't realize how heavy it was. He fumbled, letting it slip through his fingers.

The cylinder hit the floor with a lot of noise. The metallic sound reverberated through the whole basilica. Or rather, sounds, because two pieces bounced on the floor, threatening to mar the white marble of the nave. I looked apologetically at Giovanni and got up to retrieve the pieces. The plumb weight had split open. A piece of paper stuck out from one of the hollow halves. I handed it to Giovanni. After all, the weight was his, as well as what it contained. I wasn't expecting anything more, maybe, than an engineering detail about the building, perhaps a note indicating the weight of the device or indicating how to use it. The last thing I expected was the sentence that Giovanni read to us.

"'*Robustae mentis esse solidam sapientiam sustinere,*'" he said. "A strong mind is needed to support solid knowledge," he translated, adding, "more or less."

I nodded in agreement.

Giovanni shrugged, and we looked at each other in a daze. Then we copied the phrase into a notebook and politely said good-bye to our provisional helper.

During dinner we went over what we'd found. John thought that the quote could be from Galileo or Kepler, or even from his namesake, Dee. Anyway, Lazzari liked to decorate everything with anagrams, enigmas, and cryptic phrases. I also favored the idea that we had another phrase with a double meaning. We had to keep searching. Whatever was waiting to be discovered, it was worth going after. Juana was distracted, savoring her ice cream. It was sunny and she didn't feel the cold. She wasn't going to give up her favorite dessert.

John and I were so immersed in discussing the possible meanings of that phrase that we didn't realize she had disappeared. We only noticed it when she sat down again, holding a couple of printed papers.

"The next train to Rome is at five. We have to hurry," she urged.

"What about Florence?" I asked.

"The clue takes us back to Rome. And we don't have much time," she insisted.

One of her papers was, of course, the train schedule. The other sheet was a photo of the well-known obelisk at the Piazza della Minerva in Rome. A small elephant held the Egyptian monument, about fifteen feet high. We knew that the creator of the sculptural composition was none other than the famous Gian Lorenzo Bernini, and we also knew that our old friend Athanasius Kircher had deciphered the hieroglyphics there. Kircher was, more than likely, the owner of the *Voynich Manuscript* for a good number of years. What we didn't know—but found out when Juana turned the page, showing a magnified reproduction of the sculpture—was that the same phrase was inscribed on the base of the monument.

"'*Robustae mentis esse solidam sapientiam sustinere*,'" she read.

We also learned there was a cybercafé across the street from the restaurant, and remembered that Google was open 24/7.

24

Dear Juana,

We're looking over the information you've sent us. Quite substantial. It's clear that the *Voynich* has had a turbulent existence befitting its supernatural character. We knew that Cassini the astronomer was in contact with the Jesuits associated with the manuscript, but had no proof of his having any direct connection with the book.

His mentor, Riccioli, a more obscure fellow, is the envious rival of the scholar Kircher. Did you know that Athanasius Kircher was labeled "the last man who knew everything"? Since the Society of Jesus is a closed order, you can't believe all of their claims. Their nearly fanatical devotion to the pope makes them dangerous. And their missionary zeal gets them into political tangles, causing them to criticize our interests in Latin America and Africa, and even to go so far as to sabotage them. Many turn communist. They forget that poverty is the incentive necessary for the poor to seek success. Any kind of governmental assistance—either domestic or international—just supports laziness. Only hunger can make them industrious and awaken their initiative.

I'm sure you'll find something of interest in that meridian.

I'm not at all surprised by your curiosity about the book you mention. Josh and Anne-Lee Gilder are powerful journalists. Their essay on Kepler is terrific. And their last name is no coincidence. He's a cousin of George Gilder, who wrote a rave review of the book right on our Web site.

The Gilders have gone where others haven't dared: to the heart of the matter.

Josh and Anne-Lee concluded from lost letters and other items yet untranslated—heaven knows why—as well as a serious, spectrographic analysis, that Tycho Brahe was murdered by his arrogant apprentice with a lethal dose of mercury. Who else but Kepler? The book is a delightful investigation of the connections between science and technology, and of how a stubborn, obsessive astrologer, Kepler, ended up as the forefather of a politically correct abstract science. It is the science for today's weary scientists, who say they're astonished by global warming in multiple parallel universes filled with superstrings coming from vibrations out of nowhere. You have only to read magazines like *Scientific American* and *Nature*. There they pontificate on their pet theories about the ways and means of a world like ours—completely random and haphazard—without the spirit of the Creator, whose sovereignty they don't acknowledge. Brahe was an exquisite astronomer faced with Kepler's pseudoscience. No wonder the assistant had an abundance of reasons to murder his master.

Of course the book has our complete support. We'll not be stopped by any committee of scientists unable to handle the naked truth—that one of their most illustrious figures, astrologer Kepler, was a murderer. That bunch of wackos has no basis for their quirky attraction to people like him, or that horrible Darwin, the one who continues to do so much damage to our youth. They grow up faithless, thinking things just happen, as if by accident, and don't even know—because nobody dares, or wants, to tell them—that there's a superior intelligence governing good and evil, who intentionally made us separate from animals, distinctly in his own divine image.

I'll stop bothering you. You already know how I get carried away when I write.

As always, you know where and how to find us if the need arises.

And please remember, whatever the news, whatever the clues or discoveries, be sure to keep us informed.

You're in our prayers every day.

A brotherly hug,

Thomas

"We meet again."

"Yes." Juana smiled, glancing up from her computer and turning to face me. It was already dark when we arrived in Rome, exhausted from the day's activities.

Again we were staying next to Termini Station, at the now-familiar hotel that was very handy for all our comings and goings. The next day, the Eternal City would be expecting us.

"Did you bring the map, John?"

He nodded. We had only one day, and we couldn't afford much wandering around. What a shame. It was a luminous morning beckoning us to roam freely. We glanced quickly at the unfolded map. The obelisk on top of the elephant was in the Piazza della Minerva, facing the Dominican church dedicated to the Blessed Virgin. It had been a Roman temple honoring Minerva, the goddess of wisdom. Here, as in so many other places in the city, the Christian and Roman traditions merged.

"I think it's best to go back to the Piazza della Repubblica, where we had dinner the other night, and then take Via Nazionale, which will leave us just three or four blocks from the piazza—right behind the impressive Pantheon," I said.

The Pantheon, the temple honoring all the gods, that many think is the most beautiful building in Rome. There was hardly any time for us to see it, even though it was so close to our objective. We agreed to stop there, right after Kircher's obelisk.

The walk took us barely twenty minutes. Our elephant was waiting there in Piazza della Minerva, with its heavy cargo of an Egyptian obelisk eighteen feet high. A monument designed by the famous sculptor-architect Gian Lorenzo Bernini, but carried out by his protégé Ercole Ferrata in 1667. We went round and round the small animal, taking dozens of pictures. Juana wanted to pose next to it.

"Come on, let's get back to our own work. Only a few frivolities allowed." I smiled at our Mexican friend.

"You're such a bore," an extremely amused Juana replied.

"According to the guide we bought," I began explaining, "Rome has no less than thirteen of the thirty Egyptian obelisks still in existence. Egypt itself has only seven. The Minerva obelisk is the smallest of those in Rome. It's believed to have been built by Pharaoh Apries, fourth king in the twenty-sixth dynasty, 589 to 570 B.C. It had a twin, also to be found in Italy—not in Rome but in the small city of Urbino. The Romans probably removed it from its original site during the first century. Then it was hidden and buried at some unknown later date."

My traveling companions were listening attentively, so I continued.

"The Dominicans found it in about 1665 while digging in their garden—here, facing us," I said, pointing to the Church of Santa Maria sopra Minerva. "Then Pope Alexander the Seventh decided to reerect it, in its present location. This happened two years later. But the pope himself was unable to attend the solemn inauguration. He had died just two months before, in May 1667," I concluded.

"Say, Hector, isn't that church famous for something else?" John asked.

"Right, John. It's also where Galileo was forced to disavow his heliocentric belief. Exactly on June 22, 1633. The guide quotes it.

I, Galileo Galilei, seventy years of age, son of the deceased
Florentine Vincenzo Galileo, attending this trial before Your
Eminences, Most Reverend Cardinal Inquisitors, on my knees,
my gaze fixed on the Holy Gospels in my hand, do hereby declare
that I have always believed, now believe, and with God's help in
the future will continue to believe in all that the Holy Apostolic
Roman Catholic Church believes, professes, and teaches.

"What does that guide say about Athanasius Kircher?" Juana wanted to know.

"Nothing. This is only for tourists," I said regretfully.

"Then talk to us as tourists," John asked.

"The obelisk," I began. "Red granite. Eighteen feet tall. Almost forty-three feet if we count the décor, which includes the small elephant, the pedestal, and the base with four flights of stairs. Each of the four sides of the obelisk contains images of Egyptian deities and inscriptions concerning Pharaoh Apries. The message isn't very clear, but it deals with matters related to life after death, which fascinated the Egyptians."

"Enough. But it's not much. And, as for the hieroglyphics, we're not exactly up to speed yet," Juana scoffed, alluding to the *Voynich*.

"Here's the famous sentence," John said.

There was in fact a stone tablet in the pedestal, inscribed in Latin, part
of which matched the sentence we'd found inside the plumb weight at San
Petronio in Bologna.

WHOEVER SEES THE OBELISK AND ITS ENGRAVED IMAGES OF
EGYPTIAN WISDOM BORNE BY AN ELEPHANT, THE STRONGEST
OF ALL ANIMALS, WILL REALIZE THAT A STRONG MIND IS
NEEDED TO SUPPORT SOLID KNOWLEDGE.

"Apparently the pope and the Dominicans wanted to express the power
of wisdom, associating it as much with the Virgin Mary as with the ancient
goddess Minerva. The elephant symbolizes power," I explained.

"And memory, as well," John commented.

"Fine. Now what?" Juana wanted to know.

"We don't have much more," I answered, sitting on the stairs directly
under the stone pachyderm's trunk.

"No," John agreed. "We know Kircher was a devoted Egyptologist, and
he eventually wrote a book, *Obeliscus Aegyptiacus*, in which he deciphered,
or tried to decipher, some of the hieroglyphs on Roman obelisks. He published it in 1666."

"The same year the *Voynich* arrived in Rome," I noted. "Athanasius
Kircher probably possessed it until he died in 1680. Supposedly it was in his
famous museum."

"And there we lose track," Juana concluded in a rather pessimistic tone.
"Come on, get up," she said, pulling on my sleeve. "Let's go for a walk through
the Pantheon, to refresh our minds and please our eyes."

Walking around the Pantheon makes sense. Literally.

We made our way into it through the imposing portico formed by sixteen giant Corinthian columns. Inside, an immense rotunda constitutes the
largest open space built in antiquity.

"Amazing!" John exclaimed. Juana and I were speechless.

In the Roman view of the world, the Earth was surrounded by a celestial
vault, and this is the meaning of the Pantheon. If we picture a complete sphere—

inscribed in the great circular room whose upper half forms the vault—then a representation of the celestial sphere would be placed on the floor.

"'Its dimensions are beyond perfection,'" I said, again reading from the guidebook. "'Michelangelo said this building's design wasn't human, but divine. The cupola rests on a cylindrical drum, making its height identical to its diameter, which is more than a hundred forty feet. And its only source of light is that hole in the ceiling, exactly at its highest point.'"

We looked up at the oculus, the "Great Eye," an aperture nearly thirty feet in diameter at the apex of the cupola. The light coming through glided softly across a floor of the finest marbles and porphyries brought from all over the empire, and then climbed the walls, like a gigantic sundial. John noticed and pointed this out to me.

"Wait till I read the details," I said, checking my guide. "You're right, man. The building's orientation is such that every June twenty-first, at the summer solstice, exactly at noon, the aperture directly lights the main entrance."

"Well, keep on illuminating us," Juana joined in. "I love to hear you read, Father."

I basked in the praise and continued reading from the book.

"'The proportions and structure of the Pantheon represent the Romans' religious conception. The Pantheon was the dwelling of all the gods, and the Romans attempted to synthesize the great variety of cults in the Eternal City, cosmopolitan city par excellence. This circumstance was respected by the Christians, who consecrated the temple in 609, as the Basilica of Saint Mary of the Angels and the Martyrs.' In fact," I pointed out, "Masses and religious events are still celebrated here."

"Wouldn't you like that?" Juana asked, reading my mind as she nearly always could.

"Of course. Who wouldn't? It's an impressive place."

"Please go on with the story."

"'The origin of the Pantheon goes back to twenty-seven B.C., when it was built by Agrippa. A hundred years later the temple burned down, and it was Hadrian who ordered its reconstruction. It seems that he himself oversaw the work, together with the great architect Apollodorus of Damascus. The building is truly a marvel of architectural techniques, and it wasn't exceeded in weight and size until the fifteenth century, when Brunelleschi raised the cupola of his famous Church of Santa Maria del Fiore in Florence.'"

"The duomo that we won't get to see," Juana lamented.

"We can't see all of Italy in a week," I protested, and continued reading. "'The cupola rests on a wall twenty-one feet thick at the base of the dome. This encloses a complex system of vaults and brick archways that transfer the weight of the concrete to the points of greatest resistance. The filling materials become lighter toward the peak of the cupola, which is about four feet thick at the top.'"

"Isn't there a more interesting part?" John interrupted. "You know, astronomy and the like."

I checked the extensive guide and found some relevant comments.

"'Within the cylinder, given the load distributions, the design permitted the opening of eight niches, one occupied by the main door, and the other seven with alternating rectangular and semicircular shapes. These seven niches initially contained images of the seven planetary deities: the Moon, the Sun, Mercury, Venus, Mars, Jupiter, and Saturn.'"

"There we go," John acknowledged. "But only a few of them are left, that I can see."

"Yes, that's true." I kept reading. "'The Pantheon, besides its dedication as a Christian temple, has a Pontifical Academy of the Virtuosi, where famous Italian artists were buried. These tombs were all later transferred, except that of the great Raphael.' Which is still here," I said, pointing.

We approached the tomb of the Renaissance painter, in a prominent space between two of the large niches. These intermediate spaces were adorned with either sculptural groups or paintings. In all, the guidebook indicated fifteen distinct areas around the circumference of the temple, including the principal niches mentioned. In front, occupying the semicircular niche directly facing the door, was the main altar.

"What's this one?" John asked, pointing at another tomb.

"We've also got kings," I said. "Namely Victor Emmanuel the Second and Umberto the First. They're in the principal semicircular niches, not counting the main altar."

The Pantheon had a lot to offer. We found

another striking coincidence in the guidebook. Apparently, the cupola of the great American telescope on Mount Palomar, near Los Angeles, with its 200-inch mirror of Pyrex glass—the largest for decades—was modeled after the Pantheon's 142-foot diameter and identical height. While we were discussing this and other matters, Juana wandered about the interior of the temple, looking at everything. Suddenly she let out a scream that spread through the whole building.

"She probably saw a mouse, or some tourist pinched her ass," John wise-cracked.

"Don't be gross, let's go see what happened to her."

Juana met us halfway, waving her arms but unable to say a word. After a while she calmed down and finally spoke.

"Okay, guys. What part of the Pantheon will the Sun shine on through that opening around the eleventh of November?"

We gave her a look as if she'd lost it. But she went on.

"Let's suppose from the eleventh to the twenty-first, to make sure. And around noon, more or less," she added.

John started thinking out loud.

"Well, given the north-south orientation of the building, and if we know that at the summer solstice the light falls exactly at the entrance, we can look at it the same way that we saw the meridian. Around the dates Juana suggests, we'd have the sun almost on the opposite side, a bit to the left."

He pointed to a sculpture on the left side of the main altar.

"Let's say over there, for a pretty good guess."

"Fine. Let's go have a look."

Juana stayed right in the geometric center of the Pantheon, waiting. Surely she must have smiled when she heard us scream too.

As it happened, the name of the saint was inscribed on the stone base of that statue: SAINT ATHANASIUS.

"It seems like witchcraft," John said with his mouth full.

We'd sat down to eat in the patio of a restaurant right on the Piazza della Rotunda, outside the Pantheon. The direct sun made wearing our coats uncomfortable, and we were surrounded by tourists. John talked as he wolfed down his spaghetti alla carbonara.

"Lazzari brought us to the obelisk, but he really wanted to take us to the Pantheon. He probably supposed that whoever was following his clues would end up there and make the connection to Kircher's given name. Besides its being quite rare."

"Anyway, this seems like a challenge especially directed at astronomers," I said, munching on my slice of pizza. Juana ate the least. She'd hardly touched a salad and was already savoring her usual gelato.

"What do we know about that sculpture?" John asked.

I picked up the guide, regrettably making an oil stain on the paper.

"That it was sculpted in 1717 by Francesco Moderati. There's nothing more."

"No clue. He's not a very famous artist."

"Not compared to the ones around here, where we're totally surrounded by art."

"And we haven't even been to Florence," Juana sadly reminded us.

"And we didn't even find the clue to the elephant," I remarked, then smiled, adding, "Clever girl," as I affectionately swept the hair away from her eyes.

"What other sculptures and paintings are here in the Pantheon?" she responded.

"Let's see. According to the plan"—I showed her the engraving in the book—"we've got an *Assumption;* the Chapel of Saint Joseph in the Holy Land (or of the Virtuosi); *Saint Agnes; Saint Athanasius*, already mentioned; *Saint Rasius;* the chapel with *The Madonna of Mercy, Saint Anne and the Blessed Virgin; The Coronation of the Virgin;* the Chapel of the Annunciation, and the *Madonna of the Girdle*. That's it as far as religious motifs are concerned. Then," I continued, "the familiar tombs of the kings and of Raphael."

"What else do we know about Saint Athanasius?" John asked.

"It isn't in here, but I can tell you from what I know that he was bishop of Alexandria in the fourth century. He had his ups and downs with Arius, from whom we got the Arian heresy, which denied the divine nature of Christ and of the Trinity, saying there was only God the Father. For his defense of the orthodoxy, he's regarded as a Doctor of the Church," I added.

Juana kept looking at the floor plan of the rotunda of the Pantheon and its assortment of chapels and Madonnas.

"Did you bring the drawings from the *Voynich*?" she asked.

"Of course," John said, taking out a handful of papers from his beat-up backpack. "Which one do you want?"

"The one of the naked women in cans, the same one Hector found drawn by his old prior."

Juana started comparing the diagram John had put on the table and the floor plan of the Pantheon in my guide.

"Do you see what I see?" she asked.

In the old diagram, the figures of the pregnant women were arranged in two circles around a central motif. Here, it was a goat that seemed to represent the astrological sign of Aries.

"The animal can indicate a particular month," Juana started to explain, gesturing excitedly. "For example, this goat may represent the sign of Aries, when the Sun shines from the center in April. But the pregnant women enclosed in those cans are the most curious part."

"Why?" I asked.

"Because they could be Madonnas in the Christian sense. And the cans, niches. And the niches all set around a circle. That's it."

Juana was pointing at the Pantheon.

John and I looked at each other, stunned.

We were silent for a good five minutes, each of us absorbed in our own thoughts. Our interpretation of that diagram, which in times past had looked so incomprehensible, now seemed almost obvious. John was the first to speak.

"Each of the women in the niches is carrying a star, as best I can see."

"That also fits," I said, picking up the tourist guide. "'In each of the ancient cubicles of the cupola there was a bronze star,'" I read, "'set on a blue background, thus representing the firmament or place where the stars stayed firm, immobile in the classical cosmology. They've been lost in the course of time, as also happened during the exterior resurfacing of the cupola, which originally consisted of tiles and polished bronze. This occurred in the sixth century, to make use of the metal,'" I continued reading. "'Bernini in his time extracted bronze from the portico to build his extraordinary canopy in Saint Peter's Basilica.'"

"Speaking of times, how does this fit with the *Manuscript*?" Juana wondered out loud. "And with Lazzari?"

"Well, there we have the first mystery," I answered her. "Practically all the paintings and statues related to the Virgin Mary that are now in the Pantheon were created in the seventeenth and the first half of the eighteenth century. This corresponds very well with Lazzari because, for example, the statue of Saint Athanasius was installed in 1717. In this regard, Lazzari could have made the drawing fit very easily."

"Except that the diagram is much older. Toward the end of the sixteenth century, if the background information on John Dee and Edward Kelley is correct," John said, contributing his sensible English perspective. "Either we suppose that the wizard really could see the future in his crystal ball and know how the paintings and sculptures in the Pantheon were going to be placed a century later, or it's just a simple coincidence. And we see only what we want to see," he concluded.

Juana wasn't giving up.

"There must be a rational explanation," she said.

She raised her eyeglasses up on her hair and pensively rested her chin on the palm of her hand. She really was beautiful.

"And there is. Of course there is," she finally boomed in triumph.

"This girl's neurons have been bubbling over for two days," John teased.

She ignored the remark and explained.

"We do, in fact, see what we want to see. Or what Lazzari wanted us to see. Possibly neither Dee nor Kelley was ever in Rome. So who knows why on earth they thought of painting those caricatures in their time? But," she continued, "surely Lazzari saw the same things we are seeing in the Pantheon. A series of Madonnas in a circle, with the sun shining in from above, and the statue of Saint Athanasius, Kircher's given name. His obelisk brought us here from Bologna."

"I can't see where you're heading, Juana," I interjected when she stopped to take a breath.

"So now we know the *Voynich* is at the center of this whole pilgrimage. And what's most important, Lazzari knew the book in depth. And Kircher did too."

"And also Anselmo Hidalgo, the old Spanish prior, because his drawings coincide with those in the engraving that shows the Pantheon as seen by Lazzari." I nodded, finally able to follow Juana's train of thought.

"Right," practical John admitted. "Now we're sure of what we only suspected before, but where do we look next?"

"In the only unscripted part," Juana said mysteriously.

"Which is?" John and I responded in unison, overwhelmed by her amazing acuity.

"Athanasius, of course," she answered. "He can't be there by accident. The Sun always lights the same area inside the Pantheon in the month of November, so Lazzari couldn't have picked his spot randomly."

"But the statue was put there in 1717," John recalled, a bit frustrated by his inability to keep up with Juana. "Lazzari couldn't have been more than a child then."

"We'd need a crane to make her budge," I added. "They didn't even have low-fat yogurt in those days," I quipped, trying to reduce the tension.

"Someone did it before him. Or could it be that we didn't have enough

Jesuits with influence in Rome at the start of the eighteenth century?" she asked, giving me a look as if I were to blame for everything that had happened in the order for centuries.

I agreed with her. The society had enjoyed a lot of power during that period, and very easily another missing link in the chain of owners of the *Voynich* could have had the statue of the ancient bishop of Alexandria placed there.

"It's clear that the possession of the *Voynich Manuscript*, and possibly even the translation, went from father to father—all Jesuits, of course," I joked. "And it wasn't only Lazzari who hid part or all of the book. It's possible he didn't move anything and was only involved in carrying out the strategy, keeping in mind the difficult role he had to play during the first suppression of the society."

"Should we go back in?" John suggested.

"It's almost an obligation," Juana replied.

So we went back in.

"Juana, what do we need to focus on now?" I asked once we were inside the impressive Roman temple.

"On the *Voynich* diagram, of course," she answered assuredly. "Your friends realized the tremendous likeness of that diagram to the concrete Pantheon, so they decided to use it as a clue after the fact. I imagine it didn't cost them too much trouble or influence to place that statue in the area matching the key date."

Juana finished her analysis as she walked resolutely to the large statue of the saint located in a niche near the main altar. Upon reaching it she sat on the floor (nothing unusual among the tourists, some were even playing cards in that sacred temple) and crossed her legs. She was holding the copy of the diagram that John had brought.

"Fine," she said. "Would you both kindly sit with me for now?"

We sat beside her, forming a strange trio at the base of the statue of a fourth-century saint in the temple of all the gods.

"Aha!" John said after a while. "I've got something. The stars."

"What stars?" I asked.

"Come on, both of you, look at the outer circle of virgins."

There were ten pregnant figures, each holding a star. Nothing more.

"Please, Hector," he asked me. "Count how many female images there are in the Pantheon."

"Very well." I stood up. "I'll give it a go-around," I said, smiling.

The mission took me about ten minutes. I jotted in my notebook various details that I explained on my hurried return, anxious to know what the stars could have to do with all this.

"The distribution of paintings and sculptures agrees with what's written in the guidebook. We got our money's worth," I said, laughing. "Besides the eight Madonnas and saints, we can add a second Saint Agnes, appearing next to Saint Lawrence in a painting in the Chapel of the Annunciation, and another Madonna in a painting in the Chapel of Saint Joseph, where she appears in an *Adoration of the Magi*. In all, ten images of women."

"Exactly. Thanks, Hector," John said. "It was predictable, considering your illustrious predecessors in the society. Well," he went on, "one of them is different."

"I've got it," Juana shouted. "One of them has the star in the other hand."

In fact, nine of the "canned" women, so to speak, held the star in their left hands. Only one held the star in her right hand. I assumed there was a mistake in the drawing.

"Let's count then. Surely the Jesuits noticed this curious fact in the drawing, so we can expect that they've left us more clues."

"Where do you start counting in a circle?" I asked.

"What a bad Jesuit you are. They surely wouldn't have trusted you with the secrets of the *Voynich*." Juana laughed. "Obviously, with the woman indicated by the central symbol. And not to keep it simple, we'll go around clockwise."

"Which woman does the goat point to?" I continued questioning, a bit self-conscious about my obtuseness. My last cup of coffee was over three hours ago.

Showing no mercy, my friends were laughing at me.

"Hector"—Juana sympathized—"Aries is a goat. Don't we have women with a lamb over there?"

"Agnes!" I yelled, hitting my forehead.

Vincenzo Felici had sculpted for the Pantheon a virgin with a lamb, and some time later this sculpture was placed in a niche to the right of the tomb of Umberto I. According to the *Voynich* diagram, we were located five Madonnas away from the objective. We stood up and, when we got there, started walking clockwise. The fifth female image we found was a painting with the Madonna of the Girdle and Saint Nicholas of Bari.

"Definitely, the mistake is here. The count is correct."

Now they were the ones who didn't know what I was talking about. My small intellectual payback.

"Please," Juana pleaded impatiently.

"Very simple. According to Christian tradition, the girdle was a piece of green wool about three feet long, ending with small straps to be tied, that the Virgin Mary gave to Saint Thomas at the moment of her ascent to heaven. This cloth is considered a relic, and there are a few pieces of it here and there," I added.

"So what's the mistake?" John asked, wanting me to finish the story.

"It jumps right out at you. That isn't Saint Thomas in the painting, but Saint Nicholas of Bari. So," I concluded, flaunting my detective skills, "the painter, possibly by assignment, committed a deliberate error."

"And what does our precious guidebook say about the painting?" Juana challenged.

"Oil on canvas with the figures of the Virgin Mary and Saint Nicholas. Painted in 1686 by an unknown artist."

"Not even relevant," John pointed out.

"On the contrary," I replied. "It all seems perfectly planned. The date nearly coincides with Athanasius Kircher's death. That was when the manuscript began to circulate."

"Is anybody looking?" Juana was on her tiptoes, lifting a corner of the painting.

"Are you crazy?" I warned her. "That could be connected to an alarm."

But there wasn't a sound, at least that we could hear inside the Pantheon. And nobody nearby noticed. By then there were only a few tourists in the area.

"Write this down," Juana asked. "*'Mensus eram coelos, nunc terrae metior umbras.'*"

"What are you saying?" John asked, not understanding what Juana was doing.

"It's what is written here, behind the canvas," she answered.

Juana fixed the painting back as it had been. Just at that moment, I noticed a pair of temple guards rapidly approaching. My legs started trembling.

"We are closing for the day."

We left without needing to be asked twice.

Night had fallen and we were packing for our return. The following day I was to be back at the school, and a good many students awaited me with renewed energy after their Christmas vacation. John would return to his classes and research at Cambridge. As for Juana, I had no idea what she'd be returning to. This was our last night together in Italy. We ordered some sandwiches and a thermos of coffee at the restaurant and went directly to the courtesy computers for hotel guests. The two stations were occupied, so we had to wait a few minutes before we could delve into our new clue. John read from his notes.

"*Mensus eram coelos, nunc terrae metior umbras.*"

"'I used to measure the bright stars in the skies, now I measure the shadows of the earth,'" I translated quickly. "It's pretty. Clearly it seems like another clue."

"Yes," Juana agreed. "The Virgin Mary was ascending to heaven in the painting, so maybe we'll have to look for something that can be seen from above. Perhaps a shadow, possibly pointing at something."

"I think you're right," John confirmed. "And surely Lazzari's final statement would also have a double meaning. Let's try to find it."

One of the customers had finished his Internet session. Juana sat down and we stood behind her, watching the screen. Our friend typed the sentence on the Google page. We immediately got thirty-four search results, all identical.

"Mensus eram coelos, nunc terrae metior umbras.
Mens coelistis erat, corporis umbra jacet." Epitaph
by Johannes Kepler himself

"'I used to measure the bright stars in the skies, now I measure the shadows of the earth. Though my mind belonged to the heavens, the shadow of my body lies here,'" I translated. "Johannes Kepler's epitaph, written by himself."

"'Pardon me for not getting up,'" Juana joked, quoting Groucho Marx's famous epitaph.[4]

Just like us, she was totally stunned by the meaning projected on the screen.

---

4. Despite the prevalent popular belief, this line doesn't belong to Groucho Marx but is apocryphal. It isn't written on his tomb. Only his name, the date, and the Star of David appear on the gravestone. (Author's Note)

25

My week away from the school had totally disconnected me from daily chores. The community was seething with troubles, and classes were starting soon. Julian, our new prior, was no stranger to the difficulties involved in his recently acquired post, and he relieved its burdens by taking frequent short breaks. My return seemed to give him an excuse for such a detour when he stopped by my room with a broad smile on his face.

"Welcome back, Hector," he said, giving me an exceptionally big hug. "Tell me about your trip. How was everything in Italy?"

I also had a big smile, and not only from his show of affection, but for his invitation to relive the good times I had shared with my friends. I started with our arrival in Rome, and the experience of seeing the Holy Father in person for the first time. The striking impression of Saint Peter's Square, with the prayers and chants. I also told him about our trip to Bologna and seeing Cassini's meridian, but skipped the details of our discoveries related to Kircher and Lazzari. Finally I described the last day in Rome, back where we began. It was such a large city and offered so much that we preferred to roam its streets instead of a pressured visit to Florence, our one big omission.

"I think I would have done the same. Five days aren't enough to cover Italy," he said, squeezing my arms and not letting go. "I suppose you've got pictures, right? I haven't been able to go back for years."

Of course I had some photos, but still hadn't found time to download them from the camera onto my computer. I told Julian, but it didn't seem to faze him.

"Come on, get to it. Meanwhile I'll make some coffee. That is, if I can handle the strange machine you have here," he said, laughing as he inspected my espresso maker. "It'll give me a breather from the house business. We haven't had a break these past days," he explained.

I had no objection. My only fear was that Julian could mess up my treasured coffeemaker, a gift from my parents on my last birthday. While he took care of pouring the water and filling the coffee compartment, I connected my camera to the main computer on my desk. The files moved quickly from one device to the other, about a hundred high-resolution photos. I reconnected my computer to a larger, nineteen-inch monitor on a side desk. Julian mocked my manipulations.

"Cybercafé Hector—computers and coffee." He laughed while handing me a cup.

"I hope you're aware of how precarious these installations are." I laughed too. "So I humbly request a modest but necessary funding for improvements in the next budget."

"You'll have it, I assure you," he agreed. "As soon as we know where we're going to be and have the means for it."

"Is that definite now?"

"It already was, by late December. The city council hasn't shifted one iota, despite the latest efforts from Madrid. The eviction dates haven't changed. So you can continue preparing to teach computer science to one of the nuns while we're being relocated."

It wasn't a very attractive prospect. From a distance, things always look simpler. But Julian didn't seem overly worried.

"We have to accept whatever the Lord provides," he said, interrupting my thoughts. "Besides, what seems to be assured is a considerable improvement on the initial economic terms. Also, they're guaranteeing to keep the same teaching rooms and number of students, regardless of our new location. We just have to start building the new school as soon as possible, so as not to lose more than one term."

"Putting it that way, it doesn't seem so tragic."

"No, of course not. And now, let's get to those pictures of Rome."

Instead of showing the photos one by one, I chose a slide show. It was much more practical and saved me having to deal with the mouse. Given that John and Juana hardly touched each other during the trip, the most scandalous things that could appear on the screen were the antics of the young tourists. So I pressed Play and sat beside my prior. The first photo was shot from the plane.

"Wow, how the city is growing!" he exclaimed.

One after another, thirty pictures of Rome—including streets, fountains, squares, and churches, besides quite a few more Vatican moments—appeared on the screen. Julian was engrossed and commented on all of them. No corner of Rome was unknown to him. His first criticism, if I could call it that, was of the papal audience.

"Is that all you got to see of the pope?" he complained.

"That's the best I could do with the zoom on my camera," I had to admit. "Should we add to our expenses and buy a new one?"

"We'll see about that. Come on, let's keep going."

New images of Rome, and a few others with my travel mates.

Julian then asked sympathetically, "Your friends—are they sweethearts?"

"They used to be," I answered flatly.

"Too bad. I don't know them much, but they both seem like very sensible people."

I agreed with him but didn't bother trying to explain the situation. The next batch of photos were of Bologna. Julian was a little less familiar with that city.

"The Piazza Maggiore?"

"Uh-huh, the Neptune Fountain. San Petronio is right behind."

"Yes, I remember."

Cassini's meridian appeared in a dozen images. I didn't elaborate on my earlier comments about it, and continued with our second stay in Rome. The obelisk in front of Santa Maria sopra Minerva caught his attention.

"The Porcino della Minerva," he commented, quoting the popular moniker Romans use for the small elephant.

"That's right," I said. "With the obelisk on its back that was deciphered by Athanasius Kircher, one of our most famous Jesuits."

Julian gave me a look, and it seemed to me he was thinking, This guy knows too much, but I didn't sense any hidden intent. I didn't for a moment think of getting into the specifics of what we were trying to find there, and much less so when another dozen photos, showing the Pantheon, came out on the screen. The abundance of details collected didn't seem strange to him.

"The Pantheon is truly unforgettable. Unique. I'm not surprised you found it fascinating. Aren't there any more?" he asked as the screen went dark.

"I don't think so," I said, getting up to turn off the monitor.

Unfortunately I was wrong.

I'd made a big mistake. In my rush, I'd forgotten that I hadn't emptied the camera of the photos taken in the labyrinth beneath the monastery, the day before the trip to Italy. Since I downloaded them together with the others, they were appearing on the screen one by one.

I didn't know what to do. Maybe quickly turn off the computer? Pretend to have a fainting spell? I was stymied.

Julian spoke up.

"The Caracalla? No, looks like the catacombs, maybe."

I kept silent.

His words had an ironic tone. He was looking at me, but with a very different smile. He got up, thanked me for sharing my photos, left his empty cup on the desk, and was on his way out.

"I'll stop bothering you," he said. "You must have a lot of urgent matters to attend to."

"Y-y-yes," I mumbled. "I still have to prepare my classes for tomorrow."

As if I'd be able to concentrate on that.

A persistent rain was battering the classroom windows. The downpour kept my students glued to their seats, without their usual restlessness before the approaching break. Perhaps their passivity was the sheer boredom caused by my lecture, or simply the drowsiness of their first day in class after the long Christmas vacation. There weren't many kids looking at the wall clock, but few were taking lecture notes either. Immune to discouragement, I continued my explanation of orbits, maybe even more anxious than they were for the bell to ring.

"At what speed would we have to throw a rock toward the sky so that it wouldn't come back down?" I asked, my voice louder than usual, trying to wake up the audience.

"How big?" a clueless kid asked, clearly not understanding the equation I'd just finished writing.

"Size doesn't matter," I answered, smiling.

The joke caught their attention and several students laughed. Simon raised his hand, holding a pocket calculator. He was the first to solve the equation.

"About twenty-five thousand miles an hour," he said, very sure of himself.

"Very good, Simon."

I continued with the explanation.

"The answer we got from Simon"—whom they immediately eyed with ill-concealed admiration mixed with ill-concealed envy and scorn—"is the so-called escape velocity, that is, the minimum required speed for an object to escape the gravitational attraction of a celestial body. If you make the calculation now written on the board, you'll see that, for the Earth, this velocity of escape is exactly 25,056 miles per hour. Thus, whether it's a stone or a rocket, any object launched from the surface at that velocity or higher will escape the Earth's attraction."

Questions about outer space seemed to interest them. Newton and Kepler weren't that far from George Lucas, as they saw it, though Lucas wasn't much concerned with the scientific liberties he took for the benefit of his bank account.

"Given that gravitational attraction increases with mass," I continued, "it's more difficult to escape from Jupiter than from Earth. The escape velocity depends not only on the mass of the heavenly body, but also on its radius. So, if Earth's radius were smaller, even though its mass stayed the same, the escape velocity would actually be greater."

"But what if the planet were as small as a ball?" the student preoccupied with the size of things asked.

"In that case, size does matter." I smiled again. "The required escape velocity could be even greater than the speed of light. If we lived on a planet like that, we'd never be able to leave it."

"A black hole?" Simon asked

"Uh-huh. Not even light would be able to escape its gravitational pull. That is a simple way of describing it."

The bell finally rang, and the kids left class at speeds perhaps exceeding escape velocity.

Simon lingered and came to my desk with some wrinkled papers.

"More findings?" I asked, pretending to be surprised.

"It's actually a lot of fun," he said, organizing his notes and a huge pile of Internet printouts.

After dinner, I glanced at the pages Simon had brought me. The youngster was pressuring me because he wanted to go after any new leads I could give him. It pleased me to see at least one of my students so eagerly pursuing scientific inquiries. I didn't want to discourage him, apart from my own involvement in the same immense tangle. And his papers didn't disappoint me.

Simon had followed the story from the moment Johannes Kepler arrived in Prague, the capital of Bohemia, on October 19, 1600. After a few tough months for Kepler—due to his fragile health, along with family problems that too often forced him to leave the city—the German astronomer finally got settled. Quite soon, Tycho introduced him to Emperor Rudolf II, who gave him a cordial reception and encouraged him to collaborate with the Danish astronomer on the new celestial tables. Those, of course, would be completed many years later and passed on to history under the name of this emperor as the Rudolphine Tables. After that interview with the emperor, Kepler saw his life take a radical turn. From impoverished math teacher in a remote Austrian location, he was suddenly transformed into an assistant of the imperial astronomer himself. Fortune, stars included, finally seemed to smile on him.

This state of things didn't last long. A short time after Kepler's meeting with the emperor, Tycho was invited to a banquet by Edward Kelley's former patron, Peter Ursinus Rozmberk, at his palace near the bridge leading to the Prague Castle. Tycho would die a number of days later, supposedly from a urinary obstruction.

There was a new detail in this very familiar story, the appearance of Edward Kelley on the scene. By then, however, the English charlatan and swindler Kelley was already dead. Simon had investigated his life in

Bohemia, which I hadn't checked in such depth. The difference between his research and mine was my concern with Kelley's relation to the *Voynich Manuscript,* while Simon—oblivious of the manuscript—was entirely into the question of Tycho Brahe's possible murder, and focused on Kelley's life in Prague.

The kid's notes coincided with some of my own conclusions. Edward Kelley and John Dee had left England and traveled through Eastern Europe by invitation of a noble Pole, Albrecht Laski. They probably predicted Laski's ascent to the Polish throne, the only thing this credulous count wanted to hear. They accompanied him to Krakow, and from there decided to go on to Bohemia, aware of Emperor Rudolf's fame as a generous Maecenas for the occult. Laski was already ruined. Simon's historical notes identified a Spanish ambassador named Guillén de San Clemente as the go-between for the pair's meeting with Rudolf II in 1583. Nevertheless, that first audience didn't go well. The overly enthusiastic John Dee, possibly also deceived by his medium, prophesied new times of glory for the emperor, starting with his definitive victory over the Turks. To achieve this, Rudolf would only need to mend his sinful ways.[5] This did not please Rudolf. A letter that Dee later wrote to the emperor did not improve things for him. The magician then described his successes with the transformation of metals. Rudolf, an authority in this area, began to suspect the pair and ordered one of his secretaries to investigate. This resulted in an order of expulsion for both men in 1586—encouraged by Pope Sixtus V—under the accusation of practicing black magic. John Dee then left Bohemia, but Edward Kelley stayed in Trebon in the castle of Peter Ursinus Rozmberk, who offered him asylum and also spent large sums financing his secret experiments.

There didn't seem to have been a great relationship between the pair of adventurers and Emperor Rudolf II. When would they likely have sold him the book that would later become the *Voynich Manuscript?* There was no mention of it, except for some vague notes by John Dee's son, written during their flight, referring to a large amount of money obtained by his father from the presumed sale of one of his occult-science books.

Perhaps the book hadn't been sold to Rudolf II.

There was, however, practically no doubt about the topic of conversation

5. It is said that Rudolf II was a bisexual pederast, strongly attracted both to young boys and girls. He never married. (Author's Note)

on the fatal night of October 13, 1601, when Tycho went to dinner at Peter Ursinus Rozmberk's palace.

Simon had underlined a word in red: *alchemy*.

What did Edward Kelley do with Peter Ursinus Rozmberk during the years before the astronomer came to the royal court?

The kid had put together a few pages of information on this. Even before the order of expulsion from Bohemia signed by Rudolf II, the relations between John Dee and Edward Kelley were strained. Dee felt lost without Kelley's magic powers, and Kelley took advantage of this for his own benefit. One bad day, Kelley decided to stop interpreting angelic messages and cabalistic codes, and he told John Dee that he wanted to leave. Fearing abandonment, Dee signed a shameful agreement to share all of his possessions with Kelley, who claimed he did this by direct order from an angel, although nobody knows which one. Kelley was actually poorer than Dee, and lacked a wife as exceptionally beautiful as Jane Fromond, according to the chronicles. This strange pact also included their spouses. Jane Fromond would absolutely have vetoed any such clause, which—combined with the imperial order— forced Dee and his wife to leave Bohemia and return to England, where the wizard was to die, extremely impoverished, in late 1608. With Queen Elizabeth I, his champion, gone, and rejected by her successor, James I, John Dee had to sell his library, book by book, in order to survive.

Edward Kelley's luck wasn't very different, though fortune seemed to favor him during his first years under Rozmberk's protection. He remarried, to a Czech woman who gave him a son, a daughter, and a rich dowry. Rozmberk, for his part, helped him acquire several villas and farms—farmers included, as was customary in those times. Whether he was forgotten or pardoned, God knows, by Rudolf II, the emperor even knighted him and bought him two luxurious mansions right in Prague.

But then the unexpected happened, altering his destiny, just as a similar incident had affected Tycho Brahe's. He fought a duel. The motives aren't clear, but a Bohemian soldier died in the event. Duels were banned, and Rudolf II ordered Kelley's incarceration. There, in jail, the emperor's officers took advantage of the occasion. They knew of the trickster's supposed magic powers, so they tortured him under the pretense of getting him to reveal the so-called *aurum potabile*. They thought that this "golden liquid" could provide them with eternal youth. Obviously they failed. At one point Kelley tried to escape by jumping out a window, but he broke his leg. Freed in order to receive medical treatment, he had to have the fractured, gangrenous leg amputated. Things went from bad to worse. Rudolf ordered Kelley rejailed, this time under pressure from the Catholics, who still considered him a dangerous necromancer. And he attempted to escape again by the same means, with a similar disastrous outcome. Jumping into a carriage driven by his son, he broke his other leg. Facing the panic of being recaptured and having to spend the rest of his days as an invalid in prison, Kelley committed suicide, ingesting a poison he had prepared himself. Rudolf II then issued the order to have all of Kelley's possessions confiscated. This was the moment, I thought, when the manuscript could have come into the emperor's possession. There was a second possibility, even compatible with the first, in which it could have been acquired on behalf of Rozmberk, if the book had stayed in the hands of someone who theoretically claimed to understand it.

This happened four years before Kepler's arrival in Prague.

That was nearly all I found of interest in the information Simon had compiled. It certainly held its own as an entertaining collection of stories with an element of fantasy. And very well documented. As afternoon classes ended, I thanked him for all his effort and encouraged him to continue his investigation of Kepler's track in the court of Rudolf II. The possible connections of an innocuous Rozmberk, first to Kelley and later to Tycho Brahe, looked in principle like another good trail. They all had an excessive interest in alchemy. Privately I suspected that the *Voynich Manuscript* had appeared in Prague—rather than in Rudolf II's court—among the opulent possessions of nobleman Peter Ursinus Rozmberk, who was much more solvent economically than the emperor himself. That John Dee and Edward Kelley were the authors of the document now seemed almost beyond doubt, and the one who paid for it was perhaps Rozmberk, though the meaning of the book continued to be a mystery for everybody alive.

Back in my room, I lay back on the bed, exhausted. The trip to Italy had been nonstop, and my return to classes had begun too quickly. There was an overload of pending matters to be resolved, papers to read, information to research. And I felt a terrible drowsiness, just like my students, because the reentry into the classroom had hit me hard. So I gathered all my remaining energy and got up. The coffeemaker wasn't so far away. Two steps.

While dumping the grounds in the wastebasket, I noticed the coffee was looser than usual, and remembered that Julian had used the device last. I'm used to a heavier dose of caffeine. I also regretfully recalled the end of my meeting with the prior. Now with a steaming cup of coffee in hand, I went back to my computer.

The last photo was still on the screen when the monitor came on. There, immortalized in a digital moment of three million pixels, was my own photo of the insurmountable Planck wall. The flash on the camera gave it an even more impenetrable appearance than it really had, reflecting all the light that dared touch it. A brilliant and, in a sense, defiant wall. Enlarging the image and working on it in Photoshop, I played with the contrast and the contours, changing its colors, without any particular objective. It occurred to me that perhaps one could discern some unexpected opening, an entrance or an escape from the ordinary.

There was something. And it wasn't lacking in its own elegance.

It seemed that John had amused himself during our excursion by scratching into the wall with his pocketknife the words JOHN, GREENWICH. I don't know when he did it, but he earned a small booing for damaging our national as well as our Jesuit heritage. What a hooligan, I thought, laughing to myself.

The coffee totally woke me up and I completely forgot about a refreshing nap. There were too many questions to ponder for me to flop back in bed, staring at the ceiling. I decided to get up again and read. Till now I hadn't tried to translate the article by Professor Volker Bialas that John found for me. Reading German gave me a big headache, but getting really involved in an examination of the Gilders' book, by perhaps the greatest living authority on Johannes Kepler, piqued my interest.

It was only four pages. And the title already provided a hint—rather an ironic comment—concerning its content: *Das Gift der Publicity* (literally, The Poison of Publicity). The word *Gift* has a very different meaning in German than English. It means "poison." From his first line, Bialas plays with this double meaning. The poison would be what Kepler, presumably, forced Tycho, his master, to ingest. A poisoned gift. The book, obviously, was also that for its readers. And that was the premise Volker Bialas developed.

> The book is described on its flap as one of the greatest discoveries in the history of science. But it is nothing but a sensational opus, written with the sole intent of making money. Targeted by an expensive advertising campaign in the German-speaking countries—Germany proper and Austria—the public was inundated by various local and national publications. *Profil* of May 3, 2004, headlined "To Glory by Murder Robbery." In a similar manner, the May 18 issue of *Süddeutsche Zeitung* also played with words: "Mercury: The Messenger of Death in a Glass of Milk," alluding to Mercury, the original messenger of the gods in ancient mythology. Worse was the one published in *Oberösterreichische Nachrichten*, which asked for a university in Linz to change its name, which up to then had honored the memory of its most illustrious neighbor, Johannes Kepler.

The comments were truly interesting. But my German left a lot to be desired. I regretted not being able to investigate further in this language on the Internet, where I surely could have found additional opinions concerning the book and its content. Armed with patience, I started my labored translation of the second page.

> In regard to the book's content, the Gilders build two lines of inquiry. The first based on techniques of forensic medicine. And the second in reference to Kepler's biography, as Emperor Rudolf II's mathematician, and his path toward guilt, which—for the authors—seemed to be proven.

That's actually how it was. I had drawn the same conclusions from reading the book. For Professor Bialas, the biographical line had the greater importance. In this, a terrifying image of Kepler was drawn, that of a hot-tempered, violent, and totally unscrupulous man. The Gilders held back nothing, whether in compounding discredit or heaping on questionable statements:

> Without Tycho Brahe, Kepler would have been a mere footnote
> in the history books . . . Kepler lived embittered on the margins
> of society . . . the *Mysterium Cosmographicum* was a scientific
> dead end, Kepler's fascinating but poorly developed vision of the
> universe . . . Kepler was a double-dealer, making equally flattering
> concessions to Calvinists and to Catholics . . . [A]fter Tycho's
> death, Kepler was named imperial mathematician, one of the
> highest positions of honor and glory in Europe, which meant so
> much to him.

The Gilders, rather than depict a scientist, caricatured a villain. One of the most respected figures in the intellectual history of Europe was converted in their writings to a delinquent. And to an American audience—a person on the margins; a conceited weirdo; an insolent, cruel, ambitious opportunist. A criminal.

In his modest article, Volker Bialas went on to pick apart and destroy the arguments presented by the Gilders in their famous and well-financed publication. Some of the claims seemed so transparent as to make it hard to believe that readers would have accepted them. Why would Kepler have needed to kill his master, the one who'd introduced him to the emperor, obtained a lifelong post for him, shared data from his own astronomical observations, and even lent him money? The German Bialas was surprised that Kepler, a man of low social background who, thanks to his enthusiasm and hard work, gained honor and fame, could then be vilified for pursuing the American Dream.

The second part of the article gave an account of the medical and forensic aspects of Tycho Brahe's death. Of tests (with some mustache hairs exhumed from the cadaver of the Danish astronomer) made four centuries later. The high concentration of mercury found in these analyses would reveal that Tycho's death was not caused by a urinary infection or a malfunction of the liver or kidneys, but by heavy-metal poisoning, specifically by mercury. Or not. Is it possible to determine, as the Gilders claimed, precisely when the poisoning began—to an accuracy within hours—from a hair sample four hundred years old?

Like Simon, Volker Bialas had explored the matter. Tycho spent thirty years working on alchemic experiments, which he had already started by 1571, under the guidance of his uncle Steen Bille. Uraniborg was equipped with a well-stocked laboratory for, among other things, developing medicines to fight epidemics. In short, Brahe had been working with mercury for decades.

But there was another detail worthy of Dr. House[6] and which surely would surprise my inquisitive student Simon. The story of Tycho Brahe's youthful duel in 1566 was well known. He lost his nose from a precise slash by his opponent.

After that, until his death thirty-five years later, Tycho always used a prosthesis, made from an alloy of gold, silver, and possibly copper. The prosthesis needed to be attached after the wound was cleaned daily with a special product. The principal component of this type of emulsion for cleaning wounds, now generally called a disinfectant, was mercury.

Bialas suggested (and later I was astonished to verify this on the Internet) that the daily use of a certain mercury-based medication throughout most of his life could be the most logical explanation for the abnormally high levels of this metal found in the remains of Tycho Brahe's mustache.

As House would have wisely deduced from these clues, Tycho Brahe was an eccentric astronomer with a compulsion to dab his nose with Mercurochrome.[7] Day by day his mustache, the small patch of hair beneath the nose—and thus the drain for anything coming from it—and the more extensive beard below, were accumulating industrial quantities of mercury.

He could have died of almost any cause, even a bladder infection after a drunken spree. And the simplest explanation is usually the best.

---

6. *House* is a very popular American television series in which an eccentric doctor, played by the distinguished British actor Hugh Laurie, actually applies Sherlock Holmes's methods to determine the cause of his patients' ailments. (Author's Note)

7. Mercurochrome, a topical antiseptic generally known as merbromin, along with Merthiolate, was declared unsafe by the FDA in 1998. Both substances are readily available in other countries. By 2002, mercury fever thermometers were also recommended to be phased out in favor of the digital electronic type. Mercury accumulations in fish as well as the use of mercury amalgam fillings in dentistry have been discouraged as well. (Author's Note)

26

Dear Thomas,

The return trip was pretty tiring, with a lot of stops. I've got terrible jet lag, I can hardly sleep, and I'm doing everything wrong. But I'm home with my father. He seems to get older every day. The nurse who takes care of him asked me to find a job for her sister and brother-in-law in the United States. They're a wonderful family with four children, really close and loving, very hard workers and believers. I'll send you their address so you can help them.

The stay in Rome ended with a surprise. The whole scheme of the Jesuits revolves around Kepler, as we thought. They've been passing the book along from one to the other, leaving clues as to its whereabouts and its meaning. It seems that, at a certain point, perhaps due to bad blood between the scholars Riccioli and Kircher, they separated the codes. Or perhaps this was as a precaution. Who knows what was going through their heads? It couldn't have been at all easy for Wilfred Voynich to gain possession of what he thought was the main manuscript. His strategy probably involved lots of money and a good friendship with them.

I still haven't managed to find out how old Anselmo Hidalgo fits into this. Hector tells me his belongings are stored at the house. Also that he drew or copied engravings from the *Voynich,* and that several generations of Jesuits used them to protect the papers in Rome. Thanks to these small leads, we found the latest clue, Johannes Kepler's lapidary inscription on the back of a painting in the Pantheon. We still don't know what it means, but suspect that it's one step closer to the secondary code, the one that will reveal the meaning of the concealed passages of the Yale manuscript. If Hidalgo hid it in Spain, we'll know as soon as we're able to move around freely with the new machinery in those labyrinths. Wilfred Voynich mentions the Spanish priest as well as Petrus Beckx in his first will. It's fortunate that we're the only ones aware of the existence of this document, a legacy to my grandfather from Voynich's widow. God always does things for a reason, leaving nothing to chance.

Now we've almost gotten it. We only have to learn more about Kepler, even though he doesn't seem like a cold-blooded murderer to me, the way he does to George Gilder's cousins.

Lots of kisses,

Juana

"I've got terrible jet lag, I can hardly sleep, and I'm doing everything wrong." Under normal conditions, well rested after a good night's sleep, she would never have sent me an e-mail intended for somebody else. And that, for good or ill, ended up revealing a lot, almost as much as the identity of the actual addressee. I checked the heading on the e-mail. Juana and her correspondent seemed to share the same domain, one belonging to the Discovery Institute. His full name, Thomas van der Gil, stood out clearly. I didn't know Juana's reason for toying with John and me, her motive for the deception, or her ultimate goal. Her friend Thomas—clearly behind the real estate speculation plaguing us these past months—was more transparent. A treasure hunt lacking the required map, which wound up digging tunnels in any likely spot. Like a mayor obsessed with the subway lines and an upcoming election.

What about this George Gilder?

I combed the Internet. Nearly all of the articles I found placed him in the extreme right wing of the American political spectrum. He was a heavy hitter among the touted neocons backing the Republican Party. Writer, philosopher, and guru concerning almost anything related to new technology and communications. Cofounder and distinguished member of the Discovery Institute, which coined the phrase "Intelligent Design."

I was stunned. This was a frequent subject in the newspapers, a lot more topical than the alleged murder of Tycho Brahe by Johannes Kepler. The teaching of creationism, or this more palatable version of it, was now a source of fierce debate in the American educational system. I remembered discussing this with Simon when we were sifting through the exotic connections of John Dee, Edward Kelley, Enoch, and the philosopher's stone.

I kept looking for information about George Gilder. According to *Wikipedia* (he actually had his own entry), he was born in New York in 1939. Attended Harvard, where he had an illustrious professor, Henry Kissinger. There he founded various reviews devoted to political opinion. After his graduation in the sixties, he worked as a speechwriter for a number of notable figures and politicians, such as Nelson Rockefeller and Richard Nixon. In the seventies and eighties, as an independent author, he published some very popular books. In these he came off as a racist, sexist provocateur to some, or a financial wizard and high-tech visionary to others. It was in the Republican administration of Ronald Reagan that he reached the acme of his political clout. In the nineties he became the man whose words everybody wanted to hear. This was the wild time of overnight fortunes during the dot-com bubble. But in 2000 the bubble burst, dashing entrepreneurs' private and public fortunes, with shares in many cases losing 90 percent of their value.

Recently he seemed to have partially recovered his influence, dividing his time between the proselytizing activities of the Discovery Institute and his fierce criticism of certain familiar American entrepreneurs, especially Bill Gates.

Although this was all overwhelming, I smiled, impressed by the importance of Juana's friends. Rubbing shoulders with close associates of some of the latest American presidents, including Reagan and the Bushes, no less.

What they were looking for had to be pretty important.

We had a quiet dinner at the house that night.

Exhausted after so many weeks of administrative battles, our community seemed generally satisfied with the latest city council offer. Julian spoke about it optimistically and with a certain personal satisfaction. We saw clearly that we were no match for the powers opposing us. Though I now knew a bit more than the rest, it seemed prudent not to reveal it publicly. Perhaps someone in high places (on Earth, not in heaven) could be behind the operation. My community would think I'd gone nuts.

There was almost no get-together during the after-dinner coffee, and people soon retreated to their rooms. Given the opportunity, I decided to take another stroll through the underground.

I always found something new.

"Who's there?"

I shined the flashlight toward the sound of footsteps.

I was at the wall, looking closely at the scratched-out writing that I thought John had left there. The marks on the stones weren't recent, which totally confounded me. Then the footsteps grew very close.

"Come out," I demanded.

Julian stepped into the range of the flashlight beam. I wasn't surprised; he was the only real possibility.

"You?" I said in feigned bewilderment.

"Who else?" he answered calmly.

"I thought so. Why did you lock me in the other night?" I asked, recalling the fateful day of Carmelo's death.

"I was as scared as you." He smiled and sat down next to me. "I thought I was the only one who knew about the existence of the underground."

"Carmelo lent me a key a few days before he died. He himself brought me here the first time."

"I see," Julian said, clicking his tongue. This revelation of a confidence between his predecessor and me seemed to bother him. "What else did he tell you?"

I thought carefully before answering, unsure of which side he was on, or even whether he and Carmelo had held similar positions regarding the sale. But he was my superior.

"Carmelo wanted me to take some pictures down here, in case they might be of use in pressuring the real estate company," I said frankly, taking a chance.

"I guess they're what we saw together on your computer."

"You guessed right. I wasn't very discreet," I said, forcing a smile.

"Is there more?" he asked. "Did he give you anything he found down here?"

I paused again, but decided to go on, fed up with all the mysteries, and truly thinking Julian might be able to help me.

"He also spoke to me about Anselmo Hidalgo," I admitted.

"Our prior at the beginning of the century, the one in charge of building the school as we know it. I suppose there are things about him that I don't know," he remarked, seeking more information.

"No more and no less than I," I said ambiguously. "I was studying his old writings and papers until Carmelo himself took away the box that contained his records. I don't have any idea why he did this after urging me to look at them."

"I took the box," he confessed. "I didn't see anything of interest in it. Then I moved it to his room after he died, for you to find it. Fortunately you didn't suspect anything," he added with relief.

"Why did you take it?" I asked, raising my voice, which reverberated strongly inside the walls of the underground.

"Out of curiosity. I wanted to understand the original structure of the school a bit better, to compare the deeds and official records, to read the founding documents. Then I found the map of this place."

He seemed to be telling the truth.

"It wasn't hard to find an entry," he continued. "More difficult to find an exit," he said, looking all around. "Apart from going back, of course."

"Why didn't you just ask him about it?" I insisted, wanting to know, unable to forget Hidalgo's box and its contents.

"I did, but he didn't want to tell me." Again I sensed his discomfort in confirming that the old prior had first confided in me, and not him, his right-hand man for so many years. "I didn't press him. He was very sick, and obsessed with staying on in this place."

"Sick?"

"Yes. He asked me not to tell anyone. An incurable heart condition without a transplant, which wasn't recommended at his age," he said, lowering his voice. "Any more questions, Hector?"

"One more." I decided to risk it. "What do you know about a sixteenth-century book called the *Voynich Manuscript*?"

"Nothing," he said without the slightest hesitation. "Is it ours?"

I couldn't tell if he was pretending or deliberately covering up.

"No. But it could have been. It has nothing really important. Juana and John have an interest in it, and think that we Jesuits are behind its strange history, full of ups and downs," I said, withholding much of the truth.

"If I can help you," he said, getting up from the rock he'd been sitting on, "be sure to ask. I'm going back upstairs now. It's too humid down here, and I can feel it in my joints."

"I'm staying on for a bit, if you don't mind," I responded. "We don't have much longer to find out how the first Jesuits lived here."

"You're right," he said.

"And this time, please don't lock the door."

"I won't," he said, smiling as he tousled what little hair was left on my head.

My latest exploration through the underground labyrinth of the house didn't yield any new clues concerning the possible whereabouts of the *Manuscript*, or about a past hiding place. As for the scratched inscription on the wall, John himself had anticipated my conclusion in an e-mail, when he told me in all seriousness that he hadn't written anything on that big wall. The message had just reached my in-box, so I tried to communicate directly through IM. And John was still logged on.

"Hello, Englishman," I typed in a joking tone.

"Hi, Father," John answered in kind.

"Not guilty," I sent.

"Has to be a different John and a different Greenwich," he wrote back.

"Could be. But on seeing those words, I immediately associated them with you."

"The solution is simple, Hector. John Dee was born, lived, and studied, in London. He must have made observations from the hills of Greenwich. Don't forget, he was an astronomer."

"In that case we have repeated clues. Redundant. If it was Lazzari again who put those words there, they refer to the *Voynich* and to the English wizard as the author. This doesn't disclose anything new."

"Doesn't seem so. Have you heard anything from Juana?" he asked, changing the subject. "She still won't write to me. She doesn't answer my messages."

"You'd be better off forgetting about her once and for all. I think she's double-dealing and sometimes gets her cards—oops, letters—mixed up," I said sarcastically, playing with words.

I summarized for John the strange letter that had landed in my in-box. John wanted to know more about the Gilders, since he was the only one of us three who hadn't read the libelous condemnation of Johannes Kepler. But he knew about the activities of the Discovery Institute since it proselytizes all over the United States, at Cambridge, and at other U.K. universities.

"The same way they question the theory of evolution, they're also starting to question the Big Bang. That's exactly what they're doing, incredible as it sounds. They sleep with a Bible under the pillow and pull it out for the attack whenever you're not looking. They've launched their latest program right inside NASA. The current American administration adapts its scientific policy to its industrial and religious interests. From global warming to stem cells, passing over Charles Darwin—British, of course—and his old theory of evolution. We astronomers had it easy compared to the paleontologists and biologists. But now, Intelligent Design has been brought into the heart of all research. A fellow named Deutsch was appointed by the White House and later thrown out when it was discovered he lied on his résumé. As a NASA public relations representative, and Web site designer for the space agency, he was required to insert the word *theory* after each mention of the Big Bang."

"Interesting, and very telling," I commented.

"Naturally the Big Bang is a scientific theory, but the annotation served other purposes. For this individual, who professed all the tenets of the Discovery Institute, the Big Bang was not a fact, but an opinion, and one couldn't make an assertion like that concerning the existence of a universe that rejected the Intelligent Design of a Creator."

"*Whew.* Tough to swallow, even for a believer like me."

"You Jesuits are different. You've always been in the vanguard."

"Don't you believe it."

"Don't be modest. I've heard that in the Vatican a large group of Jesuit biologists and scientists are the only ones who openly defend evolution."

"There's some truth to that."

"Forgive me, Hector, I've got a doctoral student calling me. We can talk later."

"'Bye."

"Cheerio."

The next morning I returned to my classes as usual. Teaching science, especially for a priest, was becoming in many people's eyes a daring feat. But the only risk I could see in my daily duties was to die of boredom.

"And given, as we know, that the Earth is round—"

I scanned my students. No startled looks. Noticeable progress. I went on.

"—to locate a point on its surface, we refer to its coordinates. We use two. Latitude is what we call the angular distance between our point and the equator. Longitude, likewise, is our angular distance from the prime meridian, or zero degrees. In this way," I added, "we can determine for sure the position of any place on Earth."

"What is a meridian?" someone asked from the back of the class.

"An imaginary circle on the globe that passes through both the North and South Poles. So the points located on a meridian all have the same longitude," I said, drawing a diagram on the board. "The distance from the North Pole to the equator was also first used to define the meter, the unit of longitude, which was established as one ten-millionth part of that distance."

A couple of kids yawned. I wasn't discouraged. Another was raising his hand.

"How many meridians are there?"

"As many as you want," I answered. "But for practical purposes, and since the Earth rotates once on its axis every twenty-four hours, the orange got divided into twenty-four segments. Which are also what we call time zones. So"—I calculated for everybody—"each one of these lines is separated from its neighbors by one hour on the clock, or fifteen degrees, and the whole sphere, three hundred and sixty degrees, amounts to twenty-four hours."

"So where do we start counting?" the same student asked—who for once wasn't Simon. Hearing this reminded me of my own objection inside the Roman Pantheon, which finally led us to the latest, still pending, clue on Kepler.

"From London," I answered. "There's a historical reason."

The bell rang. Amid the mob uproar of kids struggling to get out, I managed to shout a request.

"Any volunteers to get the story of the zero meridian?"

But by the time I finished asking, the only one still in class was Simon. As usual, he couldn't resist the challenge.

27

The meridian at Greenwich serves as the starting point. Longitudes are measured in degrees from there. The Greenwich Observatory corresponds to zero longitude, also called the zero meridian, or prime meridian.'"

Simon was starting to read his notes up on the lectern. They agreed with mine. Like me, he had gone to the Internet and its free encyclopedia, *Wikipedia*.

"'This zero meridian was adopted as a reference at an international conference in Washington in 1884, attended by delegates from twenty-five countries," he continued. "'They signed several accords at this conference. The most important one was to have a single meridian as the reference point for all countries, and to make it the one passing through Greenwich. Santo Domingo, now the Dominican Republic, voted against this, and Brazil and France abstained.'"

"For political reasons," I pointed out, giving him a pat on the shoulder and sending him back to his desk, to keep his classmates from starting to taunt him. I continued with the relevant explanations. "Actually, though it might seem surprising, France wanted to use a Spanish island. Any ideas about which one?"

No one had any suggestions. So I told them about El Hierro, the smallest of the Canary Islands, and also the land farthest to the west in ancient times.

Because of this, it is also called the Meridian Island. In the second century, the astronomer and mapmaker Ptolemy used this as the starting point of the coordinates. There was nothing beyond it. In the seventeenth century, the French adopted the same point, with the corollary that this island was located almost exactly twenty degrees from Paris, a very happy coincidence. But London won the battle—or Greenwich, which is in the same area—since by that time two-thirds of sea traffic already used the English reference point. And that was because of the Royal Greenwich Observatory, founded in 1675 by the king of England, Charles II. The observations made there served not only to correct and refine Kepler's tables of stellar movements—not easy, given his already great precision—but also to determine location with the long-sought longitude, thus improving the art of navigation.

I was aware of this issue from my *Voynich Manuscript* research. The attempt to determine longitude concerned John Dee through his mapmaking activity with Mercator; Cassini, who found a system based on his observations of the Galilean satellites of Jupiter; and the Jesuit Athanasius Kircher, with his now-familiar magnetic declination. The problem was crucially important for worldwide shippers that centered their economy and commerce on navigation, like the British Empire. Sir Cloudesley Shovell, admiral of the British Navy, established a longitude prize in 1714 for whoever could develop a practical method to determine longitude at sea. Ten thousand pounds for an accuracy of less than one degree. The winner was a clockmaker named John Harrison, who much later, in 1773, wound up receiving a £20,000 prize from King George III. By 1761, Harrison's accurate clocks had already managed to reduce the error in determining longitude to less than a half degree.

The dates matched.

"Hector, are you all right?"

One of the kids was pulling on my sleeve.

I shook my head and said I was fine, but I ended the class, saying that I had to take care of something important.

And that was true. I went to my room in a hurry, and sat at the keyboard as if possessed, to tell my British working partner what I'd just discovered.

John Harrison. Royal Greenwich Observatory.

The clues were racing through my head. The puzzle was making sense. The pieces seemed to be organizing and regrouping themselves on their own, and I simply had to fit them together. One reconstructs a puzzle like a giant looking down on it, searching for the best perspective to locate the line of the horizon, where the surface of the sea ends and the sky begins.

The concern with longitude ran parallel to the *Voynich Manuscript*. It was the lifelong obsession of Athanasius Kircher, the man who knew nearly everything. Had he deciphered the manuscript? I kept searching through pages and pages, both digital and printed, trying to connect more pieces. His biography is so extensive, and his writings are so abundant, that one can always find new facts. I liked the ones appearing on the screen that afternoon.

In 1633, Emperor Ferdinand II of the Holy Roman Empire, aware of the great German scholar's capabilities, first offered Athanasius Kircher a position as professor of mathematics in Vienna, and later to fill the post of imperial mathematician, vacant for three years after Johannes Kepler's death. Kircher accepted the post, but en route to the court he received a counterorder from Cardinal Barberini, who summoned him to Rome. As a good Jesuit, Kircher submitted dutifully, and finally wound up in Rome, where he would conduct most of his research until his death.

Kircher was the successor to Kepler, who in turn was the successor to Tycho. One could almost see Kircher as a grandson to the Danish sage. Kircher had many accomplishments. A great many.

Before Athanasius Kircher, no one had managed to decipher Egyptian hieroglyphics. Nobody could make sense of them. Kircher studied them avidly, devoting most of his life to their interpretation. He had managed to determine, as he put it, that the ancient Egyptian language had actually been spoken by Adam, that Moses was in fact the legendary Egyptian occultist Hermes Trimegistus, and that hieroglyphics could be translated by means of a mysterious symbology unrelated to semantics.

Again the language of Adam and of Enoch. And again the legendary, fantastic figure of Hermes Trimegistus. So mysterious and unfathomable that even the term *hermetic* derives from his name. Hermes Trimegistus was probably an Egyptian philosopher and one of the fathers of alchemy. Now it is known that the works attributed to him were written several centuries after his supposed life, but his figure lives on for those who believe in his writings, though he might never really have existed.

It still seemed odd that Hermes Trimegistus was considered the messenger of the gods among the occult philosophers of Greece, Rome, and Egypt. This was due to his association with the first language spoken by human beings. Because of this, in alchemic terms and with a perfect correspondence to mythology, Hermes Trimegistus was the incarnation of the god Mercury. I kept probing the figure of this incomparable personage until I hit on the objective of my search.

Hermetism is a collection of philosophical writings, magic, astrology, and alchemy devoted to the god Hermes Trimegistus, a Hellenistic synthesis of the Greek Hermes and the Egyptian Thoth. Hermes, born in Arcadia, is Mercury, son of Zeus, messenger or herald of the gods, displaying a caduceus or staff of gold, a *petaso* or hat, and wings on his feet. An eloquent, astute god, inventor of the word and of languages, and also easily identifiable with the god Thoth, scribe of the gods and participant in the judgment of the dead. Very early, around the fourth century before Christ, he was transformed into "Trimegistus" by the translation of "big-big" (title applied to Thoth), changed by the Greeks into *"mégistos kaì mégistos kaì mégistos"* (the three times greatest).

Now I thought I understood why.

"Hector, I don't understand a bloody word."

"It's not easy to explain, John," I answered in the chat session. "Maybe it's my fault. I'm afraid I'm not a good teacher."

"I don't know what to tell you."

"I think that's why some people are looking for a second manuscript. It all fits."

"What does Juana have to do with this?"

"A lot, I'm afraid. Possibly she got on the Voynich List to gain information. She's an expert in mathematical ciphering. You know it as well as I do."

"She fell in love with me."

"That was an accident."

"And I with her."

"That was a British indiscretion."

"I think I still am."

"You're a bloody fool."

"Stop torturing me," he pleaded. "How did all of this come to you?"

"Through Voynich's last will. I suppose he probably explained the transfer of the *Manuscript* there, a secret that the Society of Jesus obliged the old bookseller to keep as part of the sale contract."

"I'll take care of looking for information on that. Voynich lived in London for many years."

"Great."

"Anything else? Do we know any more about John Harrison?"

"*Whew!*" I snorted over the keyboard. "No, I haven't had time."

"What about Lazzari?"

"Neither."

"Hidalgo?"

"I keep hoping I'll get to him, along with his predecessors."

"Kepler?"

"He's my favorite. As soon as I can, I'll keep looking into his life."

"Good. I'll try to pay you a visit within two weeks," he added.

"'Bye, John."

"Cheerio, Hector."

The one excluded for the moment from the recent outpouring of information was Juana. We hadn't talked about John Harrison and the problem of longitude in relation to the *Voynich,* about Hermes Trimegistus, or about Athanasius Kircher's theories either. Despite the fact that Juana pretended unconcern, even good humor, my reading of the intercepted letter that she addressed to the mysterious Thomas van der Gil led me to choose discretion. Not everybody, of course, did the same.

Hi, Hector, my favorite Jesuit,

Life here in Mexico is boring. I miss both of you, especially you. Researching at home can't compare with actually being there. My mind opens up much better when we're together. In spite of this, don't think I'm not working. I am, a lot.

I've returned to the cryptographic programs, but without any great results. It looks like the engraving of the calendar was the end of it all. I reproduced the mechanism of this diagram and then applied it to the Voynichian words that accompany the drawings of the virgins in cans. I even have some more heavy-paper revolving disks. But I can't make head or tail from turning them. It seems likely that this drawing has no more life of its own than the Jesuits wanted to give it two centuries later. It's probably part of the camouflage surrounding the few actual messages the Voynich contains.

I did find quite a bit more related to Johannes Kepler's epitaph. I started looking after John alerted me to the Athanasius Kircher and the Hermes Trimegistus clues. I think it would be good for the three of us to chat and exchange views.

Is tomorrow at five in the afternoon, your time, good for you? It's fine for John.

A big, spicy kiss to make you blush.

I love you like a brother,

Juana

It's definitely John—and not Juana—that I've really got to watch my words with, I thought, a bit exasperated. Even though I didn't think it was totally bad for her to continue working with us on the investigations. Once I knew—or thought I knew—about her other friends' intentions, I didn't see a major risk. The deciding factor was the possible attempt to translate the *Voynich*. I was still convinced we were very far from this, so even the collaboration of an eccentric, ultraconservative American millionaire could be allowed. The future of my house was also at the center of my problem, but from the latest conversations with Julian, I could only conclude that, in the end, we'd be getting a good economic settlement from the sale of the building. So I had to resign myself to the idea that—for the common purpose of deciphering the most complicated hieroglyphic in history—practically any travel mate, no matter how strange or self-interested, would be welcome.

Nevertheless, I was wary of Juana.

The translation of the *Voynich Manuscript* hadn't made any significant advances since the day we found the causal connection on one page between the astronomical drawing—that we had correctly identified as a supernova—and the names of the months of the year. Fortune had smiled on our supposition that the characters in concentric circles around the drawing could be turned like a combination dial on a safe. They were actually prefixes, syllables, and suffixes combined in a similar constructive manner to the suggestions made by several investigators on the Voynich List. After these surprising discoveries, the three of us—Juana, John, and I—had worked separately.

Our main conclusion as to the validity of the model was that some of the historical clues, mere conjectures till then, had proved to be correct. The date of the supernova discovered by and credited to the Danish astronomer Tycho Brahe placed the combinations of characters in their appropriate positions. Given that John Dee left writings about this stellar explosion—which Tycho himself had checked—the English wizard seemed in our eyes the probable author of the *Manuscript*. This fact was already a notable advance with respect to the translation. The duo formed by John Dee and Edward Kelley would constitute the authorship of the book, which wound up, at one time or another, in the court of Holy Roman Emperor Rudolf II.

What was the real content of the book? The interests and passions of the two charlatans pointed to a connection with the world of alchemy. Maybe in the book's concern with healing—the engravings of plants suggested that possibility—or in its most famous objective, none other than the search for the philosopher's stone. But beyond content, the enticing—and most important—aspect was the container. What was the language of this writing, and where could the keys to translating it be found? This opened a line of inquiry that still hadn't closed. Supposing that years later the Jesuits had obtained a correct translation of the book, someone must have done the work with their support.

What we were calling the Jesuit trail had proved to be fruitful. In one respect, a succession of personalities related to the society had made references—more or less directly—to the existence of the book. The first one was obviously Athanasius Kircher, who received the book—via a friend and physician in Prague, Marcus Marci—sent from Bohemia to Rome. Perhaps Kircher might also have received the translation with the book. Through him, other scholars of his time learned of it in greater or lesser degree, such as his rival and no less intelligent Jesuit brother Giovanni Battista Riccioli, with his apprentice and protégé, the famous astronomer Giovanni Cassini. A succession of Jesuits had discreetly protected the mysterious manuscript until it reached Lazzari. The Jesuits' head librarian faced the difficult challenge of guarding their most valuable volumes against the imminent suppression of the society. He dispersed their books, hiding some and dividing others. The *Voynich Manuscript*, due to its great value, possibly was subjected to both methods. The division perhaps separated the encrypted text from the keys to finding its possible messages. With only the first part—except in very simple, clear-cut cases, and by this I mean, for example, the supernova diagram with its intricate elaborations—translation was impossible.

Of the *Voynich* texts, only the coded portion had come to light, and this occurred near the beginning of the twentieth century. The book as we know it, and the way it is preserved at Yale University, was bought by a bookseller named Wilfred Voynich. The sale took place in Rome in one of our crumbling houses mired in debt. The second part of the book, the collection of codes that Athanasius Kircher probably knew, is in an unknown location. Perhaps, as some believe, Lazzari brought it to Spain. And possibly, as a few seem to think, it may still be within these walls.

Who could have translated the *Voynich Manuscript*?

Here I could no longer rely on facts, but only on suppositions. John Dee fled back to England, leaving Edward Kelley alone in Bohemia with the book. Kelley worked on alchemic questions with Peter Ursinus Rozmberk, the one who a few years later hosted Tycho Brahe on the fateful, drunken night that would lead him to his grave. Brahe shared with his brilliant assistant Johannes Kepler all of his astronomical observations on the orbit of Mars, compiled over thirty years, in an effort to untangle its peculiar movement. An authentic treasure. Couldn't he also have attempted to translate our mysterious book with Kepler, aware that it contained, or was said to contain, some of the keys and secrets of alchemy? It seems logical. If we add to this that the *Voynich Manuscript* landed in the hands of the Jesuits a few years later, and that Kepler had many friends among them—so many that he was accused and admonished by his own people for these friendships that bordered on religious treason—it is possible to think that the book passed through his hands.

If there was anyone with the creativity, intelligence, and tenacity required to translate the *Voynich Manuscript*, that person was Johannes Kepler.

28

Jesuits have always been missionaries and educators. We started schools, first all over Europe, and then all over the world. We have always admired intelligent, brilliant men who were also reasonable.

These words were the start of a chapter in a beautiful book on the history of the Society of Jesus that I found in the library. A very old, large tome. I opened it hoping to find something about Kepler.

And there was a short but very meaningful mention.

Throughout his turbulent life, Johannes Kepler had a complex relationship with us. Some members of the order had favored him with their friendship, offered him protection even when his own church withheld it. The Jesuits supported him, promoted his work, and prayed for his conversion. Once in a while there were rumors about this around Prague, the same as had occurred in Graz, but unfortunately, Kepler never abandoned his Lutheran faith.

And this despite the fact that he never attained recognition among his peers. It was the reason he was nicknamed "the Protestant Galileo." Once Jesuits arrived in Prague in 1556, we became the primary leaders, much as we had done before in Graz. It was Saint Peter Canisius who led the recon-version of Bohemia to Catholicism. In Prague we founded a new university, known as the Clementine, which like all Jesuit study centers soon became a place of influence and political attraction. Until then the initiative had come from the followers of Jan Hus, who professed a kind of liberal Catholicism, more schismatic than heretical,[8] and were the rulers of the Carolean Uni-versity after its founding in 1348 by Emperor Charles IV. Rudolf II wanted to stay out of the discussions and religious differences, as Maximilian, his father, had done. But the strong influence of his Catholic mother made him increase the pressure on the Protestant sector. He invited the Capuchins to join the Jesuits in Prague, and in this way the Counter-Reformation gained strength. In 1602, two years after Kepler arrived in Prague and by then was already court mathematician, Emperor Rudolf II declared that only Catho-lics and Hussites could stay in Bohemia, while Protestants were banished. However, Kepler didn't have to leave Prague. On one hand, his fame was well earned. He wasn't merely a math professor, but the best mathemati-cian in the empire. And on the other, his Jesuit connections prevented an-other forced exile for him. Rudolf II, rather than being an emperor full of strict religious zeal, was too busy, too concerned with his own problems, and too often subject to a deep depression. With a saddened, heavy heart, he became more and more introverted over time. His crises and hallucinations increased noticeably. Fearful of this situation, he surrounded himself more and more with alchemists and astrologers, mathematicians and astrono-mers, like Kepler himself—all wizards under any conditions, even including a few mystical rabbis.

"Yeah, like Judah Loew, Prague's chief rabbi and grand master of the kab-balah."

Simon had brought me more information. He filled my desk with more papers—as if that were possible—and overwhelmed me with all sorts of facts, dates, and nearly unbelievable events.

---

8. One of the great complaints of the Hussites (*utraquistas*) was the division between clerics and lay members when receiving the sacrament of Communion. The clerics would receive bread and wine (*sub utraque specie*) while the laity received only bread.

"And who was that?" I asked, in happy ignorance.

"He was quite an unusual guy. He might have been in the court of Rudolf the Second at the same time as Tycho Brahe and Johannes Kepler. I don't know if they met, but it's possible, according to the dates. You yourself gave me the clue, without meaning to," he added.

"I don't recall mentioning his name. I don't even know who he is."

"You gave me the Lovecraft book. He's a genius, by the way."

"I still don't see the connection," I protested.

"If I understood the book right, Lovecraft's myths are about a bunch of monsters and gods, extraterrestrials and nonhumans who got to Earth before man. And they're still here."

"More or less. A very special pantheon," I said, recalling again my visit to Rome and the pending enigma.

"Well, I liked it so much that I started a search on the Internet. I love horror and fantastic literature. Then I found the golem."

"The golem?"

The term was familiar.

"Yeah, the golem. Also the homunculus, remember? We were talking about Paracelsus."

"Sure," I said. "The word *homunculus* first appeared in the alchemic texts of Paracelsus. He even wound up saying he had created one of those false humans from bones and sperm, combined with pieces of animal skin and fur. So the homunculus is a hybrid of animal and human. This creature is totally loyal to its creator, has no intelligence of its own, and follows its master's orders literally, no matter how brutal they might be. Truly fantastic."

"Uh-huh," he agreed. "Lovecraft's myths seem to be inspired by these fantasies. And many think that the homunculus and the golem are the same thing."

"But what about the golem? What does it have to do with this Jew?" I asked again, my interest growing.

"His complete name was Judah Loew ben Bezalel, which means the son of Bezalel. He was a mystic and a great scholar of sacred texts. He spent most of his life as a rabbi in Prague. Outside Judaism, he is famous for the creation of the golem."

"And that is?" I urged Simon to continue.

"Among other things, an evolution of Pokemon," Simon joked. "But in fantastic literature, and before the golem's fall from grace, it was considered a supernatural being created out of dust, the same as Adam was created by God in Genesis. Except that in this case, its creator was human, and therefore the results weren't as good," my student went on, laughing loudly. "Judah Loew probably gave life to one of them in reality, not fiction. According to an apocryphal story, he created it to defend the Jews living in the Prague ghetto from anti-Semitic attacks. To accomplish this, he recited some canticles written in the language of Adam and Enoch. It's easy to recognize a golem because it has Emet, one of the Hebrew names for God, written on its forehead. This inhuman being probably grew bigger and became more and more violent, killing everyone who crossed its path and bringing horror to the streets of Prague. This nightmare ended when Rabbi Judah Loew, its creator, was promised that the violence against Jews would come to an end. Then he deleted the first letter from the golem's forehead, converting Emet into Met, or death. That was the end of the golem."

"Is there any truth in this whole fantastic story?" I asked, really intrigued and surprised by Simon's finds.

"Yes, though it might not seem so. The rabbi existed, and he is famous among Jews for his studies of holy scriptures. His tomb in Prague is a very popular tourist attraction. We have a confirmed date for one of his meetings with Rudolf the Second."

"When?"

"Exactly on February 23, 1592. He had been chief rabbi of Prague since 1588, and being so famous, he was summoned by the emperor. His son Sinai and his son-in-law Isaac were also present in his audience with the emperor. Their conversation was about the kabbalah, a subject that fascinated Rudolf the Second, and in which Judah was an expert. Judah died in Prague in 1609, so he might have known Tycho or Kepler, or both. There aren't any records, but it seems he had one or two earlier meetings with John Dee and Edward Kelley."

"Then"—I couldn't contain my sarcasm—"do you think that Tycho was murdered by a well-trained golem?"

"Well, the jury is still out." He laughed. "But I think poison was more likely."

"I don't," I confessed. "Maybe because I've watched too much *House* on television."

So I explained to Simon that I had my own Mercurochrome ideas. As I expected, he was fascinated and encouraged me to publish them. But where?

"Here I am."

Juana was right on time for our on-screen meeting. And soon John was there too. For a couple of minutes there were no words on my monitor, so I assumed they were having a private conversation. This was no surprise—John had told me he was going to insist—and when they finished, the three of us started chatting online.

"I tried to find out where Kepler is buried," Juana began. "And that was the first disappointment. Johannes Kepler was buried in the Saint Peter's Protestant Cemetery, Regensburg, on November 17, 1630. His funeral was very well attended. Some knew him, others had only heard of him. There was a tombstone with his own epitaph, the one we know, perhaps written in a moment of lucidity, depression, or premonition."

"'I used to measure the bright stars in the skies, now I measure the shadows of the earth. Though my mind belonged to the heavens, the shadow of my body lies here.'" I remembered his beautiful words.

"What was so disappointing?" I asked her.

"Even when he was dead and buried, he couldn't escape the horrors of war," Juana explained. "A few years later, the city of Regensburg was the center of violence during the Thirty Years' War, from 1618 to 1648. Many Protestants had taken refuge in Regensburg, and then found themselves trapped between two fires: the emperor's troops on one side, and the Lutherans' own forces on the other. In one battle, the cavalry demolished Saint Peter's Cemetery, and Kepler's tombstone was destroyed. Nothing was left. Nobody really knows where his remains are now."

"Then there's nothing?" John finally asked.

"Not a trace. Though recently a monument has been erected in the approximate area."

"Frustrating," I remarked. "Then the epitaph is no longer a reliable clue."

"Don't you believe it, Hector. Now comes the surprising part." Juana was clicking her keys so fast that she took over the on-screen conversation. "Hermes Trimegistus, or Trismegistus. According to your investigations, Athanasius Kircher thought Trimegistus was an ancient philosopher who really existed. Not only that, he had identified him with Moses, and was able to interpret the first hieroglyphics, written in the language of Adam."

"And?" I asked, a bit angry at the amount of information John had passed on to her.

"The most important contribution Trimegistus made was the so-called Tabula Smeragdina, or Emerald Table. According to legend, this is the source of hermetic philosophy and alchemy. The text was originally engraved on emerald tablets by Hermes and placed in the king's chamber inside the Great Pyramid of Cheops, or Khufu, as it's also known. Supposedly it was found by Alexander the Great himself. This whole story is apocryphal, but the text on the tables has been handed down to us, and is well known to devotees of occult philosophy, at least from the tenth century on."

"I still don't see how this connects with the epitaph, " I objected.

"You will see it if you read both, particularly if you focus on the main theme: what is below is just like what is above, and what is above is like what is below."

"That's true," John chimed in. "Kepler refers to a similar thing in his final statement. That he first looked up and then down. And then back up again."

"All of this is pure gobbledygook, though it would make some sense from the point of view of Athanasius Kircher and the Jesuit who presumably wrote the phrase behind that painting in the Roman Pantheon," I cut in again. "How does the complete text read, Juana?"

"I'll cut and paste it right now. On principle, it's believed that this text was related to the philosopher's stone, which was supposed to be used, as we know, to turn base metals into gold. Since in alchemy the Sun is identified with gold, and gold ruled over everything else, any other metal could be turned into gold and be just as valuable," she explained. "And now, here comes the complete text. The known version is in Latin, though there is doubt, logically, about whether this was the original language used. This is the approximate translation:

It is true and quite certain, without lies,
that what is below is just like what is above,
and what is above is just like what is below,
for the accomplishment of the miracle of the One.
And as all things come from One and the mediation of One,
thus all things come from this One by adaptation.
The Sun is its father, the Moon its mother,
the Wind carried it in its womb, the Earth nourished it.
This is the father of all perfection, the completion of the
  whole world.
You will separate Earth from Fire, the subtle from the gross,
gently, and with great ingenuity.
Ascend from Earth to Heaven, and back to Earth again,
taking strength equally from the superior and the inferior.
Thus will you achieve all the glory in the world,
and all darkness will depart from you.
It is the fortress of all strength,
overcoming all that is delicate and penetrating all that is
  solid.
Thus was the world created.
This is the admirable pattern of all adaptations, as I have
  spoken.
Therefore I have been called Hermes Three Times Greatest,
for I possess all three parts of the knowledge of the world.
This completes all I had to say about the work of the Sun.
Its power is not diminished, though turned toward the
  Earth.

"Kepler's epitaph can't be a coincidence," I wrote after reading the translation of the Emerald Table. "Not when I read things like 'Ascend from Earth to Heaven, and back to Earth again, taking strength equally from the superior and the inferior.'"

"That's what I wanted you to see," Juana wrote back, clearly satisfied.

* * *

And that was the end of our chat. At least with Juana, who apologized for not staying connected because her father was insisting she attend to some domestic matter. John and I had a couple more private exchanges, and he was e-mailing me his own findings about Wilfred Voynich. We kept some of this from Juana. I was now opening his message.

Wilfrid Michal Hadbank-Wojnicz, his complete real name, was born October 31, 1865, in Kaunas, Lithuania. The son of a modest Polish officer, thanks to his talent, he graduated with a degree in chemistry at the University of Moscow. He was soon attracted to anarchist and communist ideals, and joined a clandestine militant organization. Because of this, he was arrested and banished to Siberia. In 1890, he managed to return to Russia, and from there he escaped, first to Hamburg and then to London.

John indicated in his letter that this circumstance was precisely the one that had provided more information about Wilfred Voynich's life.

In London, he married Lily Boole, daughter of the famous mathematician.[9] With her and other exiles from Eastern Europe, he began working on the structure and propaganda of a revolutionary communist organization. It's known, for instance, that they smuggled translations of Engels's *Communist Manifesto* and Marx's *Das Kapital* to Russia. Wojnicz not only worked with revolutionary literature, but also translated many important Russian writers into English. That was what led him to become the essayist, translator, and bookseller we know as Voynich today. Wilfrid Michal Hadbank-Wojnicz dropped his Lithuanian name, too difficult for the English to pronounce, and began signing as Wilfrid Michael Voynich, or simply Wilfred M. Voynich. His curiosity and intelligence drew him to ancient, rare books and incunabula, and to trade in them to make money.

By 1897, he was already a very influential antique book dealer and collector. However, despite his innate business talent, it was impossible to find out how he managed to make so much money in so short a time, or how he managed to obtain such valuable collections of ancient manuscripts. In 1898 he published the first volume of a catalog of rare books, which was extended to a fourth volume in 1902, with more than 1,100 pages in a deluxe binding.

9. George Boole (1815–1864) was an English mathematician and philosopher. As the originator of Boolean algebra, the basis of modern computer arithmetic, he is considered one of the founders of computer science. (Author's Note)

By then he was already the best antique book dealer in London. His store was at 1 Soho Square.

Voynich made numerous trips all over Europe looking for books for his catalogs. In 1912, on one of those journeys, he stayed in Italy, at the Jesuit school of Villa Mondragone in Frascati, near Rome.

Here John began to repeat things we already knew. However, there was one new item. The librarian in Frascati, a Spaniard by the name of Anselmo Hidalgo—at last he appeared!—offered him a collection of several volumes, one of which Voynich found particularly intriguing. It was a small book, handwritten on calfskin, full of illustrations of strange plants, naked women, pipes, and sky maps. And composed in a disconcerting language that he couldn't make out.

Obviously, this was the book we know today as the *Voynich Manuscript*.

The rest of John's letter was very brief. In 1914, Voynich separated from his wife, Lily Boole, and moved his business to New York. In 1915, the same year Hidalgo went to Spain to be in charge of our new Jesuit house, the *Manuscript* made its first public appearance. Specifically in the *Bulletin of the Art Institute of Chicago,* which Voynich used as a springboard to inform the experts about the secrets of the volume he had acquired a few years before. This event spurred the beginning of numerous futile attempts at translation.

There were a lot of interesting findings in John's research, but there were still a lot of gaps to fill.

That afternoon I spent more than three hours working in the archives.

Not all the history of the Jesuits could be found on the Internet. I had to get my hands dirty the old-fashioned way. Just like both Lazzari and Hidalgo did. I began with the oldest ledgers, naturally. It made sense, I thought ironically, that since the Jesuits are seen as somewhat mercantile, ledgers would be the only books we're really interested in keeping. I found expense entries with the name Lazzari. There were trips to Toledo under his name, and under some other names I didn't recognize. On this there was no disagreement with the historical accounts, saying that Father Lazzari, then librarian of the Collegio Romano, had obtained an audience with Cardinal

Zelada—perhaps the most anti-Jesuit of all the cardinals under Pope Clement XIV—to request funding for the society. Zelada probably agreed, taking with him some acquisitions for his own Toledo library.

In the historical volumes about the Jesuits, I checked other data I had taken for granted. From the end of the Napoleonic War (1814) until 1824, the new pope Pius VII restored our order and our belongings. The list of main buildings is long, especially in Rome: the Church of the Gesù, the German School, the Collegio Romano, the novitiate of Sant' Andrea, the Church of Saint Ignatius, the Vatican Astronomical Observatory—of course—and the Pantheon.

I didn't know that the Pantheon had belonged to the Jesuits.

And this was true, precisely during the period when the *Manuscript* was in transit.

This fact removed doubts as to the possibility of leaving some clues there for my illustrious predecessors to follow. So I went back to Lazzari and Hidalgo. It's not known whether Hidalgo agreed voluntarily, or was forced, to head the new Spanish school built on the ruins of the old monastery that Lazzari had visited in order to protect the Jesuit library holdings—about which there were more than enough references. Hidalgo probably sold the *Manuscript* to Voynich, perhaps thinking that its secret would be well kept, since the clues for deciphering it were missing.

Or maybe it was the other way around, that Hidalgo went to Spain precisely searching for those clues. If Voynich had paid a sizable amount for an unreadable book, he surely would have been willing to pay an additional sum, perhaps much greater, for another book that could serve to translate the first one.

29

A cosmic event interrupted my research.

John's next visit was going to coincide with the approaching solar eclipse. The best place to watch it was in central Spain, on a strip of land from northern Galicia to southern Valencia, including all of Castile. A remarkable event, not to be repeated for another twenty years. My students were almost as enthused as I was. A unique astronomical event of singular beauty: the Sun would be hiding behind the Moon, leaving only a narrow ring of solar light. It was still a week away, and all the kids were prepared with their protective dark glasses and rudimentary telescopes to see the solar crown projected on a sheet of paper, or photographic cameras with the required filters. The date was clearly marked on the calendar.

Though solar eclipses are relatively frequent and may be observed in some part of the world every year, this one was particularly exciting. None had occurred in Spain since 1959, and a similar one was not expected until 2026. A lifetime. Who would want to miss it? The last ring-shaped, or annular, eclipse—perhaps the most spectacular—to be seen on the Iberian Peninsula was on January 9, 1777, 228 years ago.

"Hector, what exactly is a ringlike eclipse of the Sun?" they demanded.

"In an eclipse the Moon comes between the Earth and the Sun, hiding it. In a few days we'll have an almost total eclipse of the Sun when the Moon passes right in front of it. But because the Moon will be farther away from us than usual, its disk will be slightly smaller. Therefore, it will not darken the skies completely, and we'll be able to see a ring of light around the Sun. The word *eclipse* means 'disappearance' in Greek," I added. "There are many beautiful stories about eclipses."

"Tell us one of those stories," one of the girls pleaded eagerly.

"In the ancient world, when it wasn't possible to calculate the movements of celestial bodies, eclipses caused panic among the people. It doesn't matter which population we're referring to. Whether it was the Maya, the Chinese, or the Egyptians, people generally thought eclipses were the cause of disturbances and disasters. For instance, among the Chinese, it was thought that a dragon was devouring the Sun. Astronomers had to predict such events so as to prevent problems for their emperor. During an eclipse, all the bells in town would peal in order to scare the beast away. Two Chinese imperial astronomers were executed for making erroneous predictions. The Maya performed human sacrifices to appease their gods and make eclipses disappear. Other civilizations, in order to have someone to blame, replaced their king during the period of darkness. But with the beginning of astronomy," I continued, "it was discovered that eclipses occurred with a certain regularity. Four thousand years ago in Mesopotamia, astronomers thought that a phenomenon like this would happen every 223 months. But an accurate prediction couldn't be made until much later, thanks to the Greek astronomer Thales of Miletus in the year 585 B.C. It was like a miracle."

"Why?" Simon, who hadn't yet said a word, inquired.

I took out a book I had brought for the occasion. It was the chronicles of Herodotus. I read a short paragraph to him.

"'And day suddenly became night. This event had been predicted by Thales of Miletus, who had warned the Ionians, announcing that it would be very close to the place where it happened. When the Medes and the Lydians saw the change, they stopped fighting and quickly made a peace agreement.'"

After the reading, I continued my explanation. "Herodotus tells us here how the prediction made by Thales—who was considered one of the first Greek thinkers—ended the fighting before it really broke out in earnest. Aristotle himself said this eclipse marked the exact moment that philosophy was born."

"Hector, you're always saying the same thing," a kid complained, "that astronomy was the beginning of everything."

"And that is what I truly believe," I answered with a smile. "Since human beings began to walk on two feet, they stopped looking at the ground. So the next step, which was looking at the sky, was only a matter of time. Then questions came up—reasoning and thinking. That's how our intelligence developed."

"But intelligence is a divine gift, isn't it?" the girl in the first row piped up, the same one who always got high marks on religion tests.

"It's a whole package," I answered. "God is the Creator. And human beings are the most in His likeness. But I prefer not to look for divine explanations to what science can explain simply."

"My father says that it's impossible for a monkey to become a man. And that the Bible says differently." The skeptical kid was insistent.

"And what else does your father say?"

"That he doesn't trust Jesuits."

The whole class burst out laughing, and I did too. Luckily I was saved by the bell. That morning the kids were attacking on all fronts.

"Hector, could you come up after class? I need to talk to you for a minute."

Julian's voice on the phone sounded friendly. Our last serious conversation had been in the basement, by the big stone wall blocking the way to the long-hidden Roman sewers. Of course I accepted, out of obedience and friendship.

A bit later I knocked on his door.

"Come in," I heard him say from inside.

His desk was full of papers. To his job as administrator in charge of our survival, he had added that of prior, so that any decision having to do with our immediate future was also in his hands. That's probably what those papers were about.

"I want you to see this."

He handed me a folder with some yellowed sheets. About ten, maybe a dozen.

"What are these?" I asked without looking at the headings.

"They were among Carmelo's papers. In one of the drawers of his desk."

His words surprised me. Before inquiring further, I leafed through the folder. It was a will of some kind, written in English. It was the will of, well, Wilfred Voynich. Julian was handing me the contents of the empty folder I'd found in the office of my old prior while archiving his papers.

"The other day you were asking me about a manuscript with that name, Voynich. Later I remembered seeing it somewhere. Is this what you were looking for?"

"Yes and no." I hesitated. "Of course these documents are very valuable to me. But what is known as the *Voynich Manuscript* is something else. It's an old codex, still undeciphered, from the sixteenth century. These papers seem to belong to its modern discoverer, who found it early in the twentieth century. He was an English book dealer of Russian ancestry."

Julian gave me a surprised, wondering look. And I was ashamed that I had doubted him. Julian knew of the existence of the underground labyrinths, and he probably knew that something of value could be hidden there. The offer to buy the building was unusually aggressive for a merely urban venture. But he didn't seem to have any idea of the vicissitudes of the old document, perhaps very carefully arranged by the English wizard John Dee. I decided to offer an additional explanation.

"For some reason that escapes me," I said prudently, "the Society of Jesus has kept that manuscript hidden for centuries. Perhaps because its contents referred to inappropriate matters, or maybe our own pride and vanity made us attempt to translate it before making it public."

"Do you know where it is?" Julian asked with genuine curiosity.

"In an American university, at Yale," I answered. "Hundreds of people are studying it all over the world."

"Then where's the problem?"

"It's that nobody has been able to decode it. Some suspect," I said, again recovering my restraint, "that if it was ever deciphered by some Jesuit, he stored the codes somewhere else. There are some clues that point to Spain"—and here I reached the limit of what I was willing to share. "This is in relation to the society's regulations and our having to hide our books and manuscripts."

"Do we have them in our archive?"

"Do we have what?" I asked in response, pretending not to understand.

"The codes, of course."

"Oh, no, of course not. At least, not that I know of," I answered with an appropriately concerned expression.

"Then we have nothing to do or say about it. Keep those papers if you want."

"Thanks, Julian. I'm going back to my room."

"Go on with your work, Hector. I'll see you at dinner."

Until dinnertime, and for quite a while afterward, I was wrapped up in old Wilfred Voynich's will. The first pages were the usual lawyer's formalities, wordy paragraphs with long lists of the book dealer's belongings, establishing the conditions under which they would be distributed to different members of his family. Or to various cultural and scientific associations of his time, not always specified clearly. And these meticulous lists of books to be handed down were incomplete, and many pages were missing. The introduction made me think that the document itself had been divided after his death, each heir getting a copy of the main text plus some particular pages. In the list of heirs I found the name Oswaldo Pizarro. I concluded he was Juana's relative, perhaps even her grandfather. This would match with what she herself wrote to Thomas van der Gil.

I had in my hands a copy of Voynich's last will and testament, sent to Anselmo Hidalgo, the prior of our monastery since 1915. It was dated 1930, a year before Voynich died. Possibly Voynich didn't know that Hidalgo was already dead, but for some reason—which I would later find in the details of the dossier—before his death Voynich felt obligated to reveal some matters that had been kept secret during his lifetime.

The last four pages of the document were devoted to what Voynich called "Roger Bacon's ciphered book." Wilfred Voynich died convinced that the manuscript, which later took his name, was undoubtedly the work of the famous Franciscan philosopher and scientist. The document detailed its acquisition and the conditions of the sale. Also included was a long paragraph thanking the Society of Jesus for having ceded such a valuable work so that the scientific community could study it. The Jesuits' contract conditions expressly prohibited Voynich from revealing the book's origin, the price he paid, and the names of those who sold it to him. For an unknown reason, at least the name of Anselmo Hidalgo had filtered through, since John had found it, as well as the method the Society of Jesus followed to safeguard the code book.

So Voynich did know about the existence of a code book.

That wasn't all. The book dealer had admitted he wasn't able to find it, and thus he was returning the procedural instructions he received from the society to Hidalgo, the Jesuit representative, so that the code book could possibly be located. What followed surprised me. On the last page of the will Voynich sent to Anselmo Hidalgo, there was a deliberately inordinate version of the Emerald Table! The ancient text of the fabulous, and much fabled, Hermes Trimegistus had been used by the Jesuits to hide the second part of the manuscript, just as we had thought. So we were looking in the right direction. The next Jesuit keepers of the keys had done nothing but continue Athanasius Kircher's zeal. And I got the impression, because of the implicit discomfort Voynich showed in his final statements, that nobody was capable—not even within my order—of finding so precious a treasure again. At some point in history, perhaps due to the two suppressions of the Jesuits, or maybe because of oblivion or apathy, the transmission of information had been broken.

> *This is the father of all perfection, the completion of the*
> *whole world.*
> *This completes what I had to say about the work of the Sun.*
> *It is true and quite certain, without lies,*
> *that what is below is just like what is above,*
> *and what is above just like what is below,*
> *for the accomplishment of the miracle of the One.*
>
> *It is the fortress of all strength,*
> *overcoming all that is delicate and penetrating all that is*
> *solid.*
> *Thus was the world created.*
> *Therefore I have been called Three Times Greatest,*

for I possess all three parts of the knowledge of the world.
The Sun is its father, the Moon its mother,
the Wind carried it in its womb, the Earth nourished it.
Its power is not diminished, though turned toward the
    Earth.

You will separate Earth from Fire, the subtle from the gross,
gently, and with much ingenuity.
Ascend from Earth to Heaven, and back to Earth again,
taking strength equally from the superior and the inferior.
Thus will you achieve all the glory in the world.

And as all things come from One, and the mediation of One,
Thus all things come from this One by adaptation.
And all darkness will depart from you.
This is the admirable pattern of all adaptations, as I have
    spoken.

Now, only Hermes Trimegistus and his strange alchemic vision of the world remained for us to figure out what Lazzari and his friends had done with the book that Kircher, the last man to understand everything, had been able to read.

I immediately decided to send John the first of the five stanzas into which the Jesuits had rewritten the text of the Emerald Table. And also to Juana; why not?

John was the first to answer through Instant Messenger.

"Don't you have something more bloody difficult?" he joked.

"This isn't trivial, old Brit," I answered, blushing alone in my room, afraid I could be making a fool of myself to my friend over the Internet. "I'll copy it again," and I quickly re-sent the first part of the text that Voynich had quoted, just the first stanza.

"Well, how do you explain this?" I asked then.

"I'll tell you in one word: Kepler."

"So what else is new?" I said ironically. "Illuminate me, John," I added in the same tone.

"It's pretty simple. Almost too simple," he began. "In 1619, Kepler wrote the work he considered his best: *Armonices Mundi*, or *The Harmony of the World*. It contains the last of Kepler's theories, including his famous third law, which establishes that the square of the period of time it takes each planet to orbit the Sun is proportional to the cube of its mean distance from the Sun. Everything follows in perfect order. Therefore, the father of all perfection in the world was none other than Kepler."

"Which was what we expected," I broke in.

" 'This completes what I had to say about the work of the Sun,' " John went on from memory. "It's crystal clear. The planetary movement around the king of heavenly bodies has been solved for others by the German scholar. Everything is true and certain, and without any lies. Later Kircher, or whoever used the apocryphal Emerald text to guide those searching for the *Manuscript* codes, added the famous motto about below and above, above and below, that Johannes Kepler also made his own in his epitaph. One more clue that fits perfectly. The father of all perfection," John commented, recalling the first line of the stanza.

"Wait, we have to get to the end of the stanza," I reminded him. "What does 'the miracle of the One' mean?"

There was a period of silence on the monitors, broken by the appearance of a third guest.

"Wouldn't it be a miracle to solve something as unique as the *Voynich*?" Juana wrote.

As I feared, and maybe expected, John and Juana had been working together on the stanza I had sent. The "One" could very well be an allusion to the whole *Manuscript*. According to my friends, to "accomplish the miracle of the One" was nothing but solving the enigma of its pages. Kircher probably had read it, and judging by this first stanza, the solution to the hieroglyphic came to him through Johannes Kepler himself. And he was paying homage to him in the text we were analyzing. I was right, then. And it's quite possible that the manuscript itself had been sent to him by the Jesuit Marcus Marci, knowing that Kircher's post as imperial mathematician, as Kepler's successor, was secure. In this way, the Jesuits were assured of the possession of the treasured book, and although Athanasius Kircher ultimately settled in Rome, he probably kept the book with him always.

I thought it would be fun to return the prank of the mysterious CD they had sent me a few weeks ago. So I decided to send them the second stanza.

> *It is in the fortress of all strength,*
> *overcoming all that is delicate and penetrating all that is*
>   *solid.*
> *Thus was the world created.*
> *Therefore I have been called Three Times Greatest,*
> *for I possess all three parts of the knowledge of the world.*

Unfortunately, in this case, I had no idea of, and no solution to, the puzzle I was sending.

While my friends were racking their brains, I still had some pending matters. One of them concerned the British clockmaker John Harrison, who solved the measurement of longitude on the high seas. What did this have to do with the whole story, and above all, what was the significance of his name being written on the wall that blocked the passageway in our subterranean labyrinth?

Again, I resorted to the Internet.

John Harrison had nothing to do with the Jesuits. Nor with the *Manuscript,* or any attempt at deciphering it. Did he know something about codes, or at least about the code that would lead us to the book with the key? If Kircher had spent most of his life consumed by the problem of finding a practical method to determine geographic longitude, as had John Dee, and even Tycho Brahe, it didn't seem so strange that this common endeavor of the main personalities involved in the background of the *Voynich* would have been taken into account by whoever had hidden the keys to its translation. Those keys had to be extremely precise, as precise as Kepler had been in calculating the orbits of the planets around the Sun. And John Harrison was precision itself. The perfect clockmaker.

The problem of geographical longitude became an issue when traveling west.

Clocks had to be turned back sixty minutes from the time of the starting place for each fifteen degrees of sailing west. If we knew the exact local time in two different places, we could use the difference between the times to calculate the longitudinal distance between those two places. The seventeenth-century mariners could calculate the local time by observing the Sun—thus already having one of the two necessary points. But to be able to navigate, they needed to know the time of some other point of reference such as Greenwich. There were very accurate clocks in the seventeenth century, but they relied on the pendulum, and that didn't work very well on a ship with the continuous movement caused by the swells of the sea.

In order to synchronize a clock on board with Greenwich time, all kinds of strategies were developed. Some were very interesting, like using a network of cannons carefully distributed all over the Atlantic Ocean that would fire a series of shots in sequence. Because of the failure of these methods, the British government created a famous contest in which the winner would collect twenty thousand pounds for being able to determine longitude within a margin of half a degree or less. This margin amounted to only two minutes of real time as measured by a clock. Who would be able to construct a portable clock that precise? John Harrison.

Harrison invented and manufactured several clocks, each one more precise than the other. The best was only five inches in diameter and weighed less than four pounds. His son, William Harrison, sailed for the West Indies with one of these devices on November 18, 1761. By the time he reached Jamaica on June 19, 1762, his timepiece was only five seconds behind the astronomical measurement, based on fixed stars with respect to the Moon. The rest of Harrison's story had more to do with his difficulties in collecting the prize, which was well deserved. The last model made by this clockmaker was used by Captain James Cook during his three-year voyage from the Tropics to Antarctica. The daily deviation was never more than eight seconds, the equivalent of two nautical miles. Harrison's achievement was really impressive.

What was the motive for all this great effort?

First of all, to be able to navigate. Especially for the Jesuits, whose missions reached all over the world. Because of this, Athanasius Kircher wanted to have a precise cartography of the entire globe.

Then I remembered Kepler's epitaph.

I used to measure the bright stars in the skies,
now I measure the shadows of the earth.

Johannes Kepler and Tycho Brahe observed the heavens all their lives. And they located and measured the positions of stars and planets with absolute precision. Kepler surely pictured himself in the heavens after his death, so what would he measure from up there? The answer was obvious.

"Then is it a map that we're looking for?" John wrote from his side of the Web.

"Yes, it's that simple, old Brit. What you could see from above is the Earth itself, only smaller," I answered. "And its representation on paper is obviously a map, an extremely precise map."

"And where would we find it?" Juana interjected; she had just joined the chat.

"I really don't know," I wrote back. "I suppose we'll have to continue trying to decipher the text Wilfred Voynich sent to his Jesuit friends. Anyway," I went on, "we're looking for something with cartography from the end of the eighteenth or beginning of the nineteenth century. A result of Harrison's technological advances, and Cook's expeditions and discoveries, plus the Jesuit expansion."

"Let's see the text then," John typed. "We don't have much."

"'It is the fortress of all strength,'" I typed, repeating the first line of the second stanza. "Any ideas?"

"It seems like this refers directly to the *Manuscript*," Juana began, and then continued. "Do you think your monastery could be considered a fortress?"

"I don't think so. We don't have high walls or battlements or moats. And there weren't any in the preceding buildings."

"Then we'll leave that for now," our Mexican partner continued. "For the time being, would you say that we need a castle?"

"A castle in Castile would be quite common, wouldn't it?" John cut in. "Which one do you think the Jesuits thought of?"

"We've got dozens. And we'd be assuming that they brought the code book here to decipher the *Voynich*," I answered, disappointed by our lack of imagination. "Let's attack the next line."

"'Overcoming all that is delicate and penetrating all that is solid,'" Juana copied again. "I have no idea."

"What penetrates a solid?" I asked.

"Maybe X-rays," John suggested, not very convinced, "but they weren't discovered until the twentieth century. So, forget that."

"How about acid; who knows some chemistry?"

"I do," John responded. "Sulfuric acid? Aqua regia?"

"That last one sounds good. Explain," Juana asked.

"Aqua regia is a yellow, extremely corrosive solution, a mixture of nitric and hydrochloric acid, highly concentrated. It got its name, royal water, because it could dissolve precious, or royal, metals like gold and platinum. Very few reactants could do that," John explained.

"Well, now it sounds better," Juana spoke again, filling the screen. "If we think of alchemy, it fits very well, because the hermetic text was related to the philosopher's stone. And if we also think of a place—"

"If we think of a place," John cut in, "it could be as simple as the flow of running water, and for a royal place, I say, a castle near a river."

"Yes, that would narrow our search somewhat, but it's a bit far-fetched," I said, although I was regaining my momentum. "Let's go to the third line. 'Thus was the world created.' This is very vague."

"The world was created in six days, and God rested on the seventh. It's in Genesis," Juana wrote back.

I feared the worst, and I was not wrong.

"Don't say stupid things," John burst out. "We have the beautiful *theory* of the Big Bang to explain the creation of the universe. We don't have to go to the Bible for that."

"Yes, you're right," Juana remarked sarcastically. "It's a beautiful theory."

"Please don't fight," I intervened. "The Big Bang is a proven scientific fact, the origin of the universe as we know it. And also, believers agree on the argument, based on faith, that establishes God as the first creator."

"The one who planted the little seed." Now the irony came from John. "Please, Hector, you can't swim and stay dry at the same time."

"I don't intend to," I answered, a bit annoyed. "We Jesuits claim the father of the Big Bang, as you know. Georges Lemaître was a formidable mathematician and his physics arguments had, and still have, great scientific soundness. Edwin Hubble's observations only confirmed the results of the Belgian priest's work with Einstein's equations. If, as Hubble found through the use of telescopes, the universe is expanding, then it's logical to think that in the past the whole universe occupied a smaller and smaller space until, in some primeval time, it was concentrated into a kind of 'primitive atom.' Most scientists believe this today, but nobody had elaborated that idea scientifically until 1931, when Lemaître published an essay in *Nature*, the prestigious British journal, if I recall correctly," I added, a bit worked up from writing so fast.

"Hector, I can't believe so much heresy would be coming from you," Juana said, charging back. "You are a priest, a shepherd of God the Creator!"

"What does that have to do with anything?" I defended myself vehemently, feeling attacked on all flanks. "Lemaître was neither a priest devoted to science, nor a scientist who became a priest. He was both from the start. They are compatible worlds. Several scientists, including Einstein himself, mistrusted Lemaître's hypothesis because they thought he might favor the religious view of creation. But it wasn't so. Lemaître never intended to exploit science for the benefit of religion. He was convinced that science and religion are two different but converging paths leading to the ultimate truth. Lemaître, by then president of the Pontifical Academy of Science, was so convinced that it was necessary to clarify this situation that he advised His Holiness Pope Pius the Twelfth to avoid possible misunderstandings in his speeches. And Pius the Twelfth heeded the scientist's words."

"Well, what is it, then?" John asked, unsure of what to think.

"Give me a minute," I asked.

I searched quickly among the books on my shelf until I found the text I needed. In order to avoid having to type the long quote from the Belgian scholar, I looked in Google for the same paragraph and pasted it on the screen. It took me less than a minute.

The Christian scientist has the same means that are available to his nonbeliever colleague. He also has the same freedom of spirit, at least if his concept of religious truths is at the same level as his scientific knowledge. He knows that everything has been created by God, but he also knows that God does not put limitations on His creatures. The omnipresent divine action is essentially hidden everywhere. The Supreme Being could never be reduced to a scientific hypothesis. Therefore, the Christian scientist goes freely forward, with the assurance that his investigation cannot be in conflict with his faith.

"I'm not convinced," John wrote back.

"Me either, though for completely opposite reasons," Juana argued.

"Then the best we can do is to go back to Wilfred Voynich's text and his *Manuscript*," I pleaded. "Let's not waste any more time with this kind of discussion."

So we continued for a long while, breaking the second stanza into little pieces.

Without significant results.

30

I got more info on the golem."

Simon had burst into the classroom while all the others were on break mistreating a soccer ball. I glanced up from the tests I was grading and looked at him.

"Tell me."

"Well, the homunculi from alchemist Paracelsus and the golems from the Jewish rabbi of Prague appear together quite often. They even get mixed up."

He covered my desk with a dozen Internet printouts. All of them showed a series of strange little men in all shapes and colors. I leafed through the pages, shaking my head.

"Simon, most of these things are fantasies. Really, it's all fantasy. We're getting further away from the main topic, which is the death of astronomer and alchemist Tycho Brahe. And a serious scientist, not a wizard."

He looked at me, crestfallen.

"Well, maybe you can use this anyway," he countered defensively. "I'll leave it all with you."

And he left as fast as he'd come in.

I put my desk in order, piling up the kids' tests on one side and Simon's papers on the other, in no particular order. The page on top caught my attention. It was about the mandrake, a strange plant with hallucinogenic elements, always associated with magic rites. The tests were pretty boring, so I began reading Simon's papers.

According to his rather dubious source (it offered a link to the Web page of a science-fiction publisher), there were various kinds of homunculi, depending on the method used to create them. One involved the use of mandrake. Popular beliefs maintained that this plant thrived where hanged men, during their last convulsions, ejaculated semen that fell to the ground. The roots of the mandrake vaguely resemble a human being, like a doll or a fetish. For it to become a real man, the plant had to be collected before dawn on a Friday morning—by a black dog, to be precise—and then washed, infused with milk and honey, even with blood in some recipes. The miniature being that resulted would protect its owner with absolute fidelity, just the same as a golem.

It *was* pretty interesting.

Later, in my room, I searched for more information on that strange plant. It is believed the word *mandrake* was derived from Greek and meant "harmful to cattle." The plant belongs to the nightshade family and its chemical composition consists mainly of alkaloids, which diminish nerve impulses. Ingesting it in large quantities can be poisonous, but in smaller doses it has regularly been used as an anesthetic. I finished the part relating to botany and gardening. The pages relating to magic were more detailed and interesting. According to legend, when a mandrake is pulled out of the ground, that is, when the little man buried underneath is unearthed, the plant screams horribly, so horribly that those who heard it would be driven crazy or even killed. There was a procedure to avoid this dire situation. It consisted of tying a dog to the plant and then backing away, threatening and exciting the dog. On the point of dying from the horrendous screams, the dog would pull out the roots of the mandrake, allowing the owner to get the whole plant without suffering any harm. Besides being an anesthetic and a soporific, the mandrake is mentioned in Genesis for its beneficial effects on sterile women. It has also been claimed to have aphrodisiac properties.

Why was this peculiar plant attracting my attention so much?

Without my being aware of it, Wilfred Voynich's third stanza had been turning around in my head.

> *The Sun is its father, the Moon its mother,*
> *the Wind carried it in its womb, the Earth nourished it.*

> *Its power is not diminished, though turned toward the*
> *Earth.*

Indeed, this greatly resembled a puzzle whose solution could be the blessed mandrake, a plant that lives from the Sun, but also needs the Moon and the shadows to grow. Its seeds seem to float in the wind, but germinate in the ground. And according to legend, the seed of hanged men poured into the ground just before they died remained fertile.

It was fantastic.

Of course, the most interesting thing was yet to present itself.

The *Voynich Manuscript* was rich in engravings of exotic plants, most of them unknown or invented. I remembered a few resembling mandrakes, with bulky, fleshy roots.

I went to my computer and examined the reproduction from the book. I looked for the drawings in the last pages. Once more, just as when Jesuits used drawings of naked women in what appeared to be cans to refer to the Pantheon, the relationship was clear. A new clue placed *a posteriori* by another unknown Jesuit made a connection between the *Manuscript* and a way to find the keys to decipher it.

Engraved among the strange Voynichian characters were what looked like exotic mandrake root. But the most interesting detail was that, next to them, there were towers. Next to each one of them.

Like towers from a castle.

"Are you sure that this stanza could have been used to indicate the relationship between mandrake roots and a castle where the code book could be hidden?" John wrote.

"If not, what?" I answered. "If it's so, we would now have several clues that fit together. A castle beside a river in Castile, belonging to a king. A castle that had also been used as a prison."

"I don't get the part about a prison," John wrote back.

"Use your imagination," I suggested.

"I am, but I still don't see it."

"Think the worst and you'll be right, as they say," I offered. "The man-

drakes have to be abundant where a lot of prisoners were executed, like a prison."

"Hmm. Isn't that a rather shaky connection? And as far as I know, that Spain of yours used other methods to carry out capital punishment," he argued. "By the way, didn't you invite Juana to this chat?"

"Yes I did. But she hasn't shown up."

I was still writing my answer when Juana appeared, eagerly keying in words at a good clip.

"John, Hector," she began. "All of that business about the mandrakes is very nice, even its direct connection to the *Manuscript* and the famous page with the towers, but Wilfred Voynich's third stanza is too clear for such tangled explanations. I'm surprised that a pair of astronomers like you haven't noticed what is so obvious."

"What do you mean?" I asked, a bit annoyed with her for not being as enthusiastic about my findings as I would have liked.

"Let's see," she said. "I'm copying slowly and carefully, 'The Sun is its father, the Moon its mother, the Wind carried it in its womb, the Earth nourished it.' So I ask you, what is the effect of the Moon and the Sun on the Earth?"

"The tides?" John asked thoughtfully.

"Almost, but not quite," she wrote back, surely laughing to herself. "Another clue: what can poetically move the wind?"

"The Moon covering the Sun!" I typed back immediately.

"An eclipse?" John asked, still dazed.

"Of course. Why overthink it?" Juana remarked.

"And what is the relation between an eclipse, a castle, and the other stuff?" John argued, not seeming very clearheaded that afternoon.

Something was percolating in my mind.

And it finally came to me.

"SIMANCAS!"

I suppose my friends understood my bad manners when I wrote the name of the famous castle in all caps.[10] Everything fit perfectly, piece by piece, from the moat to the last battlement. It became clear after Juana's suggestion that the stanza referred to an eclipse. Of the many stories I'd told my students, the most popular wasn't about Thales of Miletus, but about Simancas. Maybe because it was so close to us, maybe because of the legend surrounding that fantastic event, the solar eclipse of 939. Back then, control over the lands next to the walls of the city of Simancas, and irrigated by the

10. In Internet communications the use of all caps is equivalent to shouting out loud and is considered bad manners. (Author's Note)

Duero River, was being contested between the forces of the king of León, Ramiro II, and the Andalusian troops, led by Caliph Abd ar-Rahman III. It all began when the Moors invaded northern Christian territories. The caliph managed to put together a large army and had the help of Abu-Yahya, governor of Zaragoza. The Christian king added the troops of the count of Castile, Fernán González, and soldiers from Galicia and Asturias to his own army, as well as forces from the kingdom of Navarra. The chronicles of the time describe what happened.

> When the Moors neared Simancas, there was a frightening
> solar eclipse at midday that covered the land with a yellowish
> darkness, terrifying Christians and infidels alike. They had
> never seen anything like this before. For two days neither army
> moved. Finally, Al-Andalus lost the battle, and upon returning
> to Cordova, Abd ar-Rahman III ordered the crucifixion of three
> hundred of his officers for cowardice.

An eclipse in Castile always recalls the Battle of Simancas. The castle of Simancas is located strategically at the mouth of the Pisuerga River, a major tributary of the Duero River, and very close to Valladolid, the capital of Castile. The other clues fit easily by themselves. The present castle was erected in the fifteenth century by a Castilian admiral, Don Fadrique Enríquez, and later ceded to the king. So Charles V, and especially his son, Philip II, were its royal owners. They decided to make it the general archive of the kingdom, and it's still in use today. Because of this, during the sixteenth and seventeenth centuries, many important changes were made under the direction of architects Juan de Herrera and Francisco de Mora. The castle was also used as a state prison.

Everything fit so well, including the prison.

What most caught my attention was the intelligence of the Jesuit's decision. Where better to keep a valuable document than in the massive archive of the Spanish crown? The perfect place to hide an old manuscript for decades and decades. During the sixteenth and seventeenth centuries, the Simancas Archive was the administrative center of the vast domain of the Crown. Today it is a vital research center for scholars studying European history. As a great world power during the reigns of Charles V and Philip II, Spain kept the center of its entire organization in Simancas.

Both Juana and John, who had already planned their visit, immediately moved it up a few days. They were as excited as I was at the prospect of a solid lead toward finally being able to translate the *Manuscript*. In a couple of days, we'd all be together again.

"You look wonderful today," I told Juana as soon as she got off the train.

"You don't look bad yourself, if I may say so," she answered, smiling as she handed me her familiar enormous suitcase. It almost made me fall.

We greeted each other with kisses on the cheek and warm hugs, as usual. Although, when I hugged her, it seemed to me she was shaking.

John's train was scheduled to arrive in two hours. So we decided to wait for him in the café at the train station. I didn't ask her why they hadn't met earlier, in Madrid, so they could travel together, but I already suspected the reason. Things still weren't going well for them, and whenever they needed to work on the *Voynich Manuscript*, they tried to have me with them. Or rather, between them.

I took the opportunity to ask her some questions that I hadn't dared to before, not even by phone. Now I felt secure on my own turf, my city, my place—I could almost say my castle—with a cup of very strong coffee in front of me. I summoned all my courage and started asking.

"Juana, why do you really want to solve the mystery of the *Manuscript*?"

She looked at me, startled, and after a pause, answered.

"For the same reasons you do, I suppose, the same as John's and of so many others on the Voynich List. Curiosity. We all feel passionate about mysteries, enigmas, codes."

She saw that I wasn't buying this.

"Maybe someone asked you to do it," I said.

"Well, if that was the case, what difference would it make?" she countered defiantly.

"Basically none," I answered. "But I like to be sure I can trust my friends."

"You're safe with me," she said, giving me an intense look. Then she continued. "Yes, someone asked me for help. And I owe a lot to that person. A whole lot."

"And why does that someone want to translate the *Voynich*?" I sensed that Juana really wanted to unload a heavy burden, like to a confessor, hoping for some peace of mind.

"I can't answer that, Hector," she said. "I truly can't."

That didn't satisfy me. So I was more direct.

"Who is Thomas van der Gil?"

"A friend."

"Is that all?" I was getting impatient.

"A friend of mine and of my father," she said, looking down, suddenly appearing quite vulnerable. She went on. "He helped me at the clinic, remember? I wrote to you about it."

"Yes, I remember. You've got nothing to be ashamed of," I added.

"He's an extraordinary man. You can't imagine how influential he is, and his friends too."

"I know something about them; the Internet is useful. But I don't understand why power and influence are so important to you."

"It's more than that, Hector. When he speaks, he's so convincing. He can make anyone a believer. Like a new life every day."

"I'm a priest, Juana," I interrupted, annoyed by her devotion to this character. "And even though I haven't had the good fortune to be sent as a missionary, I also know about spreading Jesus' message."

"I know, and I admire you for it. But we've already spoken about our different views of the Church."

"That's not it, Juana. It's my monastery, my house, my people."

"I don't know how you found out we're the buyers. But I'm not surprised. You're a very smart man," she added.

"But why?" I asked, angry with Juana's sudden sincerity. "What good is that pile of stones to you? The translation of the *Voynich* isn't there."

"We still don't know that," she argued, recovering her aplomb.

"You know as well as I do that the Simancas clue is promising. The interpretation of Wilfred Voynich's will is very clear."

"We also have part of that will," she replied.

"I know," I said. "I supposed that was why you decided to try to purchase our land."

"Of course that was the reason," she admitted. "We knew about Lazzari's trip to your house long before you began searching in your archives for Anselmo Hidalgo's document of sale for the *Manuscript* to Voynich. As soon as we found out, we made our first offer."

"Did you also make the threats?" I asked, raising my voice. I needed to know.

Juana seemed frightened.

"Nobody threatened you."

"Oh no?"

My patience was running short.

"No. I took care of everything myself," she argued. "And I assure you that I'm not very fond of jumping over walls at night, or writing graffiti."

I recalled that the Waldo of the List, transformed into a splendid woman, Juana, visited me the very next day after the first Voynichian graffiti appeared on the school walls.

"It wasn't directed at you," she confessed.

I was astonished. Juana knew all along that sooner or later I'd have to learn the truth.

"Isn't Hector the target of Achilles' anger?"

"No!" she said, laughing for the first time. "Achilles' anger is aimed at Agamemnon, the head of the Greek army. Don't forget the kidnapping of Chryseis and Briseis."

I didn't remember the *Iliad* very well.

"We were only trying to put some pressure on your old prior. I guess it wasn't a good idea."

Much worse than that, especially if they knew about Carmelo's condition. Besides teaching Greek at the school, Carmelo knew part of the history of the *Voynich Manuscript* from his many years as prior. He'd been mildly interested in its strange vocabulary, had kept all the pages from Wilfred Voynich's will in his desk, and besides, was the son of humble farmers. I discovered all of this after he died.

"I see. Agamemnon and his hog farmer."

"That's it. And he understood that," Juana added. "But he didn't want to hear anything about a sale. Julian has been much more receptive," she admitted. "We were truly sorry about what happened to Carmelo. We conveyed our sympathy to the new prior as soon as we learned about it. And we increased our offer."

I didn't know what to think. Julian, my present prior, had already agreed on a price for the land. We Jesuits were accused of being too interested in money. The second *Voynich* wasn't in either the library archive or the underground labyrinth, as we had thought; it didn't matter if the bulldozer leveled all that to the ground. None of it mattered anymore.

Just then, the public address system announced the arrival of the train from Madrid.

"Juana, let's go to the platform," I said, taking her by the hand and leaving five euros on the table for our check. "Your ex-boyfriend is about to arrive."

I smiled at her, and she returned an understanding grin.

More than anything else, we both wanted to solve the mystery of the *Voynich Manuscript*. There would be time to talk later.

Juana stayed in the same hotel as on her first visit—one with a lot of stars, as we'd joked then—while John accepted Julian's invitation to stay in an empty room at our house. That first night, after we left Juana resting in her private haven, John and I sat in my room, large cups of coffee in our hands. I also wanted a one-on-one conversation with him. "How are you?" I began.

"A bit confused. To be frank, I don't really know whether I'm coming or going," he answered with deliberate ambiguity.

"Why?" I wanted to know.

"It's Juana; I still love her," he admitted.

"Don't lose hope," I said, trying to encourage him.

"The problem is that she's not the same. Not since our stay in the Canary Islands. Since the argument."

"She has other priorities, other objectives. Other friends."

John looked at me, overwhelmed. He swallowed hard before daring to ask.

"Another man?"

"No, not in that sense. She's not in love, she just needs to figure some things out for herself," I answered.

"And?"

"Sometimes vulnerable people fall under the sway of a charismatic zealot. Some call it emotional blackmail. Others, more graphically, call it brainwashing. Or even *comedura de tarro,* as my kids say."

"Eating a jar?" John asked, totally baffled.

"That's slang my students use." I laughed. "Don't worry about Juana anymore. She'll be all right. And I'm sure she hasn't managed to forget you."

"I'll have to believe you, Padre. And now," he said, totally changing the topic, "give me more details about Simancas. I can't wait till tomorrow."

31

We gathered again, the three of us, for breakfast in a restaurant very close to Juana's hotel. Now facing our Mexican partner, I summed up what I knew about the old archives of the Spanish crown, and what had convinced me that this was where the Jesuits had hidden the codes for the translation of the *Voynich Manuscript*. I still had no idea what kind of document we would find. Perhaps a few pages torn out of the original. That's what I expected given the condition of the copy at Yale. It could be just a simple map, as the clue from John Harrison, clockmaker for the Royal Greenwich Observatory, seemed to indicate, or even a completely different manuscript that bore the signatures of Johannes Kepler as author and Athanasius Kircher as owner.

"Let's go back to Wilfred Voynich's will, which, as we now know, was kept in my house for years."

I began. "We already saw that the first stanza was the author's tribute to Johannes Kepler, the most likely translator of the *Manuscript*. The second stanza posed more questions. It began, 'It is the fortress of all strength.'"

"A fortress that we definitely think is a castle," Juana pointed out.

"Exactly, and now listen to this," I continued. "'The royal archive, located in the ancient castle of Simancas, was also known as the Fortress. Inside the fortress there are several fireproof chambers to protect old documents.' So it makes perfect sense with the line 'fortress of all strength.'"

"I agree completely," John interrupted. "What else?"

"The second line is just a clue to its location. The best-known acid that penetrated solids was aqua regia. We accept the details of the river and the kings, in this case, Charles the Fifth and his son Philip the Second."

"And when we come to the third line, 'Thus was the world created,' we get stuck," Juana said.

"Right," I agreed. "I suggest we skip that line; we don't need to have another debate on religion."

They were a bit taken aback, but agreed.

"The last two lines make enough sense by themselves. Notice that the Jesuit, who wrote the clue, deleted the author's name, Hermes Trimegistus Three Times Greatest, from the original Emerald Table. Why?" I wondered out loud. "Surely in order to emphasize its meaning."

"What do you mean?" John asked, engrossed in the text now before us.

Therefore I have been called Hermes Three Times Greatest,
for I possess all three parts of the knowledge of the world.

"Historically, *great,* or *magnus,* is rarely applied; it always refers to conquerors, emperors, or persons with special power. We have Alexander the Great, and Charles the Great, or Charlemagne, for example. Or saints like Albertus Magnus, and Saint Gregory, or Pope Gregory the First, the Great. At that time, who could have possessed all the knowledge of the world?" I asked.

They looked at me blankly.

"Who was king of a vast empire, like the one that comprised Castile, Aragon, Catalonia, Navarra, Valencia, the Roussillon region, the Franche-Comté, the Low Countries, Sicily, Sardinia, Milan, Naples, Oran, Tunis, Portugal, the Afro-Asian empire, all of the recently discovered America, and the Philippines. Someone on whose empire the sun never set?"

"Philip the Second," Juana said.

"Exactly. Philip the Second, the great promoter of the archive."

"And the third stanza?" John asked.

"I think Juana's astronomical explanation and the eclipses covered that. It puts you to shame, John." I smiled.

"Your theory about the mandrake doesn't seem so outlandish," Juana conceded.

"It's not as good as yours. I guess the kids are rubbing off on me. I got carried away by my fantasy," I answered, thinking about Simon, my efficient helper. "Besides, it was the famous eclipse during the Battle of Simancas that opened my eyes. From now on, I suppose we'll have to look toward the ground to find our way to the *Voynich*."

"When?" John asked eagerly.

"Tomorrow," I replied. "I've got no classes all day. And there are buses to Simancas every two hours."

I handed them a brochure for the Simancas Castle-Archive. Then I said good-bye to my friends and headed to the school to continue with my classes while they toured the city.

They would be alone at last.

" 'The historical facts about the fortress at Simancas date back much further than the actual castle.' "

I was reading out loud from a guidebook that I'd brought in my backpack, together with a lot of other papers. Though the trip to Simancas wasn't very long, I thought these could provide some entertainment as we traveled. The couple listened to me attentively. Juana had pushed her dark hair back with her sunglasses and stared at me intently so she wouldn't miss a thing. John, in turn, was looking at Juana. I continued reading from my guide for a good while.

" 'The peculiar location of the town of Simancas in the Duero Valley, where the Pisuerga River joins the Duero, was a strategic point against the Moors for León in its dominance along the river. The famous Battle of Simancas in the year of the eclipse proves this. Simancas was the most important town in the region until Valladolid started to develop and finally surpassed it. Today Simancas has only about four thousand inhabitants.' "

"When were the castle and the archive built?" Juana asked me.

"According to this little book, 'in 1467 Henry the Fourth ordered Pedro Niño, the Valladolid regent, to build a fortress in the city of Simancas. But

Fadrique Enríquez, the admiral from Castile at that time, acted first, taking over the village for the opposition forces.' Therefore," I continued reading, "'Enríquez was the first lord of the present castle. Later the Catholic monarchs Ferdinand and Isabella recovered various strategic fortresses in the heart of Castile. One of them was Simancas, which became, together with the fortresses of Medina del Campo and Arévalo, one of the most powerful of the Castilian strongholds. When the revolt of the Comuneros[11] was over, Emperor Charles the Fifth used Simancas as a prison for some of those illustrious rebels. Charles ended the war and, on his command, the castle became the general archive of the Castilian crown. The archive was renovated and enlarged by successive kings. The first renovation was by his son Philip the Second, who is credited with its magnificence, and then by his grandson Philip the Third. Later kings, like Philip the Fifth as well as Charles the Third, continued the remodeling. Today it's still used as the general archive.'"

"Pretty remarkable," John commented.

"It's one of the most important historical archives in the world," I added with pride, "surpassed in Europe only by the Vatican. It contains valuable information about Castile and all the other possessions of the Spanish empire during its greatest glory."

We were getting close to the castle.

The Simancas fortress looks similar to others of its time, and is very well preserved. According to the guidebook, there were two reasons for that. First, it had always been inhabited, with the mayor of the fortress being replaced by an archivist when the castle lost its military role—a position passed down from father to son. Second, there had been continuous restorations and expansions over the centuries. Not without cause, it's considered the oldest archive in the world to establish its own regulations.

The fortress is completely surrounded by a pentagon-shaped stone wall, with its towers, outer bailey, and embankments. The castle is separated from the wall by a moat with two fixed bridges and two access doors.

11. The revolt and war of the Castilian Communities was a rebellion against the crown (1520–1521). It was against King Charles I of Spain, who was also Charles V of Germany, and his attempts to modify the government and grant important positions to foreigners. Because of the revolt's liberal democratic ideas, a few historians think of this as the first modern revolution in Europe, and the precursor of the French Revolution. (From *Wikipedia*, Author's Note)

Juana was very impressed by its imposing medieval aspect. "No knights are coming out to receive us," she said in jest.

"It's no Camelot," John protested, letting his British pride show.

While they got involved in the history of round tables and fantastic tournaments, I was checking my guide against what I had in front of me. Four corner towers protected the castle. A turret guarded the main entrance.

"Four circular towers. As the map in the book shows."

"Are we going in?" Juana begged impatiently.

"Yes, let's," I agreed.

Inside, we found a modern lobby with modern furniture and several computers—also modern, of course. Behind the main counter, a girl gave us a friendly greeting and asked if we had come to see the castle as tourists or students doing research. Juana and John turned to me expectantly, as if I were their professor.

"First we'd like to take a tour," I said.

The receptionist handed us three leaflets.

I glanced at mine.

The archive at Simancas is one of the most important in Europe. It is indispensable for historical research from the late fifteenth century—the reign of the Catholic monarchs, Ferdinand and Isabella—to 1800, the period known as the beginning of the modern age. To its incomparable documentary value we have to add its architectural singularity, because although it looks like a real castle, it is, in fact, an archive built in the middle of the sixteenth century, which made it the first building constructed specifically for this purpose. It is a true gem both as a document repository and as an architectural marvel.

Nothing particularly new, but I kept reading.

During the reigns of Ferdinand and Isabella, and of Charles V, the castle continued functioning as a fortress, armory, prison, and monetary repository. In 1540 Charles V decided to keep the most important documents in one of the castle towers. So he had the upper floor of the northern tower remodeled, and it became known as the Archive Tower. That's how the archive began at Simancas. But it was his son, Philip II, who decided to use the entire fortress as an archive. He assigned the work to architect Juan de Herrera, who came to Simancas in 1574 and drew the plans for the present structure. He still wanted the building to look like a castle, with the outer surrounding wall, the four corner towers, the entrance turret, and the chapel.

The leaflet included a walking tour of the castle interior.

To John's chagrin, we decided to start with the chapel.

The chapel had been redesigned by the Enríquez family in the fifteenth century. There wasn't much to see there, except for a few images of little artistic merit and some coats of arms that probably belonged to this family. Then John looked up.

"Stars!"

In fact, the whole vault was decorated with stars.

"The castle of the stars," I said, marveling at this reminder of the long-gone, ancient observatory that the great Tycho Brahe had built on Hven Island.

"Not a bad start," Juana said with a smile.

Unfortunately, the rest of the visit was pretty boring.

Access was limited to certain areas, just the inner courtyard and the two large reading rooms. Nothing else. Between them was the Archive Tower, later called the Philip II Tower. He had reconstructed this part of the building, also creating an upper floor to house the archive, joined by a beautiful wooden corridor. Besides this, there was the Tower of Works and Forests, the Charles V Tower, and the Bishop's Tower, which was crowned by a showy bell-shaped roof with a lantern at the top.

I spoke very little during our tour, except to satisfy John's curiosity.

"The lantern is a turret with windows, taller than it is wide, like one finds at the top of some buildings and church domes. It allows natural light to illuminate the space."

"Like a skylight," Juana added.

"Yeah, sort of," I admitted.

"Interesting," John commented, pleased with the innovation.

We couldn't go up into any of the towers to investigate further. There was nothing at all that seemed to relate to any of the clues to the *Voynich Manuscript*.

Obviously, there wouldn't be any index card or entry for the *Voynich* in the archive.

So we decided to go back and do some more thinking over a good Castilian dinner.

"Then what do you suggest?" Juana asked.

"To plan our next step very carefully," I answered. "We don't have a direction."

"We still have two stanzas from the Emerald Table to explore," John suggested, finishing his wine. "This is excellent, by the way."

"The stanzas are very confusing, John. And most of the castle is closed to inquisitive intruders like us," I added. "Simancas is still an unassailable fortress, as the creators of the archive intended."

"And also the Jesuits," Juana said, smiling. Faithful to her meager diet, she was having only a salad and mineral water. "Regarding the Jesuits, Hector, I'd like to ask you something."

"Your olive oil mouth may ask whatever you like."

She smiled, hiding her mouth behind her napkin.

"I want to see the other archive."

"Which other archive?" I asked, unaware of how naive I sounded.

"Yours, of course. John has seen the archive in your monastery, as well as the famous underground labyrinths, but I haven't," she complained.

"I already told you there's nothing there," I answered, annoyed by the unexpected request. "I've gone down there several times. Besides," I added ironically, "soon it will be yours. Just a matter of time."

John was looking at us, puzzled. I'd told him about my talk with Juana without going into detail.

"It's no longer a secret," I told John, "that Juana has friends who are very interested in the *Voynich Manuscript*."

She lowered her eyes, looking guilty. I realized I wasn't being fair to her.

"It doesn't matter," I corrected myself, trying to mend the situation. "In fact, each of us, for different reasons, wants to solve this mystery, once and for all."

"Even if nobody had asked, I would want to know the meaning of the book on my own." Then Juana asked me, "Well, what about it?"

She was referring to her request to visit the labyrinth.

"Okay," I said. "I'll ask Julian. I returned the keys but I suppose he'll have no objection to our looking around a bit down there."

He didn't.

The following day Julian welcomed Juana and John. He agreed to our visit, perhaps the last one before handing the building over to the real estate developers. His only condition was that we had to be discreet.

"I prefer that you go at night, when the whole community is asleep. I don't think any explanations are necessary, especially after our decision to leave. And if you find anything interesting about that strange book you are looking for, be sure to tell me," Julian said. "Hector, you can quietly open the door to the library, to let your friends in."

John and Juana were right on time. Exactly at midnight they were knocking at the door.

"Come in," I said. "The coast is clear."

I had already prepared the basic equipment, batteries and flashlights, some small tools, a notebook, a camera, and some warm clothes. And a few chocolate bars.

"That's fattening," Juana protested.

"You don't have to eat them," John told her, putting the first one in his mouth.

"Come on. Let's not waste time. Julian said he would leave the keys in the lock."

We went down without any problems. I showed Juana the different rooms and paths along the way. I'd brought the drawings and diagrams in the notebook with me. She stopped to look more carefully when we got to the Roman ruins, and also in front of the Galileo quote inscribed by Lazzari. The final stretch led us to the barrier John had cosmically baptized as Planck's wall.

"We can't go any farther than this ghastly wall," the Brit said.

"Except with your bulldozers," I murmured to Juana. She pretended not to hear, or maybe she really didn't. For quite some time she stared at the perfectly aligned stone blocks.

"What's behind it?" she finally asked.

"Absolutely nothing, I'd guess. You can hear some residual water filtering from above and falling into a wider bed, possibly the same river that crosses the city. Maybe it was erected to prevent accidents."

"Doesn't it suggest anything to you?" Juana insisted.

"What could it suggest?" I shrugged and looked at John, who also shrugged.

"A stretch of stone wall, like in a castle. With the river flowing underneath," she answered.

"We're a few miles away from Simancas, if that's what you mean."

"But we're connected by the same river, aren't we?"

"Yes," I admitted.

"What makes you think that Lazzari and the rest used the Simancas Archive in a conventional way?" she kept insisting.

"Logic, I suppose," I replied.

"Is it logical to keep part of a manuscript from the sixteenth century in the general archive of the Spanish crown and not even make an entry or an index card? A very costly manuscript that possibly belonged to a nephew of Philip the Second and that nobody could decipher?"

"It's true, it doesn't sound logical, Hector," John said, siding with Juana.

"It makes sense that your predecessors would hide it there in a way we could consider atypical," she kept reasoning. "Those who wanted to suppress the Jesuit order could have searched this building to its foundation and never found a sealed room containing royal documents. And I mean *royal*," she pointed out.

"And what makes you think it's still there?" I asked, a bit thrown off by her shrewdness.

"Intuition," she said, smiling, "which is much stronger than logic."

"One option for your friend Thomas is to buy the castle at Simancas and tear it down," I told Juana sarcastically while fixing coffee for us. We were together in my cybercafé, weighing our options. John was focused on answering an urgent e-mail and paid no attention to our conversation. One of his colleagues wrote that he had discovered a supernova in a distant galaxy, very distant.

"Thomas is capable of that, and much more," Juana said with a tinge of mischief.

"And our Ministry of Culture is capable of readily selling the *Voynich Manuscript*," I said, playing along. "They love to knock down Castilian archives. Their favorite sport."[12]

"Any other brilliant ideas?" Juana persisted.

12. In 2006, the Spanish Ministry of Culture decided, in the midst of a strong social controversy, to transfer part of the holdings of the historic archives of the Spanish Civil War from the Castilian city of Salamanca to Catalonia, Barcelona. (Author's Note)

"Let's take this piece by piece," I suggested. "If your far-fetched hypothesis is true, it would mean that the Machiavellian eighteenth-century Jesuits found a way to get to the Simancas Archive without being seen, entered the fortress as if they owned it, and once there, capriciously moved the furniture and the portraits of noblemen in order to put the codes of the *Voynich Manuscript* up on a shelf, away from curious eyes," I reasoned with a tinge of irony. "And then placed this shelf in a bombproof chamber."

"Well, you've embellished this, but yes, basically that's how it was."

"And then," I went on, "they used the ancient text of the Emerald Table to indicate this hiding place, to guide the possible searchers to the book."

"Aha!" Juana exclaimed. "Once again, using clues after the fact."

"Did I miss something?" John asked, trying to rejoin the conversation.

"Basically no," I replied. "Our friend is suggesting that some hooded monks who weren't Capuchin but Jesuit took a boat and rowed from here to Simancas to hide the book."

"Well, you're very caustic today," John remarked, smiling.

"Maybe lack of sleep is getting the best of me," I admitted.

"And why don't we do the same thing? Reconstruct the scene," Juana suggested eagerly. "Like the police do."

I looked at her, at a loss. And John's answer was equally crazy.

"I'm a bloody Cambridge oarsman," he said triumphantly.

"You're a pair of lunatics," I answered, covering my face.

I had scarcely rowed half a dozen times in my life, and Juana, even fewer than that. John was really an expert, but that still meant a lot of pain. Finding a light boat for three turned out to be much easier than I'd thought.

We only had to borrow it from the modest nautical club on the river. It was tied to the dock.

The river current helped us. Even so, it took us well over an hour to reach the town of Simancas. We had to go ashore several times to avoid the waterfalls of the old mills that, even though old, wouldn't have interrupted the river flow in the eighteenth century. It was still very dark when we finally saw the lighted towers of the fortress.

"From now on, we have to watch for any possible natural landing. A cave, a hidden bend in the river, anything that may appear peculiar."

"I don't say this to be obnoxious, but it would have been much easier to do this during the day," I protested halfheartedly.

"Stop complaining and aim the flashlight at the riverbank," Juana shushed me, enjoying the unexpected adventure.

We explored several paths from the river toward town. They led nowhere.

"What's that?"

John had found what seemed to be an old iron sewer cover. It was a few yards from the shore, inaccessible from any place other than the river.

"Help me," he said, gasping.

We managed to lift it off. A terrible smell forced us back when we looked in.

"This isn't a good idea," I said.

"The outer walls of the castle must be pretty close, less than a hundred yards away," Juana protested.

"Hector's right," John said. "If this is a septic tank, surely by tomorrow someone will find the three of us, stone cold and stiff."

"Well, I'm going in."

Before we could stop her, Juana was already climbing down the rusty ladder. John looked at me, and followed her.

And I followed them, saying my final prayers. Fortunately, once we were inside, the air was better. Thank God. The corridors were similar to those in my monastery, damp and narrow, alternating with stairs that went up or down according to the terrain.

"How long since anybody was here?" John asked as he led the way.

"At least three centuries," I told him. "And we've come to the end," I said, aiming my flashlight at a worm-eaten wooden side door. "Help me push it, John."

The door gave way at the first shove, becoming unhinged. The noise was scary.

"We must be directly below the castle," Juana whispered.

"I hope there's no guard around. We're making quite a racket."

"Now what?" John asked.

We had reached a larger room. Some old furniture was piled up, along with a bunch of tools and equipment.

"This looks like an abandoned warehouse," I said. "I suggest we look behind the furniture against the wall to see what's there."

With a cloud of dust, and a lot more effort than it took to push the door open, we managed to move a couple of oak cabinets. It was enough. There was an opening in the wall, large enough for one person to go through if they crouched.

"Let me go in first, and I'll tell you," Juana said, bending down and sliding easily through the opening. In less than a minute she came back. "I think this is it!" she exclaimed, overjoyed. "There's a large cabinet on the other side. And someone made some small holes to be able to see through. It's a restored room. I can't tell what it is, but it's civilized territory."

John and I pushed again, with a little more difficulty because of the narrow space. We really were inside the Simancas Castle.

"This place isn't bad," I joked.

We had ended up in the torture chamber.

The guidebook said it was a point of interest. The bishop of Zamora, Don Antonio Acuña, had served his sentence there. As the Comunero Captain of Castile, he had fought in the Battle of Villalar. The three most famous Comuneros, Padilla, Bravo, and Maldonado, were executed the day after the battle. But Don Antonio was held prisoner at Simancas and granted the opportunity to repent. Not only did the ingrate refuse to repent, but he strangled the mayor of the fortress. Trying to flee, he was recaptured and executed in one of the towers of the castle, now called the Bishop's Tower. This was in 1521.

"First problem," I announced from the center of the big hall. "Security cameras."

"They're turned off," John reported after checking one. "They're probably only on during visiting hours. That gives us another positive conclusion."

"Namely?" I wanted to know.

"That there's no night surveillance. If the cameras are off, so are the monitors. Nobody's watching "

"And what is that?" Juana cut in, pointing at some additional electronic stuff.

John again offered his expert opinion.

"Nothing to worry about. Fire detectors and alarms. As long as we don't smoke, everything will be okay," he teased.

"What time is it?" I asked then.

"It's nearly six, almost morning," Juana answered. "According to the leaflet, the archive opens at nine thirty. I imagine the employees will start coming in an hour before."

"Then we've got more than two hours to snoop around," John noted.

"Let's go to the main halls," I said.

We roamed through the castle with almost total freedom. Except for the armored—and fireproof—rooms in the Philip II Tower, we found no locked doors, only cordons and signs denying access to unauthorized personnel. We were about to go up into the towers, the only places we hadn't visited yet, when John stopped us.

"Why don't we use our heads?" he suggested. "We don't know what we're looking for, we're just going from place to place willy-nilly," he protested.

"What do you suggest?" I stopped to ask him. "We don't have much time."

"I don't know. Let's at least check the last stanzas from Wilfred Voynich."

Juana glanced at me, then took a crumpled piece of paper with the text I'd given her out of her backpack.

"We were up to here," she said and pointed for us to look.

> You will separate Earth from Fire, the subtle from the gross,
> gently, and with much ingenuity.
> Ascend from Earth to Heaven, and back to Earth again,
> taking strength equally from the superior and the inferior.
> Thus will you achieve all the glory in the world.

"The first line is," John repeated: "'You will separate Earth from Fire, the subtle from the gross, gently, and with great ingenuity.'"

"Should we look for a fireplace?" I suggested, not very convinced.

"No. That's not ingenious at all," Juana retorted. "By the way," she asked, turning her head, "didn't we want a map?"

We were in one of the smallest reading rooms, normally closed to the public. Through its limited windows we could see the central courtyard and modest garden. On one of the walls without shelves, a large tapestry hung from ceiling to floor. It was an enormous world map.

"Could this be it?" John asked, shining his flashlight on it.

"It could be," I said. "It looks like it was made in the eighteenth century. The so-called New World is there, as well as Oceania and the southern polar shores."

"All that John Harrison and James Cook added to the maps," John remarked. "But I don't see anything special."

Juana moved closer and began fingering the fabric. She traced the soft surface all along the Americas, starting with Mexico.

"Always a patriot." I laughed.

"Idiot," she said, "don't you see how easy it is?"

I barely heard what she said because of a horrible screeching noise. A strange mechanism had started moving. Its cogwheels lacked oil as much as my worn-out neurons needed a cup of coffee.

"How did you do that, sister?" I asked, amazed to see a small door opening behind the tapestry.

"'You will separate Earth from Fire,' obviously." She laughed. "And with a lot of ingenuity."

"The mechanism was activated when a spring coil on Patagonia was released," John interrupted. "Earth from Fire surely referred to Tierra del Fuego. Literally. It was so simple."

"Right," Juana agreed triumphantly. "Now let's go inside."

The door that had just opened, as if by magic, led to an inner passageway, and this to one of the towers. The second line from that stanza is simple too.

"The Jesuits made it easy for us," Juana said, reciting from memory: "'Ascend from Earth to Heaven, and back to Earth again.' We must go up and down."

"To just go up and down for nothing is nonsense," I objected. I was tired.

"C'mon, spoilsport, there has to be something up there," John tried to encourage me, already heading up the first flight of stairs.

But we didn't find anything except the early sun, glaring with a vengeance through a long series of windows. Given the time and our collective tiredness, we decided to go back the same way we'd come in, taking all possible precautions.

We would have to come back.

32

Our trip home was much simpler. We retraced our steps, leaving everything just as we'd found it, and went back through the underground. Finally at the exit, we hid the boat among the reeds. We were exhausted, and not planning to row upstream—least of all in daylight—but instead trekked over the countryside to end up on the highway. We took the first bus heading for the city, and once home, said our goodbyes to get some rest.

Though I wasn't able to.

The coffee, along with Matthew's early call, kept me awake. Simon had been waiting for me in the library for quite a while.

"To what do I owe the honor?" I greeted him, my grogginess almost overcoming my sarcasm.

"Hector, I brought you more stuff."

"This better be interesting, or I'll give you a failing grade."

"On what?"

"On holy matters," I said, neither ready nor wanting to explain any further.

He didn't understand my answer, but that didn't seem to bother him. He was too anxious to tell me about his latest discoveries. I had encouraged him to keep bringing any interesting items related to alchemy or to mandrakes. Or both.

"Look at this," he said, handing me a printout from God knows what Web site. "'Alchemists used a tree symbol to represent the seven metals, and thus to show that these were all branches of the same tree. A shared trunk that was the source and essence of them all.'"

"The philosopher's stone all over again," I broke in, a bit grouchy, tired from the long night and dubious about Simon's fantastic tales.

"The analogy between metals and plants doesn't end there," he continued. "'For the alchemists, metals develop the same way as plants do and, in the process, don't necessarily have to be touched by human hands. The seed germinates in the ground, grows into a plant, flowers, and bears fruit, and all of this simply by natural influences. The same can be applied to metals.'"

"I don't see where you're headed. Can we plant a nail?" I kidded.

"'Everything in nature has a particular essence, which remains even when we reduce it to ashes,'" Simon kept reading, immune to my sarcasm. "'This essence persists until the remains have completely disintegrated. Certain alchemists were thought to be capable of restoring matter, making it reappear.'"

"Which alchemists?" I asked. "There were hundreds of them."

"The ones called hermetic, it says here."

"Hermetic?" I asked, now fully awake.

"Yes. One of them was able to restore a rose from its ashes in the presence of Queen Christina of Sweden. In 1687."

"Some charlatan, I imagine," I said disdainfully.

"Like all the Jesuits." He laughed, and at that point I didn't get his joke. "This guy not only studied roses, but also sunflowers. And mandrakes, naturally. He wrote a book titled *Magnes, sive de arte magnetica* that describes, for example, how sunflowers face the Sun by an invisible magnetic force coming from the heavenly body. Ancient Egyptians and Greeks already considered sunflowers sacred plants. And mandrakes too, of course."

"What else do you have on mandrake roots?" This was getting interesting.

"That the ancient Germans worshiped them, calling them *Alrunes*. They stored them in small cases, giving them food and wine, since they thought of them as little men who protected them from demons and evil spirits. Even Hippocrates prescribed mandrake roots against melancholy and depression. And the Syrians, Arabs, and Chaldeans also knew of their medicinal and magical properties. The same as the Persians,'" he read. "Kircher wrote about their occult powers, and also about the amazing results of ingesting them."

"Did you say Kircher? Athanasius Kircher?"

"Sure. The Jesuit scientist, I thought you knew who I was talking about. The one who wrote the book on magnetism, the one who restored the rose."

"Kircher wrote about many things in his life. A tremendous number," I said, trying to excuse my ignorance.

I stayed to work in the library for a while after Simon left. Then I went up to my room and started surfing frantically on the Internet, seeking more information. Kircher had actually been receptive to hermetic philosophers, though he didn't go along with the alchemists' practices. He seemed to follow a middle path, somewhere in between the two. I also fished around on the pages of the Voynich List. Every day, people were bringing in new ideas. I specifically focused on comments related to botany. According to most investigators, the only clearly identifiable plants in the whole *Voynich Manuscript* were sunflowers and mandrake roots. And sunflowers weren't well known when the manuscript was made.

For reasons that escaped me, I got the impression that Athanasius Kircher had arrived at an identical, or similar, conclusion to my own. Once the Jesuit scholar had recognized these two plants, he probably wanted to investigate them more deeply, especially if, as I presumed, he saw the possibility of translating the texts that accompanied the drawings.

A possibility that eluded me for the time being.

I kept reading screen after screen. Several pages of the *Voynich* contain drawings and engravings of what seem to be mandrakes. Almost always accompanied by medicinal vials. Or else towers. There was a difference of opinion among *Voynich* researchers in this regard. Some argued that if these were medicinal or healing plants, it was logical to think the cylindrical drawings on the left were simply vials. Others, including me, saw only towers.

I had originally associated the mandrakes and towers with a castle, although Juana's brilliant solution to the third stanza—suggesting an eclipse—made me question that.

I went back to the page with the towers and focused on additional details. If Kircher had studied mandrakes with such interest, perhaps those who hid the keys to the *Manuscript* had the same reverence for these plants, so appealing, so "human." Perhaps I shouldn't have abandoned my own conclusions so quickly.

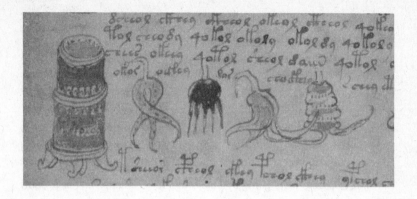

Besides, there were four towers.

One for each corner of the Simancas Castle.

And one of these had roots. Mandrake roots.

"I think the book containing the codes is in the Bishop's Tower."

"Is that from logic or intuition?" Juana asked, smiling.

We had gathered to eat. Having slept much more than I, they arrived with a freshness that I couldn't match. I tried my best to defend my theory.

"Both, Juana," I said. "The line from the Emerald Table tells us to 'Ascend from Earth to Heaven, and back to Earth again.' And on our way we found a tower in the Simancas fortress. It all fits."

"But it wasn't the Bishop's Tower," John objected. "I think it was the Works and Forests Tower, the least important of the four."

"Where we didn't find anything," I added.

"Maybe we weren't looking hard enough. We didn't have a lot of time," Juana suggested. "But the tapestry led us to it."

"I know. And that's precisely what doesn't fit for me." I was finally recovering my wits. "Logic works fine until then. Until you get to that tower. But my intuition tells me we have to look in the Bishop's Tower."

"Knowing you, I'm sure your intuition comes from some kind of reasoning," John said.

"We found the figures from the Roman Pantheon in the *Manuscript,* and I think we've found the towers of Simancas Castle there too," I explained.

"And one of them is different, the one that has mandrake roots coming out of its base."

I again showed them the drawing.

"I think it has to be the Bishop's Tower," I continued, "because this was the place assigned for executions. Where mandrakes grew, according to the legend."

"We won't lose anything by looking. I trust intuition, as you already know." Juana smiled. "Besides, we must go back. Last night we left our work only half finished."

"But this time we're going by bus," I announced happily. "I have some terrible stabbing pains in my arms from all that rowing."

The last bus left us in the town at eight in the evening. We had more than enough time to enter the underground and, from there, get into the castle. Since the night was pleasant, we sat on a terrace in the main square to work out our strategy and give a few more turns to the hermetic text used by the Jesuits.

" 'Ascend from Earth to Heaven, and back to Earth again, taking strength equally from the superior and the inferior. Thus will you achieve all the glory in the world,' " I read again.

They looked at me, searching for new ideas. I continued. "How do you achieve glory, the glory of the whole world?" I asked.

"Riches? Maybe power?" Juana tried.

"By conquest in battle!" John declared proudly.

It was simple. The preceding stanza alluded to the eclipse that had occurred during the Battle of Simancas. The triumph of the Christian troops over those of the Muslims.

"It's so clear!" Juana cried out. "In that battle, King Ramiro the Second of León received 'strength equally from the superior and the inferior.' Obviously he needed the astronomical 'superior' help of the eclipse from above. And of the soldiers from Galicia, Asturias, and Navarra, which we could consider 'inferior,' from below."

"Exactly," I agreed. "But we still don't know what to look for in the tower."

"Or even in which tower," John said, discouraged.

After waiting for another half hour, we got up and were on our way to the abandoned farm leading to the concealed entrance. After a tiresome climb up and down, and getting lost a couple of times, we got to the old sewer.

It smelled worse than the night before.

"Come on, hurry up," I pressed them, pinching my nose to keep out the intensely foul odor. "We've got to search every corner of this castle tonight."

"We're not leaving any stone unturned. Besides," John added to my comment, "I'd like to finish quickly tonight and be wide awake tomorrow morning, to be able to watch the eclipse in peace."

In fact, the annular eclipse of the Sun was scheduled—and there was no means of rescheduling its occurrence—for the next morning. It would start to be visible at ten o'clock sharp, and end a couple of hours later. Like clockwork, at 10:58 the eclipse would reach its most spectacular phase, with almost the entire surface of the Sun covered by the Moon.

"I've got to be with the kids in the school yard," I said. "Besides, I have to set up the telescopes and binoculars in advance and take care of the parents; a lot of them will be joining their kids. Plus protect all of them with dark glasses." I kept enumerating chores, with a mix of annoyance and pleasure.

"Well, less talk and in we go."

This time, as Juana had done before, she took the lead, slipping nimbly into that dark, smelly hole. After a few yards going down and a few more walking on level ground, we quickly adjusted to the unpleasant surroundings and advanced at a good pace. It didn't take us long to reach the first door and go from there to the torture chamber, our secret access to the fortress at Simancas.

"All's the same as last night," I concluded, quickly sweeping my flashlight around. "Let's go straight to the room with the tapestry."

Everything was exactly the way we'd left it only a few hours before. The small reading room seemed to be very rarely occupied and was closed to the public, its use limited to storing fairly recent documents. The computer on the lone table was the oldest item.

"Damn. It's a 286, and with MS-DOS." Juana laughed.

"The one used by Philip the Second," I also quipped.

"Come on, quit wasting time."

John had already pressed the release of the spring coil hidden behind the thick tapestry. The mechanism moved with the same horrible screech as the first time.

"It's complaining about having to operate twice in a row in three centuries. Made in Spain," John wisecracked now.

I glared at him, deciding to let him live, and one after the other we went through the narrow passageway that had opened. There was nothing new until we reached the stairway to the tower. Juana stopped us.

"If I remember correctly, yesterday we went upstairs right away, didn't we?"

"You're right, Juana," I said.

"'Ascend from Earth to Heaven, and back to Earth again,'" John coached me. "First up and then down."

"But above there was nothing at all," our Mexican friend said, continuing to think out loud.

"Nothing," I agreed. "These small stairs lead almost directly to the main staircase of the tower. There were only some narrow windows and a few swallows' nests up there. The documents of this area are below."

"There isn't even any furniture or shelving. Only the wood in the ceiling," John said, finishing my argument.

"I'm sure this isn't the tower we're looking for," I responded. "We've got to search in the Bishop's Tower, in the corner directly opposite this one."

"Then why do we need to come in through here?" Juana wondered again.

"For you to show off your knowledge of geography," I teased.

Juana paid no attention to me and hurried down the stairs.

"Hold it, crazy girl. You're gonna fall."

"Come down!" she shrieked.

When John and I got there, Juana greeted us with a satisfied smile, pointing to a new passageway, just as narrow as all the previous ones.

"Voilà!" she said eagerly. "How much do you wanna bet that this corridor runs diagonally beneath the fortress?"

It did, with a new flight of stairs at the other end, which supposedly went up into the Bishop's Tower.

"I'm not budging until you explain this," I pleaded with her.

"Hector, dear," she said, smiling impishly, "the text says that we go up, and then go back down again. Which presupposes that we had to go *down* first."

"If you say so," I muttered, and started climbing the steep stairs, not very convinced by Juana's reasoning, but satisfied to finally be in the Bishop's Tower, where the Comunero bishop Antonio Acuña had been executed many years ago.

As in the first tower, the hidden staircase led to the main one, and was concealed from it by a simple arrangement of outer and inner doors. In the opposite direction the detour was hidden by a bend in the wall.

"It's possible that the modern restorers of the castle knew of these passages. Every self-respecting fortress has emergency exits to provide an escape from invaders."

"Certainly," I seconded John's wise comment. "But these last passages don't connect with our initial path, so that the main passageway by the river stays secret."

"Like the *Voynich,* for now," Juana remarked, always on target, bringing us back to reality and our main objective.

We wound up beneath the bell-shaped roof. Its construction was more recent than that of the tower, and it was adorned with a beautiful lantern, sadly dark at night. To climb up to the lantern, there was only a long, wobbly wooden ladder, fastened to the inner wall with ropes and eyebolts.

"Does anybody ever go up there?" John asked.

"Judging by its condition," I said, shaking the ladder, "I don't think so."

" 'Stairway to Heaven,' "[13] Juana whispered, raising her head.

"I suppose you'll always hear it played the right way," I said, laughing.

"Of course," she joked back. "So John can translate it backward by tomorrow."[14]

"Definitely," the Brit agreed.

"Look at this," I said, getting back to the subject, and pointing again

---

13. "Stairway to Heaven," the title of possibly the best-known song by the British rock group Led Zeppelin, released in 1971. (Author's Note)

14. According to some fundamentalist Christian groups, if one fragment of the song is played backward, one can hear words that start with "Oh, here's my sweet Satan." Obviously the group has always denied any such content, or that there's any hidden praise of heroin. (Author's Note)

at the structure. "The tower is topped by this bell-shaped cupola without any ribs or drum, but with a beautiful lantern that is surely an intense light source during the day. If it's well designed," I added, "the light would spread uniformly in the space below the tower. There," I said, pointing at the bottom floor.

"That's fine, Hector, for the architectural details," Juana complimented me. "But here they don't help us the way they did in the Roman Pantheon."

"Maybe they do," John suggested.

We looked at each other.

"Which way do the tower and lantern point?" he asked.

"To the east," I answered, confirming what we were all thinking.

"Uh-huh," he said and nodded.

"What do you have in mind now?" Juana asked with ill-disguised excitement.

"If I'm not mistaken, John's thinking about tomorrow's eclipse."

"You're not mistaken," he said.

"At the time of the eclipse," I continued, "the Sun still won't have reached its highest point, but its rays will shine directly through the panes of the lantern. If it were any ordinary day, we'd have a wonderful, uniform glow illuminating the entire structure, including the stairs and the base of the tower."

"But not tomorrow," John remarked.

"That's right," I said. "Tomorrow, for a half hour, there will be a play of light and shadows—on the frames, wooden panels, and everything we can and can't see."

"'Ascend from Earth to Heaven . . . taking strength equally from the superior,'" Juana recited. "Now I understand completely."

"Possibly there was another eclipse during the initial suppression of the Jesuits," I suggested. "Though I can't confirm this for you now because I didn't bring those notes."

"Then what should we do?" John asked.

"Wait, of course."

Juana had decided for the three of us.

We couldn't return. First, because the archive staff would have kept us from climbing to the top of the tower without a strong justification, and any support for a story as far-fetched as ours was out of the question. Second, because it was very late. The next day had almost come. There were scarcely a couple of hours before dawn, and in about six the heavenly spectacle would start.

There was another, very practical, reason. We could hide quite easily in the space below the lantern, and weren't likely to be found by some absent-minded archive worker. No documents were stored up above.

So we sampled the chocolate bars. Including Juana.

"How much longer?" John asked impatiently.

"The Moon will start to hide the Sun in about twenty minutes," I said, keeping my voice down.

Fortunately we hadn't forgotten to bring the cell phone. A simple call to Julian had sufficed to excuse my absence on such a special school day.

"What you're doing must be very important for you to miss such an event," he said, assuring me that he would take charge of everything, and without asking for any more explanation.

"Now," I said, as my watch marked the start of the solar eclipse, "pay attention to anything that moves."

As the minutes went by, our hiding place started filling with shadows. We breathed very slowly, as if our breathing might cause some delay in the unstoppable lunar progression. In the distance we could hear a telephone ring, the bustle of the employees, chattering about the sorry state of the copy machine or about a joke coming in by e-mail.

"We're going to be able to see it," someone yelled from one of the adjacent reading rooms, undoubtedly referring to the approaching peak of the eclipse.

John and Juana looked at me with the same question on their faces.

"It's five to eleven," I whispered, "just three minutes before the maximum coverage."

"There!" Juana shouted, pointing at the staircase hollow.

It was pitch-black.

"I can't see anything down there," I said, poking my head out over the banister. John couldn't see anything unusual either.

"Please move the window frame if you can reach it," Juana asked me.

I couldn't. But on moving to make the attempt, I could make out the same image that she had probably seen. The wrought-iron latticework protecting the glass was projecting a strange pattern onto the floor. The metal openings functioned in the same way as the top opening in a meridian, and the whole tower worked like a camera obscura, the same as usually happened in cathedrals. About fifty feet below us, a ring—the diffracted projection of the combined image formed by the Sun and the Moon—pointed at the ironwork on some antique trunks stored there. These were a half dozen of the large, velvet-lined chests that Philip II had ordered to transport and safeguard bundles of papers. They were outside the locked, iron-plated cupboards that had served as strongboxes for centuries.

"Hector, it's got to be inside there. I'm sure of it!"

Juana was overcome with excitement. She had climbed the perilously unstable wooden rungs of the top ladder inside the lantern. One of the ancient iron eyebolts, rusted and corroded by the relentless passage of time, opened under her weight and gave way.

I watched in horror as John tried to grab her on the way down, but only managed to tumble with her into the hollow of the tower staircase.

33

The two ambulances took less than thirty minutes to come from Valladolid. Juana's and John's falls had produced a thunderous racket. Right away at least half a dozen people had come, alarmed by the screams and noise of the crash. John was fortunate, and despite being knocked unconscious, he only suffered a sprained ankle and a few scratches and bruises. Juana had broken her neck.

I had no idea of what to say or how to explain what had happened.

First the police and later the female judge on duty came up with a seemingly endless barrage of questions. What were we doing inside the archive? Who were the foreigners and what were they looking for? How did they fall? And who was I? Because no one could believe that I was a Jesuit priest and high school teacher. Fortunately, one of the court officials turned out to be the father of one of my students. After he recognized me, everything was pretty routine.

That is, if anything can be routine under such circumstances.

Julian came, alarmed by my call from a police department, but spared me further questions. I already had enough with the pressure from the judge and trying to explain what had happened in a more or less coherent form. For five long hours I answered, or attempted to answer, all the questions that occurred to her, trying to remain calm, praying for my friends (in the first moments of confusion, I thought they were both dead), and submitting obediently to the requirements of the investigation. In addition, I had to be careful not to mention or make any allusion to anything related to the *Voynich Manuscript*.

That night I returned to the house.

I was destroyed inside and out.

I couldn't sleep a wink during the couple of hours I spent in bed in my room. The next day, very early, I was allowed to go to the hospital and see John. He was conscious and looked all right.

"What about Juana? What room is she in?"

I didn't dare tell my friend that she had died instantly. He scarcely remembered what had happened. I lied to him, saying that she only had a few bumps and bruises and that both of them would soon be back home. In fact, at that time, her body was on the coroner's table. Only two hours later she would be sent to Madrid, and from there, by plane, to Mexico. I called the Mexican embassy in Spain and, after a lot of pleading and insisting, managed to get them to tell me that her father was waiting at the airport in the Mexican capital to receive her remains. Little else.

At noon I had to appear in court again.

"Are you better?"

The judge smiled at me, seeming more rested than I. She asked if I wanted some coffee and even offered me a cigarette. She chain-smoked. I gratefully accepted the coffee.

"Are we going to start from the beginning of the story?" she asked amiably.

I nodded.

I explained again, trying to sound more convincing than the first time, that my friends and I were at Simancas as tourists. We were very devoted to astronomy (not for nothing was John Carpenter a distinguished astrophysicist at Cambridge), and we wanted to observe the effects of the eclipse through a sixteenth-century lantern, on an occasion that could have been much like the one experienced during the famous Battle of Simancas. I trusted, on good grounds, that the judge wasn't a history buff and would overlook some of the chronological inconsistencies in my story.

"So, why didn't you ask permission?"

The question was clear, but the answer less so. I mumbled something about our being short on time, saying that my friends had to return to their universities. And since the Spanish bureaucracy was so difficult, I hadn't even made the attempt. I accepted the blame for that.

"You're telling *me* about bureaucracy?" the judge commented, taking a deep drag on her cigarette. "But go on. How the hell did you get in there? Simancas has always been a fortress, and now it's a ministerial archive with countless security measures."

I tried to convince her that this wasn't entirely so. We hadn't seen any alarms, and had taken advantage of a lapse by the guard on duty at the door, slipping through on the run. But we really hadn't done anything bad or unusual.

"Nothing unusual?" she interrupted skeptically. "If you think a woman with a broken neck is normal, let God come down and have a look."

At the mention of Juana, I started to cry. The judge sympathized and refilled my coffee cup.

"We've done a check on your English friend in the hospital," she said while I tried to recover my composure. "He's who you say he is. As for the Mexican woman, her passport is in order and the embassy vouches for her innocence. Her father is a real personality there in Mexico. We're going to consider it all an accident."

"Of course it was an accident!" I shouted indignantly. "Do I look like a mafioso?"

"Calm down," she said. "Maybe it wasn't advisable to give you so much coffee."

"She fell because the ladder gave way under her weight," I persisted, still upset. "It was rotten. John tried to grab her and fell too."

"I've spoken to the archive director concerning this. I suppose it won't be inconvenient for you to compare notes with him on a few points."

"Of course not. Besides," I added with a resigned look, "you're the one in charge here."

"It's also unnecessary to get dramatic," she replied, signaling her secretary, who returned a minute later with a well-dressed, affable-looking man a good deal past fifty.

He reached out to shake hands as the judge introduced us. He didn't seem especially worried or alarmed, and he offered very polite condolences for what had happened to Juana. There was no air of reproach.

The judge again took the floor.

"The matter of the conservation of the building could be as much of a problem for the general archive as for the ministry in charge of it," she began. "Though I must say this would occur only if the family of the victim decided to initiate some kind of legal action."

"The area of the accident," the director explained, "isn't open to the public. For security reasons as well as the general functioning of the archive itself. Without permission, visitors can't have direct access to the documents."

"I know that," I admitted.

"Because of this," he asserted with confident firmness, "in no case will either the general archive or the ministry be responsible. Much less have to indemnify any third parties."

"No complaint has been lodged," the judge explained, "though it's still too soon to know what her family may do."

"If that's so, then there's no problem," the director concluded.

"As for the general archive, does it intend to take legal action?" she asked, lighting another cigarette. The director made a face, showing his disgust as the smoke drifted into his eyes, and answered her question. "We haven't noticed anything missing. And the damages are minimal." He looked at me. "For us it's no more than an unfortunate incident in which some youngsters sneaked into our building."

Of course, the three of us weren't youngsters. It was clear that the head of the archive wanted to be done with the bothersome legal matters, and the sooner the better.

"Well," the judge declared, closing a folder as if to indicate that the matter was coming to an end. "This makes things easier. If neither party wishes to pursue a grievance, so much the better. Naturally this case will remain open for a certain amount of time, meaning that it may be necessary to call both of you again. The special reports will arrive sometime, as well as the coroner's report. But I don't want to bore you with all the proceedings and can only hope not to bother you too much from now on."

She gave us a compassionate look. I appreciated this, just as I had at the beginning of the interrogation.

"And now," she continued, "I must ask you to excuse me. I have some other urgent matters to attend to. I very much regret having taken some of your valuable time."

"Wait!"

I heard someone yell from behind. Looking back, I saw the archive director calling me, coming out the entrance door at the top of the courthouse stairs. I was just about to cross the street but stopped and waited for him.

"Thanks," he said, catching up with me. "I wanted to talk privately with you for a few minutes, if you don't mind."

"Not at all, of course not," I replied. "Besides, I need to apologize for all the inconvenience my behavior has caused you."

"You've lost a friend." He shook his head. "And that is sufficient penance for whatever offense you may have committed. Come," he said, and took me gently by the arm. "That bar on the corner has excellent coffee."

We went in and ordered. The coffee was excellent. Then he spoke.

"Can I ask you a question?"

"Go ahead," I accepted.

"What were you looking for in the archive?"

"What do you mean?" I asked, rather than answer his question, feeling a bit uncomfortable.

"The eclipse business is fine for an uninformed judge," he answered with implied complicity, "but I've spent a lot of years there and I don't believe it."

"Well, that's really how it was," I said, trying to sound convincing. "We went to see the eclipse through the lantern in the Bishop's Tower."

He sighed.

"I was very sorry to hear about your prior. He was an excellent person with a great deal of knowledge."

Now I was perplexed. What did this guy know about Carmelo?

"It seemed very strange to me to learn that a Jesuit was snooping around in our archive when the accident happened. There's more to it, am I right?"

"I can't say, one way or the other," I admitted, "but our society doesn't know much about this. Both John and the unlucky Juana are personal friends of mine. Very good in their respective areas of research."

"You see, whenever we relocate any of our documents, we find surprises. Always. Mixed bundles, chests with double bottoms, folded pages," he started to explain, ordering a second coffee. "Between books and documents, we've got more than seventy-five thousand entries in the archive. Well over seven miles of shelves, and almost thirty million pages. With endless surprises. It's impossible to keep track of everything."

This started to catch my interest. Could they have found the book of keys for the *Voynich*? He continued talking.

"And then there's the furniture. It has been the same since the fifteenth century, except for some pieces that are being added to modernize our bibliographic system and the security for the actual documents. Our experience last year relates to this. We finally had decided to retire"—he paused to finish his second cup—"some half-dozen large chests Philip the Second had personally ordered to serve as strongboxes. They were temporarily moved to the ground floor because we're having them sent to the provincial museum as soon as possible. A little more dust won't hurt them," he noted.

Had the eclipse revealed the wrought-iron locks of a chest moved last year? I crumbled inside, thinking about Juana's terrible accident. We hadn't found out anything. We had gotten caught up in a fantasy. While I lamented these and other matters, the director continued with the minute details of his alterations.

"In fact, we've renovated the main rooms. Everything's fire resistant or incombustible. It was originally designed that way. And we've installed an extremely costly alarm system that never works."

He had changed from coffee to cognac and was growing more and more voluble.

"Perhaps your friend would have had better luck if it had been properly connected," he speculated. "Actually, the security-company technicians are the ones we should sue. But, my friend, orders come from Madrid. From the interior minister. And I don't get involved in political commissions."

I was starting to lose patience.

"How did you know Carmelo?" I interrupted.

"I called him when his papers appeared," he answered.

"His papers?" I asked, my curiosity piqued.

"Yes. We emptied a large chest that had probably been hidden for centuries. It was behind a wall that had to be knocked down to install the ventilation system, precisely in the fateful Bishop's Tower. Shit, that's another—" He was starting on another tangent. "Corridors appear behind everything that gets moved. That castle is like Swiss cheese. And the people from National Patrimony do nothing but bother us."

His comparison to Swiss cheese did make sense. But I prodded him to tell me more about my former prior.

"There were papers mainly from the Spanish royal House of Austria in the chest. Things related to the Patronato Eclesiástico and the Council of Castile. The documentalists found them right away. But there were also other things that had nothing to do with the general archive."

"Such as?"

"Jesuit account books. And other books, also Jesuit."

"How do you know that they were Jesuit books?" I asked, somewhat puzzled.

"Because they all had ex libris bookplates. You know—the seal, or ownership marker."

"Yes, I know about ex libris. I'm in charge of our own library."

"Then you must also know what I'm telling you about."

I put on my blankest face, and he continued.

"Since the books neither pertained to us nor had any connection with anything previously housed in the archive, I contacted your society. Carmelo, as the prior for this region, took charge of them. We developed a good friendship after that, as I told you."

"I didn't know. Carmelo didn't fill me in on it," I said, disappointed.

"I thought he had, and that perhaps this was the reason some other Jesuit might have slipped in to search for something more. At bottom I'm pretty inquisitive myself. It must be a result of my profession," he confided.

"What were the books about? Do you remember the title or author of any of them?" I asked in a very weak voice.

"Unknown. Carmelo told me they were surely works hidden during the first suppression of the society. I don't remember any famous names among them, except for the manuscript by Johannes Kepler, the astronomer. A little book full of beautiful engravings. I suppose you must have liked it, given your fascination with the stars."

My heart practically stopped before my next question.

"Did Carmelo tell you what he planned to do with those books?"

"Send them to Rome for classification. Nothing else."

I got home after the dinner hour, so I went straight to the kitchen to put something in my body besides coffee. Julian found me there. He patted me on the back and kept silent. I told him about my experience in the courtroom and part of my conversation with the archive director. Julian didn't know anything about the old Jesuit books either.

"Carmelo became very reserved during his last years," he said. "Now you've been able to see this for yourself."

I wanted to know if there was any means of following the trail of those books.

"Hector, why don't you finally put the matter to rest?" he answered angrily. "Look at what it's gotten you."

The advice was followed by a brief and not at all subtle reprimand that was well deserved. Maybe it was about time for me to shelve my obsessions and concentrate on my students and my community, time to set my fantasies aside.

Matthew interrupted us.

"Hector, pick up the telephone in the living room. You've got a long-distance call."

I excused myself to both of them and left the kitchen. The unmistakable Mexican accent at the other end caught me by surprise.

"Father Hector? This is Oswaldo Pizarro, here in Mexico."

This struck me speechless at first; it took me a moment to collect myself.

"Yes, this is Hector," I answered. "Allow me to send you a brotherly hug from Spain. I'm deeply sorry for the loss of your daughter."

After a brief silence in which it seemed that Juana's father was drying his tears with a handkerchief, the talk resumed.

"Thank you, Father. God giveth and God taketh away. Now my daughter is with the Lord. I just recovered her body at the airport. Her soul is already in heaven."

For a few minutes we spoke of what had happened, of the strong, captivating personality of his daughter, and of the formalities with the Mexican embassy and the courts, fortunately swift. I also asked him discreetly if he planned to initiate any legal proceedings.

"No. Don't worry about that. I won't get her back with lawyers and I don't need the money," he announced. "I just spoke with the judge there, and that's how I left it."

"I think you're right; she was following her passions," I said.

"She was." And he added, "We would very much like to meet you, Father Hector. Do you think it will be possible for you to attend Juana's funeral?"

His "we" surprised me, since I thought he was a widower. Then I realized he meant his family. I hadn't even thought about the funeral (I could hardly believe that she was really gone), but I felt a personal and moral obligation to fly to Mexico. I assured him of my attendance, and we said our good-byes in a cordial and affectionate manner. Fortunately, Julian didn't have any objection to my flying to Mexico the next evening. I promised him that this would be the end of the story.

But I lied.

The next morning, even before going to see John (who now knew of Juana's fate and was receiving a strong dose of tranquilizers), the first thing I did was search through my boxes to find the general directory of the society. Once it was in my hands, I located the exact phone numbers and went to work.

After various conversations and multiple waits and consultations, nobody in our central archive in Rome was able to give me any news of some old books shipped from our house less than a year ago.

The sought-after package did not appear.

In short, the shipment had never occurred.

34

Mexico D.F. is an enormous city.

From the plane, moments before landing at Mexico City International Airport, also known as the Benito Juárez, the most congested one in Latin America, I could see an endless array of streets and buildings that barely had enough space in the already crowded basin formed by the volcanoes and mountain ranges surrounding the metropolis. The city was built on top of an ancient lake, and now it had well over twenty million inhabitants. To make a population count of Mexico City is as much of an adventure as moving through it. Automobiles and buses compete for free space with crowded pedestrians and street vendors of every variety. There's room in the city for a great number of poor people, but also for the refined luxury of quite a few.

Mexico City overwhelms any visitor, myself included.

My guidebook—I always buy one, wherever I go—asserted that this was perhaps the largest city in the world. Also the third most polluted and one of the dirtiest, with an average of seven rats for each person. I didn't see any, but even to think of its sewers made me shudder. I had little desire for any subterranean adventures. There was so much to admire, with more than fifteen hundred monuments, a hundred twenty museums, and a gigantic subway network used by over five million people every day.

Everything seemed monumental to me.

My taxi went past the incredible "computer" square. According to the driver, there are more than twelve hundred stores crowded into that place, where one finds every imaginable kind of hardware and software, licensed or not, for personal computers. An urban legend declares that somebody can go in empty-handed and come out with everything needed to build a spaceship.

There were even more immense things in immense Mexico City.

Like its cemetery.

My indispensable guide told me it was the largest in the world.

I dialed Oswaldo Pizarro's cell phone number.

"Hello?"

"Oswaldo? It's Hector, the Spanish Jesuit. I've just arrived at my hotel," I said.

"It's so good to know you're here. I hope you had a pleasant trip."

"Excellent, but I wish it were for a happier purpose," I replied.

"We just finished our neighborhood services. The famous Carlos Queiroa led the rites; he was invited by my other daughter, Mercedes. They both spoke of Juana's passing into God's presence. It was very moving."

"Uh-huh," I said, a bit puzzled by his comments until I recalled Juana's evangelical faith.

"My good Spanish friend," her father continued, "I hope you'll excuse my not meeting you at the airport. It's all too much for a tired old man like me. I'm sending a car to your hotel right away."

"No need to bother. Just give me an address and I'll take a taxi," I said.

"It's no trouble at all. Besides, we're leaving for the cemetery now. We'll meet there if it's all right with you."

"Of course," I said, and hung up.

In less than fifteen minutes, just after I'd come out of the shower, there was a call from the desk to tell me a car was waiting by the hotel entrance. I rushed to gather a few personal effects (my passport, agenda, and a small Bible, in case I was asked to say a few words) and went downstairs. Outside, waiting for me, was—oh, yes—a gigantic black limo with tinted windows. The driver was standing by an open door, waiting for me to climb in.

"Good afternoon, Father Hector," he greeted me, cued possibly by the crucifix hanging around my neck, or perhaps by my obvious awkwardness as I came out of the hotel.

"Good afternoon," I replied as he guided me into the monstrous car.

It took us more than an hour to reach the cemetery. The driver spoke on his cell phone several times, exchanging instructions during the trip. Apparently the funeral cortege had been split due to traffic, with a good part of it weaving through the city, attempting to find a clear path to the cemetery. It even seemed that the police made way for us on more than one occasion. The driver, noticing my amazement, commented simply.

"Here in Mexico there's a tremendous respect for the dead."

I nodded, satisfied with his explanation.

The burial took place in the Pizarro family's private chapel. No more than forty of us were present. I warmly embraced Juana's father, and neither he nor I could hold back our tears for a short while. And it was the same with her sister. Mercedes looked very similar to Juana, and everybody said they were the spitting image of their mother, who had died when they were little girls. An evangelical minister closed the brief burial ceremony with the reading of a few psalms, in which I was cordially invited to participate. We thus shared prayers for a few minutes. Once the coffin was lowered into its tomb, relatives and friends began to leave.

I stayed, praying silently, until I felt a gentle pat on my shoulder. It was the limousine driver.

"Please. It's late and there's hellish traffic at this time."

I smiled at the unintended and rather inappropriate adjective. I closed my Bible and accompanied him to the parking space.

He politely opened the door for me. Someone was sitting inside, waiting for me.

This time I wouldn't travel alone.

"Let me introduce myself," the stranger said, giving himself away with his strong American accent. I recognized him from the burial. He was one of the few who hadn't greeted me.

"Let me guess," I replied as the driver shut the door, leaving us alone. "Van der Gil."

He nodded and stretched out his hand.

"Thomas van der Gil, in fact."

"I don't know whether this is a pleasure," I said, equally surprised and irritated while shaking his hand.

"Please. I hope that some of our actions haven't offended you. We only want the truth to come out," he said.

I held my gaze steady on him. His small eyeglasses and elegant gray suit concealed a nervous man, lean and dynamic. One of those who surely run for an hour every day before sitting down to breakfast with strawberry jam in a garden, well tended by his wife and a handful of undocumented immigrants. I was trying to banish these negative thoughts when the car braked abruptly.

"Damned riffraff!" he shouted. And he angrily pounded the driver's-side windshield with his ringed fingers. Our chauffeur merely shrugged his shoulders in lieu of a response.

"This is an unbearable country. It's a good thing we've got its president by the balls."

"Juana was a Mexican," I objected. "And a child of God like you and me."

"Juana was an exception. Incredibly smart for a woman."

I stared at him, infuriated. His next question didn't help at all.

"You've got it, right?"

"Got what?" I said, returning his question.

"The book of keys, what else? Juana was writing daily to give me the details."

"I've no idea what you're talking about," I lied, uselessly delaying the explanation.

"And that's why you pushed her," he concluded, smiling.

I was boiling. It wouldn't have been quite right to punch him, with a crucifix around my neck, so I had to contain myself, clenching my teeth.

"The Jesuits are naturally arrogant. And let's not mention the scientists. They're accustomed to resorting to murder to get to other people's discoveries." He kept provoking me.

"There's no such book," I responded, swallowing the insults almost bursting in my throat. "We didn't find anything in the Simancas fortress. And of course I didn't push Juana. You should be ashamed for even suggesting it. There's a witness who happens to be recovering in the hospital. And with a broken heart," I added, thinking of my friend John.

"Details." He kept smiling. "Details that, as you surely know, can be conveniently modified. Please cooperate."

I shook my head.

"Do they want more money? We've already paid double what it's worth for that land. And it's quite possible that nothing's going to be found there."

"I really doubt if you know the true value of a property in Spain," I challenged sarcastically. "It's not about money anyway."

"You see," he said, changing his tone of voice along with his tactics, "we've been after that coded manuscript for a very long time. Longer than you think. Juana hasn't been the only one working on it for years, attempting to decipher it. Our best experts in sacred texts accept its authenticity without question, and are anxious to know what it says, to see if there's hidden, irrefutable evidence in its pages of direct divine intervention in our evolution. Unequivocal, conclusive proof. Intelligence is much too complex to have been created haphazardly." He added, "We're not monkeys."

"We're humans, in fact," I returned defiantly. "But with a common, furry ancestor who walked on all fours and was a total ignoramus."

"Despite your being a Jesuit and a communist"—he restarted his provocative tactics—"you're a priest. And you're denying the existence of God."

"I'm not denying it at all," I retorted. "In fact, it's much more logical to think that nature's reason reflects the action of the personal God who created it.

"A nature capable of forming successive organizations as complex and sophisticated as we could imagine. And this went on," I added, "until it reached the point when intelligent human beings could exist; but to think that this God was so clumsy as to need to repeatedly modify His own design at every step just seems insane to me."

"I notice that you brought a Bible with you," he said, looking at the seat next to mine. "But what you're saying tells me that you don't read it."

"The Bible simply teaches us that the world was created by God, and this truth is expressed in the language used at the time it was written," I said, brandishing it. "Any other lesson concerning the origin and composition of the universe is alien to the intent of the Bible, which doesn't exist to tell us how heaven was created but how to get there."

"Nice phrase. Some Jesuit, I suppose."

"Not exactly. John Paul the Second," I answered.

"All the same. Catholics," he declared scornfully. "Always believing in theories and hypotheses of scientific dreamers like Kepler and Darwin."

"The theory of evolution is more than a hypothesis," I said vehemently, unfolding a clipping that was hidden in the pages of my Bible. "'Actually, it is noteworthy that this theory of evolution has gradually entered the investigators' spirits, due to a series of discoveries in diverse fields of knowledge. The convergence of results, in no way intended or provoked in studies conducted independently, is a significant argument in itself in favor of this theory.'" I had finished reading. "I was saving this for the right moment," I added, satisfied. "John Paul the Second again."

"So what will your Holy Fathers do when the real meaning of the *Voynich Manuscript* at last comes to light?" he argued. "The Jesuits won't always be able to hide it. That much devotion to the pope can't be good."

"What exactly do you suppose we Jesuits are hiding?"

"Haven't you done your homework, sonny?" he asked in turn, abruptly changing his former politeness to an insulting familiarity. "Even a fishwife has more sense than you do."

This time I really was about to hit him. I wanted to grab his throat. By some heaven-sent chance, my hand got caught in the chain hanging around my neck, preventing it. He enjoyed provoking me and didn't react to my lunging movement. He just took out a piece of paper. He displayed it carefully and, after changing his glasses, started reading aloud to me.

"'Dear Thomas. The explanation of the Jesuits' hermetic text is nearly complete.

"'Tonight we're returning to Simancas, sure that the translation made by Kepler is hidden there. Neither John nor Hector has noticed the meaning of the last part, the most important one.'" He stopped. "Hector, would you like me to continue reading?"

I thought of the last stanza.

> *And as all things come from One, and the mediation of One,*
> *thus all things come from this One by adaptation.*
> *And all darkness will depart from you.*
> *This is the admirable pattern of all adaptations, as I have*
> *   spoken.*

What did this nonsense that Juana claimed to have deciphered mean? And why didn't she tell us anything about it?

"Please relieve my ignorance," I conceded. "I don't think anything can surprise me now."

"You'll be surprised, all right. Especially if you remember that Jesuits wrote it."

"The text isn't Jesuit," I reminded him. "It's a well-known hermetic text that the society simply used to hide the supposed book of codes. There's nothing more to it."

"What sense would you give to 'all things come from One, and the mediation of One'?"

"We were talking about it a few minutes ago. God is the Maker, the One. Appropriately written with capitals."

"Right. For once we're in agreement."

"I hope it's only once," I responded.

"'All things come from this One by adaptation. And all darkness will depart from you. This is the admirable pattern of all adaptations, as I have spoken,'" he again read. "I'm also waiting for your suggestions about this."

I didn't have any.

"Let me help you. First, let's review some history. The manuscript was found in the sixteenth century, possibly by John Dee or Edward Kelley. Then it went to Emperor Rudolf the Second, and from there to the Jesuits, possibly through Johannes Kepler."

"Uh-huh," I agreed. "It's a line of inquiry that we've been following all along."

"And didn't both Dee and Kelley indicate that the *Voynich Manuscript* was written by Enoch himself? Aren't we talking about the direct, divine granting to men of text from God himself? Didn't this help to bring them out of darkness? Aren't we faced with the original language, the one used by our first parents? Aren't our languages today adaptations of that first divine writing? Where do Greek, Latin, and English come from, as well as all intelligent communication? Why would a monkey never be able to write the *Divine Comedy* or *Don Quixote,* even sitting at a keyboard and striking the keys for millions of years?"

Van der Gil was worked up and red-faced. A vein in his temple throbbed perceptibly.

"It's God!" he shouted at me. "The revealed Word of God!"

I inhaled deeply to get some fresh air back into my lungs.

"Chance is impossible!" he announced, striking my Bible with his hand.

I attempted to redirect the conversation to other obscure points, meanwhile trying to process at full speed the information that Thomas van der Gil was giving me.

"If this were as you say, why would we stain the reputation of Johannes Kepler? Why denigrate one of the greatest mathematicians in history, the only one capable of solving the tremendous intellectual challenge of unraveling this supposed divine legacy?"

"Because, my friend, he was a criminal," he answered more calmly. "The social order can be maintained only if crime doesn't go unpunished. Punishment has to serve as a lesson and a warning for all society. It's one of the pillars of progress and prosperity. Poverty nests in the slackening of laws."

"Is all your incriminating proof based on the discovery of mercury in Tycho Brahe's mustache four centuries after the fact?"

"Any jury in my country would find him guilty. And then there's the evidence."

"What evidence, apart from the fact that Brahe disinfected his nose with Mercurochrome for almost forty years?" I asked indignantly.

"Possibly Kepler stole the *Manuscript* on the tragic night of the dinner at Peter Ùrsinus Rozmberk's palace," he answered, unperturbed, disregarding my arguments. "Rozmberk was a very influential alchemist, according to our latest findings—as much an intimate friend of Tycho as of Edward Kelley. And Kelley would have sold him the book, perhaps because Rudolf the Second, even though he was emperor, couldn't pay for it. It's very likely that during the meal, Rozmberk tried to convince Tycho to work on the translation."

I knew part of this history, but my opponent's far-fetched interpretation was driving me crazy.

"Why would Kepler want a book that presumably dealt with alchemy, a subject that didn't interest him in the least?"

"Jealousy," he answered, unmoved. "Knowing that the translation of that book amounted to a mathematical challenge, he wanted to show the world that he alone was capable of solving it. But for that, he had to eliminate his rival and master, the great Tycho Brahe. He did the same with the astronomical observations that Tycho had recorded so precisely for decades. And he stole them without the slightest qualm."

This made no sense, but my last question had to completely disarm this man.

"And how the hell did Kepler decipher the *Manuscript*?"

His response upended me. "Ask your colleagues in Rome. They'll know something."

The car had arrived at my hotel. The driver stepped out. Holding the door, he waited for me.

"I hope to see you again," Thomas van der Gil said in farewell. "Soon."

"The feeling is most definitely not mutual," I said, once more shaking the hand of a man who repelled me.

"Don't let my last words bother you too much. We've spoken with that archive director of yours in Spain. He proved to be much more cooperative than the Jesuits. And," he concluded, "much cheaper."

"What's going to happen to our monastery?" I asked.

He shrugged his shoulders. Then he smiled. "If we don't find the book of Kepler's keys, maybe we'll strike oil. Or find chemical weapons. You can always find something of value by digging," he said sarcastically.

"I hope you find the truth," I said.

"That's the greatest treasure of all."

"You better believe it," I replied.

Turning around, I walked to the hotel. Inside, I headed straight to the restaurant.

The next day I flew back to Madrid.

35

I picked up the telephone. Matthew had pulled me out of a deep slumber.

"Hector, that kid is here."

I poked my head out the window. Simon was at the door of the library.

"Hi, Hector, how was your trip?" he greeted me, waving a newspaper above his head.

"Fine," I shouted. "I'll come downstairs and open up for you."

I had slept for almost twelve hours. Never had I experienced such a strong reaction to a plane trip, no matter how long. Simon's visit would help to reactivate my neurons. He usually didn't disappoint me with his findings.

On my way to the library, I thought of John, and made a quick call to the hospital on my cell phone. The nurse told me that he'd been released first thing that morning. I wondered where he might have gone. Most of his things were still in one of our rooms. His own cell phone had been disconnected.

"Hi, Simon," I greeted the kid, giving him a strong handshake. That made him seem like an adult. Perhaps this coincided with my noticing his incipient mustache, as well as the newspapers under his arm.

"Have you seen this?" he asked before I even had time to shut the door.

We spread one of the dailies out on the table.

CREATIONISM GAINS GROUND OVER EVOLUTION IN THE VATICAN

E.G. (Rome correspondent)

John Paul II seemed to have accepted the Darwinian theory of the evolution of species when he defined it as "something more than a hypothesis." But in the Vatican of Benedict XVI, evolution and its defenders, like Jesuit priest George Coyne, are causing discomfort. He was relieved of his position as director of the Vatican Observatory—the papal astronomical observatory—after criticizing, on various occasions, the Catholic authorities who, like Cardinal Christoph Schoenborn, archbishop of Vienna, maintain that "Darwinism is incompatible with Catholic beliefs" and are favorable to the creationist movement, according to which the world and man were created exactly as described in Genesis. The dismissal of Father Coyne, 73, director of the Vatican Observatory since 1979, has been justified: he has colon cancer, is receiving chemotherapy, and has offered his resignation for health reasons. But Vatican sources quoted yesterday by the *Corriere della Sera* acknowledge that Coyne's departure was welcome in order to end his "controversial" declarations. Coyne's successor, Father José Gabriel Funes, 43, of Argentina, also a Jesuit, declared to the same Italian paper that, as director of the observatory, he should speak "only about the stars and planets, and nothing else."

"I had no idea of this," I admitted. "I met Coyne a few years ago at a symposium in Madrid. He already knew of his illness. But I can't recall ever hearing about his successor," I added.

"The paper says he's also a Jesuit," Simon noted.

"Yes, that's what it says," I agreed, my face clearly showing my distaste. "But not even the members of the society are in complete agreement on scientific matters. We have to wait for the Holy Father's pronouncements."

"He's already done that, Hector."

Simon showed me another page. It was from the second newspaper (of national, not local, circulation), and the news again captured big headlines.

It seemed that in just a few days, during my absence, the controversy had suddenly exploded.

The Catholic Church, on the Point of Rejecting Intelligent Design

Nature magazine unveils the controversy in the seminar at Castel Gandolfo (G.E., correspondent in Italy)

Nature magazine has just made reference to the approaching apparent rejection of Intelligent Design by the Catholic Church. According to *Nature*, this seems to be indicated by the remarks of Peter Schuster, molecular biologist, participant this summer in a private seminar with Pope Benedict XVI at Castel Gandolfo. Some form of theistic understanding of evolution is to be affirmed, in the sense that it represents a divine design that is maintained by the continuous action of God. Thus the radical position of Intelligent Design is to be rejected. The discussions at the meeting suggest that the Church will affirm a form of theistic evolution, establishing as a general principle that biological evolution is valid, although it was set in motion by God. It seems likely, at the same time, that there will be a rejection of the Fundamentalist principle of Intelligent Design, in which God is a clockmaker who intervenes in the details [. . .] "I got the impression that there was a general agreement by which evolutionary biology is an undeniable science, and not a hypothesis," Schuster declared.

"Well, this one seems to contradict the first one," I said, slightly puzzled. "Of course it comes from a very different newspaper," I concluded, examining the headings of both dailies. "One wants to throw us out of here. The other doesn't seem to be too concerned about the presence of a limited number of provincial priests."

From a distance, I heard Julian's voice. "Hector, are you already up?"

The reply was obvious. I turned and smiled affably at my prior.

"Please come up when you can."

I excused myself to Simon and went upstairs again.

What else could have happened in my absence?

* * *

Julian greeted me in the large hall with a hug. We talked for a while about my stay in Mexico. I admitted that I still felt very sad and exhausted.

"You'll welcome having the weekend to give you a chance to recover," he responded. "By Monday you'll be like new for dealing with the kids."

I nodded, thanking him for his encouragement and affection.

"Is there any news concerning our relocation?" I asked him afterward.

He confirmed the dates for beginning the move. He also showed me the first payment from the developer. The figure was good.

"And that is only twenty-five percent," he said, satisfied.

"What about John? Didn't he let you know that he'd left the hospital?" I asked then, totally uninterested in the financial matters.

He shook his head. "He'll be all right. Don't worry."

I tried to be positive and detach myself from the bad sensations that came over me concerning the Brit. Julian helped me accomplish this with his next question.

"Do you know Father José Gabriel Funes?"

It was the second reference to him that I'd heard in twenty minutes.

"No. Not personally anyway," I answered. "But I just learned he's been named director of the Vatican Astronomical Observatory."

"That's right." He smiled at me. "And he wants you to go work there with him."

"Me?" I asked, fascinated.

"You," he confirmed. "Someone must have told him that we had a good Jesuit astronomer and scientist here in Spain. Scholarly and capable," he declared proudly.

"What someone?" I retorted, rather vexed. Julian was puzzled by the tone of my question.

"Aren't you flattered?"

"Yes, of course," I stammered. "But I'm still dazed and poorly rested from the trip," I said, excusing myself. "And worried about John."

"Think about it." He patted me on the shoulder. "Opportunities like this don't come around very often in life."

* * *

I went back to my room.

The first thing I needed was a good dose of caffeine. I had to be able to function in short order. With the cup in my hand I turned on the computer. More than twenty e-mails were waiting in my in-box. The most recent was from John.

Received barely an hour ago.

I read it out loud, as if it were a prayer.

> Dear Hector,
>
> My plane to London leaves in a half hour. I'm well. When the doctors let me out, I ran to the station and from there to the airport (I'm writing to you from a terminal at Barajas). I couldn't stay there a minute longer. Please send the rest of my things to my house in Cambridge.
>
> The *Voynich Manuscript* is finished for me.
>
> A hug,
>
> John

Though not very explicit, it *was* eloquent.

I decided it would be best not to answer his letter right away. I needed to respect his decision. The *Manuscript* had only brought him misfortune. It wouldn't help his recuperation for me to tell him that there actually was a book of codes developed by Johannes Kepler. That the archive director at Simancas had found it. And that Carmelo, my old prior, had been able to examine it before—he sent it?—to the general archive of the Society of Jesus in Rome.

And that it had slipped through my fingers.

The telephone rang again.

"Hector? You've got a phone call," Matthew's voice said at the other end. He transferred the call.

"Father Hector?"

A marked Argentinean accent put me on alert.

"Yes, it is. Speaking," I answered. "Who is this?" I asked, already knowing the answer.

"José Gabriel Funes," he confirmed. "Jesuit brother here in Rome. Recently appointed to the directorship of the Astronomical Observatory at Castel Gandolfo."

"To what do I owe the honor?" I stammered, reviewing the anticipated answer in the form of an offer that Julian had announced to me minutes ago.

"The honor is mine," he answered smoothly. "We have shared passions, I've been told."

"That's right," I continued, somewhat calmer. "The passion for Jesus Christ and the devotion to astronomy."

"Uh-huh," he acknowledged. "And perhaps something more," he added, and I pictured a smile on his face at the moment.

"What else?" I asked, already guessing his answer.

"The passion for ancient manuscripts," he said.

Could the codes to the *Voynich Manuscript* be in Rome again? My heart started to beat almost out of control. I couldn't hold back my next questions.

"Do you have it? Can it be translated? What does it mean?"

There was silence at the other end. Then José Gabriel Funes spoke again.

"Everything in its time, Hector. For now," he said, weighing his words very carefully, "I am offering you a job here."

"Can't you translate it?" I persisted.

"I have the tools but insufficient intelligence," he admitted. "I feel like Tycho Brahe facing his data on Mars. And the Holy Father is waiting impatiently."

Then he added, laughing, "I need a Johannes Kepler with me."

Author's Note

Almost two years after my novel was published in Spain under the title *El castillo de las estrellas,* I feel impelled to acknowledge those who had faith in its international success. I again want to express my gratitude to my editor, Blanca Rosa Roca, for all her efforts both in Spain and abroad; to the literary agency, specifically its director, Antonia Kerrigan; and to Thomas Colchie, who astounded me in his first call from New York with his detailed knowledge even of the finest points in the book and whose suggestions were invaluable. Thanks also to Dolores M. Koch for her excellent translation into English and her fidelity to the original. And, of course, my heartfelt appreciation to HarperCollins (William Morrow) and personally to Rene Alegria and Katherine Nintzel, whose trust in my manuscript has brought you this book.

And I cannot sufficiently thank my wife, Mari, for her boundless patience throughout this project. I also want to thank all the friends who don't stop praising it and all those who, without knowing me, e-mailed their impressions. Their continuing to do so will be a good omen.

TRANSLATOR'S NOTE

My deep thanks to the author, Enrique Joven, for always answering my queries quickly and graciously, and to Lee Paradise, for always reading my translations. He made so many wise suggestions and helped me so much with the research that I should give him credit as my cotranslator. I also want to thank my editor, Rene Alegria, for his support and understanding, and thanks to Thomas Colchie, agent nonpareil.

DOLORES M. KOCH